First Edition

First Printing, 2017

ISBN 978-0-9909432-7-3

www.al-barrera.com

The Golden Door

Reality is that which when you stop believing in it, it doesn't go away.

-Phillip K. Dick

Chapter 1

"It's right there." Aimee pointed between the trees, the same spot she'd been pointing at for five minutes.

A rain of orange and red leaves blocked his view when the wind blew, an ocean of fall colors. A cascade of the season, overwhelmed sight and sound, filling the air with the smell of earth and the coming winter. But Aaron saw nothing even when it cleared.

The combination of frustration and her big-sister voice made Aimee unbearable, pushing everything else out. "There's nothing."

She grunted and grabbed his temples, pointing his eyes—one blue and one hazel, just like hers—at the not-there house. "See?"

She had to be pulling his leg. Houses didn't just appear between two trees when you couldn't see them from any other way.

He stared into the fall with her hands on his temples. Still better out here than anywhere else in the world. And even when she was being bossy, she was his sister. She'd get off it just like she always did, even if it took—

As if it had stepped out from behind the falling leaves, Aaron saw the remains of a beat-up old house. A shack, really. No self-respecting house would allow its label put on this wreck. His mouth dropped open. "I see it."

She kept her hands on her twin brother's head, pointing it at the impossible. "Told you."

"That's crazy, like something out of a book."

"We should go look." He turned to Aimee, her hands still on his head. "You want to see it, right?"

She dropped her arms, and her determined expression vanished. "I don't know. Dad will get mad if we're late getting home." She furrowed her eyebrows and cast her gaze to the ground. Just like when Mom and Dad yelled at her, she began to fidget with her fingers.

But Dad stayed mad no matter what they did. Besides, they had hours before dark. "Don't be a sissy. Come on." He grabbed her hand and stalked through the brush toward their target. She always found reasons to be afraid. They'd live in their room or a library all of their lives, if she had her way. It was for her own good, really. Too much fear made people weak. He'd heard that somewhere.

This part of the woods was as far behind their house as they dared go. Beyond these paths lay Here Be Dragons, and even Aaron's courage faltered there. Or at least, the voice of reason spoke a little louder in his ear. Mom always told them stories of people getting lost around Umber Gardens. Monsters that *everyone* knew lived out here ate up bad boys and girls who were a burden on their parents. It sounded too much like a fairytale. They wandered further every day and had yet to see any monsters. Today had been the boldest excursion of all.

This far out, with no trails, the brush and plants rose to their waists. They had to duck under and around branches to get anywhere near the shack. As they moved on, the bushes grew farther apart, though from a distance they hadn't seemed to. The limbs of the trees towering above them formed a tunnel that led straight to their destination. The ground flattened out, and footing came easily where moments before it had been treacherous.

The light filtering through the red and gold canopy illuminated the ground as birds sang all around. One bird asked its high, shrill questions: *Keee kee? Keee kee?* Another honked a low cry: *Hoooorrrk!* Aimee's grip loosened; a moment later, Aaron wasn't dragging her at all.

"This is weird, right?" she asked. Cautious, but not afraid.

He shook his head. "No way, this is awesome." It wasn't just a lucky clearing leading to the beat-up shack; it was a path. An old one, but there nonetheless. He smiled, giddy with the thrill of discovery. Finding something exciting in a book was one thing, but this? This was real.

The structure drew closer. What might have been white paint had chipped off in patches. Most of the shingles had fallen away to untold time. No glass remained in the windows, and if there had ever been a door, it was gone now. Small red and white mushrooms sprouted in a circle around it. The place couldn't be very old, but to

3

his imagination, it was ancient. Timeless. It had stood there since humanity fell to Earth from whatever place in the universe it had originated. The first man had lived here with his twin sister, and they had spread out over the world to explore it, leaving only this battered shell behind.

Birds he'd never seen before stood on the roof. They were robins but purple and pink, brilliant colors the birds of Tennessee didn't display. He and Aimee had wandered in these woods often enough to know that much about the wildlife. Something *other* hung in the air. It almost had words.

"Do you hear that?"

She cocked her head before nodding, but she didn't slow down. Neither did he. "It's like a song."

Not just the birds but the wind. The creaking of the shack. The swaying of the leaves, even between gusts.

Aimee reached out as they approached, tentative for a moment before touching the weather-beaten wood. "I can't believe we almost didn't see this."

Aaron walked right in. Why not? These were their woods. This was their place.

But the inside held none of the outside magic. A table and the remains of a chair took up the center of the room. Shelves with empty glass bottles lined the walls. Leaves littered the floor up to his ankle, crunching as he spun. Nobody had been here in a long, long time. Just a little bit of garbage in a moderately interesting find out

4

in the woods. His heart sank a little, but such was the nature of exploration. Not every building held treasure.

"Aaron," Aimee said from outside. "Look at this."

He stepped back out. The way they'd entered looked like a path, a straight shot from the two big trees with the view of the there-but-not-there shack between them. But the path didn't end at the shack, only ran by it. He followed it the way Aimee stared, even further the other way. Past the shack and into the beyond. The light shone a little brighter there, and the leaves glowed golden. More weird birds stood in the trees, cocking their head at pair as if unsure what two children were doing so far from home.

And something else. A string on the ground, a yellow piece of yarn leading them further in. He bent to pick it up.

"Don't touch that!" She grabbed his arm.

"It's just a piece of string, sissy."

She hugged herself, looking around as if someone might be listening. "I don't know. Maybe we should just go back. This is weird, right?"

Aimee had always been the smart one, but she'd never try anything without her big—by two minutes—brother to do it first. "It'll be all right. I just want to see what's down there."

She let go of his arm, allowing him to pick the string off the leaves. He tugged it, and it rose in a spring of golden leaves along the path. He glanced back at her, and she smiled her brave smile. When he flashed his own, hers grew, like it always did. Smart, but not brave. Not by herself.

5

And she didn't need to be. That's why there were two of them. He followed the string hand over hand, leaves crunching underfoot, past the edge of the clearing with the shack and into lands unknown. They passed older trees, bigger, like the ones guarding the entrance to the little building. Here, they hadn't given up their fall bounty yet. Both the ground and the sky radiated the colors of the season, brilliant red and burnt orange. Seeing the blue of the sky through the canopy brought to mind thoughts of rainbows in fall's bleeding colors.

Ahead, the woods thinned out. "This is different," he said.

The forest parted. Aimee gasped, and Aaron dropped the string. It couldn't be real. They were dreaming. *He* was dreaming.

The chill of the air begged to differ. No dream, then. Aimee searched for his hand and squeezed when she found it. Woodland gave way to a clearing on a hill, and in the distance, the ramparts of a castle.

"What is this?" Aimee asked.

Aaron looked back over his shoulder. There was no indication the landscape behind them would suddenly end and give way to an open plain like this. "I...I don't know." It was as if one world stopped and another began. He cleared his eyes with the palms of his hands.

Aimee stared at the castle, so far away yet so close. It couldn't be there. It was a trick of perspective. A downtown building seen from a different angle. There were no castles in Tennessee.

She turned to him. A gleam in her eyes had replaced her earlier fear. "Let's go look. Just to the top of that hill." She pointed at the one nearby, bald except for the knee-high grass.

For once, it was his turn to be afraid. "We shouldn't. We might get lost." He wasn't worried about that, not really, but the grip of reluctance around his guts wouldn't abate. Something was off about this place. Even the atmosphere felt different, like the time Mom and Dad had taken them to the top of the mountains near Chattanooga. Every intake of breath was fresh and crisp. The wind against his face spoke of flowers and adventures just out of sight.

But he knew better. If Mom and Dad had taught them anything, it was suspicion.

"We won't get lost. It's okay. Don't you think so?"

When Grandma came to visit, there was the sense that everything would be all right. The bad things that happened at home behind closed doors wouldn't find their way out when she was around. This was the same feeling, though he couldn't tell why. But that didn't mean they should go further.

Still, he didn't resist as Aimee pulled him up the hill. By the time they reached the top, they both huffed for air.

"Oh my gosh!" Aimee covered her mouth with her free hand.

It was indeed a castle, and before that, another forest surrounding a town. Not a city like Umber Gardens, but a village— thatched roofs and all. There were people down there, far enough away that it was impossible to make out any details. The edges of the world vanished into the blue sky, as if it were all an island floating in the clouds.

He glanced at Aimee. Excitement lit her eyes, and he wondered if he looked the same. "What is this?"

The colorful birds flocked overhead, flying toward the castle. They sang to the duo as if inviting them in, but they didn't need to. It pulled at Aaron. It called out the same way home did after a few days away. Better, even. This was more than home.

It was magic. It had to be.

The fear melted away, as if the gentle summer heat of the place had broken it down to its base parts and cast it into the wind. Aimee was right. They had to see more.

"What's that?" Aimee tugged Aaron's arm.

"Hmm?" The castle held his attention. What secrets might they find in a place like that? Certainly more than in that little shack.

"Aaron." He finally followed her gaze.

Someone—a small person that looked yellow from a distance— was coming. He was following the path from the village toward them, bouncing with each step.

Aaron should have been afraid. Strange place. Stranger people. Every warning bell well-honed at home should have been going off. But they weren't. He couldn't so much as find them, let alone ring them.

The small, yellow man, his skin sagging, approached them. He skipped as he hummed something wordless under his breath. He didn't look scary; he looked like a candle half-melted. Round and chubby, he waved when he saw them watching, smiling with what passed for a face.

"Aaron!" Aimee tugged on his arm as she stared at him.

"I see it too." Whatever it was, it certainly wasn't a person.

He held Aimee's hand and waited for the thing to come closer, but he wasn't afraid.

When they walked back out between the guardian trees leading to the shack, the sun had fallen away to night. Aimee stumbled on the roots of the silent giants, but Aaron caught her arm before she hit the ground.

"Are you okay?" The giddy delight of the secret world had faded, and all that remained was the exhaustion. It bit into his bones and pulled at his eyes. It must have been what Mom felt like after a day at work when she complained of an aching back and even more achy feet.

But this was different. It had been magic.

Magic.

She tilted her head to the side as if the question didn't need an answer. Even by the light of the full moon, her confusion made her appear younger than eight. "Did all of that really happen?"

Prince and princess. Another world. Lord and lady of all they surveyed and beneficent rulers of a fantasy. They'd been there for weeks. Or days? Had it only been hours? Even now, just out of the Kingdom, he could recall it only through a fog of memory, as if the waking mind were trying to speak to the sleeping one. That fantasy had spit them back into a universe where the rules were harsher and always applied.

The little candle that walked and talked like a man, fawning and pawing like a pet, had told them it was theirs . Aimee and Aaron laughed and stared in wonder.

"What do you mean ours?" Aimee had asked after he had babbled for minutes.

He cocked his head to the side and considered her with his big, black eyes. Drippy, as he wanted to be called, was a dog running up to you after you'd been gone from home. The smell of the house after a long day outside. Drippy was Grandma coming to visit, and there was nothing to be afraid of in that.

"What do you mean, what do I mean? I mean what I say and I say what I mean!" He waddled in a circle around them, clapping. Little bits of him flew off and vanished into the air. Sometimes the pieces became leaves, others turned into butterflies, but he never seemed reduced for their loss.

Aimee laughed at the nonsense. "We don't even know where we are!"

Drippy stopped in front of him and smiled at them. "You're home. This is yours."

But now that they were gone, Aaron didn't know if it had happened either. "I think so?" He hadn't meant it to be a question.

For the first time, Aimee noticed the darkness. "Oh my gosh. We're late getting home."

His mouth dropped open as he stared at the moon. Kingdoms and candle men half-remembered paled in comparison to what Dad did when they returned home late.

He shook his head, clearing his thoughts. In the distance, the shack still stood. Waiting for them. Drippy had said he'd wait for them there, but they had to go before it was dark. "We'll tell Dad we got lost. He won't be mad if you cry."

She didn't need the cue. The glow of the stars revealed eyes full of tears. "You think?"

"It'll be fine. Come on." He grabbed her hand and started back the way they'd come, tearing his gaze from the shack and the mystery beyond. It wouldn't be fine. Nothing here ever was. But *there…* What was it? Why couldn't he remember now? Colored birds and a castle. People that weren't all people. Everyone cheering as Drippy led them onward toward their castle. All the memories faded into little more than pleasant warmth the longer he was away. When he turned his back on the shack, they vanished.

But they weren't in that make-believe place, and they certainly weren't home yet. Animals and the ever-present threat of getting lost loomed over them at night. Eyes bore into their back, though were was nothing when he turned to look. Or there was, but he never caught glimpse of it. Something waiting, watching, as the cold bit into their fingers. Aimee hated it out here at night, but Aaron didn't. This place belonged to him. He wouldn't get lost. These were his woods. This whole place was just an extension of his kingdom.

Their kingdom.

They trekked through the woods using moonlight to walk. The blessing of the cloudless night vanished sometimes as one passed by the moon, leaving them in utter blackness for horrifying moments while they waited for it to pass. When it finally did, they inched onward toward home, going slower than would save them, not that there was any speed for that now.

He squeezed Aimee's hand. The tension grew around them like a shroud, and it would swallow both of them before Dad got the chance if he didn't say something. "We can go back," he said. "We can go back whenever you want." Not a brave girl, no. Not always. But she didn't have to be. He could be brave for her.

She finally broke her silence. "Really?"

"You want to, right?"

He could almost feel her smile. She'd forgotten the fear of their surroundings and home for a moment. "Yeah. I want to stay there. Don't you?"

He did, even if he didn't know why. Even if he thought they couldn't, he wanted to.

The lights from their house appeared in the distance. The flood lamp attached to the sliding door on the porch lit the woods for a half a mile. He braced himself for the worst.

In the light of day, it looked normal. Old brown siding and a shingle roof on a home that sat at the outskirts of town. Only the rusted railing leading up the stones to the front door gave a sense of the inside. Because inside it was as rotten and rusted as the people who lived there. And for every spec of dirt on its outside, there was a mountain of it on the people in. He hated it here. He hated everything about it except Aimee.

At night, it couldn't hide its ugliness. Crooked and dark, like the people who owned it. A hag sitting on the side of a hill, leering down at all the people who drove by, as if it would spit on them if it could. Maybe it would. Maybe it had; maybe that's all their parents were— the spit from that angry old house, coming through the front door every day to make the whole town angry and ugly like them.

Their mother sat on the back porch, smoking a cigarette. When they emerged from the trees, panting, sweaty, and dirty, she regarded them as if the branches had swayed in the wind, nothing more.

"You're two hours late."

They stopped in front of her chair. Aimee folded her hands at her waist and stared down at her feet, an appropriate expression of shame painted across her face.

Not Aaron, though. He wasn't afraid. If she weren't mean about this, it would be something else. Being afraid didn't make it better.

"Your daddy's still up." She flicked the butt of her smoke into the darkness, the red cherry fleeing the scene of the crime. "You better just go inside and get your whoopin'."

"Momma, no!" Aimee looked up at her, her brow furrowed, tears in her eyes. "We didn't mean to! We got lost is all!"

Aaron hated hearing her talk to their parents. Those people were dumb, and she acted dumb around them, trying to appease them. He walked past without another word, sliding the door open. She said whoopin', but it was a beating. The kind of beating that came from a man who knew how to hit without leaving marks when his kids had to be in school the next day.

"You better just follow your brat brother." She pulled another smoke out of the pack and lit up.

The pleas wouldn't help. Aimee knew that. She followed Aaron inside.

Wood paneled walls, ugly as sin, lined the room. The whole place stank of smoke and garbage. Dad sat in his chair, watching a basketball game on TV. He had a beer in his hand and a TV dinner on the tray in front of him. His big arms jerked as he jumped in his seat every time the men on TV did something. A trash-man surrounded by his trash home.

"These fucking weasels are useless. JV bullshit." He didn't as much as look at Aaron, who made his way behind the chair, trying to remain unseen.

Aimee wasn't as lucky. The door clicked as it closed, drawing his attention. Aaron could smell the beer on his breath and see the red tinge to his eyes. Sports always made it worse. They got him fired up. Made him mad.

Really, if Aaron were being honest, everything made Dad mad.

"Fine fuckin' time to come home. You think you can just do as you please around here, missy?"

She didn't dare lift her gaze from the floor, and her hands remained folded in front of her. "No, Daddy."

He took another swig of his beer and turned his attention back to the game. "Don't 'no, Daddy' me. You do whatever you want 'round here. We were about to go looking for your stupid asses in the woods."

A bold-faced lie. He wouldn't piss on them if they were on fire, not unless they happened to be on the way to the bathroom. This place was wrong. Everything here was wrong.

"It was my fault."

Noticing Aaron for the first time, Dad looked over. "'It was my fault,' what?"

"It was my fault, *Dad*." Aaron knew damn well it wasn't the word he wanted to hear, and he didn't care. The filth of the real world had settled in once more, but he was still giddy with the high the Kingdom had left him. The people there who had been thrilled to meet them. The feeling that nothing bad there could ever happen.

Had it been real?

Dad shook his head, setting his beer aside and standing. "You're one disrespectful little shit, you know that? Just like your mom." He undid his belt, pulling it from around his waist. "That's where you get that from." He stumbled over his own feet and nearly fell. When he looked up at Aaron, his face shone redder than before. "From that fucking bitch."

Aaron wore a scowl. He wouldn't cry. Dad made Aimee cry all the time, but Aaron would stay brave for her. He tried to signal her, telling her to go. Hide under the bed. Get the hell away.

She stood and stared. Little Bambi watching big-brother Bambi get hit by a truck. Dad reared his arm back as he got in whoopin' range, and Aaron squeezed his eyes shut, a sneer still painted across his face.

It struck him hard across his shoulder, almost on his neck. He opened his eyes to see Dad's foot catch him in the chest, sending him flying into the bar chairs behind him as he screamed.

"You're in my house!"

The belt whipped his upturned hands. Pain flared in his right fingers before they went numb.

"You'll do what I say!"

It hit his hands again. This time the tip of the belt wrapped around and struck him in the cheek.

"My fucking rules are law, boy!"

Dad reared back to swing again, but the blow didn't come. Aaron, shaking, peeked out from behind his hands. Aimee had grabbed the belt hanging over Dad's shoulder.

It took Dad a moment to figure out the problem, an expression like a drunk caveman on his face. His eyes widened when he did, and he spun on her, lifting a foot and slamming it into her belly. Her eyes grew as big as baseballs as all the air exploded from her. "You think you're getting off, bitch?"

She curled into a ball on the floor, gasping. Dad stood over her, the belt dangling from his grip, his chest heaving. Aaron's bravery vanished as his twin-but-still-baby sister struggled to breathe. He wrapped his hands around Dad's ankle. "Please, sir. Please. We'll be good."

He stared down at them, an angry god taking out his wrath on his weakest disciples. Aaron expected another blow. Another stinging slap of the belt, or another kick. Maybe a broken leg, same as the time Dad had thrown him off the porch.

This house was bad, and only bad things happened here.

Dad tossed the belt onto the floor instead. "I'm missing my game. Pick her up and go to bed."

Aaron didn't need to be told twice. He grabbed Aimee's arms as she struggled for air on the floor. Dad stepped over them and returned to the game. He stared at the TV, his eyes seeing nothing, his jaw clenched.

Without a word, Aaron helped Aimee to her feet, and they walked down the short hallway to their room. As soon as the door shut, Aimee began to sob.

"Shh. Shh. It's fine. It's done." She had to be quiet. If Dad heard her, he might come back. They'd gotten a whoopin' for crying about a whoopin' before.

They'd set up their room like they'd seen other kids do on TV. Posters of comic book characters they liked and drawings that Aimee had made. On the shelves were all of Aimee's dolls, though she was quickly outgrowing the desire to ever take them down.

But it was just a thin coat of paint over the sickness that pervaded this place. "No," she sobbed. "It's not fine."

Seeing her face crunched up made him want to cry. Her tears always brought his to bear. He gazed into her eyes, his own reflected back at him. One blue, one hazel. Special eyes, or so Grandma had said once. The kind of eyes that saw deep.

The only thing they saw here was hate. The place reeked of it. He didn't know what they'd done to make their parents despise them. He didn't know why they treated them nicely sometimes and broke legs others. There was no rhyme or reason to it. He didn't understand how his mother could watch it all happen and not help them. This kind of thing wouldn't happen in his kingdom.

Their kingdom.

Off to school the next morning as if nothing had happened. It didn't do any good to rat on parents. Mom had told them stories about the little boys and girls who tattled at school. The first thing they'd do would be to call the parents.

"Oh, no! We spanked them for back-talking. Just a little swipe on the butt. I have no idea where they get these stories; they have such active imaginations."

Dad said he'd make it worse if they didn't take it like adults.

And so they did. Every day they put up with the hard words and hoped it didn't turn into hard actions. Some kids dreaded school, but not them. School became a release, a place to get away. The walls of the library were lined with books and a million places to escape to. Story after story of children from bad places rising to overcome. But he understood that those were just stories, and he suspected Aimee had figured out the same. There was no real escape there.

Until now.

"You remember it, right?" Aimee asked as they walked to the bus stop. She didn't bring up what Dad had done. She never did.

"A little. It's weird. It's like trying to remember a photo. I know it was there, and I know what it looked like, but I can't picture it myself."

"Exactly!" She smiled. "We should go back today."

"We can bring Brian."

Brian, their best friend at school. In many ways, their only friend. The other kids called them poor or made fun of them for wearing ratty clothes. Not Brian. Sitting with them at lunch, talking about movies with them, inviting them over after school. His mom made them dinner and told them that she loved them. It had been weird at first, but not bad.

Aimee shook her head, dismissing the idea out of hand. "I don't think we should."

"Why?"

"That place is special. Isn't it? It's our place." She shrugged. "I don't want to share."

If she didn't want to share, they wouldn't. They should make sure it had really happened before they invited the neighborhood anyway. It wouldn't do for them to take Brian only to find out that shack, and the weird little kingdom beyond, were nothing more than a figment of their imaginations.

Aaron boarded the bus with that in mind, and the day passed as it always did. The two of them sitting next to one another in class. Going to the library with Brian during recess. Brian and Aaron discussing the finer points of Batman and the X-Men while Aimee chimed in about the characters she preferred.

Brian and Aaron were the loudest of the three, and Aimee watched, quietly listening. Speaking up when one of them said something particularly silly. She never felt the need to fill the silence the way other kids did. The library's sanctity offered a peace lacking everywhere else in her young life. She'd told him once that it felt like talking in church, though Mom and Dad only took them there when Grandma came to visit.

To Aaron, that calm was a promise. Even as he laughed with Brian, even as he ate his lunch and smiled, pretending everything would be okay, it lurked in the back of his mind. One day this would be their life, and they'd never have to go home.

They didn't return home after school, instead going straight to the guardian trees. Back to their secret world. No fears there and no worries. This time they made it back before dark. The memories faded again, but not as completely. Little by little, visit by visit, it stuck in their minds.

The Kingdom had been waiting for its rulers, after all.

Chapter 2

Aaron had never been to an intervention before, but as far as he could tell, this one was a bust. Ten minutes in and the screaming began. Name-calling followed shortly. Marie started to cry, and Brian stopped listening. Ambush tactics probably weren't the best ammo against a guy coming down off a three-day drunk. Whatever fucking brain trust had come up with that one deserved a slap in the mouth.

"Aaron, please, just listen!" Marie crossed her arms, a surefire sign she wasn't taking her own advice.

"Putting me in a circle doesn't make this anything other than the same talk we've had a hundred goddamn times." He fished in his pocket for his smokes. The same brand Mom had sucked on for thirty years, Marlboro Reds. Another lovely trait handed down in the proud family tradition of fucking over your children.

"We care about you. We don't want to lose you at twenty-four."

The scratch of the lighter gave way to fire, and he puffed a long, smooth drag before blowing it toward Marie. "We" was a pretty loose use of a plural pronoun when it was just his buddy, his girlfriend, and the guy she worked with that Aaron had only met twice. He didn't even know the asshole's name.

"Why is he here anyway?" Aaron pointed at the blond goober. Goober. Apt name. Goober it was.

Marie opened her mouth but didn't speak. She shook her head and waved helplessly at Brian.

"Don't look at me. I told you this was a bad idea."

"Are you kidding? Grow up!"

It would be funny if they weren't trying to *It's A Wonderful Life* him. "You might want to read a pamphlet on the subject before you wait in the shadows of someone's apartment like an intervention assassin, sweetheart."

Sweetheart. The same sugary-sweet nickname he'd used their entire six years together. It didn't fit anymore. Get a college degree. A good job. A nicer apartment. Suddenly, your old boyfriend isn't so much fun anymore. Out of nowhere, party animal became dirty words, and suddenly the fun guy had turned into the junkie.

"Please. Are you even eating anymore?"

Aaron ignored her and searched the room for something to stare at. Anything. This whole stupid plot twisted his stomach into knots. This was their problem, not his. If they didn't like it, they could leave.

Goober sat on the edge of the couch as if lounging would be too much of a commitment. He glanced at his phone every few minutes, looking for an escape route.

Aaron finally snapped his gaze back to Marie as she droned on. "Why don't you just say it? Nobody wants to be around me anymore because I use heroin. See? Was that so hard?" It wasn't, but it *was* trying his patience. "And you know what, that's fine. Get the hell out if you don't like it."

Brian finally spoke up. "Dude, using the 'I' word was too much, but seriously, we're just checking on you."

Ever calm. Ever quiet. Forever giving no shits, even when the world was on fire. "You could have called for that." He shook his head. "I want Goober out."

Goober, who had been checking his phone again, glanced up. "Me?"

"Yes, you, asshole. I don't even know your name." He looked at Brian, shutting Marie out. "Why is he here?"

Marie's earlier rage returned as quick as a coastal storm. "You don't know his name? You lived on his couch for two weeks! It's Mike, you bastard!"

Mike. It clicked back into place. Marie had been living with her parents, who hated Aaron, and Brian had been out of town after ditching when the lease was up. Between things with nowhere to go, Aaron had hooked up with Mike at Marie's behest. The nice guy who'd only been a little uncomfortable when he caught Aaron shooting up in his living room. Marie had moved in with him at his old apartment a couple weeks later, the asshole landlord giving them both some vague threat about "paying their shit on time," as if other people were clawing at the gates to move in to his roach motel.

23

Aaron scratched at his five o'clock shadow, clearing away the cobwebs. How the hell could he forget that? Fuck it. "I don't care. Get out." He put on his best bored-sovereign expression and stared at the ceiling.

Mike squeaked a few times, nearly forming a word on the third. The nice guy. Buttoned-down shirt, blond hair, and blue eyes. Always willing to go out of his way for a lady, the question of whether or not he wanted to get into her pants forever hanging in the air. He finally gave up on speaking and stood without a word.

"No! Mike, stay!" Marie commanded, a harsh owner demanding obedience from her dog. Her big, goober dog.

"No, no. It's fine. I should go. This is a personal thing." His face had gone from white to red in the time it took to open the door and close it behind him.

Marie watched him exit, her plan crumbling around her. Fairly fucking classic. Great intentions, bad executions; Marie all the way up and down. "You know, he likes you. He asks about you all the time. He said you were cool."

Everyone thought drug dealers were cool. "So?"

Brian shook his head. "Jesus, dude."

That was saying a lot coming from him, but this had gone on long enough. "I'm going to say this as nicely as I can: Fuck both of you; now get out." He pointed at the door, his patience gone.

They had some goddamn nerve coming into his home and laying this on him. He didn't bother them with his life. She wanted space, and he gave it to her. Brian didn't give a fuck if he called, and so he only called when a new movie came out. This wasn't about him; it was about them soothing a guilty conscience, and they could shove that right where the good lord split 'em. If he wanted to forget things, he was allowed. If his lifestyle didn't intrude on theirs, and they didn't like it, then they could just stop coming around.

Marie wouldn't have it. "I am so *sick* of this bullshit." She grabbed an empty beer bottle on the kitchen table and flung it across the room, shattering it on the far wall by the door ol' Goober had just fled through.

Aaron raised an eyebrow at the new hole. It didn't do much to improve the apartment's back-alley ambience. It looked just like something Dad would have done. The only way this could be better was if Mom were watching it all with a smoke in her hand.

"We fucking get it, Aaron. Your sister died and you're sad."

The words brought his attention back to Marie like a splash of cold water.

"What the hell do you think she'd say if she were here now? Huh? You think she'd be shooting up smack in a roach motel with you? She be as sick of your stupid shit as the rest of us, you crybaby! Grow up!"

Every ounce of blood in his body rushed to his head. He stood up, turning over the table as he did.

"Marie!" Brian was angry, but not as angry as Aaron. "What the hell is—"

"Who the fuck do you think you are? You never even met her, you stupid bitch!" His dad's words. A stupid bitch, same as Mom.

Regret might have fired a shot across his bow if anger hadn't already sunk him. "She'd have been disappointed with my taste in women, you dumb cunt. That's about it."

Marie didn't back down an inch. She laughed in his face as she rose from the chair. "Fuck you, Aaron! You're a goddamn whiny junkie just like every other crackhead on Broad Street!"

He balled his hands into fists. "What the hell do you know? You think getting a job and a degree makes you anything but a burnt-out party whore, you bougie bitch?" He wanted to punch her, to wipe that smug sneer off her face. Maybe grab her by the hair and throw her off the second-story porch. Maybe just tell her to fuck off and never call her again.

Brian stepped between them. "Marie! What the hell?"

"No! No! This is bull—"

Aaron slammed his fist through the kitchen drywall as if it were paper, punching a hole straight to the hallway. The upstairs neighbor screamed and pounded on the floor.

"Big man, huh?" She was itching for a fight. Maybe that had been her whole reason for coming here. Look for a reason to be mad. Find a way to call it done, finally walk away, and never come back.

"Get out." He pulled his hand back through the hole, drywall crumbs falling to the stained carpet below.

"No, we aren't done!"

But Aaron was. He walked into the bedroom hallway, shaking his head, his temples pounding.

"Yes, Marie, we're leaving."

Aaron turned around to see Brian dragging her by her wrist toward the door. Brian understood. He knew what had happened.

He didn't have to pull her far before she moved of her own accord. She yanked the door open, bashing it into the wall and leaving yet another hole. The neighbor continued to pound on the floor and shower them with curses. "We're done, Aaron, you goddamn junkie." And then she was gone, into the hallway, out of his life.

"No shit," he yelled after her.

Brian looked back and forth between them. Indignant. Angry. Helpless. "I'm sorry, man."

"You think her and Mike are fucking? You think that's what this was about?" The same old paranoia. The anger. All of it always lurking just beneath the skin.

Brian shook his head. "No. I don't. Call me, okay?" Simple as that. Nothing left to say, time to go. Good luck with this bullshit; sorry we couldn't help.

Aaron waved him away. He entered his bedroom as the click of the door closing echoed through the apartment. Good. Let them go. They could make choices for themselves, and he would make his own. If he wanted to get high and forget for a while, so what? He deserved it. Did that give Marie the right to come here and throw Aimee in his face? To drag her out of her grave like the goddamn Ghost of Christmas Past and parade her in front of him?

He stared at his sister's picture on the dresser as he sat on the bed, the upstairs neighbor still screaming. She and Aaron standing

27

by their guardian trees in the forest, Brian behind the camera. It had sat there for years, but he never really looked at it anymore. Why would he? No good memories lived in his past. Or his present. His future didn't look much better.

Gone almost ten years now. Her life cut short by her own hand.

The mental images that always preceded the pain parade marched through his mind. Her crying alone. Her wishing Aaron would come back. Aimee finally having enough and blowing her brains out with one of Dad's old gun.

He turned his eyes to the ceiling, willing the thoughts away, but as usual, they didn't budge. He glared at the water stains above him before turning his attention to the clothes and empty beer cans all over the room. The smell of the dirty sheets burned his nose. The closet door that squeaked every time it opened. He looked anywhere but inward, because as dirty as this place was, it was worse there. Something ugly lived inside that little black box, and if you showed it even a little bit of light, it would crawl out and eat you whole.

He took a deep breath. No tears today. Even if Marie didn't see them, somewhere, on some level, she would get some sense of satisfaction out of it. He piled his anger on top of the emotions, trying to crush them and make him forget for a little while. He didn't need drugs to do it. He wasn't the monster Marie had painted him as in her head.

He'd never hit her, and he never would. He never hit anyone who wasn't asking for it. Not after everything he and Aimee had lived through in that house. But he wanted to, and that was a sure sign she shouldn't be around him. Maybe it was for him; maybe it was for her. After so many years of this back and forth shit, she had to be as tired as he was. If she wanted to flush six years away, he could deal. Getting the hell away from his problems had become an art since he was a kid, something he could do as easily as breathing.

He grabbed his backpack from his closet, the door squeaking on the rusted hinges. He needed to get his mind off this, and he was running short on weed anyway. Time to make a little trip.

Not ten minutes after Marie and Brian had left, Aaron followed. He half-expected to see them in the parking lot, still arguing about how things had gone. Still strategizing about how they could reach him, fix his problems, and make him a real boy again.

They weren't. They'd gone to take care of their own lives, or to forget about him in peace. He clenched his jaw until his teeth hurt, angry with himself more for giving a shit than for them leaving. He hopped into his beat up 90s Mustang and threw it into gear, peeling out of the parking lot of his shithole apartment and onto the streets of Umber Gardens.

He pounded his steering wheel before the first red light. How could Marie bring her up? It had taken three years before he could tell her about Aimee. He couldn't even think about his sister most days. He'd found a nice quiet corner of his mind to lock all that shit away, a CIA prison so deep and dark it never saw the light of day, and Marie had unlocked the door.

And Brian. Ever the best friend, and what a sorry title that had become. When things got hard, he moved out. On to bigger and better things than hanging out with his friend who maybe partied just a little too hard. Aaron wasn't easy to be around. Maybe he used a little too much. Maybe he talked a little too aggressively. A little too mean. But fuck, they'd known each other for almost twenty years. Twenty fucking years. Now the guy could barely muster any give a damn during a supposed intervention.

He tried to push it out of his mind as the downtown streets passed by the window, but that word stuck. Intervention. The *I* word. Number one on a guy's blacklist when he liked to go out and have a good time.

The irony of going to pick up a pound of marijuana after a failed intervention was not lost on him.

Chapter 3

"You look like shit." Devon looked him over with an upturned eyebrow and a scowl.

"One of those days, man." Aaron plopped down on the couch. Devon's apartment had all the style and class lacking in his, even if it did smell like bong water. Tasteful Art Deco, a white carpet that was actually white, and a beautiful view of the mountains out the window. It looked like he was aiming for Tony Montana and doing a fair job.

The TV flashed commercials for fast food and diet pills before coming back to reality-show bullshit, the same brain-rotting crap Devon had on every time Aaron stopped by.

"You got anything for me?"

Devon didn't take his gaze off the TV. "Yeah. Yeah, man. I got you."

He left the room once the commercials returned. He had the air of a pro about him. No small talk. No bullshit. None of the crap anyone who watched too much news thought every drug supplier came loaded with. Not one pit bull to be seen and, as far as Aaron knew, not a gun in the house.

He returned a moment later with two big bags under his arm. "Got some shit from California this time around. Sour Diesel."

Sour Diesel. The good stuff. A nice high that lasted a while and hit like a truck. Most of the guys selling skunk weed on the street didn't know a sativa from a hybrid, but Aaron had always been a bookworm. After ignoring the after-school specials and toking for the first time, he'd hit the books and done his homework. A well-informed dealer was one that made money, and Aaron had jumped into the game quick. Jobs that required a time clock were for the birds.

"Nice. I ran out a few days ago. I've been getting phone calls out the ass."

"Better go make that money, boy." He gave Aaron a sly look. "I heard you *ran out* at BJ's after staying there for a few days."

Nothing stayed a secret in this shithole town. "Moonshine, man. Moonshine and a few golden girls."

Just thinking about heroin got his blood burning for it, but he could stay sober if he wanted. He wouldn't say he wasn't a little addicted, but he wasn't sucking cocks for rocks, and he didn't need his so-called friends bombing his place with their bullshit.

Thinking about Marie talking about Aimee didn't help that craving though. Remembering the look on Brian's face didn't do much for it either.

"I got some in the back if you want to take a little brown sugar home."

He had fourteen hundred dollars in his pocket, enough for one pound of weed. Devon didn't cut his stock. You bought it by the unit or you went home empty-handed.

His foot did the junkie jive just thinking about getting high. He wanted to put this shit day behind him. Take a hot shower, throw on some music, and just lose his fucking mind for an evening. Maybe grab a beer or two and tell this day to fuck itself good and proper. Wrap up in a heated blanket, smoke a bag, and chill.

What Marie had said about Aimee stuck in his mind, though. The snotty look on his sister's face when he'd do something stupid flashed through his head, and his face grew hot. That same expression she'd given him when he stayed out too late, knowing well and good there would be hell to pay for it. He couldn't fathom what she might think of him now, and that thought punched him harder than anything Marie could have said.

He didn't realize he'd been staring into space until Devon spoke. "You all right? You have a little party earlier?"

A smart addict stayed out of jail by making sure he didn't mix business with pleasure. "No, man. I'm cool. Like I said, just a shit day." He wasn't cool; he was pissed. He wanted out of this crap. He wanted to get the hell away. But Aimee's memories lived in this town. Their home. Their schools. The door to their secret kingdom.

That made him smile. He hadn't thought about it in a long time. "I'll be all right."

"Good. Blow it off. Shit comes, and shit goes."

The pothead anthem. He paid Devon and left him to his programs, texting his missed calls and connections to get some paper in his pocket. He'd sell his fourteen-hundred-dollar purchase for more than twice that, keeping the lights on and his stomach full for another month. Things were always tight since Marie left, but that wasn't news in his life. Things had never been great.

He made his rounds, dropping off an ounce or two here, a half or three there. He didn't fuck around with dime bags; it wasn't worth his time. Tapping the steering wheel as he drove around filling out his friends "prescriptions". This whole gig was a waste of talent as it was. Everyone wanted to rub elbows and be his friend to try to get free weed. Some dumb fucks even tried to dime him out to the cops when he wouldn't, as if the cops gave a shit in Umber Gardens. Bad enough that this bullshit was what he had to do to keep the lights on; he wasn't going to do it for ten dollars at a time.

Most days he sneered in the car and smiled at the door, but not today. Today all thoughts drifted on the river of the mind, past selling weed, past the would-be intervention, and back eight years. Back to Aimee.

Her name rang in his ears as if a nuclear bomb had gone off. For eight years, he hadn't thought of her when he could help it. Not her or that house, or the horrible people who lived in it. There had been times he couldn't help it, of course. When that awful *Alice in Wonderland* movie had come out, the posters everywhere reminded him that Aimee had missed her favorite movie. It sent him hiding in his bedroom, the tears perilously close but never quite there.

Other times it was more insidious. A voice on the street that sounded like her. A dream of the room the two of them had shared. Finding something in his closet she had once even so much as touched. Anything and everything ran the risk of stabbing him through the heart and sending him down that spiral to the comfort of needle-shaped oblivion, because everything felt better there. Why go through a few decades of therapy when you could drop thirty bucks and fly away to a golden paradise? Cheaper than Disneyworld with twice the thrills.

He drove and drove, his phone and "clients" forgotten for a while. The afternoon traffic ebbed and flowed like the tide, and Aimee was the seashells washing ashore. Unpacking that baggage wasn't easy. The good memories inevitably led to the bad, a straight line from point A to suicide no matter where he started. Everywhere except that stupid kingdom of theirs in the woods.

A dumb idea two kids had made up to escape their abusive parents, but even now, the ghost of a smile touched his lips thinking about it. When they were ten, they said they'd live there forever. She'd packed her backpack, toy tea set and all, and he'd helped her lug it all out to those two trees, to the little shack where they stopped to rest. The path out there had become as familiar as the one from home to the park up the block. They could have found it blindfolded.

"Do you think they'll even notice we're gone?" She leaned against one of the walls, the glass jars overhead shaking as her back smacked against it.

The air out there always smelled like spring, even in the winter. "Who cares? We'll never go back, right?"

She turned the question over for a full minute. "We'll have to if we want to go to the library. The one at the castle only has the books with the weird words."

The ones that shifted and changed every time they looked at them. Sometimes symbols with an air of menace about them, almost coming off the page. Other times just little squiggles. Sort of Chinese, but not quite. They'd asked Drippy about it, and he'd told them it was their kingdom, but that didn't mean everything in it belonged to them. He'd suggested they stay away from those books, and after that, they'd never been able to find the library again.

The castle at the heart of the Kingdom was always like that. Shifting and changing. One trip, what might have been a swimming pool before was now a tower that led upward forever, giving a grand view of everything around the Kingdom. From the edges of nothingness where it vanished, all the way to the path that led back to the real world.

They hadn't thought of this world, with its shitty traffic and drug problems, as the real world. This was just the world they were forced to go to every night. Drippy had made it clear they couldn't stay in the Kingdom past sunset, though what time the sun set in the Kingdom seemed fast and loose.

But they had thought the rules didn't apply. How could they have? At home, they were miserable, and in the world they'd made, they were rulers. Why not stay forever? So Aaron had nodded along with her stupid idea. "Good idea. We'll get a whole bunch of books if it works. We can keep them in the throne room." It wasn't stealing. Libraries let people borrow. They would just be borrowing it forever.

None of it had been a good idea. When they lay down to sleep in that outrageous castle, they'd woken up in the woods by the trees. All their carefully packed bags filled with childish bullshit were spilled around them. No indication how they had gotten there, and no sign of the shack where Drippy always waited to greet them. Aimee cried all the way back, fearing that they'd never be able to return for breaking the rules. Just as bad, Dad had beaten them within an inch of their lives.

"We almost called the cops, you little shits!" Lies and beatings. The only gifts he'd ever given them.

He sneered at the thought but froze as he pondered it. They had gone somewhere. They hadn't just gone out to the woods and waited there, playing until nightfall. They'd been somewhere else, then wound up back home despite their best efforts. No imagination was that strong.

But it didn't matter. As they always did, the memories went sour. It wasn't Aimee and Aaron playing in the castle library; it was Dad hitting Aaron so hard he saw double, and punching Aimee so hard one of her baby teeth came out. The past left a bitter taste in his

37

mouth. Aaron shook away the memories as he made another house call. No small talk this time.

Aimee would frown and turn away if she could see him now, and he would call her a stupid snob for it.

But she was dead, and the Kingdom was fake. It always had been, and they'd been fools to believe otherwise.

Chapter 4

By the time the sun started dipping below the horizon, Aaron had sold plenty more than enough to get a burger and a few beers. He parked his car out by the park where he, Aimee, and Brian had played as children.

He leaned against the front bumper of the 'stang while he chewed without tasting, checking his phone as often as Goober had earlier. He didn't give a damn about selling more stock. He wanted Brian or Marie to text him. After all day thinking about them and Aimee, he wanted something, anything from that time, to connect to. He didn't care if they were mad, not deep down. He might give them some shit about it, but he'd let it go back to business as usual if they would. He wanted to know if they gave enough of a damn to call and follow up on their crap. For once, he wished he wasn't so goddamn alone. Nobody could ever replace Aimee, but fuck if he didn't just want somebody… anybody.

They apparently didn't. They had moved out, hadn't they? They'd been calling less and less for months now, growing more distant every day. A little less, "What's up, man?" and a little more, "Hey. How are you?"

He put the phone away and stared at the rusted swings and dented slide. He and Aimee had slid down it a thousand times. The bench not ten feet away was where Brian had told him, sworn to silence in solemn confidence, that he'd always had a crush on Aimee, a fact unnoticed by absolutely nobody. Over there, by the piss-stinking trashcan, was where Aimee had whispered to Brian about the Kingdom, offering to take him if he promised not to tell a soul outside their gang.

Aaron smiled at the thought and took a swig off his second beer. Brian had never seen the kingdom. ID checked and entry denied at the door. It remained their little fantasy. Their secret place. A land where only the fantastic and the Vasilica twins were allowed to roam.

He'd knocked on the big trees when they found them in the woods. "This is it?"

Aimee and Aaron looked at one another. There should have been a path between the two trees. The ones that looked like they were older than the world. But there was nothing. No path and no shack.

Aaron shook his head. Drippy had seemed uneasy at the prospect of trying to bring people in, but he hadn't forbade it. He'd rubbed his paws together and looked away, mumbling under his breath. "Might not be as easy as all that, sers."

But he hadn't explained further. Aaron felt like a fool as Brian laughed at the good joke they'd played on him. A real knee slapper. He took the picture that even now sat on the nightstand by Aaron's bed.

It was easy to see the problem now. Of course there had been nothing there. The Kingdom had been nothing more than a stupid, childish fantasy. Had they thought it was real? Dragons and fairies. A man made of wax. A kingdom filled with loyal subjects whose problems could all be solved by abused children. The invention of terrified children to lessen the horror of coming home.

The swings rocked back and forth as the wind blew, silent phantoms at play in the shadows of the woods. They'd always thought they were so smart, but they couldn't see the obvious.

He threw the empty beer bottle at the playground. It hit the top of the slide and shattered into a thousand pieces, a shower of glass sprinkling down on the toys. He might have cared if anybody came out here. This was *that* section of town. Good parents didn't let their kids play here, and the kids with bad parents knew better. They had to stay away from junkies and drug dealers like Aaron. Brian had only been able to sneak out and play there with them by lying to his mother.

It brought a sneer to his face. He pulled his pipe out from under his driver's seat, stuffed it full of Sour Diesel, and went back to the hood of his car. He lit up and took a long puff as the sun vanished, plunging the world into twilight. A thick cloud of smoke hung in the air before gravity pulled it down. Without waiting, he took another big toke.

Fuck them. Fuck Marie and Brian. He wondered if they would call him a junkie for smoking pot at a park and decided it didn't matter as he took a third hit. He held it in until his chest burned as he looked out over the rusted childhood in front of him. He could almost hear Dad screaming, "*Get your asses in the truck, we got places to be.*" He let his breath out as he tapped the char out of his pipe and put it away.

A smarter man would have driven away and left this park with its mixed bag of memories. His dad had been a moron most of the time, but he'd dropped some wisdom on occasion. "Sometimes the day is a wash. You say fuck it, and you have another beer." Aaron did just that instead of leaving as he should have. He grabbed his last beer, lit up a Marlboro, and waited for the high to set in. A THC high wasn't as good as a nice big bag of skag, but it would do in a pinch. He was just a guy who wanted to blow off steam. A guy who didn't give a flying fuck about a bank account or a nice place. They didn't like him because he didn't put on airs. The fucking illusions of grandeur as tall as the sky so many built across their lives, only to be eighty-year-old half-dead corpses living atop them. They could keep that shit. He did just fine in the gutters.

He rolled his eyes as he sat on the hood. He really did sound like Dad.

The darkness set in deeper and deeper with every passing minute, and the world slipped further and further away. Turned sideways, as some junkie or another had said once. Everything stretched out in the dim light of the nearby streetlamp under the cloudless sky. Everything mellowed just a little bit. It became a problem on a shelf. Still a problem, but set too far away for him to give a damn.

He stared at the forest on the far side of the park as the high settled in and the beers did their thing. Those woods were the place he and Aimee had spent most of their childhood. They'd loved the library, but it had just as many rules as home, even if the consequences were less dire. Out there, surrounded by nothing but hills and trees, they'd found freedom. They became masters of their own kingdom, even if it was fake.

Aaron laughed aloud at his own mental joke. Masters of their own little kingdom. *The* Kingdom. Just him and Aimee.

And now just him. Just him for eight years.

He took another drag and chugged the rest of his beer. He didn't want to be alone anymore, but nothing filled that hole. In losing her, he had lost a piece of himself. People with missing limbs didn't just get over it. They noticed it every day, even if they learned to adapt. Aimee dying was the same pain, the same daily recognition of absence.

He stood, swaying slightly in his less-than-sober state. He should go out there. He should be in that place where they'd been together so much. He'd done it enough times as a kid that he could find it blindfolded. Aimee wouldn't be there, but her memories would be closer.

He walked toward the wood line, throwing the empty beer bottle at the playground and missing by a mile. He staggered past the old equipment, their three-man gang silently flashing in front of his eyes. He and Aimee on the swings. Dad screaming for them to get in the truck and come home as Brian watched with his mouth open. Brian asking Aimee to the eighth-grade dance and Aimee laughing until he turned red and she felt bad.

The forest engulfed him, and the light of the rising moon dimmed beneath the canopy. He stopped as his eyes adjusted. People got lost out here all the time. That sort of shit played on the news weekly during the summer months. Campers vanishing in the blackest sections of the woods. Warnings from wildlife officials that Umber Gardens was dangerous no matter how experienced an outdoorsman you were. Way more people missing than could be accounted for by "accidents". Ten times the national average. But he had never been afraid. Not as a kid, and not now. Too much fear made people weak. He continued forward, lettings his memories guide him, feeling his way as much as seeing it.

The hills and meadows of Umber Gardens radiated menace at night. Infinite eyes of unknown things pressed in on every side. Legends about the insane asylum that had burned to the ground somewhere in these wilds were told around campfires every summer and laughed off. Stories of a killer who'd stalked the city since pioneer times, painting the floor of his old church to keep the monsters in. All of it silly. All of it exactly the kind of macabre bullshit that people in this town ate up. But alone, out here, it was easy to believe. Easy to think the old trees didn't appreciate having people around.

Or that could just be the weed. Paranoia and poverty, the junkie's best friends. He shook his head and flicked his smoke into the underbrush. Silly bullshit. Childish garbage. They had spent every day out here for years and years. There were no more monsters here than there were anywhere else. Grandma had laid it all out for them.

"You two. You two are special. You never be afraid of anything, hear?"

She visited every chance she had, though the drive from New York to Tennessee grew harder for her each year. The idea of asking their parents to go to New York to visit her never even crossed Aaron's mind, and he knew what the answer would be regardless—a smack across the face.

Grandma hated Dad as much as Aaron and Aimee did, though she was careful never to say anything in front of them. She was from the Old Country, and in the Old Country, people had rules about that sort of thing. Dad was always on his best behavior around her as well.

"That old witch might fuckin' poison me," he'd said to Mom once after Grandma had left.

But Grandma coming to town held the same reverence from the twins as Christmas and summer. More, even. Nothing changed during the holidays, but everything was better when she came. There were trips for ice cream. Praise. She told stories while Mom and Dad

45

went out to drink and she sat in the house with her grandchildren. Stories of the Old Country. Of myths and legends. Stories of other people born with the special eyes, and the things they had been able to do.

Aaron and Aimee had looked at one another during one such story, a tale about a young girl who could talk to animals and walk through trees to secret worlds as numerous as the stars in the sky. She'd saved her village from bandits by calling the animals of the forest to her aid, but then she'd been cast out to wander and explore the worlds beyond her own forever.

They didn't need to ask each other if they should let her in on the secret of their kingdom. It crossed between them in the same unspoken language so many things did.

"We have a special place too, *puri daj*."

She had been pulling a cigarette out of her purse, but she stopped with her hand hovering over it when Aimee spoke. "Yes?"

Aimee glanced at Aaron before she continued. "It's out in the woods, and only the two of us can go. It's like… It's a whole kingdom."

Grandma leaned in close. "You imagined this?"

Both of them shook their heads in unison. "No, Grandma. We go there a lot. We can do anything!" A note of excitement entered her voice. "It's—"

Grandma covered her ears with her hands. "Tut, tut, tut. That is a place for you, not for your *puri daj*. You keep that secret, and you never forget it. Hear? And don't be scared of it. You are special. You fear nothing."

Aaron sized her up then, as if seeing her for the first time. She looked older than even the guardian trees out in the woods, and she always wore that red scarf around her head. Aaron had never seen her without it. Mom said she didn't have hair underneath.

And strangest of all, she believed them. He could see it in her eyes.

"Isn't a little fear good, *puri daj*?" Aimee smiled the way she did every time she thought she'd asked a clever question. Ever the apple-polisher.

Grandma pursed her lips. "No. Not for you. You are special. You have the eyes of a god, and don't you forget." One blue, one hazel. Their pass to the Vasilica secret club. Better than a decoder ring.

She reminded them of that the day she left for the last time.

"Your dad, he's stupid. Your mom, she's stupid and weak. You aren't stupid, and you don't let yourself be weak. Hear?"

They nodded in unison. She kissed the tops of their heads and got into her Volkswagen, waving bye at Mom without looking at Dad. She didn't smile. She never smiled.

Grandma wouldn't look him in the eyes if she were around to see him now. *Why do you fill your body with poison? Stupid boy.* He could almost hear her. She'd be on his case no different from anyone else. Still, thinking about her made the walk a little easier. He weaved through the brush, heading steadily deeper, a piece of the

47

night making its way toward the secret heart that led to his childhood kingdom.

He never lost his way, not even high as a kite and eight years rusty. Before long, he found the familiar trail that led back to their old house one way, and toward the guardian trees the other. He stood on it for a moment, drinking it in, looking back and forth. Their feet had stomped and tripped here a thousand times. They had whispered secret conversations so frequently on the worn trail he could almost catch them in the quiet murmurs of leaves. They vanished as suddenly as they began. Dead whispers on phantom lips.

He walked on. Past the bends. Over the old creek on the log. Well away from the noise of the city, and past where hikers ever came. Out to a place where the forest resembled a jungle in South America more than a stretch of woods in the rural Tennessee.

The guardians were impossible to miss. Giants among giants. Their girth easily tripled the next biggest trees around them. How could they not find this place as children? Of course they'd have been drawn here eventually, and of course they'd think it was special. Even in the moonlight, it impressed myths and legends on the waking mind. Surely it did the same to the sleeping one.

He wiped his mouth. Memories played like silent film images projected onto years of fog. The first time they'd come here. The last. The times he'd sat here after she'd died, screaming at these sentinels. Begging them to let him in. Wondering why he wasn't allowed to go back to the Kingdom anymore.

Tears and snot streaming down his face, he'd gouged at the guardians with his pocketknife as if they could feel pain, as if he could share his fury at their rejection. The blade had broken on the right one, leaving a scar on his hand. Their way of saying they didn't give a flying fuck about his temper tantrums.

He touched the place where he'd left the bark scarred. Still there. Those marks as irrelevant as ever.

"You're just a tree. You've always been just a tree, haven't you?" They rose up forever, touching the bottom of the moon with their branches, as though he could climb up to heaven and find Aimee there. "And it was all bullshit, wasn't it? Never real. Just a way for some scared kids to get out for a little while."

He balled his hand into a fist on the wood. Why the hell had he come out here? There weren't any answers, and certainly no comfort. Just some old trees in an old forest in an old, shitty town.

"If you've got a door here, open it the hell up. I'm sick of being alone out here." He plopped onto the ground as wind rustled through the plants. The same eerie quiet had always pervaded this place. Lighting a smoke illuminated the area as if it were a cave. Aaron stared at the guardians through the flame. Would they burn if he lit them? Would it bring any pleasure or relief to watch this place and its memories turn to ash?

As if to answer him, a single bird called from somewhere beyond the two trees. Long and sullen, it wailed for a nearly a minute without changing pitch, then stopped.

He froze with the cigarette in his mouth. No bird in Tennessee made that call. More like one of the colorful things so common in the Kingdom. He waited for it to cry again.

It didn't. The adrenaline faded, and he smoked his cigarette down, watching the cherry in the dark. The booze and the Sour Diesel kept him mellow even when he wanted to crack up. When the butt was spent and he'd flicked it into the woods, he sat in solitude, trying not to think of anything at all.

The magic of the place hadn't faded in all the years away. "What the hell is this place, huh? What are you hiding?"

The trees, as stoic as the Earth itself, didn't respond.

"Why did we come here as kids?" He stood and wiped his ass off, ready to leave, but something between the trees caught his attention.

The barest glimpse of a roof in the moonlight.

Aimee's words rang back after twenty years. *It's right there.*

"What the fuck?" He could almost feel her hands on the sides of his head, pointing him in the direction of the shack.

See?

He did see. His mouth hung open. Shingles on a roof. The hint of white below them. Far enough away that he couldn't be sure but close enough that he couldn't stop staring.

"No goddamn way." It hadn't been real. Not the shack, not the Kingdom, and most certainly not the people. Childish fantasies.

The guardians groaned as if a strong wind had moved them, a deep crackling that issued from somewhere inside.

He took a step back. There was no wind.

The thousand eyes of Umber Gardens stared holes into him, reminding him how alone he was out here. If he screamed, there was nobody for miles around to hear.

In the distance, one of the exotic birds called again. Another answered, closer. The trees moaned once more, and the shack taunted him, trying to draw him closer with the seduction of secrets and things long forgotten.

"No. No way."

The noises continued, and the moonlight brightened, illuminating a path that hadn't been there before. A yellow piece of string lay in the brush at his feet. Not the first time. It had been there once before, on a cold fall evening a long time ago.

For one maddening second, he felt the urge to embrace it. Grab the string, get on the path, and follow wherever it would lead. Back to the Kingdom maybe, to Aimee? To the answers everyone who maybe used a little too much was looking for deep down?

But things that enchanted as a child terrified as an adult. This couldn't be real. It was the weed or the beers. The stress of that goddamn intervention, or thinking about Aimee for the first time in a long time.

The stories of the monsters and madmen that roamed the woods whispered in his mind. He retreated a step and the spell shattered. The noise continued, the moonlight still highlighted the string and the shack, but he wouldn't follow. He ran, the calls of the guardians and the exotic animals following him as he fled into the night.

Chapter 5

"Ser. Ser, come back."

A black, endless void surrounded him, filled with things the size of planets that moved just out of sight. Hulking monstrosities of flesh and thought stared at him as he flailed in eternal fall.

"Your kingdom needs you, ser."

There was no up and down. Only the here and the not-here. Careening through the here into the not-here toward an inevitable death, but never reaching it. The soul-crushing fear in his guts was the steel to the magnet at the center. He tumbled through the dark, monsters and madness just out of reach. Every heartbeat pounded against his chest, a hammer on an anvil.

"Ser, come back."

The ringing of his cellphone brought him out of his dream. The steady beeping pulsed in the nothingness. *Beep. Beep. Beep.* A chiming beacon leading him out, away from the dark place between worlds with its dark sentinels. *Beep. Beep. Beep.* It grew and grew at the edge of sense, finally tugging his eyes open.

Still on the couch where he'd fallen asleep. Oprah spoke on the TV, the volume too loud. He'd left every light in the apartment on. He rubbed the sleep from his eyes. There had been trees, and the old path back to the Kingdom. A trip down memory lane that had been a bit too literal for his half-drunk, fully high mind.

Beep. Beep. Beep.

It had been so real. He remembered going out there. Drinking. Breaking the bottle on the playground and internally bitching about his family.

Beep. Beep. Beep.

The ringing broke through his thoughts, and he answered it without looking. "Hello?"

"Aaron?"

Marie. Her voice punched him in the gut, and he sat up straighter. No thoughts of old forest paths or getting blitzed in the wood, just that voice pushing everything else out. The way she greeted him—tentative, almost shy—could only mean one thing. And the sudden rush at the thought of her that used to last for days vanished as quickly as it came.

"Aaron, I'm sorry."

Always sorry. After every fight, like clockwork. He didn't say anything, but he dug around in the couch cushions and found the remote, muting Oprah as she consoled a crying mother.

"I didn't mean to get so angry yesterday. I'm just scared for you. You… Things have been so different lately."

He sat and listened in stony silence, still only half-awake.

"I love you."

They did this dance every time. Every goddamned time. He knew the steps by heart. Get together, things would be fine, he'd have a good time, she'd flip shit, they'd break up, pause, and reset. The Imperial Russian Ballet Company couldn't time it better. And much like an actual dance recital, it was fucking exhausting.

He opened his mouth to speak but thought better of it. Why? Fucking why? All of this same shit over and over again. She got nastier every time. Bringing up Aimee? Nothing was sacred with them anymore. Their entire relationship had become a race to see who could be nastier, who could both be hurt the most and do the most hurting. He deserved better, and so did she.

"Are you there?"

Thoughts of his sister brought him back to the night before. Running through the woods. The sounds behind him. Birds that had no place in Tennessee screaming, trees groaning as if the forest were having a conversation even with no wind. Driving home blitzed and terrified to sit on the couch, eyes wide until he passed out. He was lucky the cops hadn't nabbed him. With as much weed as he had in the trunk, that would've been the end of the line. White or not, he wouldn't have gotten away with it.

"I'm not mad at you. I'm mad at the drugs. I'm mad at what we've been putting ourselves through. I'm mad at myself."

The noises. The weird hallucinations. Stuff like that didn't just happen, no matter what Grandma had once told them.

"Aaron, would you please say something?" That quiet in her voice, that mousiness, reminded him of Aimee when she would talk to Mom and Dad. Afraid to say the wrong thing. Afraid they'd fly off the handle. Marie was one step away from her flinching when he raised his hand.

He said the most decisive thing he could, nothing at all, and pressed End Call. The phone clicked off as Oprah spoke silently to a bratty-looking kid with her arms crossed. Pleading with her eyes the same way Aaron imagined Marie did when she talked to him like that.

He wasn't going to do this with her anymore. He'd cracked up last night and tripped balls in the forest on nothing but two beers and a dime. The stress of dealing with their bullshit was mounting.

And equally importantly, maybe more importantly, she deserved better too. He'd dragged her into this life. He'd done nothing but bring her down for years now. It hadn't always been like that, but it was now. He gave her no reason to love him, but she did, and that kept them coming back together like shit-covered magnets. Maybe it was time to let her find someone better, someone like that dumb Goober who could give her the kind of buttoned-down life she was already making for herself. Lord knew his broken ass would never be able to give it to her.

She'd said he was fun once. Called him the adventure in her life. He'd made her bold—brave like he'd always thought he made Aimee. And here he was, leaving her too.

Just thinking it hurt. Tearing Marie out was like tearing another hole in his chest, right next to the Aimee-shaped one in his heart. Maybe not as big, but an opening none the less. But why not? What was any of this worth? If she could still find something to love in the world, he should let her have that.

Everything hurt him, but he knew what would fix it—a nice little pile of white lady. Some horse to make the day pass by a little smoother. He tapped the remote with his finger, thinking about it. Not the outrageous crackhead high they showed in the movies. A guy passed out in an alley, a needle sticking out of his arm. Just something to make life go down a little easier, disgusting as it might be. A bag up the nose. If it had been a terrible day, shoot it between your toes or in your groin.

After that, all you had to do was chill. No wild rides. No crazy bullshit. Not eating someone's face off like it was goddamn bath salts. Just fucking unwind. And if you wanted to keep it going a little while longer, just take a little more. No more dead sisters, no more bad memories or weird woodland sounds, and certainly no girlfriends nagging you about your problems as if they were hers. Just the chill, and the ugly realization that you were the drug problem in America.

He threw the blanket off and rubbed his face. Not today. Not after yesterday. He wasn't a junkie. He wanted it, and he wanted it bad, but he didn't *need* it. He wasn't like the crackheads on Broad Street.

He jumped into the shower and turned it up until it burned, keeping a cup of water and a beer on the toilet to ease himself out of the hangover. He'd gotten himself filthy screwing around in the woods. Dirt from the guardian trees swirled and vanished down the drain. Hallucinations. A bad day. It wouldn't be the first time he'd imagined something while relaxing after a troubling afternoon. Never on just weed and beer before, but that didn't mean it couldn't happen.

By the time he'd finished, the clock read 1:00 pm. He put clothes on and hit speed dial one. Brian. It only rang twice before he picked up.

"What's up, G?" Cool as a cat. No mention of interventions or holes in hallway walls.

"What are you up to?" Aaron lit a smoke as he leaned back on the couch. Oprah had given way to some family sitcom bullshit, the kind that kids from bad homes daydreamed about. Dinner on the table by five every day, and Dad *never* touched Mom, though the question of whether or not they fucked remained on everyone's mind.

"Writing something up for work. About to go grab lunch. You?"

The perfect sister, brother, and father mouthed silent witticisms on the TV, and everyone smiled. He could almost hear the laugh track. He hated this shit. "Mind some company? Yesterday got nasty, and I need to get out for a bit."

"I need to get out," had become code for, "Don't leave me here alone" during their teenage years. Brian sighed as if he were considering it, but caved like he always did. "Yeah, sure, man. Meet at the office in half an hour?"

"You got it." Aaron ended the call without another word.

Chapter 6

Marie picked at things. She scratched at scabs until they bled, and questioned until someone blew up. Not Brian. As long as there wasn't a wall to run into, he kept on going as if everything were fine, even when it wasn't.

Aaron clicked off the TV and left down the stairs that looked every bit as disgusting as the rest of the building. Water-stained, creaky, and with peeling paint. The parking lot filled with weeds wasn't much better, and as usual, Umber Gardens looked as if a storm was brewing overhead. Dark clouds, the occasional grumble of thunder mixing with the shouts and rumble of trucks from the factory across the street. The stink of sulfur in the air from the paper mill up the block. Even the nice sections of this town screamed, "Kill me" loud and clear, and yet it lived on. Day after day and year after year, it crawled through time, a living corpse bloated with maggots like Aaron.

He jumped into his car. The city flew by out the window, and it didn't take long to reach the storefront of the local rag Brian wrote for. From school newspaper to local journalist, he was living the dream. Sure, that dream might be writing articles about house bands or a function UNICEF was doing for charity, but a writing job that paid the bills was further than Aaron had ever gotten.

He'd droned on and on about doing it as a child. "*The New York Times*?" Aaron said as they sat around the lunch table at school. "That's shooting a little high, don't you think?"

Brian raised an eyebrow at him, and Aimee tsked. "I think you can do it." She smiled her perfect smile, long blond hair falling down her back. "You're really good."

"Thanks." He turned to Aaron. "It's no more fantastic than being a bestselling author, jerk."

Aaron took another bite of his sandwich. "It's all about how you sell it, man. You don't have to write a bestseller, you just have to make everyone else think you did."

Aimee's mouth dropped open. "You're already slacking, and you haven't even started yet!"

They laughed through the rest of the lunch period at that and the other in-jokes only the three of them shared. That night they'd gone to Brian's house for dinner. His mom took care of them as if they were her own, always supporting and encouraging them in ways their parents never had. She told them they could be anything, and when she said it, it was easy to believe.

They were young and invincible that year. On the cusp of moving past childhood to better things. Best-seller lists for Aaron and a Pulitzer for Brian. Aimee would go to school for psychology and help kids who suffered at home as they had. All of them were so sure of themselves, and yet so utterly unable to see tragedy just around the bend. That had been six months before he ran away. Seven before Aimee took her life.

Aaron sighed as he parked a few spaces up the street from Brian's car. He eyed the newspaper office. It wasn't the *New York Times*, and there was no Pulitzer in sight, but it was something.

Brian jogged up and knocked on the window. "Yo, girl. You want me to buy you some lunch? I'm a local celebrity."

Aaron stepped out of the car. "I'm not fat enough to be one of your girlfriends."

"Well, let's fix that. Tacos?" He nodded at the taco cart up the street. Uncle Pedro's Perfect Carne.

"I don't think anyone named Uncle Pedro has ever had anything to do with that abomination."

"Good tacos anyway." Brian started toward the place, but they didn't make it ten feet before he spoke up again. "Sorry about yesterday."

Aaron shrugged. "Don't sweat it. I imagine it wasn't your idea." Though if he were a betting man, he'd wager Brian hadn't done anything to stop it.

"Obviously. I didn't get the full scoop until she had me in the car."

He believed it. Brian had always been a live and let live kinda guy. Sure, he might get pissed when Aaron smoked in the apartment. He'd asked Aaron not to run his "business" out of their home, but he'd never gotten on Aaron about drugs. He hadn't even complained when Aaron had tweaked out one night and demanded Brian drive him to the hospital at 4:00 am after a bad trip and a lot of alcohol.

Brian let it all slide, so Aaron let it slide. No different now than any other time. He wanted to unwind and forget, and hanging around the other member of the old gang always aired out the bad feelings, at least a little. It was as close to Aimee as Aaron ever got anymore.

They ordered their tacos and ate on the hood of the 'stang.

"I don't want to beat it up, man, but she went too far talking about Aimee. If I had known she was going to do that, I wouldn't have let her get that crap started in the first place."

Aaron took his first bite. "It is what it is. She can be a bitch."

"She does it because she cares. We both do. I don't think that shit is going to help anyone, though."

He hadn't expected a comment like that. "Help? Usually, when people want that, they yell 'help me' in a loud voice."

"Don't be shitty. You know what I mean."

Aaron stared at the blue sky. The previous day's frustration bubbled up inside him. "No, I don't. I want my friends to just fucking accept it when I say that I'm fine."

Brian raised his hands, half-eaten taco and all. "Relax. I'm not going to start it up again. I just wanted to say I'm sorry about what she said. It got to me too. I think about Aimee a lot."

"Like I said, it is what it is." But inside it was more. He wanted to tell Brian to drop it. He wanted to tell him if he hadn't insisted Aaron had a problem, they could have just hung out and drunk a beer

62

like they used to. He wanted to be mad at someone for having to think about Aimee.

Brian looked as if he would say something more, but he never did anymore. For a long time he'd talked about how he took care of Aimee's grave: kept it clean, got rid of the weeds, put down flowers. Later, after the paper hired him, he'd talked about writing an article on suicide awareness and prevention.

Aaron couldn't bring himself to go to her grave. Not once since the funeral. What if he sat down to talk to her and couldn't find the will to get up again? Even now, thinking about it, he wanted to buy a big enough pile of junk to die on and just say goodbye. Go out with a bang. Ride up to see her on a golden cloud.

He didn't want to forget Aimee, and he didn't even understand moving on, but he didn't want to talk about it, either. Some things were too close even for best friends. Better to let it alone. Keep those things quiet. Everyone in the world was too damn familiar with one another. They didn't understand what it was like, and he wasn't going to waste breath trying to explain.

"You still trying to write?"

Aaron glanced over out of the corner of his eye, giving Brian a sly smile even as his heart ached. "Only unicorny bullshit."

Brian laughed so hard that bits of taco sprayed from his mouth, and he started to choke.

"Unicorny" became the official code word for bad writing when Aimee insisted in middle school she could do it just as well as Aaron and Brian. The result was the story of a unicorn that learned to live among humans. Tropes, run-on sentences, and ugly verbs from front to back.

She sat them down at the table in the park, ignoring the stink of piss that wafted up from under it. "Don't be too hard on me, okay? I think it's pretty good, but it probably needs some work."

Aaron rolled his eyes. "I can either be honest or nice, but probably not both."

She fixed him with the bossy-sister expression he hated so damn much. "I'd like to remind you, Aaron Vasilica, that I'm doing better in English class than you are." She didn't quite put on a smug smile, but it was close. That holier-than-thou attitude of hers killed him.

"Fine. I'm sure it's amazing. Will you shut up and let me read?"

It wasn't as promised. It was so bad that Aaron had to stop himself from laughing aloud more than once. While Aimee leaned against the table, staring off into the woods behind the park, Brian and Aaron made eye contact over their pages, both trying not to giggle. Brian's face burned red from the effort.

"It's adorable!" She turned around as Brian and Aaron set their copies back down on the table. "Isn't it?" She stared at Brian, waiting for his praise.

"It's...it's...great." He plastered a fake smile across his face.

She looked at Aaron, her grin nearly touching her ears.

"Aimee, I love you."

She smiled and glanced away, embarrassed by what she thought was a compliment. The picture of a talented young woman poising in an appropriately humble manner. Eyes downturned. Grin sheepish, yet accepting.

"But this is unicorny bullshit."

The wind died, and even the birds stopped singing. Her mouth dropped open as if she'd been slapped.

Both Aaron and Brian burst out laughing. Aimee turned red as Brian slipped off the bench and fell to the grass.

"Screw you, Aaron!" She stormed to the swings, not looking back, her hair swaying in the breeze. "Screw you both! You're just jealous!" Her voice went hoarse as she screamed it over her shoulder.

Aaron watched her sit with her arms crossed before he turned back to Brian. "Like, really bad."

Brian rolled on the ground. The infectious laughter spread, and soon Aaron couldn't stop, either. To nobody's great surprise, Aimee didn't join in.

Ever since, unicorny had been their go-to slang. Even now, more than a decade later, it hadn't gotten old. She'd never missed a chance to show off her intelligence or talents, and Aaron never missed a chance to poke the bear.

"Aimee rolls over in her grave every time you say that."

And for a moment, laughing was okay. As it tapered off, Aaron dropped his taco, and it started anew. Like the old days, if only for a while.

"Her stuff was really, really bad." Brian smiled as he took a bite, wiping a tear from his eye with his free hand.

Aaron rubbed the dirt off his meal. "Yes, unbelievably bad, and you never had the balls to tell her."

Brian shrugged. "What can I say? Your smoking-hot sister had me wrapped around her finger."

"Ugh. Dude. She wasn't fat enough for you to date, either."

"Nobody could replace her. I had to lower my standards after that."

"You two didn't ever bang, did you?"

Brian scrunched up his face in disbelief at the question, though Aaron didn't know if that meant he was about to tell a lie or not. "No."

They ate in silence for a while, and that was okay too. They hadn't spoken about her this much since a few weeks after the funeral. Flexing those joints hurt, but it was a good hurt. They'd been locked up a long time.

Brian blew out a breath. "She was the best, man. I miss her."

Aaron couldn't look in a mirror without seeing her, but he couldn't say that to Brian. "Me too."

"So is the writing going that bad?"

"A few hundred words over a few hundred days. I'd say yeah."

"What are you trying to write?"

Aaron set the taco down and ran a hand through his hair. "Fuck, dude. At this point I'd write to prison pen pals with a foot fetish if I thought it would get me going."

He would too, with pictures of his own attached. He'd crawl across broken glass. He'd do anything except the actual work. Every time he sat down, it vanished. The good ideas, the perfect sentences in his head; every time, every one, gone. He'd dropped out of college after half a semester for the same reason. Brian had gone on to get his bachelors in journalism. Without a doubt, Aimee would have finished her degree if she were still around. She hadn't been wrong when she said she was smarter than Aaron; he just hated to hear it.

"Just keep at it." Same advice, different day. "You ever consider writing a story about that imaginary kingdom you and Aimee had?"

The dark forest full of speaking trees and exotic birds. The feeling of being chased out of the woods at night. For a moment, he was back there, not on a day-lit street next to his best friend. It was so vivid, he dropped his taco again. "What?" He froze, any follow-up stuck in his throat. Why would Brian bring that up now?

"You remember, right? You and Aimee convinced me you found a secret castle and town out in the middle of the woods. One day we went out there, but we never found the shack the two of you were talking about."

Aaron's mouth went dry. "Yeah, I remember."

"You guys had all sorts of crazy stuff. The weird animals, and the waterfall that fell out of the throne room and down a cliff. You actually convinced me it was all real."

The mention of it twinged something in the back of his mind. That waterfall, the one where Aimee had sailed the little paper ships. The ones she said would find Grandma on the other side after she'd died. He'd folded them. He cut his thumb on one. That cut had been on his finger for weeks. It had stung every time he'd done anything.

"I think the best part was how you couldn't go there at night. Like, why not? What was there that you guys weren't allowed to see?"

Something. A monster, or monsters. Drippy had never told them about it, only mumbled under his breath while escorting them out.

"No! No sirree, sers!" He had practically pushed them down the path as the sky turned red with the colors of sunset. The wax of his body had been warm as it fell down Aaron's arms, but it always vanished as it hit the ground. "Even royalty must obey, and thus you aren't allowed to stay! Now get, gone, go away! Come rule again another day!"

"But why!" Aimee had literally stomped her feet on the dirt path, taking the princess thing as far as she could push it. "If it's our kingdom, we make the rules!"

But all Drippy said was, "When you're older!" before nudging them past the shack with one final shove. When they'd turned around, it was all gone. No hill. No castle. No strange people. Just the afternoon Tennessee woods, not even dusk yet out in the real world.

He remembered that. Their kingdom, but even they had rules to follow.

Brian was still staring at him as Aaron broke free of his memories. "That would make an amazing story."

Aaron needed a fix, badly. All this Aimee talk was too much. Too many old memories and too many questions about that place. Too much heartache with Marie. Too many thoughts of Mom and Dad and all the shit they'd wrought. He wanted something that would wipe him out. Make those weird questions stop. Make it all— the day, the week, this life—seem okay.

"I need to go." Aaron stood up without looking at Brian. "I forgot I have some stuff to do." He tossed the remains of his taco into the street, nearly hitting a passing car.

"Is it the Aimee talk? We can change the subject, man. Go see a movie or something."

His way of reaching out. *Let's just forget about the world for a bit.* There were better ways to do that than movies.

"No. It's fine. I just gotta go. Call me, all right?"

Brian watched as Aaron climbed into the Mustang. "Okay. Sure. Be safe." He had to be used to it by now. The sudden shifts. The unpredictability. How could he not be? He'd lived with Aaron for years.

"Yup." Aaron shut the door and started the car, pulling out into traffic.

Time to fix this shit. He could carry on just as well gorked out of his mind as most people could sober. He had to. He had to do something to block out the bad memories that always rode the good ones in like a tick. Memories of Dad and his fist. Memories of Aimee crying at Grandma's funeral. Getting beaten up at home for getting beaten up after school.

He waited until he couldn't see his best friend and interventionist's assistant in the rearview anymore. As soon as he turned a corner, he popped out his phone and dialed Devon.

"Hey, bro. Still got any white lady lying around?"

Chapter 7

A quick trip to Devon's with his fingers tapping the wheel the whole time yielded exactly the medicine he needed. The drive back home had been carefully blank. Not a junkie. Junkies needed to take a hit right away; he had things to do first.

Now the baggie sat on the kitchen counter like an accusation. He'd worked around it, making a lunch out of four-day-old pizza and beer. Pretending to clean, even though a flamethrower and a prayer couldn't get the job done in his shithouse apartment. Anything but taking, because he wasn't a junkie. Always playing the stupid games that let him know he didn't have a problem.

Don't take it right away. You don't need it, right? Just a little to take the edge off later. Maybe after you do some writing?

When that didn't work, and his palms started to sweat, he looked at anything but the bag, thought about anything but the sweet release inside.

He wondered who made bags like that while he tapped his fingers against his lips. Did some drug dealer who worked in a corporate office at a plastic factory say, "Hey! I have a great idea! Sandwich bags for your drugs." What the hell else could you use them for?

And who stocked them? It wasn't like you could go to the store and ask for dime bags to sell your weed in, if you were the kind of stupid hood who slung that amount. Maybe all the Nancy Reagan-bot drug busters kept tabs on those kinds of bags. Maybe cops watched anyone who picked them up from whatever bodega they found them at, keeping a registry of every skuzzball in the city who needed either tiny sandwiches or just a little bit of drugs.

His mental questions became more frantic as he chewed the pizza. His gaze drifted back to the bag. Instead of giving in, he went to the living room and turned on the TV. Shit had been coming at him hard and fast for a whole day now, and he was just coming down from a three-day binge. He tapped his foot against the table in the living room and lit a smoke while he waited for the inevitable. The acceptance. The acknowledgment that he wasn't a junkie, he just liked to use to unwind. To feel better about the world. To feel anything.

Just a taste. Just a tingle.

That was all it took. He jumped up and pulled his rig out of the desk drawer in the bedroom. If he was going to fuck himself up, he was going to do it right. The same old spoons, the same syringe with a different needle. Cotton swabs and the same cup for water every time. He took it all into the living room and set it neat as could be on the table, then put on some music, shut off the TV, and got to work.

It didn't take long if you knew what you were doing. Within a few minutes, he'd mixed it up and filtered it into the syringe. Custom-made and ready to rock. The light from the hole in the drapes struck it as he examined his work. Golden and delicious. A goddamn lifesaver. He never understood how people coped without something like this. What the hell did straight-laced people do when it got to be too much? Jack off? Beat your kids?

He pulled his shoe off and wrapped a constricting band around his ankle, waiting for one of the good veins to show up. The other foot was starting to look a little cracked out. Little holes between the toes. Bruises. The whole foot looked infected, and he didn't want to lose it. Better to move on to greener pastures, and only a dumbass of a drug dealer used a vein a cop could see.

When he found the vein, he didn't hesitate. Pop it in, push the plunger, and take the ride. Just a little spoonful, a bit of medicine to make life go down smoother. Another way to fall into that big, dark void, but at least this one made you forget for a while.

He tossed the contraption aside and closed his eyes. Relief washed over him before anything else. No more anxiety. No more overthinking. The stains on the walls and carpet ceased to exist. The stink of the paper mill and the constant noise of trucks coming and going on the highway vanished. Everything would be okay. That drug inside him wasn't just a solution; it was comfort. The family dog grown in Afghanistan and delivered to your door. Everything else would drip away. The fat of life always burned off in the oven once you found a way to turn that fucker on.

It didn't take long for the first sweet fingers of the Golden-Eyed Girl to caress him. A little tingle. A little euphoria. They said it was never as sweet as the first time, and that was true to a point. Some of the guys he'd known over the years had come to Jesus and quit. It wasn't fun for them anymore, or a way to relieve stress; it was just a burden. But as the tickling in his toes and fingers set in, he didn't mind diminishing returns. It might be expensive and suicidal, and never as good as that first bite, but who gave a fuck once you were high? Feel great for a while then pass out, and if things got bad when you woke up, do it again.

Fuzz covered everything around him. Some stupid fool had turned the world into a fist wrapped in velvet, one hammering him down, down, down into the couch. It molded him into putty, smearing him all over everything. Aimee and her silly castle, *their* silly castle, faded into distant memory. He put Marie and her bullshit on the backburner. They'd make up, then they'd get back to it. They always did.

Right now, only that high mattered. That swirling, larger-than-the-world-but-fitting-in-the-palm-of-your-hand-gem to cure all your troubles. Better than being Spider-Man, a porn star, and the president all at once.

A shadow passed his eyes, and when he blinked them open, something had changed. It wasn't all velvet, not now.

The world pulled a little further away than it usually did. The living room stretched out forever. Somewhere, way in the back where sober Aaron lived, an alarm went off. The front door swung open and closed, a mouth trying to carry on a conversation without a voice.

Oprah flashed back on TV, but she wasn't interviewing a mom and her bratty kid. This time, it was Aimee and Aaron. He watched himself speaking to his dead sister on a lonely soundstage, and the first tendrils of anxiety wormed themselves in through the high.

"What the hell?"

He tried to sit up, but failed. When he tried again, the couch slid toward the TV, giving him a good view of the show. He could almost make out what Aimee was saying, but not quite.

"I miss… so much."

Whatever muscles were supposed to take him away from this nightmare didn't work. Instead, his hand sought the remote of its own accord, grabbing it and turning up the volume as that golden gem in his hand fell and shattered on the floor, and the fear moved in to grab the pieces.

He shook his head. That at least still worked. "No." Bad trip. Heroin didn't gork people out like this, but maybe it wasn't pure. Maybe it was some new shit, or Devon was trying to teach him a lesson. "No!"

The door continued to slam open and closed with blinding speed. One by one, the lights in the apartment vanished as he struggled to sit up. Shadows behind. Shadows in front. The kitchen light gone, and suddenly the only one left was the one right above him. Spotlighting him in an empty, black void. The numb shock of fear dulled by drugs raised the hair on his arms. He could be OD'ing right now. This could be his brain running out of air. A bad trip all the way down the hole in the cemetery where they'd bury his stinking corpse.

He finally managed to sit up, but he wasn't in control, and he fell face first onto the carpet as the last light went out with a final, defiant *click*. As quiet as the grave and loud as a gunshot.

He tried to scream, getting only a mouthful of stone each time until he remembered to lift his head. The drug still dulled him, but not so much that he didn't know how fucked up it was. He had to get to his phone and call 911.

But the phone was in the apartment, and an empty sound stage on a studio lot surrounded him. Near black and filled with ghosts. That anxiety beat to the tune of his hammering heart, the drugs backing away just a little. It was made for people ten times bigger than him, all the furniture oversized, the stage itself as big as a basketball court. Not real. An *Alice in Wonderland* world made for shooting TV.

"Aaron, why would you leave Aimee when she really needed you?" Oprah stuck the comically large microphone in his face. He couldn't understand how she was holding it. The visual didn't line up, but he couldn't figure it out. How had he gotten on the stage?

His words were mush. The world was empty but for the three of them.

"Aimee, how did it make you feel?"

He saw his sister for the first time as Oprah turned the mic toward her.

Aimee stared at him. His eyes reflected back at him in the face of a beautiful teenage girl who'd left the world before her time. The big hole in her head where the bullet had blown out the back remained. "I was so alone, Aaron. I told you I was too scared to go."

He couldn't look away from that red crater in her skull. The casket had been closed at the funeral. He hadn't seen it then. He gripped the edges of the huge chair for dear life. This wasn't real. He'd fallen asleep on the couch after taking a little too much skag was all.

But he had to tell her anyway. He'd never gotten the chance when she was alive. He fought through a handful of cotton to get the words out. "I was going to come back."

Oprah nodded, her expression close to tears. It might have been fake on anyone else.

"I couldn't wait. I'm sorry, Aaron. Do you know what it was like? Do you know what Mom's boyfriend did to me?"

The wound on her head, the small one in the front, oozed a thin red line between her eyes. His euphoric high was gone. This didn't feel like a bad dream. Everything shone a little too brightly, the textures a little too crisp under his fingers. He scratched the inside of one of his fingers with his thumb, and it hurt.

But none of that mattered. The words poured out of his mouth as if he weren't in control, echoing across the empty studio. "I suspected. I told Mom. She laughed in my face. Called me melodramatic." He gazed down at his hands, unable to take her stare. Those hands were far away, in another galaxy. "I was going to kill him. I had the gun… The same… One of Dad's old guns." Tears blurred his vision, smearing everything in Vaseline. "I'm so sorry. I didn't mean to leave you alone. I wanted you to come with me."

Aimee shook her head. A droplet of red flew from the bullet hole and landed on the arm of his chair. "Shh. It's okay. I know you didn't mean to let anything bad happen."

Oprah nodded again. "Do you forgive him?"

She smiled her sad smile, the same one he'd seen a million times when they told each other about the places they'd escape to when they were grown. So close, but so far away. "There was never anything to forgive. I'm the one who should be sorry."

He wanted to close the gap between them and embrace her, drugs and leaden limbs be damned.

But as he stood, both she and Oprah vanished, leaving him alone on a sound stage. One by one, the lights shut off—first in the wings, then out in the audience. When only the one above him remained, a buzz filled the room like static on a television. Out where the audience should be, a giant screen appeared from nothing. It showed his living room. He sat on the couch, passed out, his head lolled to one side.

Behind him stood a figure covered from head to toe in black armor. It stared at him through the screen. Watching. Everything in the apartment was going as insane as it had been before he'd ended up here. The doors opened and closed; a wind picked up pieces of garbage and dirty laundry, flinging it all around the room. But whatever that thing was, it stood still at the eye of it.

He jumped from his chair as a primal fear stirred inside him. Death. He had to run. He had to get away before it touched him.

A voice from the darkness offstage called out as if reading his mind, "Come with me, ser. I can help you."

He tried to run toward it—anything was better than here—but the world had become molasses. "Help me! I can't get away!" The sound stage melted around him. The colors bled over one another, leaving only a terrifying black void. He ran in vain toward the voice just below the screen. Something swooped overhead as he whimpered in panic. Giant leathery wings and a great red eye, gone in a flash. "Get me out of here! Take me home!"

"No, ser. I don't think anyone can do that now. No ser, no ser. Gotta go a little deeper if you want to get away."

Something about the voice brought back distant memories of another time and another place. The last of the stage vanished, leaving him alone in the blackness. The floor was the final piece to go. It hadn't disappeared as much as become insubstantial. Dissolving like sugar in water beneath his feet. When it did, he tumbled into the void beneath him, but the screen above didn't disappear. It followed him as he fell down, down, down into eternity, screaming.

The Black Knight reached for his prone form on the couch while the invisible storm on the TV tore apart his apartment. The static grew louder. If that hand touched him, he would die both here and out there. He could feel its icy fingers behind him, inching ever closer.

"I'll do anything! Please, help!"

Something grabbed him by the shoulder from behind as the terror in the screen did the same, and his heart went cold. That voice, the one that had been below the screen, spoke over the buzzing of the oversized TV. "As you wish, ser. Better hold on."

Chapter 8

Between the old trees and down toward the hidden shack, he'd walked the path a hundred times. A thousand. He'd walked it until the sun had set and turned into night twice, and soreness burned his muscles. His heart sat in a sack inside his chest, a burlap bag filled with shattered pictures of a family. A dead sister. A dead grandma. A mom and dad who'd long since given up.

Still, he walked. More empty woods leered down at him.

He'd gone right after the funeral. He still had his nice clothes on. Nice, for him, was black slacks and a button-down shirt. He hated that color on clothing. It was overdone, and Aimee had once remarked that it made him look like a skater punk who was trying too hard. He laughed for a moment before killing the smile, wiping the sweat from his head onto his ruined clothes. She'd always made fun of him, and she was the only one who could.

That hole was too big. As if a piece of him the size of her had been replaced with the fires of Hell, it burned and burned, so hot it left no place for denial, or anger, or sadness. Just action.

He was alone, but he didn't have to be. They had a Kingdom. If he could find it, there might be some comfort there. They had always been able to make the world into almost anything they wanted. They had even opened up a hole into the universe and sailed the little boats to find Grandma in whatever happened after life.

But what if they'd gone a little further? If he went to the throne room and demanded a door to find Aimee. Would it be there? A golden thing, ten feet high and inlaid with a tiles showing the thousand adventures they'd had? He would make it. He would find her again.

His thoughts raced as he paced back and forth between the two trees. Up the trail to them, around them, through them, looking up at them, studying their roots. Each action and passing second stoked the rising tide of mania whipping harder at his back. It had to be here. She was there. She had to be. She wouldn't leave him, she'd promised. They'd promised each other so many times.

He walked up and down where the trail should have been, past the guardian trees and toward the shack. But there was no shack.

"Where are you?" The first day, he'd muttered it under his breath.

"Where are you?" By the first night, he said it aloud, his search growing frantic.

"Where the fuck are you?" He screamed it again and again, his words bouncing off the trees back at him. "Where?"

After two days, his legs gave out. He collapsed against the left guardian, as impartial to the impact of his body on the wood as the

82

trees were to his suffering. He stared back the way he'd come, back to home. Back to an empty room he'd shared for sixteen years. Back to a mother who didn't care. To a world that had no place for him, and one that now had no safety net to catch him. That had always been her. She'd been the one to get them out of there. He'd watch out for her, and she'd set the path. Like a captain and the navigator.

He dropped his head between his knees, closed his eyes, and wept for the first time in… maybe forever. He didn't know anymore. He didn't know anything as the saline drops fell from Aimee's eyes and into the uncaring Earth below.

The Kingdom wasn't here. She wasn't here. There was nothing.

The clothes he'd worn to her funeral were ragged and torn from thrashing through the bushes. He hadn't slept in days. The world spun around him, though he suspected that was from a lack of food. He didn't care. His whole universe, everything he'd ever known, had crumbled. Had they really thought there was anything out here besides some big trees and a place to hide?

He was a teenager again, the willow of a boy who would grow into an oak of a man. A man who would slowly kill himself with smack. He'd wanted to find the Kingdom after Aimee died. Maybe she was there. Maybe he could find a way to her. At the very least, the people there could make him feel better, give him that sense of home he'd never found in the real world.

But that wasn't right. He was a grown man with a dead sister. A grown man with a shitty apartment and a bad habit. That young boy had gone out to those woods a long time ago, after something terrible had happened. He'd stopped thinking of himself as a boy that day. An angry man had come back out. That angry man who fell, and fell, and fell, in every way he could.

Everything slowly focused above him. The high had vanished as quickly as it came, leaving him sober as a stone in the middle of a dark forest. He lay on his back, staring at the canopy, just as he had those years before after the funeral when he'd needed to find her.

Nothing registered. He'd been in his apartment. No, that wasn't right, either. He'd gotten high, and then he'd been somewhere else. He wore the same clothes and no shoes.

The memory of the Black Knight reaching for him clicked into place, and he shot up. Instead of a shitty apartment or even a soundstage, ancient, giant trees surrounded him, spaced out with plenty of room between them and reaching forever upward to the sky that must have been there. But no stars glowed overhead, despite there being enough light to see by. An ambient glow permeated everything, as if a black blanket covered the world but a nightlight still illuminated the room outside. A few hundred meters away in every direction, black mist obscured his vision. Darkness compounding darkness.

The fear crept, wrapping itself around his guts. Nothing stirred the branches, and no sounds marred the silence. He stood, disoriented. "Hello?" Someone had put him here. The voice from the bad dream. "If someone's out there, speak up."

His own voice died a few feet past the nearest trees, as if he were in a small box and not the open woods. He'd grown up playing

84

in forests. He knew how to find his way by the stars but could see none. There was nothing there at all, the firmament just gone.

Fear turned to panic. He had to find a road or a house, but while the surroundings looked familiar, he wasn't in Umber Gardens anymore. He pinched the back of his hand, confirming his suspicions. This wasn't a dream.

All the lessons they'd picked up in books and experience fled him. All the little tricks to make sure you didn't get lost disappeared in a haze of anxiety. Everything looked the same. Every direction was the very picture of the next.

But he couldn't stand still, not with nobody looking for him and no knowledge of how he got there. Devoid of options, he picked a direction and started walking. One foot in front of the other, past the slumbering giants. Through the pea-soup fog. Across nearly barren fields alive with only a few limp weeds and brush.

Some sense of purpose returned. That haze of fear parted, just a little. He had power out here. He knew the tricks. Find a river or stream and follow it down. Without stars, there were other options. Follow trails left by planes. Look out for mountains or any other defining features of the landscape. A man familiar with survival was never out of options.

The first fifty feet yielded trees and brush that looked the same. The next hundred brought the sinking suspicion that this place wasn't natural. Ten minutes later, he was certain.

Every tree was the same tree, right down to the markings. Every few square feet of brush were the same as the last. It was as if the landscape had been painted on, not grown.

Sweat beaded and fell down his face. This had to be a dream. Real sensations or not, this couldn't be the waking world. "Hello!" he yelled into the woods, hoping for something in return. Anything. "If someone's out there, please help. I'm lost!"

The stale air lay on his tongue, the taste of mold in a dank basement. The humidity was unbearable. More a swamp than a forest. But there were no bugs. No birds. No anything. The quiet was so perfect that he began to doubt even his own thoughts.

Something caught his bare foot. A yellow piece of yarn ended where he stood and stretched off to some unknown place in the distance.

He had to be still sitting on the couch, drooling on himself in a drug-fueled delirium. The terror of the last hour vanished in morbid fascination. He'd seen that string before, and not just yesterday.

With a shiver, he realized what was familiar about the trees. They were the guardians. The gatekeepers to the Kingdom. A thousand of them. A million.

He slapped his palm to his forehead. Once. Twice. Then again and again. The only thing it accomplished was a headache. "Gotta wake up, Aaron. You got some bad shit. This isn't real!" He spun where he stood, staring out in every direction at the unnatural darkness. He looked back down at the string under his foot, leading off into the nowhere land.

If it was a dream, then it had to play out. You couldn't fight it. Once you knew it was a dream, if you couldn't wake up, you had to ride it through.

With a shaking hand, he picked it up and followed the string. It remained taut under his fingers, as if someone on the other end were holding it, waiting for him. "Bullshit thought, Aaron." He nodded as he stepped over and around the little foliage on the ground, his feet making no sounds. "Gotta stay focused, bro. Follow this shit back home."

Time lost all meaning as he pulled on toward wherever it might lead. One hand over the other, the feel of cotton under his fingers maddeningly real. The woods never changed. More than once, eyes drilled holes into his back, but when he spun around to catch whoever his phantom stalker might be, he saw nothing. Shapes glimpsed only from the corner of his eyes moved in the blackness, but there was no sound.

He stopped looking, his heart hammering a funeral dirge in his chest. This was it. He'd died and gone to Hell. He'd follow a little yellow string into eternal night forever, hounded by the shapes of monsters and killers.

"Bullshit thought, Aaron." His feet felt frozen, even though the soil underneath was loose as if it were spring, not winter. Everything felt frozen here, as if the very spirit of winter had come here to roost. Maybe it had. Maybe some little pixie thing that brought the snow lived here in the off seasons, and maybe the weatherman was full of shit.

He shut down the rambling. "Shut up, dipshit. Just keep walking."

He managed to keep his thoughts carefully blank for nearly a full minute before noises sprung up around him. Moans. Yells. They started at the edge of hearing, and his ears perked up as he stopped following the string.

Closer now. A cold sweat broke out over his body as he realized what he was hearing. Those were voices in pain. Angry things. Clips of not-quite speech and raw emotion encased in parade of sound, all of it hurt.

All of it angry.

Whatever it was, he didn't want to find out. A scream pierced the night, growing closer with every second. The hairs on his body stood on end as he hunched and walked faster.

In the distance stood a small building, the string pulling him ever closer. He dropped it and ran as the noises drowned out his other senses. A chorus of pain echoed across the dead landscape, lighting the world with nightmares. A shadow fell over the already darkened world, as if some impossible specter loomed over him, ready to swoop down and consume him to the cheers of the deafening crowd.

He panted as the shack grew closer, the scream just behind him. He wouldn't make it. Whatever made that horrible noise would pounce on him and devour him before he could reach it. A whimper of panic escaped him between gasps for air.

Five hundred feet.

Four.

Three.

Close enough to make out the shingles on the roof and the empty spots where windows and a door had once been.

The scream blared in his ear. He spun, falling down and hitting the ground hard enough to knock the breath from his body, waiting to face whatever demon had come for him.

But the woods were quiet. Just an empty, black forest forever.

His eyes bulged. No bad trip could do this. It had to be Hell. "Oh, God." He put his face into his hands and rocked back and forth. "Please let this be fake. Let me be imaging this. Please, don't leave me here."

Was this his punishment? Had he died and been cursed to wander forever in the woods where he'd promised Aimee he'd come back for her?

"Ser?" asked a small voice behind him.

Aaron jumped, rushing to his hands and knees and turning around.

Chapter 9

The magic there-but-not-there shack of his childhood stood before him. The wood had molded, rotting in his absence. The glass jars that had lined the walls were scattered in shards on the floor, broken glass glittering through the open door.

A short man squatted in the doorway. His yellow flesh constantly ran down his oblong body, leaking to the floor and vanishing before it touched. Two black eyes and a giant gaping mouth marked his face, and two stubby arms jutted from his sides. He had no hair. His body was perfectly smooth other than the rivers of goo cascading down him.

It was horrific—this thing. That shack. These woods. Aaron screamed and scrambled backward, trying to distance himself from the creature.

The candle man waddled forward.

"Get back! Stay the fuck away from me!"

Still, it approached. "Ser? It's you, in'it?" It narrowed its eyes, taking Aaron in. Globs of flesh reappeared at the top only to ooze back down its naked body. His nauseating flesh looked more like wax than skin.

"I said stay the fuck back!"

It stopped only a few feet from him. "You're him, right? You're the prince? Prince and the princess sitting in the keep, W-A-L-K-I-N-G!" There was no hint of mirth in its voice as it spun in a circle and stopped to stare at him with those black eyes.

Aaron jumped to his feet and ran back toward the woods, his heart screaming, his extremities numb with fear.

The candle man yelled behind him, "Not that way, ser! The dark lights live out there!"

He ran. The path that should have led back home didn't exist, only endless forest in every direction. But if he ran long enough, he'd find something or he'd wake up. Every nightmare had an end.

The black mist swirled closer and closer with every inch, a wall of darkness blocking everything. The candle man's voice followed him. "Ser! They'll eat you up! They'll swallow you in one big bite!"

The mist drifted in, almost swirling into shapes but dissipating before they fully formed. Cones and triangles turned into circles and boxes. He stopped dead as it closed. A star. A rod. A hand beckoning him. The walls moved in, no longer fifty feet away but twenty. Ten. An arm. A leg. The outline of a skull. The shapes mesmerized him.

The whispers of a thousand people trying to tell him a secret all at once rose as the mist became empty-eyed figures floating toward him.

"Should have been you."

"Killer."

"Everything you touch dies."

Reaching. Caressing. Their eyes vacant spots in a shadow form, their outlines a black light in the deeper dark. Their icy aura chilled him to the bone. He should have been terrified. He should have run screaming. He should have tried to get away while he could.

"Left her."

"Junkie."

"Kill yourself."

He stood there, hypnotized by their words. They were right. Not just them, but everyone. His mother. His father. Maybe they hadn't been so bad. Maybe Aaron had always been rotten. All the good had gone to her and all the evil to him, so much of it that he'd twisted his father, the future boxing champion turned machine repairman, into a drunken monster. By virtue of his corruption, he'd transformed his mother the stage actress into a petty hag.

They were right, and he deserved to die for it. He stumbled toward them.

"No ser, no ser." The candle man stood next to him, a dim radiance emitting from his mouth. "Not today, shadow things. Back and back you go, where you stop, nobody knows." The glow in his mouth flashed brighter than the sun, so bright it hurt Aaron inside and out, burning away the terrible feelings. The creatures flew away screaming, their shapes solid. Corpses hovering above the forest floor, a thousand years dead. They returned to the mist, and with them gone, it was as if Aaron had come up for air after a dive.

His head swam. He exhaled in a ragged gasp, the spell broken.

"Not safe, ser, not safe here at all. Not supposed to come here at night. Not ever." He sized Aaron up. "Though I guess you are old enough now."

Aaron stared at the creature that had just saved him from the floating horrors as the lingering fingers of dreams still beckoned him into the fog. "What is this place? Who the fuck are you? What are you?" He grabbed his head as the world tipped over and spilled him onto the ground.

The candle man seized Aaron's leg before he could protest, dragging him back toward the shack. "Who, what, who, what? Not very princely questions. Shouldn't do for you to forget where you came from, no matter how long it's been."

"Wha—" His head struck a rock—*thud*—as his vision started to clear. "What the hell are you?" He rubbed the stinging spot on his scalp.

"It's me, Ser Aaron, Drippy, your most humble and loyal of servants."

Servants?

Clarity returned all at once, and he latched onto the ground. Was this thing really telling him he was back in the imaginary place he and Aimee had made up fifteen years ago? It hadn't been real. Just a stupid old ranger station in the woods two abused kids had turned into a fantasy land.

"Let me go! Let me the fuck go!"

Drippy dropped his foot at once, although Aaron didn't know if it was because he had said to or because they were at the shack.

He jumped to his feet. "Where are we really? What are you?"

Drippy sighed and plopped onto the ground, his waxen butt making a *squish* sound as it hit. "We're home. We're in the Kingdom, ser." He looked around, his face transforming into sad features. "Though it isn't what it once was, or what it would have been if things had been different. I suppose that's always true, though."

Aaron examined his surroundings. The endless forest to his back. The path the led up the hill, past the shack and to the Kingdom beyond. The piece of magic floating in the sky that he and his sister had found so long ago. It had taken their breath away. It had saved their lives.

He looked down at his toes, at the needle hole he couldn't see in the dark. Bad shit. Some low-grade skag had done this. "No. No. Nope." Aaron scanned the woods behind him. It hadn't been like this. There weren't monsters. "I'm going to wake up. I'm going to wake up on my couch, and I'm never going to touch junk again."

Drippy's face turned passive once more. "Doubt it. Ain't easy to wake up from what's real, even if it's fake to you." He cocked his head. "Where have you been, young master? We waited and we waited, and even when things got to be bad, we waited s'more. Have you finally come to fix it?" It clapped its misshapen hands together.

"This isn't real. You." He pointed at Drippy, who continued to melt. "You aren't fucking real."

"Everything's real here, ser, even the things what ain't. You know that. This is all yours. Yours to make and yours to keep! Don't ya know? Can't ya recall?"

He did remember.

He and Aimee placing decrees on their subjects. The people bowed before their rulers, the children touched by the hand of some unseen god and blessed with the voice of rule.

"Are the people here real?" Aimee had asked as they walked past the village and toward the castle on their first day. There had been so many, and not all of them appeared normal. Bright lights surrounded some. So bright it was hard to look at them. Horns sprouted from the heads of others. When they'd first entered the village, Aaron had caught sight of a man with the lower body of a horse.

And they'd all come to see Aaron and Aimee. Some bowed. Most nodded. Aaron didn't know what to make of it. If it was real, then magic was real. Mom had said Grandma lied about everything, but if she was right, what else was out there? Werewolves? Vampires? Demons? All the bad things from the stories?

Aimee waved and smiled, looking just like the little kid she was. The little kid both of them were, he supposed. She was asking the same questions he was about how real this place was, but not in the same way.

Drippy walked in front of them, glancing back over his shoulder as often as the trail would allow. He kept checking as if they would disappear, as though he could scarcely imagine his luck at getting to meet them. "Some of them are more real than others. You rule here. This belongs to you. But not everyone here comes from here. Some of 'em visit from far, far away. From worlds without names where only the bravest knights dare to tread. Don't ya know?"

The baker in town had given them fresh donuts and apple cider. The sweet taste of it tingled on Aaron's lips as they waved goodbye to her and continued to the castle. "This sort of thing doesn't happen where we're from. None of it."

Drippy arched an eyebrow when he looked back. "Well, it sounds to me like you sers are from a silly place indeed." He hopped into the air and clicked his heels together, laughing. "Who rules your kingdom out there?"

They looked at one another as they strolled through the woods, but neither had an answer.

"Well, sers. It don't rightly matter anyway. This is yours. It'll be what you need it to be when ya need it. Not much more matters."

Aimee had asked Aaron if they could stay here forever. Much later, she had made him promise he would come back, right here in front of the shack. And he had, but it had taken him ten years, and she was already gone.

His eyes misted as that lump, the same one from the day of her funeral, formed in his throat. This hadn't just been his; it had been hers. Theirs. The memories trickled back. A hole in the dam of shit that had built up since she died.

"Drippy!" They'd been coming for what felt like a lifetime. Even if their memories faded in the real world, they remained at the shack whenever the twins returned. Aimee and Aaron spoke in hushed whispers at night about what they would do the next day. They sat on their thrones in the castle. Sometimes that was all they ever did there, come to the castle and relax. Put the ills of an unkind world behind them for a little while.

Drippy ran toward them from the door of the throne room when she called. He was never far. "Yes, Princess?" He bowed before her, one leg out.

"How much longer can we stay today?"

Aaron had been wondering the same thing. Time moved differently here. What should have been hours sometimes became weeks, and other times they stayed for minutes before they were escorted out to the shack and saw their way home.

"All the time you need, ma'am, but not all the time you want!"

She giggled, amused by his nonsense the way only a child could be. "Very well, let's have a feast before we go."

And they had. They danced exotic dances from a world where people were made from pillars of sand that moved and spoke. A travelling salesman brought them exotic fruits that tasted like memories of days spent on a beach that stretched toward the stars. After hours and hours of it, Drippy finally informed them it was time. He took them to the shack and waved as they left, always waiting for them to come back.

This place with its black mist ghosts and haunted shacks had been as real as that fucked-up apartment back in Umber Gardens that stank of loneliness and failure.

"No." Aaron stared off into space, the sudden recollection hitting him harder than any drug. It was always like this. The memories stayed at the shack, just like Drippy. "No. It can't be real." Aimee and Aaron. Their secret place. Their secret world.

"'Tis, ser. 'Tis." Drippy bowed to him, one leg out as always. "Welcome home, Your Majesty."

Chapter 10

Aaron stared at his most loyal subject, the one who had always greeted them. The one who had always consoled them when they entered the Kingdom crying and covered in bruises.

"The lady said she would return as well. Promised the royal siblings would set things a'right when you came. But…" He cocked his head as if listening to someone speak far, far away. "She was here and never left. Or she never left even when she did. It's hard to hear anything anymore, ser. Everything's gone bad. Everything turned rotten. Black and black, and black and dead; that curse upon the Black Knight's head."

Aaron hardly heard Drippy as he stared down the path leading to the village and their castle. "It's all still here." A sudden desire to see it overcame over him, just like that first day when Aimee's hands had been on his head. When she'd been the brave one and he'd wanted to turn around. He needed to lay his eyes on it. To let those memories wash over him. He needed to walk the same paths he and Aimee had a thousand times or the aching inside would kill him.

"Of course it's here, ser. Where else would it be?"

Aaron started walking toward the Kingdom, but Drippy grabbed his arm. His flesh oozed, soft and warm. "You need to understand, ser, it isn't safe here now. It's night forever, and you aren't supposed to be here at night." Drippy glanced around the forest surrounding them, taking it all in. "You aren't a child, but there are things here that eat big folk as well as small."

Aaron tugged his arm away. "I don't care. I want to see it."

Aimee had found it for him, showing him with both hands on his head. He could almost feel those hands. He could almost feel *her*. His heart ached, even through the fear still tickling his spine. Whether it was a bad trip or Hell didn't matter; he'd take both and more to feel his little sister again.

"The Black Knight made it all bad, Ser. Bad, bad, bad and sad, sad, sad. He took away the sun and the moon and the stars from the sky."

The words made no sense, but none of this did. He could recall snatches and glimpses of the Kingdom. More than just vague memories. He remembered Sir Horace teaching him how to ride a horse. The time the Romani had passed through and been shocked to find two American children wandering in their secret places.

Aimee had seen them first, pointing them out as they eyed the village. It wasn't so unusual to see new people. Drippy had told them it was their world, but it wasn't *just* their world. Still, neither of them had ever seen people who looked like they came from back home in the Kingdom.

The handful of men and women stopped and stared as Drippy and the twins approached. All looked wary, an expression not often seen there.

Aimee had hung back, but Aaron marched right up to them. "Hello."

And still they stared. All around them, villagers went about their business. At length, a woman so old that she walked with two canes hobbled toward them. Her eyes were milky and glassy. The colors of her clothes were faded with age, and her lower lip trembled constantly. She limped to Aaron, leaning against one of her canes and using her free hand to grab his face. He took a step back, his confidence that nothing bad could happen here shaken by this ancient woman before him. It was a gentle touch, though he still pulled away in fear. It had been the first time he'd ever felt that here.

"The eyes of one touched by gods." The old woman spat on the ground and gestured with her fingers the same way Grandma did. She'd called it the evil eye, and said it warded off bad spirits summoned by even the mention of their names. "Is this place yours?"

He and Aimee looked at each other for a long moment. She spoke this time. "This is our Kingdom. Who are you?"

The old woman smiled, revealing a mouth with almost no teeth. "Just travelers. Not like you. We go now. Don't be afraid, little ones."

Aaron had wanted to ask her a million questions but never got the chance. The travelers followed the trail back toward the hill leading to the shack without speaking another word to the twins. He didn't know where they were going, but he suspected it wasn't back to Umber Gardens. Things came and went from their kingdom all the time with no apparent rhyme or reason to where that path led.

He shook his head, clearing away the memories of days long past, of times when this hadn't been a stinking, dark mess. Then, it had been light and the trees green.

Now?

He stared into the terrible mist covering everything. The trees devoid of animals. The air empty of sound. The smell of decay hanging heavy over it all. "What happened here?"

Drippy glanced at him. "You left, ser. You left and you never ever came back. The princess couldn't fix it all alone."

"The princess? Aimee? She was here?"

Drippy nodded. "All by her alonesomeness. She said you'd gone far, far away. That was just before the Black Knight broke the world." He reached with his misshapen fingers as if to grasp at the celestial bodies that weren't there. "Took the sun, and the moon, and the stars from the sky. He locked them away. No more wishes here. No more magic, leastwise not the good kind. Ain't seen her since then, but I can't seem to recall her going anywhere."

She hadn't been here. She'd died. Alone. Her brother, the co-heir apparent to the kingdom, gone. His mother had told him on the phone in detail about the blood on the walls. About the red stain she couldn't get out of the bathroom. Her voice quivered when she spoke, as if she might pretend to care for his sake, but she never did. Not once.

"No. She died. She…" He couldn't say it over the burning that threatened to choke him and rain tears from his eyes. This was too close to her, like stepping on her grave. "She died."

"Nothing ever dies, ser, it just changes."

He had to see it, monsters be damned. He walked the path that led to the village. This time, Drippy followed.

"Don't be concerned, ser. Things is bad, yeah? But you can fix them! Issue your royal decrees, just like old times!" He bounced back and forth, an obscene little monster in a kingdom of them. Had he always looked like that? How had it not terrified them as children?

The path through the forest opened before him. The thousands of guardian trees were rotten and bent. The animals had fled to parts unknown. The monsters, the dark lights, still waited in the mists. The occasional shape formed and beckoned to him, but this time he looked away. This wasn't the Kingdom. This was a nightmare.

He pressed on, the path familiar even after all these years. To his left, the spot where Aimee had fallen and scraped her knee on a rock. To the right, the place where the Romani woman had waved goodbye and told them to listen to their grandmother, though neither had mentioned her.

And then, the hill peaked and opened to a view of the entire Kingdom. The endless black of the sky, and the edge of the world at the borders. The path that wound through the hills. The village. The castle in the woods beyond.

But this wasn't the view he remembered.

The only lights in the world, the harsh light of torches and fire, came from the village and castle. A bonfire, a huge affair visible even from so far away, lit up the town center. The black mist and endless night covered everything else, leaving the impression it all floated in some eternal nightmare void.

Aaron lost his breath looking at it. This had been his home, his real home. That place where his family slept had been nothing but bad memories. They'd giggled about this place on the bus going home from school. They'd read their library books here day after day, year after year. When they imagined the future, they imagined it here.

Now, that castle in the distance wasn't a poor man's Camelot, as Aimee had once called it. The stone had gone dark, matching the world around it. Terrifying shapes danced in the shadows cast by the lights on the spires. That wasn't their old home; it was where nightmares ruled.

"How?"

Drippy stared at it too, the wax of his face contorting into a frown, the mounds that passed for eyebrows furrowed. "You left, ser." He whispered the words as if to soften the blow.

He left. The same curse he'd been hurling at himself for a decade now. He left, and Aimee died. He left, and his real-world house became worse than when Dad was around. He left, and the Kingdom crumbled. He'd killed his sister.

A dull ache pulsed behind his teeth and seeped into his skull. He closed his eyes and put his hands to his head. A horn sounded in the distance, a bass note that vibrated the ground. It turned into the up and down wail of a siren, a warning of something terrible approaching.

"Time to go, ser."

"What?" The pain behind his eyes ratcheted every second, quickly reaching unbearable. "What's happening?"

"You'll come back this time? We need you, oh yes we do!" Drippy danced around him in circles, repeating nonsense rhymes.

Bad trip. Bad drugs. The only explanation.

"Yes, yes indeed. Get to the castle, God save the queen!"

The ache became a wall of pain, pushing him forward, stealing his balance from him.

"Don't fear, ser. Remember your first time as a boy? Can't stay long. Just a peek. Just a little lookie-see."

He tried to catch himself, but the siren continued its endless note as gravity pulled him over the edge and down, down, down to the ground.

But he never landed. He fell endlessly with Drippy's mirthless voice in his ears.

"Everything will fall apart if you don't come back. Just like last time."

And then even that was gone, and it was just him, the pain, and the siren as he fell forever.

Chapter 11

"Think he'll be back?" Brian asked, swinging on the rusted playground set. They'd been there all afternoon, neither speaking a word. Cars zipped by on the cracked asphalt nearby. The trees watched closely, and the knee-high grass whispered as it swayed. Despite all of that, the Earth held its breath. Nothing moved outside of those swings, not in the entire world.

Aaron stared at the sky. "I don't know." It would be dark soon. Aaron's mom wouldn't care, but Brian's would be worried sick. She would call Aaron's house. She'd come looking. And when he got home late, she wouldn't slap him in the back of the head, or worse; she'd hug him and say in a stern voice, "I was worried sick." But that voice would be the hardest thing about her.

It made him angrier, but Aaron would have liked nothing more than to go over there and live with them forever. Take Aimee, grab a bag of clothes, and never look back.

Because Dad had left for a pack of smokes, and despite what everyone kept saying, he wasn't coming back. Everyone knew the drill but was too afraid to say it, as if he'd been some shining example of a father before then. As if he hadn't been half a step out the door since the day he walked through it. Mom hadn't stopped throwing a fit for days now. Aimee didn't know what to do.

Aaron loved her, but she was goddamn stupid. They should be having a party. Throw a parade. Ding, dong, the dick is gone.

"How're you holding up?"

Aaron shrugged. How could he explain the burning in his chest? The absolute delight when he should feel terrible. The bit of guilt for being so happy when everyone else was so mad, which made the whole thing that much better.

Maybe that he could explain. But the other half he couldn't. That sickness dropped into his gut like an iceberg. The constant looking over his shoulder and expecting to see his old man. Maybe he'd pull up in that stupid truck, open the door, and say, "Get in. I'm finally taking you on that camping trip I always said I would." And Aaron would be mad, but not forever. And if that became the rest of their lives together, maybe he wouldn't even hate him.

It would be better than the hot tears pressing behind his eyes, or the angry, screechy yell he could feel building in the back of his throat.

"Fuck him." And why not? Shouldn't they be honest and say it was great he was gone? "He was a fucking loser. I hope he chokes on those smokes. I hope he dies of lung cancer. I hope it takes years, and he suffers the whole fucking time." How long were he and Aimee supposed to wait to have real parents? How long did they have to suffer while everyone else got to be kids, like Brian's mom always told them to be?

Brian stopped swinging. "Jesus, dude."

But the words were out, and so was that burning. "No. Fuck him! Do you have any idea what it was like going home to him every day?" Aaron laughed. "I'm stoked! I hate them! I hate all of them! The only people worth a damn around here are you and Aimee."

That manic glee in his chest turned to cold bile as he spoke. People should feel safe in their home. They shouldn't walk on eggshells and lie to their friends and teachers to cover up for the people who hurt them. There was no safe place for him and Aimee here, maybe anywhere. He wasn't sure there ever would be.

Aaron's next words were a whisper. "Mom thinks it's my fault." His eyes welled with tears, and the first one crested.

But he wouldn't let it fall. Not now, not ever. That was weakness, pure and simple. He slammed the back of his hand into his eye so hard he saw stars, then dragged it across his face and out of his life, just like Dad.

Brian stared at the dirt beneath his sneakers. "I didn't know my mom was going to call the cops."

The anger in Aaron's chest simmered beneath the skin. "I'm glad she did." He finally looked at Brian but couldn't meet his eyes. "It's not your fault." Aaron pulled out his pack of cigarettes and lit one. Brian and Aimee both disapproved, but they never said much about it anymore. He'd only been smoking a few months, and they'd made one hell of a deal out of it then.

"We're only fourteen!" Brian had yelled.

But most fourteen-year-olds didn't have parents that broke bones and knocked teeth out. They didn't live in a house where garbage piled up everywhere except their bedroom.

"As long as you don't smoke in the Kingdom, I don't care." Aimee had finally acquiesced after weeks of riding him about it. "You aren't going to make our castle smell like your filthy hair."

Our castle. What did that even mean anymore? It didn't protect them from anything. It only put a Band-Aid on a bullet wound. The memories vanished when they left, dumping them into a world that claimed it would do anything to protect them while it watched, impotent, as they were bloodied and bruised.

More and more, year by year, he wondered what it meant. He wondered if it was anything at all.

Even as he fell through that endless darkness, the anger was fresh. It kept burning long after everyone involved was gone. There had never been a home for him. Never a place where he felt safe.

Nowhere except the Kingdom, and that was gone too, if it had ever been real to begin with.

The darkness parted as a car passed by the living room window, honking its horn. Aaron jumped off the couch, his vision blurry and his muscles aching. All the classic post-binge signs. The pain in his head hadn't subsided.

But there had been a place, or a thing. He and Brian had been swinging, and the Kingdom…

He searched the room, disoriented by the sudden change in scenery. Everything was just as he'd left it the night before, right down to his used needle and gear on the table. He stumbled to the window and threw open the curtains, letting the blinding sunlight in.

No monster shapes in black fog. No candle man. No flaming castles. Just the stinking paper factory across the street and the freeway traffic. Just the sun riding high past the noon mark, burning up over the world.

And yet his head still hurt from where he'd bumped it on the rocks. He rubbed it as he looked at his feet still caked in dirt and sore from walking through the forest barefoot. A piece of brown grass stuck up from between his toes.

"What the fuck?"

He opened every window in the apartment, turned on every light and opened every closet, but nothing was out of place. No indication anything had happened at all. He threw open the front door to see the lady who lived across the hall walking out with her dog. She jumped and scowled, and the dog began to bark.

But there were no answers out there, just the maddening sense he'd been somewhere else, and a maddening lack of ways to prove it.

The shower washed away the dirt, but it did nothing for the questions or the impression he had travelled bodily to some nightmarish *other* world.

He'd strode back and forth in the apartment, his thoughts racing. Maybe he'd gone outside and tripped balls. Maybe he'd travelled back to those woods and those trees and pretended he was a fucking hobbit in the forest or some stoner shit. Junkies did weird shit.

He caught himself at that word and stopped dead. Not a junkie. A user, but not a junkie.

The apartment closed in like a vice, so he grabbed his keys and wallet and went cruising. Tunes up, windows down, and nothing but the stink of a half-dead city to keep him company as he tapped on the side of his door, arm out the window. Umber Gardens drifted by unseen. Had he just wandered outside while he was high as a kite and forgotten about it? Did that explain the dirt on his feet or the marks on his clothes that suggested he'd been dragged through the muck?

The ghosts from the Kingdom haunted him even at sixty on the freeway. He chain-smoked cigarettes while he thought about it, his hand shaking. Maybe worst of all, Aimee had been sitting right across from him. He'd felt the lights on him in that nowhere studio. And that place, the Kingdom. He hadn't imagined it.

Had he?

He'd seen heroin do some nasty things to people over the years. Someone seizing and biting off their tongue. He'd been at a party once where everyone was using. Party was a liberal term for a bunch of assholes nodding off on the couch, but that's what they'd called it. One poor kid had taken too much and stopped breathing, dying right there on the couch next to Aaron. Everyone had left. He didn't know who owned the house, but he wouldn't have wanted to be that guy the next day. Another time, a buddy swore he saw shit and heard voices when he was lit, but nothing like that. Acid and a few other drugs, maybe, but not heroin.

Aaron tapped the steering wheel as he lit another smoke with the butt of the last one, taking a deep drag before the first one was even out the window.

And the most fucked-up thing, the icing on the cake, was that he wanted more. Both because of the stress and because he wanted to go back. He hadn't seen that place in a decade. He'd almost forgotten it was there. But he'd gotten to see Aimee. He'd gone back to the secret fort of their childhood, the one place from his youth not dripping with terrible memories. If it took a little skag to get there, well shit, that was just perfect, wasn't it?

"Fuck." He stared out the window, seeing nothing as the light turned from red to green.

But it scared him too. The things in the mist. The burning castle on the horizon. Drippy, innocent and cute as a child but horrible to look at as an adult. All that shit they'd made up as kids to get away from Mom and Dad. Or was it?

He scratched his neck. There was one way to find out. Go back to the guardian trees in the woods and look for the entrance. If he saw the shack and the yellow string again, he'd have his answers. More questions than answers, really, but he'd at least know he wasn't just a crazy junkie. He'd never lacked for courage. No reason to start now.

He turned his car that way. For the first mile, he was ready. During the second, he doubted. By the time he reached the park, he couldn't get out of the car. Wind blew through the trees, and leaves fell to the ground. No nightmare mist here. No ancient plants of unknown origin. Just the Tennessee foliage changing like it had every fall of his life.

But in the spaces between trees lay a silent threat. If it wasn't real, then he really was cracking apart. Their cute little intervention had a valid point. Normal guys who had a good time with drugs didn't sit across from their dead sister, and they certainly didn't visit magical childhood kingdoms.

And if it was real... Well, that was worse.

Tired, aching, and scared, he turned the car around and pulled out his phone. Marie picked it up on the first ring.

"Aaron?"

He had to get out of his head, to get away from the night before and try to sort himself out for a minute.

"Dinner?"

Chapter 12

No one ever ate at the deli down the street from the Pacific Applied Biology and Technology building where Marie worked as an executive assistant. Like most parts of Umber Gardens, it wasn't a good neighborhood. Marie didn't give a shit.

"That's cute!" she'd said when she got the job and he'd voiced his concerns. "Little boy from the suburbs is going to lecture me on the ghetto."

She hadn't known then about what kind of home he'd grown up in. He wasn't scared for her; he was warning her. Another year had passed before he'd told her everything. He sometimes wondered if she would have stuck around as long as she had if he'd spilled the beans sooner.

When he'd called, he'd wanted to tell her everything. The Kingdom. The drugs. All of it. Get it all out on Front Street and test the waters, see what she said. But he knew damn well what it would be.

"You're losing it! It's that fucking smack!"

"Go to rehab, baby, for me?"

"I can't deal with this. Not right now."

Same tune on a different station. Better to try to forget it for a while. Push it all away. He was good at it. That was his go-to move.

She arrived ten minutes after him, the evening light framing her perfectly as she stepped through the door. He stared as she walked over. She might be a pain, but she put up with more shit than most people would. And by God, she was a looker.

"See something you like?" She sat down.

"Yeah, the woman behind you had an ass that wouldn't quit."

She rolled her eyes but smiled anyway. "Well, you look like shit."

The words hung in the air. His heart sank. It had been a mistake to come here. He was going to get the same attitude she'd given him at the intervention, and he couldn't handle that today.

But she didn't. Her smile faded a little as she sensed the tension, but the hard words vanished. "Getting any sleep?"

He shrugged. "No more or less than usual."

She set her purse on the floor next to her. "So, no. At least that isn't news, I guess."

He tried to smile. "Well, you look great." He wanted to go off script this time. No fights, no talk about drugs, just the two of them having an early dinner like they had in the old days.

She ran a hand through her hair, shifting in her seat in a mock provocative way, chest out and lips pursed. "Thanks, I work out."

The waitress stopped to take their order before the awkwardness could set back in. By the time she walked away, he knew what he wanted to say.

"I miss you."

It had sounded better in his head.

Marie grabbed his hand across the table. "I miss you too. I-I'm sorry. I'm sorry about the whole thing. I just—"

He held up his other hand. "Let's just enjoy dinner, okay? Please? We can talk about…" He waved wildly in the air. "Whatever, later."

She smiled but dropped his hand. "All right."

She kept her word for a while, but it was painful. It hadn't always been like this. They had laughed a lot once. Kissed every chance they got. Fucked like rabbits. They spent so much time together that Brian had wanted to ask her for rent. When he had left and Aaron needed the help with rent, it had been only logical for her to replace him. But then college ended, and with that, her partying did too. Late nights weren't as fun as they used to be when one person had to be up at six. And then it just stopped. All of it. She needed space, and he had a problem. She moved out a few weeks later.

Now she took every opportunity to drag him along for a ride on the guilt wagon. She had to end the good times for everyone, only they weren't good times anymore. Not really. Maybe they never had been.

But she'd stuck around. That was more than anyone else in his life had ever done. It was more than he'd done for Aimee.

"I worry about you, Aaron."

The waitress cleared away the plates as he shook his head. "Can we not?"

"I'm not going to rag on you, and I'm not ever going to do something like that intervention again. I promise. I read an article about them, then I found a book on it. Next thing I knew, I had this big plan in my head, and…I'm sorry. I'm really sorry."

One of them was always sorry these days and suddenly, not telling her about his wild ride the night before seemed like the best idea in the world. "It doesn't matter, all right? It's over."

She stared across the table at him with an expression that said she had more to say. "It isn't over, though. Is it?"

"Fuck. Here we go." He put his face into his hands.

But instead of the angry wrinkles on her forehead appearing as they always did when she stared yelling, her eyes misted. "I love you, Aaron. I love you so much. I'm just scared for you. You remember Mitch? And Connel? I don't want you to end up like them. I don't want to find out on the news that you died because I didn't hear from you for two weeks."

"I'm not going to die. I didn't end up homeless when you moved out, and I'm not begging for cash on the street to keep the lights on. I'd be more likely to end up there if I was actually writing."

"Yes, and the writing? Remember when you said it was the only thing you loved more than me?"

Not the most romantic thing to say on their anniversary, but it had gotten a laugh out of her. "What about it? I still write sometimes."

She glanced away as more tears fell. He wanted to leave, but her tears were worse than her anger. Nearly as bad as bringing up Aimee. "It just doesn't have to be like this anymore, you know?"

"Like what? This is life. You work, you have fun, you die. It's pretty straightforward."

She held his hand, looking him straight in the eyes as tears dripped from her face and crashed upon the table. "Let's just get out of here. I can take a job anywhere we want—New York, Seattle, LA. My parents even have that little place in Kentucky. Kutawa. We can go there. Wherever. Let's just get the hell out of this town and go away. Leave all the crap behind. No more drugs, no more fights, just me and you."

This was a new act to the play. "What?"

"Yeah. We could be out of here in a month. We don't even have a lot to pack. We can fresh-start it wherever we want. I've got the money now, and the resume."

She didn't get it. She never would. Some ghosts followed you no matter how far you ran. He'd learned that lesson young. "No. I can't do that."

Her face fell. "Why not?"

Last time he'd run away, his sister had killed herself. He'd been a hundred miles away, sleeping in a stolen car. On the night it happened, he had a dream. He and Aimee alone in a room with white walls and no doors. She'd started crying, but every time he tried to speak, no words had come out. A *boom* shook the world, and he'd woken in tears. When he called the house on the payphone the next morning, his mother had told him everything.

He hated this town, but it was his prison as much as his home. He wouldn't leave again. He and Aimee had run these streets as kids. This place once held the entrance to a kingdom only the two of them could see. Maybe it still did.

He pulled his hand away from hers. "I can't, okay? I just can't." He stood to leave, and he could almost hear her shatter as he did. Just like every other time he'd hurt her. Just like Dad. Just like Mom. If he'd wanted something to distance his mind from the previous evening's nightmares, he'd hit the jackpot.

She grabbed his arm as he started to walk away. He looked down at her. He couldn't remember her ever looking so pathetic.

"I love you, Aaron. I really do. You know that, right?"

"I love you, too."

He left without looking back.

He felt better with food in his stomach. The jitters and lethargy that accompanied coming down still lingered, but not as much. He'd wanted to clear his head, and he certainly had, but he still didn't know what to make of the trip back to the Kingdom.

A message from a god he didn't really believe in? A hallucination? He tapped the steering wheel as he drove around the city, unable to face the thought of going home. He didn't want to be still. He wanted to move and jive, to skitter and run, anything but facing that apartment after the night before.

He stopped when he realized how much he was shifting and twitching. He wouldn't do the junkie dance. He wouldn't validate their goddamn intervention or Marie's tearful offer of amnesty. He wasn't a loser. He'd kept it together through shit that would have driven most people to an early grave.

He pulled out the phone and called Brian, but it went straight to voicemail.

"Fuck." He started tapping the steering wheel again but stopped immediately.

The streets bled together as he drove and the sun set. By the time the last rays of light were cresting the mountains, he was back at the park. He stepped out of the car this time, his courage bolstered by a day to think.

He lit a cigarette and sat on the hood, staring into the forest. There could be answers out there, or there could be nothing. He almost jumped down half a dozen times, but he couldn't bring himself to do it. The implications were too big either way. Right or wrong, he lost here.

By the time he returned to his apartment, night had settled in hours ago, and he was no closer to answers.

He hadn't cleaned up the apartment, and his rig still sat on the table. Evidence that at least those memories weren't faulty. He picked it all up to put it away.

Just touching the syringe triggered that craving, an earthquake inside his guts even though he was perfectly still. Seeing a gas station on a long, lonely highway when his meter had read E for miles. A goddamn nuclear bomb going off inside his head, and the only fallout shelter was inside a syringe. Just a nibble to take a little heat off the top. Something to even him out after feeling crazy all day.

He didn't have anything left to take, and after the last twenty-four hours, that wasn't such a bad thing. It wasn't as if he needed to use every time he got stressed out. He hadn't taken anything after their intervention, had he? No Broad Street crackheads here.

He rolled a joint and sat on the couch. Only a prude would accuse a man smoking pot of having a problem.

And it did so almost instantly. Within minutes, he felt better. Not great, but better. More able to get out of his head. He flipped on the TV. Oprah appeared on the screen, and he changed the channel immediately. Every one had something horrible on it. CIA torture. Two cops dead. Black men gunned down in the streets. He, Aimee, and Brian had joked as teenagers that channels one through nineteen were reserved for depressing events. That hadn't changed, even if everything else had.

When classic cartoons flashed across the TV, he stopped and lit up. He didn't smoke as much as he had two nights ago. That had been asking for trouble after the intervention, and he wasn't going to make the same mistake twice. He took a few puffs and put it out. No shotgunning a tampon's worth tonight. He needed something to bring him down, not stress him out. It was no heroin, but it sanded down the harsh edges of the day.

Aimee would probably scowl and disapprove, but she'd been a teenager. Maybe if she'd grown up she would have been smoking right there with him, though it was hard to picture. He pushed the thoughts aside. They were a constant companion, but also the last thing he needed right now.

For once, they vanished on command instead of haunting him for hours. Within a few minutes, the pot did its thing. The bad thoughts and ugly memoires were still there, but they didn't matter as much. Better to lose yourself in *Tom and Jerry* than to dwell on shit you couldn't control.

For the first time in years, he laughed at the cartoon cat getting its ass kicked by a mouse. The colors were a little brighter, the rancid smells of his apartment a little stronger, and the bad shit he didn't feel like dealing with was a lot farther away. He sank into the couch and wished his thoughts away. Hid behind the laughs. He smoked his Marlboros until they were gone, and ate the last of the pizza in the fridge, the taste foul after a little too long in there.

Brian could go blow himself, and Marie could move wherever she liked. He didn't have a problem, and he was fine where he was.

Chapter 13

At some point, he'd drifted off. He opened one eye to see through the still-open curtains that morning hadn't yet dawned. *Tom and Jerry* had given way to some bullshit 80s cartoon about talking cats, and the lights were still on.

Something had woken him—a creak of a floorboard or stomping upstairs. The sense of someone right behind him. He shifted to look, but there was nobody. But the gnawing eyes drilling a hole into him didn't vanish. If anything, the feeling intensified. Anxiety replaced the lingering high that softened his thoughts.

"Ser."

The word snuck in from a great distance, a whisper across a crowded room. He placed the voice right away.

He leaned up to look behind him. He didn't want to see anything but the hallway. The thought of ending up in those woods again made the rotten pizza in his stomach threaten to come up. Not tonight. He couldn't handle it tonight.

Nothing, just the hallway as he'd hoped. Still, the word drifted from somewhere.

"Ser."

He jumped off the couch, nearly losing his footing in his daze. "Get away from me, man. Leave me alone."

Nothing answered.

He didn't need this shit. Not tonight, not ever. He would go for a drive, find some bright diner, and chug coffee until the sun came up. Cruising around a little stoned might not be the best idea, but he'd gotten by for a while without a record. Anything was better than more questions and crazy thoughts.

The hair on his arms stood up as he snatched his keys and wallet off the table and slipped his shoes on. He didn't know if this all meant he was a nut, and he wasn't going to stick around to find out.

"Ser, please."

He shuddered at the depressing urgency in the words that came from everywhere and nowhere. A rising tide of panic nearly overpowered him at the idea of it originating from inside his own head. Without looking back, he stepped to the door and twisted the handle.

It wouldn't budge. Not even to jiggle the whole shitty thing in the doorframe as it always did.

"Ser!" The voice was closer now. Not a whisper anymore, but someone speaking in another room.

He broke out into a cold sweat. Tug. Tug. Pull. When that didn't work, he shouldered it, grunting with the effort of trying to break it down. "Fuck, fuck, fuck." He punched and kicked the door, but it didn't move. The first hint of bile rose in the back of his throat. It couldn't be happening. Aimee had died years ago, not gone to a fantasy land.

The air grew heavy, as if too many people at a party had been breathing too hard. It stank of rancid meat and dirt, and it was too damn hot. He gave up on the door and squeezed his eyes shut, willing himself to turn around, afraid of what he might see. With a deep breath, he spun around, prepared for horror and maybe a fight.

An empty apartment. A place that had been the cream of the crop forty years ago now barely holding water. Dirty floors, water stained ceiling, rot along the edges. Nothing waited for him. No magical Kingdom and no intruders.

Except...

The TV was off, and the lights from the factory had vanished. He stared out the window before realization grabbed hold, and a horrified whimper escaped his lips. It was all the lights, not just the ones from across the street—even the stars. A big black blanket had been thrown over the world, like in his nightmare adventure to the Kingdom.

He dropped his keys and wallet. "Is this some kind of game?" He balled his fists as if he could fight this. "Huh, motherfucker? Come out!"

Nothing responded for a long, silent moment.

"Ser. Please, help."

126

The words shook him. That desperation. That pleading. No different from a little girl and boy who didn't want to get black eyes when they returned home late. He wouldn't look. Whatever it was would go away. He could stand here until Marie called or Brian came over.

No sooner had the thought occurred to him than his phone rang. Saved by the chime of modern technology. He fumbled it out of his pocket and stared at the unknown number, his hands trembling so hard he could barely see the screen.

"Hello?" he said as he put the phone to his ear.

"Ser! Things is bad, and they're like to get badder if you don't help."

He dropped the phone and watched it sail to the floor as if in slow motion. It bounced once and lay face-down at his feet as he tried to back away from it. He could still hear Drippy begging him to venture back and set the Kingdom right. Make things the way they used to be.

But things could never be the way they used to be, and it was all just a bad dream anyway. A sure sign Marie and Brian were right. Proof positive that Aimee would shake her head if she could see him now. Maybe she'd cry over the man he'd become. Maybe she'd hate him for who he was, just like everyone else.

As if on cue, her voice floated out of his bedroom. "I could never hate you, Aaron. Never."

No mistaking that voice, even after a decade.

"Aimee?" He craned his neck to peer into the hall but gained nothing for it. Sweat broke free of his face and rained down onto the floor as he took one childlike step toward her. "You can't be Aimee. She died."

"Yes, I'm sorry, Aaron. It wasn't your fault. I was just so lonely. I didn't mean to leave you." She sniffled. "I didn't know what else to do. I was so scared." A hiccup echoed from her direction, and the low moan of a crying teenager followed.

He teared up. His feelings mirrored hers, same as ever. If she cried, he cried, as if they didn't just share the same birthday but the same heart. "No. Don't. I shouldn't have left. I'm so sorry, Aims. I'm so, so sorry." He strode toward her. Maybe it was like the imaginary soundstage. Maybe there was nothing in that room, or something dark and ugly like those black-light creatures, but he didn't care. Aimee needed him. She'd always needed him, and he'd abandoned her. He wouldn't do it twice.

"I promise I will never leave you again. Do you hear me? I'll stay here until this place burns down."

The darkness of his room, a gaping maw of shadow and terror, yawned before him. So be it. Into the belly of the beast. He walked toward her cries, into the black, in open defiance of his fear. He found the light switch on the wall and flipped it up.

To his surprise, the light flicked on. But there was no crying sister. No monsters. Just a stinking room with a messy bed and clothes everywhere.

"Aimee?" He hadn't been hearing things, not this time. "Aims, where are you?"

Nothing answered. Not Drippy or Aimee. Just silence. Outside the window, he could see the lights of the factory and the stars above. She was gone all over again, and just as suddenly as the first time.

His heart sank. He wished he'd told her he loved her. He wished he'd said he would always love her, and that he would have died for her if she had let him. He could almost hear the million whispers into his tearstained pillow in the quiet. He'd never shed those tears when Marie or Brian had been around. Never spoken about them. He would beg god, any god, to bring her back, or at least let him see her one last time. He did it knowing it wouldn't make a difference, that it couldn't be done. But now he'd had his chance and missed it. And it had probably never been there to begin with. Just a waking dream or the aftereffects of some shit drug.

"Fuck." The heat behind his eyes pushed and pushed, but he wouldn't cry. Not now. Dad had told them it was only good for getting you a beating, and he hadn't been wrong. Tears didn't fix anything.

She was dead. Moved into the great beyond. Not in the Kingdom and certainly not waiting in his bedroom. Just vanished, like everyone did eventually.

He stared at the ceiling, the catch in his chest keeping the breath out, tears blurring everything. Slowly, very slowly, he mastered himself the same way he always did.

"Get a fuckin' grip, man. Grow up and handle your high. Fuckin' JV shit."

Harsh, but it did the trick. Dad had been an asshole, but he hadn't always been wrong. Sometimes being tough was better than being soft. In fact, it usually was.

When his composure finally returned and his heartbeat approached something normal, he turned to the bathroom to wash his face, to stare at Aimee's eyes looking back at him in the mirror.

No monsters in there, either. Just a man with a tenuous grip on reality. He turned the hot water on and dipped his face down. No sister. No magic. That shit wasn't real. File it into the box marked "forget by breakfast," never to be thought of again. Just another sign he was losing it. Another check in the junkie column.

When he looked up, the figure in black armor stood behind him. Gauntleted hands grabbed Aaron's head in the same place Aimee had all those years ago when she'd showed him the shack and the entrance to their secret kingdom.

He screamed in horror, forced to gaze into Aimee's eyes by the monster behind him. But there was no escape. His whole body rigid as a board, he screamed and screamed until his throat was hoarse. Saline drips fell lose and splashed against the porcelain of the sink. He might have pissed his pants. He didn't know. He couldn't think, couldn't see anything besides that visor. Waves of hate poured out of it, paralyzing him.

Aimee's voice spoke from behind the mask. "It's right there. See?"

He screamed as the lights went out and darkness consumed him.

Chapter 14

"What are you gonna do, stupid?" Joey Curry took Aimee's book and held it over his head. He was big, round, and mean, and teased them mercilessly. "What are you gonna do? Cry and tell your mommy?"

Other kids stopped and stared. Everyone at school treated them with scorn, or at least it felt that way. That hadn't changed from elementary to middle school. Even some of the teachers looked down at the dirty kids who missed more class than anyone and never had a good excuse.

Aimee smirked. "I'd call yours, but I don't have a pork chop to stop her from eating my leg."

Aaron grabbed the book from behind Joey as the rest of the class chuckled and he turned red. Aimee didn't need him to look out for her, but he did it anyway. They took their seats while he fumed at the front of the class.

"Don't worry about him," Aimee said quietly. "He's so dumb he'll probably get held back anyway."

But if it weren't him, it would be someone else. It would be people making fun of them for wearing the same clothes all year, or the holes in their shoes. It would be someone teasing Aimee for her three-year-old backpack or the tangles she sometimes had in her hair. For two poor kids from a bad home, it would always be something, and he was just now realizing it at twelve.

That night, he stomped back and forth in their room after dinner, a rare one where Mom and Dad had both been in a good mood. "I think I could take him." He threw a big haymaker in the air. "I could blindside him. He wouldn't know what hit him." He paced back and forth in their room. "I bet after I did it once, he would never mess with us again."

"Just let it go." Aimee watched him walk back and forth across their room. "If you get in trouble at school, you're going to get it from Dad."

Aaron rolled his eyes. They would get it from Dad no matter what they did. "So, what? We just put up with that crap all the time?"

"We have somewhere else we can go where that never happens." She leaned back in bed. "What else do we need?"

It didn't go away on its own, and Aaron didn't fight back. Every day Joey had something to say. Pretending he would trip them, or sucking in as if he'd spit as they walked by. More and more, others started to laugh when he showed off.

It finally came to a head a week later. Joey got off the bus early and followed them as they walked from the bus stop to the park. He smiled, showing off his buck teeth, as he saw they weren't going home but toward the woods.

Aaron moved to turn around, but Aimee grabbed his hand. "Don't, Aaron. Just leave it alone. He won't do anything in the woods. Keep going."

"Where you going, Trash Twins? You got a pile of trash out in the woods you like to play in?"

Aaron balled his hand into a fist.

"Don't."

"You going to go out there and fuck each other, perverts?"

The vulgarity of it stunned Aaron, and he stopped, straightening his back.

They were halfway across the park when Joey began laughing hysterically. "You do, don't you? Gross! I'm going to tell everyone."

Aaron's rage must have been clear on his face as his lips twitched, because Aimee tried to grab him by both shoulders. "Don't!"

Aaron spun on him. "Why don't you fuck off, you fat piece of shit!" He dropped his backpack and took two steps toward Joey, his hands up like Dad had taught him.

The laughter stopped. "What did you call me?" The cruel smile on Joey's face fell away.

Aaron could feel the red in his face and hear the ocean in his ears. "You heard me, lard-ass. Leave us the fuck alone, or I'm going to pop you in your stupid mouth!"

Joey's eyes widened, and pleasure coursed through Aaron. It was good to know some bullies in life could be forced to back down. It was something he needed.

But Joey wasn't backing down. He clenched his jaw, and his cheeks burned red. "You got a real smart mouth on you, trailer trash." He strode toward Aaron.

Aimee stepped between them. "Why don't you go kick rocks?" She furrowed her brows and curled her lip into a sneer. The best attempt at looking fierce a little girl could muster. "You're nothing but a bully!"

Aaron wouldn't have it. It didn't even occur to him that this big, round child wouldn't hit her. He had never so much as touched her before. Still, Aaron pushed her aside, ready to tell this turd what was what and knock him out if need be.

"Stay away from my—"

A big, meaty hammer struck him across the face, sending a crimson spray through the air. Joey laughed as Aaron tumbled into the dirt chin-first. "Call me fat again, trailer trash. Do it one more time and I'll—"

Aimee was on him in a flash, slapping and scratching before he realized what was happening. "You fat asshole! I hate you!"

Aaron had never heard Aimee cuss before. He'd never seen her hit someone.

The bully reared back to punch her too, but her foot found his crotch before he had a chance. With a *thwack*, she hit him in the nuts as hard as he'd ever seen Dad hit anything.

Joey doubled over. "You bitch!"

He gasped and held his nuts, but Aimee wasn't done. She slugged him across the face, and he fell to the ground opposite Aaron, his nose crooked.

People on a porch across the street stood up, staring at the spectacle. A bad neighborhood it might be, but that didn't stop people from gawking. Aimee looked down at Aaron, her breath heaving, her hair wild and feral. The people left their porch and walked toward them. They'd call parents, and Dad would hear about it. They'd get a worse beating from him than anything Joey could dish out.

Aaron put his hands under him, his head spinning like it did when Dad hit him, and jumped to his feet. Aimee didn't have time to say a word before he yelled, "Run!" He grabbed her hand and took off toward home as people crossed the street to see what had happened.

It wasn't far, but by the time they made it, they were sweaty and gasping for air. Aaron looked up at the house, at the rusted railing leading up the stairs to the faded, dented front door. "You go inside first. If Dad sees me like this, he'll get mad."

She stared at him as she did her best to catch her breath. At length, she did as he bade.

But they both knew the truth. There was no hiding what had happened to his nose. Bloody and bent, even more so than Joey's. The first time it had ever been broken, but it wouldn't be the last.

Dad would see it and ask what happened. He'd get mad as a bull seeing red, and he'd charge the same way.

Still, he wiped the blood off and tried to set the nose like he'd seen on TV. Palms on either side and turn. Instead, he yelled in pain, and it remained bent. There was no fixing it by himself. Dad could. He'd been a boxer for a long time. But he wouldn't.

Aaron walked to the back door and took a deep breath before opening it. The stink of trash and beer seeped outside as he stepped in. Dad dozed on the couch, eyes closed. Small miracle there.

But the door clicked too loudly when it closed. "Keep it the fuck down, boy." His red eyes opened, taking a good look at Aaron. He never left the couch. He'd hurt his back working at a lumber yard and collected disability ever since. He'd ruined his boxing career doing it, and then his wife and kids had ruined his life, according to him. "What the hell happened to you?"

He wasn't really voicing concern; it was a game he liked to play. When Brian's mom asked what was wrong, she wanted to know. When Dad asked, it meant something bad was about to happen. "Nothing. I fell down." Aaron tried to walk by.

Dad moved to throw the beer bottle sitting in his lap, but dropped it instead. The sleep in his eyes vanished in an instant, replaced by white-hot rage. "Don't fuckin' lie to me, you little shit-bag. You got your ass beat because you're a pussy."

Aimee peeked from behind the corner to the kitchen, and for half a second their eyes met. Dad followed his gaze and saw her standing there. Just like that, his rage shifted from him to her, just as it always did. Eventually, Aaron would guess correctly that his father hated women. He was a no-class, trailer-trash wife-beater, and he took it out on everyone around him.

"What the fuck are you looking at? You're just like your mother. Think you can sneak around and do what the fuck you want in this house just because he did something stupid."

Aimee took one timid step back. That fierce child of the forest with the wild hair and flying fists had been replaced once more with the meek little girl who loved bad fantasy books. She cast her gaze to the floor in a way that wrenched Aaron's heart out.

He had to do something. She'd saved him; he would return the favor.

That same red hot anger he'd had with Joey jumped back into his chest, up his throat, and out his mouth. "If I'm a pussy, it's 'cause I have a pussy for a dad!"

Aimee knew what to do. She gave him one final look before vanishing around the corner. This wasn't a war movie where you could rescue your fallen comrades. Once they were down, they were down. They'd get right back up again to be knocked down again the next day.

"You motherfucker!" Aaron had never seen Dad move so fast. He jumped off the couch, nearly falling over the beer bottles at his feet, and closed the distance in an instant.

Time slowed as Dad wound up. As weird as it was to notice, Aaron thought his dad looked like the college boxer he'd always said he was. Back straight, chin down, and guard up. Aaron did his best not to flinch as the first punched connected with his already broken nose, but he couldn't help it. He screamed as it shattered further, and he flew into the wall behind him hard enough to crack the plaster. Blow after blow rained down on him until he was numb with terror. He cried out, begging for it to stop, but it didn't. He wanted to hate himself for being so weak, but there was no room for it, only fear.

It went on for what felt like an hour. Finally, Dad stood over his prone form on the floor, gasping for air as they had when they'd run home. Aaron wanted to look up to see if there was any remorse on his face, though he knew the answer. Dad couldn't feel remorse. He'd either killed it a long, long time ago, or never been able to feel it to begin with. The results were the same either way.

"If you ever talk to me like that again, I'll fucking kill you. You understand me, boy?"

Aaron tried to tell him what he wanted to hear. There was no room for defiance any more. But he'd bit his lip from one of the blows, and he couldn't move it like he wanted to do.

Dad didn't seem to mind. He went back to the couch and sat down, leaving Aaron in a ruined pile on the floor. There was no sign of Aimee, and that was the only comfort. When Dad got like this, there was no telling how he would react if someone else intruded. He became a wild animal, rabid and dangerous.

But nobody told Mom that. She walked in with an armful of groceries not ten minutes later to find Aaron still unmoving on the floor. Everything felt like it was broken, and he was scared to move. Scared that if Dad saw him, it might start up again.

Mom, staring at Aaron, slammed the groceries down on the counter. "What the hell did you do to him?"

Aaron peeked up. Dad set his jaw the same way he had before he'd lost his calm. "Not now. Don't fucking get on me about this now."

She knew as well as Aaron where it would lead if she pushed the point. She scooped Aaron up off the floor. It hurt, and he cried out in pain.

"Shut up," she said. "If you didn't have such a smart mouth, this kind of thing wouldn't happen. I bet you deserved it." There was no pity in that house. She placed him in his bed the same way she might set down a sack of potatoes. No concern for her bruised and bloody child. No words of comfort like Brian's mom would have given him.

Aimee ran from where she sat at her desk as their mother left and knelt next to the lower bunk. Her eyes shone with tears before the door had even closed. "I'm so sorry! I'm so, so sorry!"

"Not…" Aaron swallowed and tasted blood. "Not your fault." He couldn't open his left eye all the way, and his nose was a knot of pain in the middle of his face.

He didn't go to school the next day, or the day after that. His arm hurt in the middle, but nobody took him to the doctor. It was hard to breath for a week. The bruises on his face healed long before he could walk without a limp or move his whole arm.

Three weeks passed before he went back, and not a single teacher called that whole time. At Mom's orders, Aimee told the school he'd had to have his appendix taken out. Rather than ask questions, they loaded her up with his assignments, and that was the end of that.

Aimee did his homework that whole time, and brought him new library books when he finished the old ones. Mom wouldn't let him leave the house. She stared at him with contempt when she bothered to look at him at all. "What would people say if they saw you like that? They'd take you away and put you in an orphanage. You'd never see Aimee or us again. Is that what you want?"

He wanted to get away from them more than anything, but the thought of never seeing Aimee again left him in tears. He was trapped. They both were. The systems put into place to protect them didn't amount to shit for those who fell through the cracks like they had.

Those words left him aching now, just as they had then. He woke in bed with tears still running down his face. Sunlight broke through the open curtains, insisting his eyes open. Everything blurred as he did. It took a moment to realize he'd been crying. In another, memories from the night before clicked into place.

He threw the covers off and looked around the room, unsure if he was still dreaming. The sound of cartoons drifted from the living room, and the lights were on. Had he wandered in here after getting high last night?

His heart hammered. He jumped out of bed and looked at his feet. No grass or dirt this time, no signs he'd been anywhere but his apartment. No signs that Aimee or anyone else had been there.

Because she was dead and gone, same as everything they'd had together. If life had taught him one thing, it was that eventually, everything broke and fell away eventually. Your twin, your secret Kingdom, your girlfriend, and your best friend. One day he'd find himself faded too, living off the tracks in some cut-rate nursing home by himself until even his body failed him, and then he'd slip into whatever came next.

And maybe that would be better, because maybe Aimee would be there.

He sat back down and covered his eyes with his palms, trying to hold back the heartache. Even in secret, his tears were shameful. *Men don't cry.* Not real men. Dad made sure he knew that. If you cry, you get it worse. The golden rule of the Vasilica house.

A hot drop slipped between his fingers. How did people go on? Every day was a minor tragedy compounded by minor tragedy. A slow and certain march toward annihilation. People existed only as the meat machines of some capricious god or a universal accident, take your pick. You were born, you hurt, people died, you went mad. Cap it all off with your own funeral. And for what? So some prick could say he knew you when? So your kids or your grandkids could forget you, your name stricken from everything but the family tree by the time you were a hundred years dead?

A single sob escaped his lips. He sucked it back in as if Dad would hear across the years and charge through the door to make up for ten years of missed beatings.

"Fuck," he whispered under his breath. No time for that. Even if he had nothing to do and nowhere to be, there wasn't time for that kind of soft business. Little by little, he pushed it back down. The tears retreated. The tender parts inside hardened again, and he wiped his eyes with the back of his hand. "Get a goddamn grip." Same as he would have told anyone he saw blubbering. Tears didn't solve problems, and self-indulgence wouldn't make the hurt stop.

Not that kind of self-indulgence, anyway. He wanted a fix. Something to block out any chance of ever hearing Aimee in the night again. Fuck it. Marie, Brian, and ol' what's-his-face… Goober. They could call him a junkie if they wanted. Let them throw him on Oprah and say he was tearing their lives apart. He didn't give one shit. He wanted to fuck himself up. He wanted to replace that hurt with a bit of liquid sunshine.

But all he had was a beat-up old Mustang, a shitty apartment, and 1/100th of a novel. That desire, though, blocked everything else and replaced the pain with need. It would have to do for now.

"Fuck," he repeated, a little calmer. He had no idea what happened the night before, and he didn't care. He needed to get out.

Without changing, he hopped out of bed and made for the door, leaving every light on and the living room basking in the Technicolor glow of cartoons. His keys and phone were where they'd been when he dropped them in the dream.

He scooped them up with shaking hands and fled.

Chapter 15

Within an hour of leaving, the clouds had moved in. You never saw them coming in Umber Gardens until they were above you, a wall of roiling gray flesh dashing across the horizon and ending the world beneath. They turned a bright afternoon into something more suitable to his mood as they wept their payload onto his car.

He couldn't process the dreams, the odd visions, or the sudden resurgence of godawful childhood memories. One more box checked in the junkie column. He'd met people like that, the ever-popular Broad Street crackheads. The sort of assholes who couldn't separate fact from fiction in their own heads. Once upon a time, he'd sold weed to them, listening to their sad stories, telling them to get lost when that sad story involved getting free pot. That had stopped after a while. There was no money to be had in people who panhandled to fix themselves up.

But those stories. He couldn't forget those stories.

"My dad went crazy. Nearly killed me and my mom when I was a kid."

"I fought in Iraq. Can't even remember what it was like now."

"Government cut off my meds. Had to go free and clear the hard way. You're the only thing keeping me going."

He could just as easily imagine himself out there, telling his story.

"Mom and Dad drove my twin sister to suicide. Just as much my fault. Left her all alone."

How close was he to that? How many of them had almost kept it together and slipped up? The shiver that ran down his spine was from more than the rain. Everyone liked to imagine they were driving the train, even if they were tied to the tacks.

He crushed the thought. He wasn't like them. He was smart. He made money. He could quit when he wanted; he just didn't want to.

Right then, he might have killed for some H. He gripped the wheel harder and rubbed his mouth. A little jolt of electricity ripped through him at the thought of that sweet, sweet bliss. Cheaper than it cost to fill his gas tank. But he couldn't call Devon. He didn't want to buy twice in three days. The guy was his boss, his *associate.* If he thought Aaron was turning into a bad investment, he might cut off the supply of weed. If that happened, Aaron would be just like those assholes on the street he had so much contempt for. He slapped the wheel with his palm and blew out his frustrations on the storm as the day grew darker and darker, buffeting the car back and forth.

He drove everywhere and nowhere. When he ran out of gas, he filled up and kept going. Brian and Marie, either sick of his shit for the week or busy living their own lives, didn't pick up when he called.. They could be at work for all he knew. He'd stopped keeping track of what day it was a long time ago.

He turned down his old street without thinking. Past the park this time, straight to the old house, slowing as it passed beyond the window. That rusted stair guard still stood, same as ever. But the roof had been replaced and the siding changed up. It would always be ugly to him, but someone had put a lot of care into unfucking the dump. The rain suited it perfectly. It was a dour, hateful place, and the same sort of weather ought to forever remain above it until fate saw fit to knock the fucking place down.

He wondered if the new owners knew what went on there. Did they know about the little girl who killed herself in the master bathroom? Did they suspect a loser and a drunk had driven one of their kids to suicide?

He stopped as he saw a woman standing at the window. Early thirties. Good-looking. A book in her hands as she adjusted the curtain in the living room. Maybe she'd made happy memories there. Maybe she and some handsome lawyer had shit out a bunch of kids now playing with their toys, creating the good memories children should.

Or maybe she drank like a fish and the house still stank of trash and beer. Maybe Daddy was busy bitching out the kids as Mommy used her new Nicholas Sparks novel and a handful of Valium to make life go down a little easier.

She caught sight of him idling in the middle of the street, staring at her. For a second, their eyes locked through the rain, and he saw fear there. Every young woman from a decent home received a thousand and one warnings about men that looked like crackheads and the things they liked to do to women.

She watched him like a woman wondering what was happening to her neighborhood when the bad elements of town were idling outside. They'd fixed it up and made it their own. But to him it would always be a black spot on this town. They'd be doing everyone a favor if they just burned it down.

He drove away as she wrapped her arms around herself and, calling to someone, walked away from the window. *John! There's some weird-looking man outside the house.* He could almost hear it.

He watched the lawn in the rearview, the same lawn where Dad had once tried to teach him baseball. Playing catch for a while before getting bored and going back in the house. He'd tried to teach Aaron boxing in the backyard once too, fitting him with kids' gloves and getting his own out of his trunk in the master bedroom. The only clean spot in the house.

Aaron stood outside and waited for him. It couldn't be real, not in *this* house. Dad didn't do things like that. They didn't go camping or fishing. They didn't play games together or go out. The people in the house had grown as stagnant as the air, and what was left of Aaron's desire to play with his father had too.

Almost. Dad taught him how to shuffle and dodge a bit, then he'd poked at Aaron with jabs. Aaron, stony faced, dodged and weaved as he was told, tripping over his own feet as much as staying on them. Dad laughed when he did. He honest-to-god laughed and helped Aaron up. Out of habit, Aaron glanced over his shoulder to see if Aimee had heard it too, but she was inside. She wasn't going to believe it when Aaron told her, if she wasn't watching out the window. Aaron scanned the back of the house for her.

"Keep your guard up, son!" Dad fake jabbed twice and hooked. "You drop your guard like that, and you get knocked out first round." Dad tapped him on the forehead to make his point and smiled.

And Aaron laughed, while his dad taught him like dads should.

"When are we going to do another lesson, Dad?" he asked at dinner two days later. "I really want to learn more."

Aimee stared into her mashed potatoes. Aaron had gushed about it, and she had said little. He knew what she was thinking. That it wouldn't last. Sooner or later, everything would go back to the way things were. Their roles had been reversed, and now she was the too-young cynic. It didn't take long to see how right she'd been.

It didn't end in violence or tears. It didn't end with Dad beating the shit out of anyone in the house, or with the police. It ended with a story while Dad sat drunk on the couch one night two weeks later. Aaron had stopped asking, but that spark of wanting still glowed in his chest, just a little. As if any day Dad would come around.

Aaron got up from the kitchen table where he'd been doing homework when Dad grunted and waved him over.

The beatings hadn't started up again, but you could always tell when one of Dad's phases was coming, just like the moon. A little angrier at dinner. A few more beer cans in the trash. Mom would start a fight with him and spend more time out of the house. Then, *boom!* Someone had a black eye. Maybe everyone did.

So Aaron kept his eyes down and his posture meek, and he hated himself for it. He hated himself enough to push out that laughter with Dad in the backyard and the hope that had come with it.

"I was almost a champion," Dad said once Aaron stood between him and the TV. "Did you know that?"

Aaron nodded, but he didn't believe a word. Even a kid knew drunks lied.

"But it all went to shit. Fucked up. Got the wrong job. Messed up my back. Had kids. You know what that's like?" He furrowed his brow at Aaron, stopping when he realized no answer would come. "You don't know. But I'll tell you. It's fucking hard, kid. He stared into his beer can as if it would tell him a secret. Maybe it did, and that was why he drank so many of them. "You want to know how I got to be a champion?"

The rest would come like clockwork, and Aaron nearly opened his mouth to add almost before champion just to be spiteful. Instead, he shook his head, and his toes twitched at the cowardice of it.

"My dad beat the fuck out of me. Every day. I mean, he knocked us out like you wouldn't believe."

That time, Aaron's lips twitched. Like he wouldn't believe? He'd been beaten half to death. He'd missed weeks of school. He and his sister lived in utter, pants-pissing terror of him, and the man who caused it thought he wouldn't believe.

149

"So I got tough like that, and when I was old enough, I knocked that piece of shit out, just because I could." He glared at Aaron, the same glare that said someone was about to get hurt. "But don't go getting no fuckin' ideas about it. I'm just tellin' you." His expression softened, and for just a moment, that man who'd laughed with Aaron returned. "I want you to be better than me, you hear?"

"Yes, sir."

Dad looked past him at the TV. "Good. Don't ask me about the boxin' again. Now get out of here."

Acid dripped in Aaron's guts and left a trail of hate behind him as he left to his room. He'd been so damn blind to think anything would ever be different. Aimee hadn't said a word, because she wasn't spiteful like he was. She let it drop and never so much as mentioned it.

But he never forgot. And he never would. Suckers hoped; winners hit back. Nothing had changed about that man until he'd been gone. Brian's mom having the guts to stand up to him had been the only thing to shut him down, and even that had only made matters worse.

So long ago, but still so fresh. That hope. That disappointment. The beatings that had started up again only a week later. And maybe the worst part was, Aaron hadn't been a better man than Dad. Not if he was being balls-to-bones honest with himself. He looked around the car now, at the trash and cigarette butts. Not so different than the house had been. He glanced down at the phone his girlfriend and best friend never called him on, as if it might spring to life and save him from the truth. It didn't.

Marie and Brian had done this. They'd dragged up a lifetime of shit with their little stunt. It was true that things were never good, but they weren't always bad either. They'd summoned Aimee's goddamn ghost to haunt him in his apartment at night. It was already more than enough to see her staring at him every time he looked in the mirror. Those memories chased him often enough without the visual reminders of what a fuckup he'd turned into.

He shook his head as he opened the contacts on his phone. Fuck it. Devon wouldn't cut him off. He'd get enough junk for a few days. Make some bullshit up about passing it on. Things would be tight this month, but he'd made it through worse. He could make it work.

He always did.

Devon looked him up and down. The second ambush in a week. "You know you're the only guy I nickel and dime with this shit, right?"

He could read the subtext easy enough. *I don't want a goddamn junkie knocking on my door for a fix.* He'd said everything was fine on the phone, but the TV was off when Aaron walked in. Devon never had the TV off. Now Aaron stood in the middle of the living room like he was on goddamn trial. Again.

"I know, man. I appreciate it, too." He kept himself still as stone despite wanting to shake into another dimension.

"You sure you meant to ask for a bundle?"

A way out. A chance to back away and say he wanted less, or none at all. But he didn't. He wanted a stash. He wanted enough to snow himself in when Aimee or the goddamn Ghost of Christmas Yet to Come showed up at his place.

"Yeah, man. I think I might be able to pass a bit off. Make a little more paper on the side." His eye twitched as he lied.

Devon leaned back on the couch and stared at Aaron. "Don't bullshit me, man."

He already felt like an asshole just standing there, and he did his best not to blush at Devon's frankness. He opened his mouth to speak but didn't get the chance.

"I've known you for a few years now. I know the circles you run in, and I know the places you get your heroin. I also know you sell weed. No dope, just weed. Am I wrong?"

He could have lied more. He could have said he needed it to make rent this month, or he knew a guy going through a bad time. At least the last one would be true. Or better, he could tell Devon to fuck off with the questions. "I'm having a bad week. I just need to get some shit to stash away for those rough spots, you know?" And his last dealer had been nailed to the wall for minimum mandatory for possession with intent to sell; otherwise, he would have been over there.

"I don't like junkies. I don't like the kind of attention they attract."

The words sent him straight from one to ten, but he held it down. His eye twitched again, and he balled his hand into a fist in his pocket. Who the hell did he think he was? Having Aaron stand in front of him like this like he was Daddy laying down the law. Practically having his business partner standing at attention. Who let themselves get grilled like this? Bitches. Punks. Chump-ass junkies who…

He grabbed ahold of himself. Getting mad at Devon wasn't going to do shit but lose him his only source of income. But he wanted to. Hot damn, did he want to slap that smug look off this shitbag's face.

"Are you a junkie?"

Aaron bit the inside of his cheek. "No."

"Are you sure?"

Fuck you. "Yes. Like I said, rough week. It helps me keep even." Understatement of the year. It didn't keep him even; it kept him together. Every second he stood in this inquisition, he needed that a little more.

Devon only stared at him, that smug expression making Aaron's fist itch more and more.

"I've always brought you money. That isn't going to stop now." If he was going to plead, he might as well go for broke. "Selling is the only income I have. I'm not going to screw that up. I don't want to share a box with those assholes out on Broad Street. I just want something to help me relax at night, that's all." He left out the part where buying that much H would put him at almost twice his monthly budget. Fuck it. Go big or go homeless.

153

Devon stared out the window and nodded. He'd started this, after all. Aaron had never gone to him for anything but weed. He'd offered. "All right. This is the last time, though, do you understand? You make me too much money to let you go and off yourself with smack."

Talking to him like a kid. Giving him that condescending look. Aaron had knocked people in their fucking mouth for that more than once.

Devon must have picked up on it. The lines of his smile tightened. "And don't think just because I've never smacked the fuck out of you, I won't now, hear?"

The same kind of threat Dad had given him every day. For one insane second, he nearly jumped the distance between them. He would knock the pretty teeth out of this asshole's smile and grab whatever the hell he wanted. Devon didn't know where he lived. He didn't know jack shit about Aaron besides who he liked to get high with and how much money he made. He was being treated like a punk, and that kind of shit didn't fly.

But that thought was insane. Junkie shit. Devon wasn't trying to bring him down a peg; he was getting personal for the first time in their relationship. His own private intervention. For money, maybe, but that's what it was.

The anger vanished as quickly as it appeared, leaving behind a simmering pool of resentment. He didn't need so many goddamn nannies. "I hear you, man."

Devon disappeared deeper into the apartment. He returned with a brown paper bag sagging at the bottom. He never took his eyes off Aaron, who never took his eyes off the bag. They exchanged money and drugs.

"You might want to think about taking a break once that shit's gone. And don't forget what I said. Last time."

"Thanks."

He closed the door behind him and spit on the wall as he walked down the stairs. He had a lot of problems right now, but heroin wasn't one of them.

Chapter 16

Nothing waited for him when he walked into his apartment. No candle man, no Aimee, and no Black Knight. Just roach motel-quality housing at roach motel-quality prices. He threw the bag on the table and zoned out for a moment, staring at the cartoons on the screen. No more *Tom and Jerry*. Now it was the good stuff, *Dexter's Lab*. The show Dad had actually sat down to watch with his kids, laughing the whole time.

It didn't hold his attention long before his gaze was back on the bag. A bundle. Ten doses if you did it right, five if you did it really right. Enough to get him good and fucked up, nodding off and dozing half the day to wake up and take another hit in time for bed. This was going to turn the week around. After this, he could regroup and try again next week, whenever the hell that was.

And he wasn't going to wait.

He pulled out his gear and cleaned it off, grabbing a new needle. His old dealer turned prison pen pal had always made fun of him for being so fastidious about drug hygiene. "If yours is the only arm it's going in, who gives a fuck?"

He'd grown up watching the afterschool specials about how everyone would be in a gang and HIV positive by the year 2010. While the year had come and gone with none of that bullshit happening, those nightmare images stuck with him.

He attached the needle and started cooking two doses. One for now, one for later. The best way to achieve a good high was to get a dose going in the start, then push a second once the first one began dying off. You ran a higher risk of hitting those two terrible letters, but it hadn't happened to him yet, and he'd been a pro for a while now. Junkies and dumb fucks overdosed, and he was neither.

He didn't have the patience to find a vein in his foot. He took his pants off and found the big bastard popping out of his thigh like an earthworm. He poked at it for a moment, squeezing the muscle so it sprang up nice and tight. He slid the needle in and eased down on the plunger. The sunshine vanished from the syringe and into his veins.

He took the needle out, dabbed away the blood with a wet piece of paper towel, and sat back. Pay for the ticket, take the ride. Catch the dragon by the tail, if he hollered, let him wail. Once you caught him, you better never let the fuck go, because you won't catch him again. He didn't always show up, but sometimes just catching a glimpse was plenty. Aaron settled into the couch and waited for it to show its mug.

It started tiny, like it always did. And fast. A little tingle, a feeling like happiness in your guts. A physical, visceral thing that crawled out to your arms and legs. Up to your head where it infected your brain. It hotwired you into thinking maybe the world didn't suck so much, even when you had evidence proving otherwise.

After a few minutes, everything slowed down. The cartoons on the screen were moving at a different pace than the rest of the world. Their spastic, over-the-top shenanigans juxtaposed with everything else happening in the apartment. The noise outside bled in as if a black hole at the window were trying to pull it all to the event horizon. Light moved out of the bulb so slowly he could see each ray. It showered him, bathing him.

The cartoons were too much. He shut the TV off and stared at the wall, which moved further and further away by the second. Everything felt fuzzy. Life was one big Saint Bernard, and he was petting it.

The white lady's warm fingers stroked his face, pushing him deeper into the couch. He could almost hear her.

"Shh. Just relax, baby. You've had a long day."

He closed his eyes and smiled at the imaginary woman. "I have. It's been a long week." She looked just as good as Marie. She *was* Marie. The Marie he got sometimes when everything between them was great. There had never been a more beautiful or perfect woman in all the history of the world.

A hand caressed his cheek. "I know, baby, I know. If it's too much, you could always take that other one too." She pressed her breasts into his face. "Come lay down with me for a while."

He shook his head, clearing away the image. That would be silly. You always wanted to max out that high. Do everything just right and string it out. But it wasn't worth choking on your own vomit and dying from lack of oxygen. He laughed and rubbed his arm, enjoying the feel of it, imagining the white lady cooing at him more. She didn't, and that was fine too.

He nodded off. When he opened his eyes again, he didn't know how long he'd been out. Couldn't have been more than minutes, or the high wouldn't still be in full swing. He lifted his head from the back of the couch and glanced around.

Nothing was out of place. His shit was sitting on the table. The TV was off. His apartment still stank. But something had changed.

He touched his legs. His pants were back on. Had he put them on when he passed out? He stared at them, cocking his head like a dog that had heard a strange sound. It didn't compute.

The colors of the room had changed too. They were wrong. A little lighter than they should be.

No, that wasn't right. They were bleeding. The color from the ceiling leaked down the walls, running across the white paint and leaving a yellow blotch. The black from the edge of the TV sloughed off, turning the grayish carpet that should have been white into sludge. He stared at his hands as the white of his skin became too literal.

Anxiety nudged the high out of the way, just enough to make room.

"What the fuck?"

The shapes changed. The room's perfect squares weren't lines drawn on the real world; they were pencil scratchings of what a trashed apartment might look like, complete with smudges and creases. Erasure marks smeared the top of the TV where the clumsy hand of God had decided he needed a redo. Aaron looked at his hands again.

He was a drawing too.

He screamed, but there was no noise at all, just the quiet of the page. A bubble appeared over his head, holding the words he couldn't get out.

"What the fuck is happening!" He moved to grab his head but hesitated, afraid of what he might feel. "Someone help me!"

A different string of words rained down from the ceiling. "Keep it the fuck down, crackpot!"

He shook his head, staring at his penciled world, his heart beating out the soundtrack to cardiac arrest. *Boom, boom. Boom, boom. Boom, boom.*

"Help! Please!" He wasn't dreaming. He felt everything. His hands grazed his jeans, the ones he shouldn't be wearing. Rough denim under his fingers. All of it as it should be, but the world had come undone.

Boom, boom. Boom, boom.

160

On the paper's edge, blackness spread. Some cosmic klutz had knocked over the ink jar, and now Aaron would suffer for it.

"No!" He jumped up and down, pounding on the ceiling when he could reach it. "Help me, man! Help!"

Boom, boom. Boom, boom.

"Keep it down you fucking loser. I'm going to kick your ass!"

The blackness crept past the door, moving closer. He ran into the kitchen, trying to put distance between himself and that stain.

Boom, boom. Boom, boom.

"Someone! Please!" His throat burned from screaming. Tears, as drawn onto the world as everything else, fell down the page and onto the ground at his feet. "Please!"

Only a few more seconds and the ink would wash over him, rubbing him out like the rest of the world. Limbs poked out in places, hints at other poor souls lost in its darkness.

"Please! Please!"

Boom, boom. Boom, boom.

Arms and faces reached out of the stain. Grinning at him. Leering at him. Beckoning him forward as it drew closer. The dark lights. The things from the Kingdom.

Boom, boom. Boom, boom.

He was going to die here. Marie would find him and cry, or Brian would stand over him and say, "I knew you when." Or maybe they'd only find a crumpled piece of paper with a screaming Aaron drawn on it and an ink stain covering half. All the things he'd ever done wrong flashed before his eyes, quicker than a deck of cards cascading to the floor.

The ink hit his foot and climbed up his body, taking him into the blot that obscured the rest of the page. The dire cold of the grave froze him to the spot. Blackness crawled over him like some horrible growth. The last thing to go was his mouth.

He screamed until the ink oozed inside.

Chapter 17

No light pierced the gloom. He fell forever, but this time he remained conscious of it. No dream. No illusion. Just the sensation of his body flung through a sky with no stars.

His eyes open or closed made no difference, but he kept them shut anyway.

"God, please make this stop. Please. Please."

But the nothingness continued eternally while Aaron prayed to the deity he didn't believe in.

Until it didn't.

He hit the ground with enough force to knock the wind from him. It should have killed him. He'd been falling for hours, or days. Maybe years. His eyes shot open as he gasped for breath and stared up into the Kingdom's starless sky, the blackness above as perfect as that which he'd arrived through. As he struggled to breathe, he looked at his hands. No lines. No drawing. Just hands.

He groaned as he rolled across the ground. The nightmare images from his apartment flooded him, dropped into his lap in one giant tangle of fear and sweat. Tears formed and fell as he gasped, trying to catch his breath. This was too much. Everything had come apart for him in one short week. He didn't need any further proof he'd lost his mind. Whatever certainty he'd had in the stability of the real world was gone, replaced by the fear that at any moment reality would be unmade beneath his feet once more.

He didn't bother trying to get up. A place like this, a place like home, all of it was nothing more than a big ball of bullshit and bad memories.

"Cryin' ain't never done anyone any good, ser."

Aaron looked up as Drippy emerged from the forest.

"It comes from fear. Too much fear makes people weak."

Aaron sniffled and rubbed his runny nose. "Get away from me. You aren't real. None of this is." But his voice lacked conviction. How could he say what was real and what wasn't? How could he be sure after what happened in the apartment?

"Afraid it is, ser."

Aaron sat up and examined his surroundings. Mist clung to the landscape, same as the ink that had covered his apartment. Overhead, the dark universe stretched on forever. But the forest of guardian trees loomed before him, not all around. The hill he had once studied the Kingdom from with Aimee was to the left, standing silently over the landscape.

The well-worn road beneath him ran across the level plane of the world, trees occasionally marking the way. The lights of the village gleamed in the distance, the dwelling place of the Kingdom's subjects—*his* subjects. The wind carried moans and screams from that direction. Every hair on his body stood on end as one shriek, louder than all the rest, burst from down the road.

"You came back though, ser. I knew you would!" Drippy waddled over and brushed the dirt off him.

Aaron pushed him away. "Don't you goddamn touch me!" He wanted to yell that none of it was real, but the cold, hard ground under him protested. The silence, broken only by pained moans, didn't have the air of a dream. No happy thoughts that would allow him to soar among the clouds. The absolute oppression of this place couldn't exist anywhere but the real world.

"Ser…" Drippy kept cleaning him off, heedless. "It isn't safe here."

The mist swirled around them, waiting.

"I don't care."

"We need to get you to the castle. You can make things right from there."

Aaron stood, wiping the tears from his eyes. "It doesn't matter. None of this matters." He surveyed his domain. No life. No hope. No anything.

"If it doesn't matter, why not go?"

He'd said the same thing to Aimee the first time they stood on the hill and looked at the Kingdom. Drippy had bounced foot-to-foot, spinning in circles and clapping as they'd whispered to one another.

"What do you think? I'm not scared. It's…" She stared off into the perfect blue sky as she searched for the right word.

He wasn't so sure there was one. "I'm not scared, either. There's nothing bad here." The same words undoubtedly spoken by thousands of children before they vanished forever. "Aren't you curious?"

She looked down. "This is just a dream anyway. I'll wake up and nothing will be different."

He gazed out at the magic and wonder everyone had always told them wasn't real. "If it doesn't matter, why not go?"

Aaron stared at the same hill now. No light. No dancing candle man to ease their transition into a friendlier world. Now everything had teeth, and the candle man cowered in a shack at the edge of it all, waiting for them to return.

"The princess came this way, you know. The Lady Ser."

Aaron turned to him. The drugs had worn off the moment he'd been pulled from his apartment, but his head spun as if he'd just taken another hit. "What?"

"After you'd gone, gone, gone, she wanted to fix us. Like I told you last!" He turned in a circle and struck a pose as pieces of himself flew into the air and vanished. "She went to the castle but never left. Never, ever, never."

She'd died. He'd been at the funeral. He'd run his hands over the casket as they laid it on the lowering device, nearly overcome by the insane urge to throw it open. He had to see her to know. He had to be sure she had died.

But he didn't. Mom smoked as they lowered her daughter into the earth, not a single tear shed.

"Step back, son." The priest put a hand on his shoulder and guided him back to the little crowd as they chucked his sister into the ground like garbage.

He'd never looked, but he'd heard the stories. Brian had seen. He'd helped Mom get everything ready for the funeral.

"No. You're lying. She died out there." He pointed in the direction where the path back to Umber Gardens had once been. "They put her in the ground. She's not here."

Drippy shrugged. "Can't say if she's here or not, ser, but I can say she was." His big black eyes stared up into Aaron's. "She told me to wait for you. Help you find her if you came back."

"She what!" He grabbed Drippy by his runny chest and walked him backward. His hands sunk into the wax, which had the texture of skin. He latched ahold as if grabbing a dog by the nape.

Drippy put his hands above his head, but he didn't resist. "Ser! Ser! I'm only tellin' what she told me!"

"Why didn't you say anything last time!"

The warm wax under his hand jiggled as Drippy trembled. His eyes were as wide as tea saucers, reflecting the eerie light emanating from nowhere. "I did, ser! Sure did, yes, ser! I said she went all alone and never left! Nothing leaves here once it comes, ser!"

Aaron shook him. "Make sense! I left, didn't I?"

"Did you, ser? Aren't you here now?"

This pitiful thing didn't have answers. Aaron released him. His waxen body reshaped instantly, absorbing the marks Aaron's hands had left.

"She never left?"

Drippy cocked his head and closed his eyes, listening for something Aaron couldn't hear. Seconds dragged into minutes as the mist roiled around them, close enough to fear but not enough to harm.

Aaron paced back and forth. The sound of his steps didn't carry far. They died in the air, as if the world were hollow. He glanced at Drippy, but the little candle man's eyes remained closed. What was he doing here? How had he gotten to this place? How had they ever arrived here? Now he could recall it all so clearly. The touch of the grass on bare feet and the taste of perpetual spring in the air. Even without Brian, this had been a magical paradise for them. Not quite another world, but a door into one, perhaps. An escape they had needed.

And one they had probably fooled themselves into thinking they had, as imaginary as Dad's promise of a better life. No different from Mom's promises to do all the things for Aimee that Grandma had never done for her. Lies and lies and lies.

Just as Aaron's patience reached its limits, Drippy spoke. "Dunno. Can't hear nothin' from there. But she never came back this way, I can say that for sure."

Aaron rubbed his eyes and took a deep breath. Too much was happening too fast.

But he'd promised, hadn't he? Right there in front of those trees outside. And he'd swore he'd come back, and he'd said goodbye, and she'd died. She died without him, thinking he'd left alone with Mom and her rock-star boyfriend like everyone else had.

If he had the chance to see her again. Even in a dream…

"Fine. We go to the castle."

Drippy stared, his face passive. "Will you fix us, ser? Will you set all the bad things a'right here?"

Aaron walked toward the village. "I doubt it."

"But you can, ser, you can." Drippy caught up with him. "You're royalty. The Black Knight will hear your voice and obey."

The trees bent over the path, looming as if they would strike him down. In the perpetual gloom, they took on grotesque shapes. A one-armed giant. Corpses piled twenty feet high. The limb of some ancient monstrosity piercing the soil.

At one point, decorations and ribbons had hung from the trees, gifts from the townsfolk grateful to have the royal siblings return to them and more than that.

"Each ribbon is a wish," Drippy had told them as they walked past one day.

Aimee stared at a large red one, like something that would decorate a door on Christmas. "Who's wishes?"

Drippy skipped toward the village, his arms swinging wildly at his side. "The wishes of people who pass through here, or at least them that would like to. Don't you know anything about ruling the world?"

Aaron cocked an eyebrow at all the decorations. They sure didn't look like wishes. "So what are we supposed to do with them?"

Drippy smiled. "Maybe one day you can grant them all! It's your kingdom, in'it?"

It was, and it felt more like it after every trip here. But was he telling them they could grant people's wishes in the same way they changed their own little world? Was that something they could do here?

If it had been, Aaron had never found out. He'd left before he had even a hope of understanding this place. As kids, they'd only seen the sunshine on the water, never thinking to ask about the things that swam beneath. Now there were no wishes left, just good memories covered in bad reality. "How did the Black Knight do this?"

"You left, ser. Once you did, something had to fill in that space."

"So it was like this before we came too?"

Drippy shrugged. "'Before'. That word don't mean much here. You was always here when you was here."

Riddles piled on riddles. "I don't understand. What was here before we were?"

Drippy shrugged again. The casual gesture crawled getting under Aaron's skin. "Who knows, ser?" Nightmares and strokes didn't need logic; why the hell would this place?

The shapes of the trees changed every time he glanced away. Here a giant arm, now a big black tongue poking erupting from the ground. First a monster from the sea, now a crow with dead leaves for wings.

He glanced at the trees to his right and froze in his tracks. Two yellow eyes and stained yellow teeth grinned from a shadow high in the branches, and then it was gone.

"Did you see that?" Aaron touched Drippy's shoulder.

"Aye, ser. Pay him no mind."

Aaron looked at all the trees, trying to figure out where it had gone as they morphed. A giant cock. A willow with mouths in the bark. An oak like a bloody stake thrust through a heart. No monster eyes. No yellow grin.

"What the hell is it?"

Drippy continued to walk, forcing Aaron to catch up. "Just another unwelcome visitor, ser. Even the ones that speak can't be trusted. If he talks to you, remember; he always lies, even when he's telling the truth."

Talking in circles. The wails grew closer, pushing the thought out of his head. The phantom sensation of being watched, the itching between the shoulders, didn't stop.

He and Aimee had really walked down this path and thought it was a dream once.

She picked flowers at the bases of the trees. A rainbow of colors flooded the ground around them. Some of the plants Aaron knew— roses, lilies, posies. Some were foreign—giant purple leaves with a blood red center, pumpkin gourds with soft, yellow leaves, bright pink stems covered in green rose petals.

Aimee picked some of those last ones. "They're for the baker. For the cake she made last week."

There were always cakes. Half the time, Aaron and Aimee hadn't even had to ask. Their words could change the very shape of the world, but it couldn't change the people, at least not that they'd ever seen.

Aaron had asked Drippy about it once as they sat in the throne room, looking over the waterfall Aimee had made there to see the infinite stars of the universe beyond.

"Change people?" Drippy furrowed the yellow mounds of his eyebrows. He stared quietly at the floor as if giving the idea serious consideration. "I suppose you could, if you tried hard enough, but why ever would you want to? That sorta thing ain't good magic, ser."

Aaron wanted to know if he could change his parents. Make them into the kind of people he'd always wished they were, or make them disappear altogether. But he couldn't. No matter how commandingly he spoke, or how often he wished it, nothing outside of the Kingdom ever changed.

But the citizens of the Kingdom were eager to do whatever they could for the twins. They were certainly their own people, even Drippy, but they loved their rulers as if they were their own children. And so the baker made them cakes and cookies every time they came to visit. She put their favorite colors of icing on top, and everything she cooked was hot and fresh out of the oven. The only cookies they received in the real world were the ones Grandma brought when she visited. There were no birthdays or after-dinner desserts at home, and certainly no cakes.

Aimee picked flowers every time the chance arose. Drippy had informed them it was always good to reward a subject's loyalty, and so they did in the only ways children really knew. "You think she'll like them?"

"I'm sure they're fine."

They'd been visiting the Kingdom for years now, though every time they left, it seemed like the first time they'd ever been. Aimee had stopped questioning after a while, but Aaron never did. He rained questions on Drippy. Always poking. Always wondering if it would be there tomorrow, or if he and Aimee would wake one day to find it had all been a dream.

Drippy had asked him to stop. "Don't ruin it for her, ser." He hadn't said it to threaten, only to caution. Don't rock the boat. Just accept it for what it was and let it go. It didn't matter if it would be here forever. It didn't matter if it was real or not. They were both allowed in, after all, so what was the harm?

And so Aimee had collected her flowers, and Aaron walked with her, and when they found the baker, she gushed about how lovely they were. The people welcomed them the same as ever. The twins issued their royal decrees, keeping their subjects happy, even if they couldn't really understand why as children.

A fresh wave of cries drifted from the village. No more happiness here. No more cakes from the baker. No more flowers. No more Aimee. Miles away, torchlight glittered on the castles' ramparts. Could she really be there? If she died out there, did she return here? Was this her heaven even as it became his hell?

"What's making that noise?"

"The people, ser."

"Why?"

Drippy searched the trees around him for any uninvited parties to their conversation. "The Black Knight. When he took away the stars, he took away food and drink too."

"What? Wouldn't everyone just die?"

Drippy's gaze fell away, seeing another place or maybe another time. "He took that as well."

Aaron shivered as images of zombies prowling the town flashed through his mind. A stone dropped into his guts. If he hadn't seen the dark lights and the starless sky, he would say it couldn't be real. But he'd seen Aimee twice in the last few days, and she'd been dead for years

The violent, flickering torches were closer now. In the strange glow of the Kingdom, the fire brought no comfort. They invoked images of witch hunts and angry mobs. Villagers carrying pitchforks to raid the mill in which Frankenstein's monster hid.

He saw the first one at the outskirts, an emaciated man. His hair hung from his head in strings. Sickly pale skin stretched over visible bone. His eyes were sunken in his skull. He leaned over, grabbing his belly and screaming.

Aaron halted, anxiety bubbling over. "I don't want to be here. I can't do this."

Drippy stayed a step behind him. "Me neither, ser. But we have to. It's the only way to the castle."

"Then I won't go."

The dark mist swirled around them, growing closer. The absolute cold chilled him to the bone, but he couldn't see his breath. He looked back the way they'd come. He could see the hill in the distance, but the path had vanished along with the shape-changing trees.

"What the hell is that?" No stranger than everything else here, but no less unsettling.

Drippy glanced back. "Just the way of things here, ser. Paths change. You know that."

He didn't. He didn't know anything. Had he died on the couch, choking to death on his own vomit after taking too much smack? Had Dante seen moving trees and living mist when he ventured into the Circles of Hell?

"The only way anyone can ever go is forward." Drippy tilted his head. "Unless, of course, you walk backwards, but then you might trip." If he was trying to be funny, it didn't show on his face.

"Is it safe?"

Drippy entered the village. "No, ser."

Chapter 18

Here, the wailing grew worse. A hundred voices screamed in
agony. Some came from the streets, though only one person was
visible, if indeed it was a person at all. The rest pierced the walls of
the stony houses that made up the town, hinting at the dark horrors
inside.

The village had been laid out in haphazard order. No streets per
se, just avenues between buildings. A narrow alley might lead to the
back of a barn or the front door of a smith's forge. A street that
appeared to go all the way to the end of the village might turn right
when it hit a sudden cluster of buildings. At the center was the well,
but that was all Aaron could recall from his youth.

Now, though, the homes and shops twisted or leaned over the
paths. Shutters opened and slammed on their own. Doorways gaped
like mouths, hungry and ugly. A thin layer of the same black fog
from outside the village hung over everything. He'd seen pictures of
war-ravaged villages in far-off countries that didn't evoke the feeling

of absolute despair pervading this place. Nothing could warrant whatever doom had visited here.

"Do you know where were going?" Aaron had to speak louder over the cacophony as they walked on. He hunched lower as they passed the first building, afraid of discovery, afraid of the eyes he felt on him even when nobody could be seen. Whatever made those noises couldn't be human. They would drag him away into the dark, and he'd become another screaming voice in the background of this horror story.

"Aye. I know the way. The way knows me." Drippy continued as if he heard none of it.

They passed the wailing man, his hands still wrapped around his head. Aaron couldn't help looking. He stopped as a pang of recognition tugged at his heart. It was Sir Horace, who'd taught Aimee and him to ride a horse. The kind gentleman who'd said he'd been a knight and a poet a long time ago, far away.

"Don't be afraid, young miss, just step up." He'd lifted Aimee into the saddle, where she froze.

Aaron nudged the old nag he rode over to her, hoping to comfort his sister. He'd picked it up as naturally as breathing, but she was terrified of horses. "Don't be scared. Horace won't let anything bad happen."

He hadn't. He'd watched after them as if they were his own children. He'd walked her around the riding yard for hours, week after week, until she could finally do it on her own. Never a word of complaint. Never a sullen look. It had been his idea to name her horse Animus. He said it meant courage where he came from.

"Horace?"

The emaciated creature before him kept ululating, not looking up.

"Horace! It's Aaron. Do you remember?" He reached for Horace before he had time to consider it. The flesh of his shoulder was cold as ice, and Aaron recoiled in revulsion.

Horace jumped back and cowered, crouching with his hands above his head. "Please! No more! No more! *Misericordia!*"

Aaron's heart sank. Was this really the kindly knight who'd practiced swordplay with him?

Thwack, thwack, thwack. Their wooden practice swords bounced off each other as they drilled the forms. Aimee watched from a distance, sitting at the edge of the forest and sharing stories with Drippy. When Horace had offered to teach her, she replied she got enough of that at home. Aaron had rolled his eyes. It was just like her to find a way to be snobby, even here.

In the movies, swordplay looked much looser, as if it was a matter of outwitting your opponent. Here, Horace ran him through drill after drill. If they struck high, you blocked like so. If they thrust, you parry like this with a shield, and like this without. Should they charge with all their weight, you turn like so, deflecting both them and the blow.

It was as much schoolwork as anything else, and Aaron had no talent for it. He didn't doubt Horace had noticed as well, but he was much more interested in the man himself than in what he had to teach.

"How did you get here, Sir Horace?"

Thwack, thwack, thwack.

"I come from long ways away, and a long time ago."

Aaron had heard that before, and the same as then, it told him nothing. "Right, but where did you *come* from?"

Horace held up a hand, and Aaron stopped swinging. He pulled a handkerchief from somewhere along his belt and dabbed it across his forehead before returning it from whence it came. "Why the curiosity, young master?"

Everyone always asked why he wanted to know something instead of just answering it. The truth was he wanted to know more about the Kingdom. He'd always wanted to know more. What was it? Where did the people come from? Why were he and Aimee able to do the things they could do here? Perhaps most curious of all was why anyone would listen to children.

Instead of a direct answer, Aaron lied. Every time he brought something up here, he was shut down. Told to wait. All might be revealed when he was just a little older. Sit back and enjoy it for now. "I want to know what kind of fighter you were. If I wanted to learn another type of swordsmanship, I should be able to explain myself." Horace had spent the whole first day teaching him the proper terms for things. It wasn't sword fighting, it was swordsmanship. In the same way, it wasn't lying if he needed to know more about the man, it was creative questioning.

Horace gazed up at the sky above, perfect and serene. "I fought in wars for countries that by now are nothing more than stories in a book. I can't go back to those lands anymore to discover for myself. I doubt anyone there now would know the styles if I were to name them."

That was more than he'd ever said on the subject before. "Why can't you go back?"

He smiled. "Everything has its time in the world, Master Aaron, and every world has its time. But there are many worlds. Your time expiring on one doesn't mean it has expired on the others." He took a deep breath. Flowers and grass scented the air. "I rather like it here. It's peaceful." He raised his sword. "On your guard. Speaking of times past is well and good, but the present time calls for the sword."

The cold, screaming thing in front of him wasn't that man. He had been strong and full of life. He'd always had a wry smile and a knowing glint in his eyes. Aaron knelt next to him, his fear not forgotten but set aside. "Horace. Horace." He reached out to touch him again but stopped short.

"No! Please!"

"Horace, it's me, Aaron."

He shook, half-naked. "Please, Your Grace! Hurt us no more! Let us free of this curse!" He grabbed the hem of Aaron's jeans, tugging himself closer. Aaron backed away, startled, pulling Horace to the ground. "We've done you no wrong!"

This wasn't the man who'd named a horse after courage, or fought in wars.

"Punish us no more! My lord! Please!"

Aaron stumbled backward into Drippy, his breath escaping in panicked gasps as Horace began moaning once more. "What is this? What's he talking about?"

Drippy eyed Horace as well. Pity pulled his features downward. "They can't make sense no more, ser. They're broken. All broken up and dead inside now. Nothin' old can leave here, and nothin' new can come. But you can fix it if we can get to the castle. You can make it right."

Aaron stepped away as Horace screamed in agony, the veins on his neck bulging. He could do nothing but stare at the dirt as he continued into the village. What could have done this? What even was this place? Those questions nagged through the screams and the terror, but the one that nagged the most scared him. Why did Horace think Aaron had done this?

"Mercy! Mercy!" Horace's cries joined the din.

An elderly woman with no shirt on pulled her hair out by the handful, her body as ruined as Horace's. Two men embraced one another, screaming as they lay in the dirt outside a house. Across from them, another man held the pit of his elbow to his mouth, either screaming into it or biting it, Aaron couldn't tell which.

Madness. Aaron didn't mean to lean in close to Drippy as if for protection, but he did. "Why don't they stop? Why are they hurting themselves?" He yelled as loudly as possible to be heard over the nightmarish concert.

"They can't, ser. The Black Knight made it so. He forces them to hurt all the time."

One question kept returning over and over. "Why?"

Drippy carefully avoided looking at the people around them. "Maybe he wants somethin', though I can't imagine what. Maybe he just likes to see people in pain. Maybe there's a monster under all that armor."

What a creature like Drippy would consider a monster was beyond him, but Aaron's heart sank further thinking of it. He had a shitty apartment and a complicated relationship with heroin; he wasn't equipped to fight monsters. He had to get away from this. There was a path here, or there had been once, but he couldn't focus. The screaming drowned out his thoughts, shattering them to make room for the suffering in the air. It filled the space around him so completely he couldn't be sure he wasn't screaming himself. He hurried on, though he had no idea where to go. "Get us out of here, man!"

Drippy skipped in front of Aaron, his juvenile actions at odds with his meek expression. Whatever path he was taking, Aaron couldn't discern. They turned down alleys to find narrow openings between two buildings. They passed a storefront with the windows shattered, a little girl rolling in the glass as she shrieked. Aaron stepped on a piece of glass as they passed, but he barely noticed. The cacophony had replaced any sense, even pain. The deeper they travelled, the worse the cries grew. The misery expanded, and it pressed down on him, pushing the air from his lungs and the thoughts from his mind. He tripped over Drippy, walking so close he could have kissed the creature.

From outside, the village appeared to be only a few buildings, but inside it stretched on endlessly. The world spun with the howls and sobs of hundreds of people. The buildings looked familiar as they walked on. When they found themselves at the storefront with the girl again, Aaron grabbed Drippy.

"What the fuck is this, man?" he yelled as loudly as he could. It did nothing to stop the deafening lament. "Get us out of here!" The din of the crowds bled through his fingers and into his ears. Oozed into his soul. Images of an inferno filled with suffering pressed against him, pulsing from all sides until his entire world became a little box of noise and the heat of ten thousand bodies.

The Dark Knight hadn't just taken the light from this place; he'd turned it into hell.

Drippy's gaze darted from building to building. He danced from foot to foot. Aaron could see the mania in his eyes. He was starting to panic too. "I'm not sure which a'way is which and where, ser. Something ain't right. Nothing ain't right here!"

Aaron kicked him, leaving the imprint of his bare foot on the creature, a streak of blood from where he'd stepped on glass blemishing the wax for half a second. "You told me you knew the fucking way!"

Drippy put his head into his misshapen hands and rocked back and forth. "Gotta be quick and quiet! Wanted to be! Can't be seen!"

Gibberish again. Gibberish to compound terror and noise. The screams pierced through his hands and rocked his eardrums, every noise amplified a thousand-fold and blasted at him. "Can't be seen by what? What didn't you tell me!"

"Lots, ser! Lots! If the Black Knight finds out you're here, he'll get you. He'll eat you all up, or make you hurt forever, too."

Aaron stared at the girl rolling in the glass. An impossible amount of blood for such a little girl pooled under her. He saw himself doing the same. Foaming at the mouth. Emaciated. Stabbing his eyes with shards of a windowpane and tearing pieces of his flesh with his teeth.

He picked a direction and ran. He'd deal with all the dead things floating in the forest. At least out there he could think. There had to be an end to this village somewhere.

The wails pursued him. He didn't know if Drippy was behind him and didn't turn to find out. Despair and pain, everywhere he looked.

One turn brought him to a dead end, and he nearly tripped over Drippy backing out. More people poured into the streets. Did they know he was here? Had they heard him speaking, even over everything else?

He ignored them as they grasped at him from their doorways. He wasn't their prince, and he wasn't going to save anybody but himself. Still, begging hands reached, and people prostrated themselves as legions filled in around him. Gaunt and damned, thin flesh stretched over near invisible muscle and protruding bone. An eternity of hot flesh pressing in closer and closer, consuming him in search for relief.

Two more turns brought him down a wide lane with a dozen stores. The doors were opening one at a time. The screaming, bleeding masses approached. They crawled on hands and knees toward him. Limped to him, seeking an end to it.

Drippy grabbed his hand and yelled something.

"What!" Aaron couldn't hear him and couldn't focus with the mob approaching. His whole world had become a shrieking void.

"There, ser! Go there!" He pointed at the two-story building in the center of it all. A sign overhead displayed a foaming mug. A bar.

A steam horn blasted from the direction of the castle, muting the villager's cries. In its wake was sudden, total silence so complete after so much sound that the abrupt void gave him vertigo.

Dread snaked into Aaron's guts. If the reaper were to announce his presence, that was how he'd do it.

The villagers threw themselves to the ground, prostrating and pleading as soon as the note ended. Drippy grabbed Aaron's hand as the darkness overhead swirled with a strange glow, hurricane clouds of black light that multiplied the Kingdom's terrible gloom. The eye of it was a literal, a ghostly blue thing crisscrossed with veins and staring down.

"He knows! He knows! Run, ser!"

Drippy dragged Aaron as he stared overhead. The clouds shot rays of light the color of blood at the village.

Searchlights.

"Run!"

Another low blast from the horn drowned out the villagers' anguished cries as the lights drew closer. A thousand lights washed over the whole Kingdom. Aaron looked over at the hill he and Aimee had walked a thousand times, bathed in crimson light as it vanished in horrifying light. The cone swept over the miles between here and there instantly, drawing ever closer.

Only a few yards from the door and whatever safety the building might provide. The enormity of it all struck him like a blow to the head. What kind of place was this? Same as he'd asked Horace so long ago. Even over the terror, he wanted to know. Maybe more than ever, he *needed* to know.

Drippy's concerns seemed more visceral. He dragged Aaron on as the red cone from the hill swept up the street behind them. His hand was almost on the door as the light washed over the villagers in the street.

The candle man tugged the door open and ran inside, pulling Aaron in only a second too late. The red light encircled him for a fraction of a second as he stared open-mouthed and blank-minded at the sky.

Time stopped as the red light absorbed him. For an instant, it held everything in one perfect picture of anarchy and madness. The people running, Drippy looking back at him, the door so close that he would almost feel the warped wood under his fingers.

Something jerked him backward as if he were a puppet on a string. For a moment, he saw through two pairs of eyes. The carnage of the village was set alongside the idyllic plains and forest that had once been a Kingdom. Then he wasn't Aaron any longer; he was Horace, or at least he was seeing what Horace saw as he sat on a stone outside of town. Aimee and Aaron weren't there, though Aaron didn't know how he knew. That answered at least one question. He'd always wondered if the Kingdom simply vanished when they left.

But before he could wrap his mind around seeing the Kingdom as it had once been, that terrible horn blasted from the direction of the forest, and a haze of darkness rose. The Black Knight entered the Kingdom the same way Aimee and Aaron had for years. He strode down the path, and where he walked, night followed. Aaron saw a flash of Drippy cowering in the shed, but the Black Knight paid him no mind. He had other goals to accomplish.

The stars vanished as he crested the hill. The villagers looked to the sky, not scared, just curious. Fear wasn't a concern here. Things didn't hurt. People didn't die. Wicked creatures couldn't enter, and black lights never followed in anyone's wake.

Horace watched the knight stride down the path, the sky darkening as he stepped, and a dread he hadn't known for two thousand years coated his heart. This thing walked as the shadow of death. The rider of the pale horse galloping across the world, leaving only decay in his wake. He didn't know what it was, but the wind that it brought spoke of change. A new era of nightmares to usher out the light.

He turned to the little girl playing with a hoop in the nearby street. She had stopped to stare, and the hoop kept spinning off toward the Black Knight, falling to its side a little ways down the road. "Hide! Run and tell the princess she isn't safe!"

That word echoed in whatever nowhere void Aaron was seeing the world from. "Princess". It had to be after she had died. They'd come together that last time before he ran away, and the world hadn't been the nightmare it now was. The Black Knight had come after.

But there was no time to consider that as the vision of things past continued to play. The girl Horace had yelled at stared at him, not understanding.

"For the love of all that's sacred, run, you stupid child! Tell the princess!"

Horace never raised his voice. The girl jumped, squeaked, and fled toward the castle.

The dichotomy of light and dark in the Black Knight's wake brought to mind a solar eclipse, the sun and moon's clever way of showing every person how insignificant they really were. It hurt to stare at it. Horace broke his gaze away, running into the village. "Run! Hide! Flee! There are monsters here! Get away!"

The image blurred, falling away to pieces and shattering like a broken window, as Drippy pulled Aaron inside the bar. He collapsed to the floor, and Drippy hopped over him, slamming the door shut as a blast of red light framed the space they'd stood seconds before. The sound outside cut off at once, leaving only the accordion music and dull thuds of glasses hitting the bar. Aaron could barely think, as if his mind had been stuffed into a taffy machine and ripped apart.

He grabbed his head as it swam and the room rocked, looking up to see half a dozen undying villagers gaping at him, and a giant woman standing behind the bar.

Chapter 19

Drippy grabbed Aaron under the arms. "This won't do at all."

The music didn't stop, but Aaron could barely hear it. Pictures of the Black Knight entering the Kingdom flashed before his eyes, the afterimages of a bright shape in a dim room. He couldn't see anything else. Even the horror of the last ten minutes paled in comparison.

Drippy scanned the room and kept tugging on Aaron's arm. "We have to keep a movin'. Choo choo, keep the train on the tracks, ser!"

A walking eclipse. A meteor striking the world. The Black Knight wasn't a who or even a what, but a force of nature. It couldn't be stopped any more than an earthquake, especially not by a sister-killing junkie.

"What…"

Bad accordions screamed from nowhere and everywhere, as if the whole world were nothing more than a sound stage, and the music in the pit flooded from off-scene. It chased every thought from his head, until only feelings remained. *Dead sister. My fault. Dead sister. My fault.*

The woman behind the bar held up a hand, and the music stopped. Solid black eyes watched them from a face covered in so much makeup he couldn't discern her complexion. Unlike the other villagers, she wasn't skinny or covered in wounds. A cigarette poked out from between each of her fingers, and endless shot glasses had been piled on the bar, many having spilled onto the floor to form a layer of shattered glass. Her clothes left almost nothing to the imagination, and her saggy, sallow skin folded over itself, covering what might have been a crotch without underwear.

"Who the fuck are you?" She took a puff on one of the cigarettes, licking the butt as she squinted at them.

He lurched forward as the sudden absence of the music created a physical void. Only Drippy prevented him from collapsing to the glass below. His ears rang with the manic thoughts of the music, and the images of the light Kingdom juxtaposed with the dark one around him. None of this made sense. Not being here, not the glass on the floor or the red lights outside, not even Aimee and him having been born.

"Well?"

He could hardly see her through the smoke in the air. The entire place reeked of piss and vomit, and black dirt or yellow smoke stains covered every surface. The patrons drank from the wooden mugs in front of them, stopping only to slam them down and gasp for air.

One man leaned over the side of the table and vomited water on the floor, only to continue drinking.

"I asked you a question. You running from something? You bringing your troubles into my house?" She scratched at her crotch.

"No. No, ma'am. Just passin' through." Drippy dragged Aaron to his feet.

Slam, slam, slam. More mugs hitting wood.

She spit onto the floor. "Don't lie to me. You caused trouble outside, and now you run in here because you want me to save you. You think I don't have better shit to do than that?" She stepped out from behind the bar. "You just want to ruin everything. You're like a child. Children always ruin everything."

Aaron couldn't think straight. The images of what Horace had seen the day the Black Knight found the Kingdom were etched into the back of his eyes. "What was that light? Who are you?"

Slam, slam, slam.

She leaned against the bar, an ugly Amazon of a woman. "Maybe you should just kill yourself." For a moment, the woman had his mother's voice.

It wasn't the first time he'd heard those words. "What?"

He'd gone home for the funeral, and he didn't have the heart to leave afterward. How could he? This was his home. If he hadn't left in the first place, Aimee might still be alive. His absence led to hers. What more good would come from his leaving?

And it was more than that too. They'd believed in magic once. It had of course been nothing more than childish fantasy, but what if

192

he was wrong? What if her ghost lingered on in Umber Gardens? Everyone else's seemed to.

His mother carried on as if nothing had changed, as if she'd never had a daughter. He sat at Brian's house with the only other person who cared that Aimee was gone, both crying or sharing memories in turn. A week passed like that, until one day he returned home to find all the pictures of Aimee gone. Only rings of dirt and bent nails marked the spots where they'd hung.

"It was just too depressing," his mother had said. "I don't need that kind of thing staring me in the face and reminding me of my failures as a parent." She stared at him as if he might deny her own self-recrimination. Her eyes seemed to plead, *Tell me I'm a good mother. You're the only one I have left.*

But he wouldn't. Fuck her. She'd been here when Aimee died, and she'd done nothing. Where had their mother been? What could possibly have been more important than keeping the only person in this family worth anything alive? She'd always been jealous of Aimee, and she'd never thought of Aaron as anything more than a burden. It was all in the way she looked at them.

No, not them. Not anymore. Just him. And so he only sneered at her and walked away, staring at the blank spots on the wall where the ghosts of his sister had lived.

Aaron cried often, sniffling and red eyed, until his mother had not so politely asked him to keep it down or stop being around her. She hadn't shed a tear. She had in fact become happier over the last few weeks, going out and drinking with her loser boyfriend every chance she had. Living big on the disability check he received, no different than Dad. Aaron hung around the house like a funeral shroud, but she never seemed to be there. She avoided him and it as much as she could, and when she was home, she was wasted. More wasted than she'd ever dared be when it was her and Dad. Part of him wondered if she wasn't trying to drink some pain away, but the rest of him knew she'd never given one shit about her kids. Or if she had, he'd never seen it.

No, people like her couldn't feel hurt like he did. They weren't really people at all. Anything that looked like it was only a close approximation in a hunt for sympathy, and all of his had died with his sister. Their mother could drink herself to death for all he cared.

And her goddamn boyfriend never left. A fucking loser without a job, not unlike Aaron. The big difference being that Aaron was a teenager, and this asshole was in his forties. A slob with illusions of grandeur for his shitty band and their shitty music.

He'd had the audacity to come out of their bedroom once, reeking of pussy and liquor, to sit next to Aaron staring at a picture of Aimee. His robe, one of their father's old ones, lay half-open. "Don't worry, kid. We'll make you a new little sister." He'd laughed as if he'd made some stupid joke.

But it wasn't funny. None of it was. Everything was different now, as if the world itself had become a shade darker and the sun wouldn't shine again. "You're a loser, you know that?"

The laughter stopped. "What did you call me?"

Aaron put the picture, the last one of Aimee left in the house, in his pocket. It would go on his dresser in the apartment years later. "I said you're a fucking loser, and your music sucks. The only reason my mom sticks with you is the money. That and you're the only asshole pathetic enough to stick his dick in a mess like her."

Rockstar stood up, his robe flying all the way open and his cock flopping out. "What did you say, you little shit?"

The same thing Dad had called everyone in the house before he'd go off on a rampage. But Aaron wasn't a kid anymore, and there was nothing left to protect or care about here.

"You're a fucking washed-up loser. You aren't shit. You never were, and you never will be." He stood as his face heated up, and he imagined it turning red the same way Dad's had before he lost it. "Why don't you go back to living with your mommy, you fuck?"

Rockstar was bigger than Aaron, but not by much. A kid standing up to him had taken the wind from his sails. Instead of puffing up further or taking a swing, he closed his robe and slunk back into Mom's room, slamming the door behind him.

Aaron stormed out too, angry and wanting to find something to hurt. Maybe find the biggest, cuddliest dog and kick it in the ribs. It was past time to make something tremble the way he did.

Instead, he went to the park near the house, watching the ghosts of his childhood play on the swings until all that anger was gone, and the only things left were tears. They'd sat at the same bench once and made fun of Aimee's writing. That little path just up the way probably still had her footprints on it somewhere, at least until the wind and weather took them away.

He tapped the edge of the table. He could find those footprints and walk in them for a little while. Better than going home to a mother who had no time for anyone but herself, and… nothing. That was all he had now.

A single tear hit the table as he got up. The path remained the same, ignorant of Aimee's passing. Still, he walked it, trying to find the peace he'd known out here, gone since Aimee died. But the Tennessee wilderness didn't fix anything. The world had fallen apart, and the Kingdom was gone. He spent three days searching with only a cut on his finger to show for the effort. The memories faded to almost nothing, another relic of a sad childhood, just like Aimee. Nobody but he and Brian gave a flying fuck that his sister was dead.

It hit him all at once—he could kill himself and be with her. Mom hadn't thrown away the gun. It still sat in Dad's old cabinet, collecting dust with all the others as though it hadn't destroyed his life. Brian would be upset, but he would understand. Or maybe he wouldn't. He couldn't possibly know what it was like to be this alone. He'd always been a whole person. He'd never had a second half. He didn't know what it was like to lose a living, breathing piece of himself.

Aaron returned home that night and pulled the gun from its case. She hadn't even unloaded it. He stared down at it, his anger bubbling. How could his mother have let it happen? How could

Aimee leave him alone? After all they'd survived together, how could she not hold out a few months while he found work and a place for them to stay? How the fuck could Brian not see what was happening?

But he wasn't mad at her or Brian. He wasn't even mad at Mom, if he was being honest. The only person who really deserved his anger was the one staring at him in the mirror through Aimee's eyes. How could he have left her alone with the woman who treated her piss-poor because she saw in Aimee all the things she'd never been? Pretty, smart, friendly. How could he have left her with the washed-up musician that undressed her with his eyes every time she walked in the room? The man who walked around with their father's old robe wide open so everyone could see his swinging cock.

The shiny metal called to him as the kitchen light glinted off it. The black absorbed it all, as deep as a moonless night. He'd written a note to Brian, an explanation and apology of sorts. It had been shitty. Unicorny bullshit. He crumpled it up and threw it in the trash. He didn't owe anyone an explanation. Brian hadn't killed Aimee, but she hadn't gone to him for help, and Brian had never been one to come out fighting for his friends. Aimee was equally dead either way.

Aaron's hand shook as he pulled the slide back and let it slam forward. The sound made him jump. He didn't realize he'd been sweating until he saw greasy marks on the metal.

Would it hurt? What if he fucked up? Would someone find him, a twitching mess on the floor? Would some bitchy old nurse end up spoon-feeding him until he died of bedsores in two or three years?

Afraid of fucking it up, maybe, but no fear of death. He didn't feel that anymore. He felt nothing but a hole in his chest, a swirling void of rage that died down to an ember only to be replaced by tears that wouldn't stop. It had to end. He couldn't live like this anymore.

As he lifted the gun, a key turned in the front-door.

He froze, gun halfway to his mouth, as Mom and the Rockstar entered. He'd assumed they were sleeping off another mid-day bender. Judging by the smell, they were just getting started on the evening edition.

He didn't have time to think as they stared at him. He didn't put the gun down.

Rockstar shook his head. "Jesus fucking Christ." He walked to the bedroom without another word.

"What are you doing?" his mother asked in the same way one might ask the time.

For a moment, he saw himself from the outside, a wreck of a teenager with no out but the business end of a bullet. He burst into tears and set the gun on the table.

She didn't touch him, and she didn't comfort him. She stood over him as if he were a rabid dog, an animal one shouldn't get too close to lest it bite.

"I miss her so much, Mom. I don't know what to do. It won't stop hurting." He covered his face, ashamed of the tears. Ashamed of being less than a man and knowing someone had seen it. "I can't even sleep anymore. It's my fault. I shouldn't have left her all alone. I'm sorry. I'm so sorry."

He sobbed in the chair as she stared at him, never blinking. Never moving, beyond the sway of inebriation. A statue of a parent witnessing her son's breakdown. The reek of pot and booze oozed off her. She stank of the sleaziest dive bars.

He finally composed himself enough to glance up. She looked at him, her expression devoid of any emotion a mother should have for a grieving son and a dead daughter.

"If the world is so terrible, maybe you *should* just kill yourself."

The words hit him in the gut as strong as the whiskey on her breath. Then she smiled that smile, the one that said she knew she'd gotten under his skin. And he ran, tears dripping down between his fingers, the gun forgotten on the table. Dad might have been a monster, but he wasn't the only one. She wasn't just weak; she was sadistic. She hated everyone around her as much as she hated herself.

He wouldn't kill himself. He wouldn't give her or that fucking Ziggy Stardust wannabe the satisfaction. He made the silent promise to Aimee's ghost.

But how did this barbarian bitch in the Kingdom know? Her nearly bare chest heaved with every breath as she grabbed a bottle from behind the bar and poured herself another shot.

Slam, slam, slam.

"Ser." Drippy tugged on Aaron's arm as clarity returned. The woman looked nothing like his mother but resembled her in every way. "She got here after the Black Knight," he whispered. "We shouldn't be here."

"Shut your ugly mouth, you limp-dick little turd." She threw the bottle at Drippy but missed and hit Aaron in the leg. He stumbled back into the door. "Why the fuck would you come back here, huh? You think your sister is here, you sniveling brat? You think anyone cares enough to say goodbye to you before you fucking croak?"

The images of the Black Knight and the memories of the last night at home danced before his eyes. The screams of the villagers and the horns still echoed in his ears. It hadn't been like this before. There hadn't been a bar in the Kingdom, and nothing like her, either.

"You were always weak, weren't you? Never good enough for anyone but still clinging onto them like shit on an ass."

Slam, slam, slam.

Every eye in the bar watched him. The townsfolk continued drinking and puking, and the clouds of smoke choked him with every breath. He didn't recognize any of them. If they had always been here, he'd never known their names. But their stares bore into him. He couldn't think.

"You always got so angry at everyone else. Blame Daddy 'cause he hurt you." Her voice was mockery and hate. "Blame Mommy because she didn't help. Blame your sister because she left. How about you blame yourself?" Her words bounced off the walls back at him, louder every time. "You're a fucking junkie, just like the rest of them. An anger junkie. A sex and money junkie. A fucking self-righteous shitbag just like your sister."

Her words wove around him as she approached him. With every step, she grew bigger, more menacing. Her hair touched the ceiling as she strode forward. A few more feet and she had to hunch to walk.

"Don't listen, ser! Close up your ears!" Drippy put his hands to the sides of his head.

But her words tickled the back of Aaron's mind, inserting themselves and becoming part of him. Beating him down even as they defined him. She wasn't wrong. He'd said the same things to himself a million times.

"You're pathetic!" She grabbed him by the front of his shirt and lifted him off his feet, holding him in midair as Drippy screamed. The patrons slammed down their drinks and puked them back up onto the floor, their eyes round and wild.

"I'm not." The denial came from a place where an eleven-year-old sister had once taken care of him for receiving the beating meant for her. "You were always a monster."

Slam, slam, slam.

"Shut your mouth!" The slap that followed darkened his vision. His nose bled. "I wish I'd had the balls to just blow my brains out when I wanted to, just like your bratty little sister! That's how you make me feel! Can you imagine what that's like, having your kids hate you so much you hate them in return? Like it was my fault your life is so miserable? I wish I'd never uncrossed my legs and shit out a couple of troublemakers like you!"

It wasn't his mother, yet it was—the same woman who'd watched her children beaten within an inch of their lives. The same one who'd brought the would-be Rockstar home. The one now standing before him, repeating words she'd once said to him at the dinner table in their dirty, hateful house.

"Just kill yourself."

The gun in his hand hadn't been there a moment before, but he knew it by feel. He could sense the hate in it. This was Dad's gun. The one that had killed his sister.

"*No!*" Drippy wailed over the echoes of her damnation.

Slam, slam, slam.

The chance to end it all. A few seconds of pain and he could be with Aimee, whether she was in the Kingdom or not. He could find her if he was free of his mortal shell. He could finally tell her how sorry he was.

I forgive you. I'm sorry.

The words whispered to him by her ghost twice now. Aimee would have said that if she were still alive, because she'd always been better than him, better than all of them. And she wouldn't hate him. She wouldn't hate Mom or Dad, or even Rockstar. She'd moved past it.

And they were two halves of a whole.

There was no gun in his hand. There never had been.

"We blamed you because it was your fault."

The silence that followed fell onto the room with a physical weight. The floor creaked, the shelves buckled, and Aaron felt as if someone had just poured water on him, though he was dry as a bone. The bartender jumped back, dropping him. Her swirling words and insults vanished, leaving only his proclamation in their wake.

"Master! Be silent! Hide! Run!" Drippy grabbed the waistband of his pants and tugged.

"Shut up!" Aaron yelled.

The words reverberated back at them, growing louder just as hers had. Drippy stopped talking, and the patrons stopped drinking. The whole world watched the family drama play out.

"You." He stood up, staring at the giant beast. "You were terrible. You were as bad as Dad. He was a mindless monster, but you were a manipulative asshole." He stepped forward, and she retreated, shrinking. "I heard you tell him we did things when you thought we weren't home. I saw the look on your face when he hit Aimee. You hated her. You hated your own daughter because she was good and pretty, and you were rotten and ugly."

She raised a hand that ended in a claw, the cigarettes still sticking out. "I'll kill you!"

"Sit down!" He wasn't a child, and he hadn't been for a long time. She couldn't control him if he didn't let her. Power flowed from his mouth.

Her legs collapsed, spilling her onto the floor. His voice was the authority of the land, the prince returned to set his kingdom right. Drippy stared from his side, his melted mouth a perfect circle of surprise. She backed away from him.

"You are nothing. You're the one that was worthless, not us!" He strode toward her, his anger free. He wanted to hit her. He wanted to take out a decade of beatings on her as she shrank further, revealing the wretched crone underneath the facade.

He stood over her, his chest heaving. This thing, this part of the woman who had ruined his life, cowered beneath him, its bluster spent. Its hold on him had been revealed for what it was—a lie, a fiction he'd repeated over and over his entire life.

It looked like his mother had the last time he'd seen her. Old and beat-up. In a hospital bed after Rockstar had caught her flirting with the bartender at a gig. The guy was nowhere to be found. Just his mother, old and alone, looking every second of her almost fifty years of life.

"Son." She reached out to him from the hospital bed. Her eye was black. There were stitches in her scalp. Dad had sent Aaron to the hospital more than once, but never Mom or Aimee. "Son, I'm so glad you came." She looked as though she might cry.

But she had never cried for Aimee, and she had never called him son.

He said the same thing he had then. "I'm nothing like you, and you can't hurt me now."

But he saw more now too. The woman who'd taken beatings for her kids and kept working to put food on the table after their father vanished. The same one who brought the would-be Rockstar home because she'd been so lonely after her husband of fifteen years left. The one now standing in front of him, looking as sad and pathetic as she had when she'd reached out to her son in the wake of her daughter's death, only to be brushed aside like Dad had a million times. Not a good person, but maybe not the monster he'd assumed.

And then, it was just… gone.

The bartender opened her mouth to speak, but he wouldn't allow it.

"Go away. I don't have the energy to hate you anymore."

Pressure bore down on the room, as if gravity had doubled. The shelves collapsed. Shot glasses piled on the counter rolled off and shattered on the floor. Some of the lights overhead exploded, raining shards down on him.

Now just an old woman, the bartender screamed. Her mouth gaped open, impossibly large. Big enough to fit a head in. Bigger. Her black eyes grew to the size of basketballs. Any moment she would burst and shower them in gore.

But the scream petered into a whimper. She shrank further, her skin sagging from the bones. All at once, she melted into shadow and fell into the floorboards. Gone.

The smoke from her cigarettes cleared as if a warm breezed had blown through the bar. The stink of piss and vomit receded a little. The pressure returned to normal as Aaron stumbled backward, the rush of his condemnation giving way to terrible exhaustion and a head rush like no drug had ever given him.

Then he was falling.

Drippy caught him before he could hit the ground, and set him down gently. "Ser… Your voice."

Aaron stared at the spot where the creature had been. He'd commanded it to leave, and it had, just like when they were kids. The same as when they'd commanded the throne room to be a waterfall and sailed their little paper ships to find Grandma in whatever came after.

Drippy put out a leg and bowed in front of him. "The prince has returned."

For a moment, the silence was absolute, even in Aaron's head.

"Your Highness." One of the men at the table stood. "Does that mean you can help us?"

Aaron turned to him. Another one of the Kingdom's lost souls, unable to find peace. Could he fix it?

"I release you from your curse."

The man stared at him as if he didn't understand the words, but the mug fell from his hand. It hit the floor with a *thud*, its contents spilling into the cracks in the floorboards, vanishing as the bartender had.

Time froze. The patrons looked at him. They glanced at one another. But they didn't drink.

A dozen voices rose in jubilation as more mugs hit the floor and melted. A decade of pain, suddenly cured. A disease removed by their prince.

"Oh, ser!" Tears welled in Drippy's eyes. "You're doing it! You're making things that got done by the Black Knight undone! You're fixing!"

"Fixing" meant something different to Aaron than it did to Drippy, but right then it didn't matter. In the distance, the horn that had played on the cliff at the end of his last visit wailed once more. It called to him somewhere deep inside, its bass note touching his heart. This one seemed to mark the turning of the world, and as it rang out, Aaron found it impossible to stay awake. His eyes closed of their own accord. His body slowly, slowly drooped to the floor.

The panic that had vanished with his proclamations returned in full force. He couldn't keep himself conscious. Was this some trick of the Black Knight? Another monster come to get him?

He grasped at Drippy but missed. "What's happening?" Sweat beaded on his forehead and splashed onto his shirt.

Drippy grabbed his hand as he flailed. "No fear now, ser, no fear. Too much fear makes you weak."

The world gave way. When he should have hit the floor, he kept falling down, down, down between worlds. Thoughts of Aimee and the Kingdom drifted away into blackness.

Chapter 20

He could smell her perfume from across the table. Marie laughed and drank, danced and flirted, told stories and listened, all in equal measure. When she was around, he could forget everything else for a little while. Fuck school that wasn't doing anything but killing his writing. Screw Mom's bullshit, and let Aimee's ghost rest for a moment. When this chick was around, things were pretty damn okay for the first time in a long time. The only thing different tonight was the look in her eyes—a glint and a stare that people didn't use unless they wanted to fuck.

They hadn't had sex yet, but something told Aaron that would change in the next thirty minutes. The way Marie bit her lip. The way her chest heaved when she laughed. The fact that both of them were getting trashed at a restaurant that hadn't carded. And above all, her foot on his dick.

Ten minutes later, they walked out as casually as possible, leaving only a note that read *Better luck next time!* sticking out of the check holder. He held her hand and laughed as they fled down the street, awash with the exhilaration of minor crime.

He'd been with a few girls before her, but none like this. She threw him down on the bed, ripped his pants off, and took him in her mouth before he knew what was happening. She climbed on top of him and rode him until she came twice, both times screaming so loud that the upstairs neighbor pounded on the floor.

When she pulled his hair and stuck her tongue down his throat, he couldn't hold it in any longer. He pulled out and exploded all over her. His entire universe went blank as she wrapped her hands around his cock, stroking until nothing was left but the terrible sensitivity. She didn't let go, laughing as he jumped and pleaded, squirming to get away.

They went at it three more times that night and once more the next morning.

It had to be the best night he'd ever had, hands down. He loved her. It would be a cold day in hell before he told her that, but that didn't make it any less true. Instead, he said, "It's easy to be with you."

Not much of a snuggler, she rolled onto her side of the bed. "Because we fucked?"

He lit a Marlboro for each of them. "Four times, but no. You've got your shit together. And you're cool. And your jokes fucking suck, but you tell them anyway."

She laughed, basking fully naked and unashamed in the light flooding in from the window.

"I enjoy your company." The most romantic feeling he'd ever shared.

"That's sweet, but I think I could do better."

He choked on the smoke as he laughed. "Me too. Brian! Come in here!"

Brian and Marie hadn't met yet. She grabbed the sheet and pulled it over herself. "What are you doing?"

"Brian!"

Footsteps sounded from the hallway followed by Brian opening the door. "What's up— Jesus Christ, dude." He covered his eyes as Aaron sat naked on the bed with a stranger, cackling. "Seriously?"

"I think she can do better. You should give it a shot. She's good to go if you want to take her for a spin."

Marie grabbed a pillow and smothered him as Brian walked out of the room, shaking his head. Aaron gasped for air as he giggled.

"You are such a pig!" But she laughed too.

"It's okay," Aaron said, his voice muffled by the pillow. "He likes the big girls. You're safe."

In those days, it had always been fun, even when he was being an asshole. The drugs hadn't become a problem yet, and the words youthful hijinks were thrown around more than addict or asshole. He told her about Aimee and about growing up. He told her about crying at night sometimes, even years later. He told her about the rage so thick it choked him when he thought about the guy Aaron suspected had driven Aimee to suicide. Mom's boyfriend.

"How do you know?" Marie had asked as they sat on the couch a year later.

"Just a feeling. She had mentioned she didn't like the way he looked at her, and he always walked around the house drunk and naked." Aaron hadn't connected the dots until later, that Rockstar might have touched her, might have done something that drove Aimee to the point where she saw only one way out. It wasn't until almost a year after Aimee had died that he put the pieces together.

"And your mom just let him do that?" Marie had grown up in the ghetto, but only because her parents were poor. They still went to every PTA meeting, took her to soccer practice, and helped her with her homework every night. She'd never said it, but there was little doubt that nobody had ever laid an angry hand on one another in her home. She couldn't relate, and so every time he told her of his childhood, it seemed a horror story to her.

And to most people horror stories weren't real. Or at least, they were meant to entertain. His story wasn't fake, and it wasn't for their joyful fucking consumption.

She squeezed his hand, but he pulled away. He didn't want her pity. She had asked, and he would tell her, but that was it. He didn't want to share his grief. It was a meal he dined on alone.

"I pulled a gun on him at a bar. That was the last time I saw him."

There was more snow than they'd seen in a decade. He trudged through it to the same dive bar Rockstar played every weekend. He had no proof, but after a year of fuming over Aimee's death, Aaron had to do something. If he didn't, he would go mad. He hadn't told Brian where he was going that night, just walked out of the spare bedroom at Brian's mom's house without a word. He didn't expect he would return.

The gun Aimee had used to kill herself, the one with which he'd almost done the same, stuck out of his belt. He pulled it out once inside, feeling the cold steel in his hand, ready to shoot that prick in the face. They hadn't bothered to card him at the door. It was just as dark outside as in, and the whole place reeked to high heaven of pot and cheap cologne.

The bouncer started choking him from behind before he even reached the bar. Aaron screamed and fought back, but he didn't stand a chance as two other monstrous men closed in from the front and worked him over. He never so much as saw Rockstar, but his mother was there and she saw *him*. While the bouncer dragged him to the back door and out into the alley, she slapped him across the face.

"You've tried to ruin my life for the last time."

Nobody wanted to call the police. Instead, the bouncers beat him half to death.

The big one who'd grabbed him from behind held his gun up and pointed it right between Aaron's eyes. "Come back to my place with a piece again, and I'll fuckin' kill you. Hear?"

Aaron spit at the man, but that got him a boot to the teeth. They walked back inside, leaving him alone with his mother for a moment longer before she went inside too.

Her smoking a cigarette, her eyes following every punch, seared itself into his mind. It could have been any given weekday of his childhood, but as an almost adult, it hurt more. As an almost adult, he could see he'd never had any family besides Aimee, and she was gone. All because he'd run away, and she'd been stuck with these people.

He lay bleeding in the snow, with nothing but the streetlight for company. He tried to imagine she'd watched to make sure it didn't go too far. She couldn't do anything, after all, so maybe she was protecting him the only way she could. Maybe that was all she'd ever been able to do.

But it didn't fit. She didn't care. She'd be happier if he was dead.

He told Brian he'd been in a bar fight. It was years before he told anyone the real story.

"Oh my god." Marie sat still as if seeing him for the first time. In a way, she was. By that point, the good times had started to fade. She hadn't given up the party life, but she was ready to. Now he was the drug-dealer boyfriend, and she was the one with prospects. Not quite the same as Mom and Rockstar, but not entirely different. She'd started to see the dark waters under the surface, and she wasn't pleased. "Why?"

"Why what?"

"Why would you shoot him? Could you really have done it?"

He would have pulled the trigger with no regrets. His eyes, Aimee's eyes, drilled into her. He swallowed hard, pushing down the urge to call her a stupid bitch for asking a question like that. He looked away to try to avoid the mental images of Aimee wondering why he hadn't stayed and saved her. He never could.

He wished Marie had never brought it up.

"Why didn't you—"

"I'm done talking about this."

"Aaron."

But he was already out the door, off to get drunk or high. Who could recall? It was all just a memory in the blackness between worlds, a play acted out in his mind as he endlessly sought to hit bottom, not asleep but not awake. Out in dark space with the gravity turned on, falling to the floor of the universe that never came.

That last part, though, the drugs—that stuck with him. Twice now he'd used, and twice now he'd ended up in the Kingdom. It had dream logic to it, the kind that came from crumbling thoughts as they fell away and turned into something else. The kind usually forgotten when awake.

But there was no Kingdom, and no dark place between worlds, filled with monsters and doors to places best left alone. He thrashed in the sheets as morning sunlight burned his eyes. His chest and leg hurt, and he backed away from blurry images of dressers like candle men and deep-shadowed doors like monstrous bartenders. For a moment, he was just an animal, a frightened creature waking up in captivity.

He tumbled off the bed, hitting his head against the dresser as he took up position in the corner. Better to die there with your back to the wall then on your bed like a chump.

But there was nothing to kill him. Just an old apartment and old memories.

And not-so-old ones. Of Drippy. The Kingdom. Horace. The woman at the bar.

The drugs. The thing that brought it all together. His addiction and his habit, his keys to the Kingdom.

Breathing heavily, sleep still insisting it might have been a dream, he looked at his chest. Large red claw marks stood out through tears in his shirt where the woman at the bar had held him.

Chapter 21

It had to be more than coincidence.

He didn't bother showering before he left the house, just grabbed a new shirt and threw it on, out the door in a flash. He couldn't be there any longer. With nowhere to go, he just drove instead, trying to put his thoughts into focus.

Horace, Drippy, and the Kingdom. That feeling. Knowing something important had happened the night before, even if he wasn't sure what.

He'd considered taking another good hit right then. It terrified him, but aside from the obvious upshot of getting high, he would know for sure. If he stuck that needle in his arm and ended up back in the Kingdom, he'd be one step closer to knowing he wasn't crazy.

Exhilaration gave way to stomach-turning fear. The drugs had worn off, and the painful comedown had settled in. More than that, his giddiness scared him.

He had to know. He needed someone to watch him while he used. It was the only way. Marie wouldn't do it, and he wouldn't dream of asking Devon or anyone else.

The only option was Brian.

He called four times, but Brian didn't pick up. It could be a weekday, putting him at work. Aaron turned the car around and headed toward downtown.

Brian's car was in front of his office, as predicted. Aaron parked behind it and entered, the bustle of the street giving way to the quiet of an office. Steel gray walls, glass everywhere, and potted plants. Brian had once remarked that it looked more like a caricature of an office building than an actual office building, yet here he remained. The security guard in the lobby eyed Aaron up and down as soon as he walked through the door. Aaron tried to pass him without making eye contact, but the man caught his arm.

"Can I help you, son?"

Between the junk in his veins, the comedown, and the abundance of anxiety, he didn't have the patience to deal with an overweight rent-a-cop. "I'm here to see Brian Richards." He shrugged out of the guard's grip.

He didn't have to hear the words; he could tell by the look on the guard's face it wasn't going to happen. There was a particular condescension that existed only to be aimed at the poor. Aaron had seen that set of the eyes and subtle uptick of the mouth to know it from afar. "He's expecting you?" Just another asshole ruling his little roost with an iron fist. Invested with the authority of absolutely fucking no one, he would make sure everyone knew how important he thought he was.

"If you don't believe me, go get him." Aaron held up a hand. "Yea tall. Brown hair. Doesn't have that slack-jawed country look currently plastered across your face."

The guard's expression shifted from bored and business to angry in half a second. "Get the fuck out of here." He stood up.

Aaron wanted to knock the guy out. He wanted to scratch at his own neck and shake, do the junkie dance. He wanted to rage. He wanted to go home and get high for a thousand reasons. But knowing was more important.

Fortunately, Brian walked by the glass doors at the back of the room as the guard was about to make the mistake of putting his hands somewhere he would lose them.

"Brian! Hey!"

Brian looked up, and his face fell, a shift in demeanor saved for unwelcome relatives. The *thanks for coming, please don't ever do it again* expression. There had been a time when Brian would never have looked at him like that.

The guard backed up as Brian poked his head out the lobby door. "It's fine, Frank. He's here with me."

The guard glanced between them, and for a moment, Aaron thought he was still going to get grief. "He's got a goddamn mouth on him."

Aaron patted Fat Frank's belly as he passed by. "Don't stress out so much, tons of fun. Might give yourself a heart attack."

The guard's face turned red, but not as red as Brian's. Aaron ignored both and joined his friend in the empty hallway leading deeper into the building.

"I need you, man," Aaron said as the door closed behind them.

Brian ignored him and kept going. They entered a honeycomb of hallways, all as slate gray and sterile as the last. Brian moved as if he had a stick up his ass, giving a curt nod to the people he passed. They reached his office in a moment, only stopping when they were safely inside with the door closed.

His lifelong friend turned on him in a flash, his brow furrowed and face still crimson. Aaron couldn't remember ever seeing Brian this pissed. If there were any more blood in his head, it might pop. "Are you out of your jackassed mind? You are a goddamn pimple on the ass of humanity!"

Aaron jumped back at the sudden insult. "Is this about that fat prick up front? He was giving me grief."

Brian sat on the edge of the desk and wiped his face with his hands. "You look like a fucking crackhead. There's blood on your shirt, for fuck's sake."

Aaron looked down to see the claw marks from the bartender had bled through this shirt too. He pulled his jacket closed and shook away the shame. "That's not why I'm here." There had been a time when Brian would never have made him feel like that.

219

"You're dirty, you stink, your hair's a mess; it looks like you wandered in off the street. It's his fucking job to keep people like you out. Why the hell *are* you here?"

A fucking crackhead. A Broad Street regular. "Not even a goddamn hello before you lay into me, huh?"

"This is my work!" He threw his hands into the air. "My fucking job. It's how I pay my bills so I don't end up on the street slinging dope to make ends meet. I know you've never had one, but they frown on it when employees bring in their friends during the day, especially if they look homeless."

Aaron sneered at him. "I don't sell dope, you asshole, I sell pot. And you never complained when it paid the bills."

"Aaron." Brian put on his faux calm middle-class face. "Fuck off, I'm at work. I'm not mad at you, I'm mad that you'd show up here like this. Are you high? I'm asking seriously, are you high right now?"

"No." Aaron bit off the word. "And before you ask, I don't need money."

Some of Brian's old calm, the kind he'd had when Dad would show up and scream at the three of them on the playground, returned. It even extended to his mom chasing their father away. Always so calm, until one of his friends didn't fit the square life, or showed up at his job, apparently. "What do you want?"

Aaron's face grew hotter with each word, though from shock or anger he couldn't say. Was that what they thought of him? Just a fucking burden to be brushed aside? "I need your help."

Brian shook his head. "Whatever it is, it can wait." He opened the door. "Get out."

He wasn't even going to escort him back. Brian didn't want to be seen with him. He couldn't stand the looks and the shame the other squares might pile on him, the talk that would go around the oh-so-fucking-important office. Aaron had become a burden to his friends. Someone they felt they had to take care of and sneak out the back door. A fucking stray dog.

And Brian was still the only person Aaron could turn to.

"Will you call when you get off?"

Brian didn't move from the door, nor did his face soften. "Yes."

Aaron left without saying a word.

Now that Brian had pointed it out, he saw the glances. People giving him a wide berth, wondering what a guy like him was doing in a place like this. He pulled his jacket tighter over his bloody shirt, but it wasn't just that. There was junk in his veins, and not just the kind he put there with a needle. Well-off people could smell the trash on people like him, and they would always hate him for it.

He wanted to use. He wanted to grab the extra skag he'd made the night before and forget. Would it prove them all right? Maybe, but he didn't care. How did you deal with something like that? How did normal people live with the look of disgust on someone's face when you'd disappointed them? Did they know what it was like? Did they care?

He entered the lobby through the glass doors. The security guard stared at him. "Didn't get any cash, did ya? It's all over your face."

He turned toward the guard. He would knock his fucking teeth out. Stomp the shit out of him and show just how tough his XXL uniform really made him. The guard sat up straighter and sneered, as if he could see what was about to happen and welcomed it.

Aaron thought of the look on Brian's face. The shame. He imagined what it would be like to try and explain how he'd gotten into a fight on a thirty-second walk out the door to the street.

He left instead.

"See ya later, junkie," the guard said as the door closed.

Aaron drove away, still feeling the gazes of the people on the streets as much as in the building. He looked at himself in the rearview. The bags under his eyes had worsened over the last few days. Dirt smudged his face, and the bloodshot eyes staring back at him looked less like Aimee's and more like a monster's.

He couldn't remember the last time he'd really examined at his reflection, but it hadn't been like that. Maybe they had some small point. Maybe things *were* a little out of control. It had been an out-of-control week. If he could get Brian to see what happened when he shot up, he could prove it wasn't just in his head. He could prove he wasn't crazy, or a junkie. The Kingdom was real.

And maybe, just maybe, that meant Aimee was there, too.

He'd skirted around the thought all day, but as he drove home, he forced himself to embrace it. She couldn't leave Umber Gardens when he'd asked her to all those years ago, and maybe she couldn't now. He'd been able to pack up and leave, convinced he could find a better life. They didn't need a fantasy world. Leave the childish dreams to children. They could get away and break the cycle.

But she couldn't. She'd grown up too scared to be brave when he'd asked her to be, and he'd left her. He gripped the steering wheel tighter just thinking about it. Maybe some part of her was still trapped in that place. Maybe something of her remained in the Kingdom. It wasn't a normal place, after all. The rules of the real world didn't apply there.

If she was there, he would find her. He would make everything right.

Chapter 22

He hadn't noticed the dirt on the sheets until he returned home. Big streaks of mud splattered across the bedding further proved something was happening when he used. He rubbed the sleep from his eyes, trying to focus through the fog. This sort of thing didn't happen to a normal person—or a normal junkie for that matter.

Aaron froze with his hands on the sheets as the word he'd used sank in. Not a fucking *junkie*. Normal guy. Dude. Fella. Motherfucker who liked to have a good time and apparently travel between worlds. Not junkie.

He grabbed it all and took it into the living room. He'd show Brian. If he could see why Aaron suspected his habit was literally taking him to another world, he might not walk out the door.

As he sat on the couch, he eyed the syringe full of heroin. It had separated a little, as it did when you used a high concentration mixture and let it sit for a while. Filter it out, and it was good to go.

He wanted to do that now. Just a little taste before Brian arrived. Something to make him less nervous about how it was going to play out, a little less afraid his best friend would call him a lunatic and slam the door in his face.

He paced instead. He had control. He didn't need, he just wanted. He could wait. The syringe and the heroin went into the drawer where he kept his gear. Without the temptation in the room, the craving fell down a peg, enough for him to turn on the TV. Oprah popped onto the screen. She was tearing some jerk a new one for taking advantage of women on dating sites. He changed to something less terrible. The news reported flash flood warnings and severe storms heading toward Umber Gardens. He changed that too, finally settling on cartoons again. Last bastion of the civilized mind.

Even with the distraction, the hours crawled by. He watched the clock turn from one to two then two to three. By four, he thought Brian was standing him up. By five, he was certain. As he finally caved and picked up the phone to call him, Marie rang.

He stared at the screen as the phone vibrated. Had Brian told her about his visit to work? Called her and said Aaron had finally lost it? That he was roaming around downtown looking like a crackhead?

He didn't have the heart to answer and find out, so he watched her name shake a little every time the phone rang. In a moment, the screen turned black once more.

She wanted him to leave town. Both of them, together, running away from his problems and finding a better life elsewhere. But there was no better life. Running just meant you died tired. The only thing that could fix him now would be finding out what it all meant.

And maybe, just maybe, finding a piece of Aimee somewhere in the Kingdom.

One Message From Marie flashed across the screen in green letters.

Or maybe he was fucked up, and she was right. Brian too, in his own too-scared-to-say-it way. Normal people didn't see ghosts or monsters. They didn't take some dope, go down to the local bar, and use magical powers to kick the shit out of a souped-up version of their drunk mother. Not that he'd ever heard of anyway.

He nearly called her back. *Say you're wrong and ask forgiveness. Tell her you'll go with her to a place where you don't know any dealers, maybe even go to rehab. Stand up every week in front of a bunch of drunk losers like you and tell them you're a sinner, just like them, and prostrate yourself until they tell you you're a good person despite always acting like a piece of shit. Maybe have a bunch of kids and beat them like your dad beat you because life didn't turn out like you expected. Maybe your wife develops a drinking problem and turns into a passive-aggressive dickhead because she feels the same way.*

He couldn't do it. Not to himself, not to Marie, and not to Aimee's ghost. There was a way to fix all of this right here in town. All he had to do was reach the castle.

And to do that, all he had to know is if he was really going there. But before he could call Brian, the phone rang again.

Aaron answered. "I thought you were blowing me off."

"No, man." Awkward silence filled the line. "I'm sorry I blew up, but you surprised me, and you insulted a guy who's worked here for twenty years. People get fired over that kinda thing, you know?"

Another way people distanced themselves from things they found distasteful. One had to put a little extra space between themselves and the alleged junkie, after all. *It's not you, man. I'm just too much of a bitch to get in even the smallest bit of trouble.*

There would be time to deal with it later. "I need you. There's something I have to show you."

"What is it?"

"I can't explain it. It's better if you see for yourself."

More silence. There had been a time when Brian wouldn't have asked questions.

"Please? It won't take long. I need your help."

Was he waiting for an apology? Then, finally, "All right. I'll be there soon." He hung up.

Be there soon he might, but he didn't sound thrilled about it. If Aaron were right, that would change. If it turned out to be real, it would change everything.

Someone knocked on the door. Brian didn't wait for an answer before he let himself in. "'Sup, G." He eyed the surroundings as he closed the door, his gaze lingering on the hole in the wall before sweeping back to Aaron.

"Hey, dude." Aaron wiped his hands on his pants. He hadn't changed or taken a shower and wished he had. In fact, now that it was time to share what was going on, he intensely didn't want to. This would only end one way. *You need help. Maybe another intervention? Hey, we could stick you in rehab and then let you out on the streets to fend for yourself.*

Aaron kept rubbing his hands on his pants, his knees shaking. When he stopped, the expression on Brian's face didn't change.

"What's the thing you needed to bust into my office for?"

Aaron rolled his eyes. "I didn't bust into your office, I stopped by. And—it doesn't matter. I need your help with something."

Brian held his hands up. "Well, I'm standing right here."

Aaron ignored the snarky tone. He wanted to pace, or run his hands through his hair. His finger twitched at his side, jonesing to scratch an invisible itch. "It's hard to explain." He picked up the sheet and held it so Brian could see the dirt and mud.

Brian shrugged. "You brought me over here to look at how you shit the bed?"

Aaron took a deep breath and blew it out slowly, willing his anger down. "Something is happening when I get high."

"Yeah, no shit. You're frying your fucking brain."

Aaron threw the sheet down. "No, you prick. I..." Now or never. "I think I'm going somewhere else when I shoot up." It had sounded so much more eloquent in his head. *Tell him you're travelling to some magical nightmare realm. Make him watch to see what happens.*

"What? You're sleepwalking? I don't have time for this. Call me when you've been clean a few days and can act like a human being."

Aaron stepped around the table. "I'm going to the Kingdom. You remember? The place that Aimee and me told you about."

"Jesus Christ." Brian set his hand on the knob.

"I'm not making this up. Twice now, I used and woke up there sober as a stone. When it ends, I wake up here, but not where I left from." He lifted his shirt to show Brian the marks on his chest. "I'm not doing this shit to myself."

Brian didn't let go of the doorknob. "You sound like a mental patient. You got high and stumbled into the grass. It wouldn't be the first time."

True enough. Sometimes he'd wander outside to watch the stars, or fall asleep with the rain on his face. The cops busted people for that kind of shit, but cops didn't bother with this neighborhood. Just some white slums and factories, most of the time. They were too busy harassing the black neighborhoods to bother here.

But he remembered those times. He'd known what he was doing. This was different. "That's not what happened."

"Why did you call me here?"

He stared at Brian. That set jaw. Those hard eyes. "I need you to stay here to test it out."

"Test what out?"

"I need to get high while someone's here and see if anything actually happens."

Brian started to speak, but Aaron interrupted him.

"I know how this sounds. But something's happening. I keep ending up back there, and I think Aimee might be there too."

Brian actually laughed at him, though it was free of any mirth. "You think I'm going to sit here and watch you kill yourself anymore? No way, man. No way. Is this because we talked about Aimee the other day?"

That "live and let live" attitude was gone, but so was Aaron's patience. Just hearing Aimee's name put him on red alert. "You fucking owe me, Brian."

"She's fucking dead! Gone!"

The upstairs neighbor pounded on the floor.

"And whose fault is that?" Beneath the anger, a tiny pang of guilt flashed through all the muck inside him. Not just because deep down he knew it was his own fault and no one else's, but because of Brian's expression. His whole face collapsed. Of all the words in all the worlds, nothing could punch him like that. "Yeah, that's right! Who the fuck was just a few blocks away when she blew—" Aaron looked away as his throat caught and his voice broke. "When she died."

Brian opened and closed his mouth a few times. "This isn't about Aimee." All the anger had vanished.

"You owe me. If you want to walk away afterwards, fine, but you owe me this."

Brian's eyes narrowed. "I owe you? I've been watching out for you since she died. I sat here while your life spiraled out of control, trying everything I could to help you. Me and Marie both. I've been babysitting you for years."

Aaron's fingers twitched as he stared into his best friend's eyes. The calm in the room following those words was deafening. Even the constant scream of the highway vanished for a long, sullen moment. "Is that how you see our friendship? A burden?"

"Right now? Yeah."

Each watched the other, close enough to touch but never further apart. Had this been a long time coming? Had Brian held this inside the whole time?

"I won't do this for you." He opened the door.

"I'll go to rehab." The words were out before he gave them a second thought. "If you do this and nothing happens, I'll go to rehab. I'll get a real job. I'll admit there's a problem."

Brian spun around, and Aaron did his best to look as sincere as possible. *Something* was happening. Whether he'd lost his mind or really discovered some other world, he didn't know. He hoped the latter; he needed vindication.

"You expect me to believe that?"

"Have you ever known me to go back on my word?"

Brian closed the door. "No bullshit?"

"Cross my heart."

"You'll go? You'll let me drive you first thing in the morning to the clinic when I see how insane this bullshit is?"

Junkies would say and do anything to avoid the problem. They'd say their friends had done it. They'd make excuses about how hard life was. They'd invent anything to avoid the big admission, but Aaron wasn't a junkie.

He stuck out his hand. "I promise." And he meant it. If it took this to get the people he cared about back on his side, he'd do it. Aimee was out there. Drippy and that ass-backwards nightmare world were too. They had to be.

An internal debate raged in Brian's eyes. To be or not to be. *Behind door number one, we have your best friend dead from an overdose. Do we want to see what's behind door number two?*

He finally shook it. Both of them stared at each other, steel-eyed and clench-jawed. Not two friends hoping to find the lost pieces of their heart, but two enemies meeting on neutral ground. That hurt, maybe more than the Kingdom and the possibility of seeing Aimee again.

It was all so familiar, just like when Brian had confessed in tears that he should have done more to save Aimee. A promise to make everything right. A teenage vow to help Aaron do what he could to make it okay at any cost.

"Be honest with me. You don't think Aimee is really alive, do you?"

Aaron didn't answer. He walked into the bedroom and grabbed his gear. He expected to hear the front door open and close before getting a *fuck off* text. But when he returned, Brian had taken a seat on the couch. Though, judging by the crossed arms and hundred-yard stare, he was considering it.

Aaron filtered out the old junk and cooked up a new batch, mixing them together into one mother of a hit.

"Jesus, dude. That's going to kill you."

Aaron's hands shook as he worked. He wasn't just nervous about Brian watching him, something he'd never done before; he was hurting for something to smooth out the rough spots. He hadn't been mad at Brian in a long time. Not since Aimee died.

The completed product looked like golden candy, and it would taste a lot sweeter.

Aaron didn't bother with a toe or leg this time. He threw the constricting band on his arm and pumped his hand until a vein appeared. He popped the needle in.

"Do I have to watch this part?"

Aaron pushed the plunger, slowly releasing the heroin into his body. "No."

Brian looked away. He'd seen Aaron high plenty of times, but he'd never watched the whole thing. Back then, Aaron would do it in his bedroom or the bathroom. But with nobody to impress anymore, heroin etiquette went out the window. The living room had become just as good a place as any, though he still did it in private when there was company, which meant never.

It was a big hit, but Aaron had taken bigger. Depriving the brain of oxygen killed heroin users, and that was usually a result of questionable purity. If something hit a lot harder than you were used to, and you took the same amount, odds were good you'd end up dying on your couch.

Aaron's eyes glassed over. He wasn't some stupid kid doing it with his friends on the weekend. He wasn't some tweaker who cared more about getting that heroin dick in him than taking his next breath. He was better than them. Even poor and raised in the dirt, he was better.

But today? He threw the gear onto the table and lay back. Aaron didn't give one fuck. If it killed him, it killed him. At least that would put an end to the stress.

"So what happens now? You fly out the window and off to fairytale land?"

Aaron rubbed the blood off his arm. "I don't know. It's different every time."

"Uh-huh. How long does it last?"

"Smack doesn't last more than a few hours. Real high is a lot quicker than that. It's not about that, though. Shit gets weird."

"Weird how?"

The lights overhead flickered. "You'll see."

Injection worked fast. It wasn't that everything changed, more like life kicking into a lower gear. Dropping some torque and pulling everything closer to the center. Making it all a little cozier.

Aaron sank into the couch as something hit the floor in the bathroom and the lights flickered again. This was it. He would have smiled, but the muscles in his face had mutinied from his control. He blinked back the euphoria that blossomed at being both high and correct.

"Is someone else here?"

Aaron shook his head. Any feeling of vindication quickly vanished as the junk took control. "I told you; things get weird."

"I'm not here to fuck around." Brian stood and walked into the hall. Something else moved in the bathroom, this time into the tub with a dull *thud*.

Aaron glanced at his best friend, the guy who would do anything for him. The man who thought of him as a terrible burden to bear. "It's going to get worse."

He hit the light switch in the bathroom, but nothing happened. "What the fuck is this?"

Something shifted in the TV's reflection—a shadow between Brian and Aaron. Something like the Black Knight. The memory of him standing behind the couch as Aaron sank into the Kingdom the first time intruded on the high, and Aaron shifted as the high started turning sour. Visions of him invading their secret world followed, bringing darkness into the Garden of Eden. Just like Horace had seen.

Had he come from here? Did the Black Knight live in the real world? Could he hurt Brian?

"Brian?"

"What?"

Aaron stood on jelly legs and searched the room for any sign of an intruder, but there was just Brian, staring at him from the hallway.

The sun hadn't set yet, but each time the lights dimmed, the room darkened as if it were midnight. Aaron had to struggle to care. Lady H, the freedom from life's endless stream of bullshit problems,

235

had come once more to soothe away his fears. He blinked hard, trying to stay focused.

"Electricity problems aren't magical, Aaron."

Laughter echoed from the bedroom, not one or two voices but a dozen at once, soft and far away.

"Fuck this." Brian stormed into the bedroom.

Aaron's legs only carried him two feet before they stopped working. His eyes wouldn't stay open, and despite the fear, he couldn't stop smiling. That only made it worse. The Black Knight would drag Brian into the Kingdom with Aaron. He would get his best friend killed.

The lights went out, and Brian's footsteps stopped.

Aaron tried to dash toward the hall, intending to get him the hell out before something went wrong, but he only stumbled into the wall, bracing against it and laughing despite wanting to puke. He shouldn't have brought Brian along to begin with. Aaron had always been a goddamn coward. Too afraid to go alone, and too willing to drag people down so he didn't have to.

"Brian!" He started shimmying along the wall, getting lower and lower to the floor with every step. The front door slammed open, but no light entered from the exterior hall. A thousand hands on a thousand arms ten feet long grabbed him. The laughter was behind him now, the ghosts of dead children—dead sisters—looking for company.

"Brian!" He fell forward as they grasped his legs and yanked them out from under him. No response from the bedroom. The certainty he'd made a horrible error in judgment, that he'd dragged his best friend into his personal hell, overcame him. He couldn't think straight. The drugs shrouded everything in haze. The world had no edges for him to grab. Everything in his body and mind had turned to burnt trash and blown away on the wind.

"Brian!"

The hands pulled him backward with a sudden force that knocked the air from his lungs. He rocketed through the front door into the absolute darkness of the nowhere place. His apartment grew further away. The midnight world closed in, suffocating him as phantom limbs stole him from the world at impossible speed. This was it; this was how he died. And instead of fear, the White Lady had replaced it with indifference.

They let go when he lost sight of his apartment, dropping him into the void. Just another nothing, falling forever.

Chapter 23

He screamed as he dropped, but he couldn't hear his voice. Silent, invisible sentinels to his descent watched, things so small he couldn't see them even if the light of day spilled into this hole, and others so large they could devour planets and stars. Black, shapeless beings passed in and out on their way to other, tastier places. Ones that radiated fear and terror in waves like ants crawling across his convulsing body.

"Not like that, dear." Mom grabbed Aimee's hand gently as she tried to apply the red nail polish to her own pointer finger. "You have to brush it gently, or it'll leave streaks and clumps. People will notice."

Aimee looked up at Mom with that admiration that always turned Aaron's stomach. "Will people really notice? I mean, from a distance?"

Or, normally it turned his stomach. Today was too good to ruin, even for him. Aaron watched from the couch, pretending to be looking at *Dexter's Lab* on the screen while Dad slept in his chair nearby. The back door was open, and a spring breeze ghosted through the house, taking a little bit of the stink with it as it escaped from the front door. Weeks had passed since anyone had been hit, yelled at, or made to feel like maybe they shouldn't have been born. That always meant it was coming. But now? The sun waited on the front doormat as if asking to be let it, and Mom gave her daughter lessons on the finer points of being noticed.

"Of course they will. People always look for reasons not to let people in. Especially if you're ever hoping to make it in the theater, or lord forbid, Hollywood."

Aaron raised an eyebrow but said nothing. If Mom knew anything about her daughter, she would know Aimee wanted to a vet, or a doctor, or a nurse, or... well, anything but that.

But Aimee only nodded and scrunched up her face the same way she did at school, filing that tidbit away for future use. "Did Grandma teach you that?"

Mom laughed a laugh Aaron had never heard before. Not a mean one—those always sounded like she was laughing *at* you. This one was bells, like the kind the beautiful, impossible people on TV laughed. Something inside ached while she laughed that laugh.

"The only things your grandma ever taught me was that I wasn't good enough and all Mexicans are thieves."

"Why would she do that, Mama? You can be anything, right?"

Aaron stopped pretending to stare at the TV and turned to watch the mother-daughter drama unfold. But instead of that angry, condescending face, Mom stared at the table, the nail polish brush hanging in her hand. Aaron knew that look. She wasn't staring at anything in *this* world but at things gone by. Back to when Grandma had said something, and what she had said. He knew that look well enough. Aimee wore it all the time.

But the stinging in his chest for their parents was new, and he didn't care for it at all. You didn't get to treat your family as badly as they treated Aaron and Aimee and then beg for pity.

But Aimee was taken in. "What's wrong?"

Mom looked up, shaken from her memories, and smiled at Aimee. She started brushing her next nail on the table. "You know I wanted to be a dancer when I was your age?"

Aimee shook her head.

"Oh, child! I would practice all the time. I danced, and danced. I danced at school. On the way home. At home. Do you know what your grandma said to me?"

Aimee shook her head again, her attention rapt.

"She said I was too fat to be a dancer, but maybe not too fat to find a decent husband." Mom glanced sidelong at Dad in his chair. The kindly-mother facade shattered, and the hateful person Aaron knew returned.

But just for a moment.

"Mama, that's awful. I bet you were a beautiful dancer."

She dropped the nail polish brush into the bottle. "Were?" With a dramatic flourish, she rose from the table, pushed her chair back, and spun three times before striking a pose, her back arched, one hand delicately reaching behind her as if to grasp a distant star.

"I was going to go to Broadway." She kicked her leg in a way Aaron wouldn't have believed she could as her children stared in wonder. "I would go to Hollywood and be a star like Debbie Reynolds." She delicately glided across the floor, her arms painting pictures while her body and feet told their stories. The spring breeze kissed her, blowing her hair behind her in a dramatic mane while the sun reflected like a spotlight set on a dancer for the world to see.

Slowly, slowly, she came to a stop. Her hair settled, and she gasped for air after only a moment of such wonderful movement. She'd shared her secret message with her children, and now her energy was spent, and her spotlight turned off to highlight some other woman with her own secrets.

"I was going to take the whole world by storm, sweetheart." She pulled her chair back to the table and lit a cigarette as she sat in it. "And your grandma made me feel awful for wanting that. Said I was dreaming above my station, and it wasn't for me. She berated me every day until I ran away from home."

Aaron stared, his jaw still open. Had that really been his mother? Had something from the Kingdom come and taken her shape?

Was the grandma they loved so much really so awful?

"I'm sorry, Mama. I think you're a beautiful dancer." Aimee grabbed her free hand. The adoration in her eyes was something Aaron had rarely seen at all.

Mom squeezed her hand back. "You are good enough to be anything. You and your brother both, but you especially. Don't ever let anyone tell you otherwise."

Especially you. He turned to stare at the TV with hard-set eyebrows and a clenched jaw.

"You can still be a dancer, Mama."

Mom laughed. "No. But…" She glanced at Dad to make sure he was still sleeping. "But I'll take the chance to dance the first time it comes along. Everyone needs to dance sometimes, sweetheart, especially when times are bad."

It all faded into smoke as Aaron fell through the endless void. So long ago but so fresh. He'd forgotten about Mom's beautiful dance and the tender mother-daughter moment he was never meant to see. The hurtful little barbs she managed to stick him with even then. How badly Aimee had wanted to be a real family.

But that dance while her children watched... That might have been a wonderful mother to have.

Far below, the ghostly vision fled him as a red light twinkled. It grew rapidly, two dots now instead of one. A castle on a hill and a village below. Individual houses. Individual torches. Terrible shrieks of agony.

"Oh fuck!" Wind buffeted his face. Cold bit his lips.

Too fast. Too fast! Any brilliant plan to save his life refused to form as he rocketed toward the ground, fixing to slam into it at terminal velocity.

All the breath exploded from his body as the ground met him full-force. His vision blurred. The cries of a hundred people surrounded him, but he wasn't dead.

He rolled on the ground, doubled over in pain, trying to make it stop. Something wet covered the side of his face. Pieces of people wiggled on the ground—an arm twitching, fingers grasping. A head staring at him, its mouth speaking soundless words.

Horace.

Aaron blinked twice before the monstrous image registered. He pulled himself to his feet in numb horror. Blood stained the village square. It covered his clothing, red, red, red stains pointing at him like an accusation. He backed away from the head and nearly tripped over a leg behind him. He couldn't take his eyes off Horace. His guts turned to ice as the mouth worked continuously with wordless articulations. He moved to cover his eyes with his hands, but red stains coated those too. Red everywhere. He whined in panic. There was no escape from it.

Despite the horror assailing him from every direction, he remembered his best friend and the laughter in the bedroom. Brian had to be here too. He could be in this very pile of corpses, screaming his wordless screams, wondering why Aaron had done this to him.

"Ser!"

Aaron screamed as something touched his back. He spun around, swinging wildly. It was only Drippy, carefully stepping between the parts of the people Aaron and Aimee had once called subjects.

"We need to go, ser!" Drippy grabbed Aaron by the hand and dragged him. He resisted, but the grip was solid, the little candle man was stronger than he looked.

"Let go of me! This isn't real! You aren't real!" It couldn't be. Because if it was, those people were in a hell he had created. If none of this was just the crazy ramblings of a drug addled mind, then all this terror was real, and he couldn't escape it.

"No!" Drippy dragged him until Aaron's feet began to move of their own accord. "Such things need to be unseen! Yes, ser. Yes, ser!"

They passed more bodies. Nothing remained intact. One man was just a pile of twitching gore. A woman nearby was cut in half at the waist. She screamed and pulled at her legs as they kicked.

Aaron closed his eyes. He couldn't see any more. He'd die on the spot, or go mad. Nobody could look at this for long and remain sane. "It's not real." He chanted it under his breath as the contents of his stomach climbed his throat. "It's not real. Not real. Not real." Had he really wanted to prove it was? What a stupid fool.

Drippy pulled him through streets and alleys like before, but this time he moved with a purpose. The sticky texture of blood still matted the side of his face, but the cacophony began to fade. With the screams dying, some of the anxiety eased too, but the overwhelming terror of it still hung overhead. It would be impossible to move out of its shadow. Even if he left here and never came back, this was part of him forever. Maybe it always had been. He shuddered at the thought. He'd never be able to sleep again.

It was quieter here. The packed road underfoot gave way to grass and dirt, but still he didn't look.

"Ser, I found the way out. I did it while you were away."

Aaron shivered in the darkness.

"Ser?"

How had he and Aimee ever thought of this as a dream? What dreams lived here?

"It was the Black Knight. He was angry. You freed the people he cursed, and he made them pay. Yes, ser."

Aaron finally opened his eyes. Drippy stood in front of him, hunched over and drawn in tight, looking everywhere for unseen foes. "He'll get us too, ser. He'll chop us into little twitchy pieces and make us stay alive after. After, after, after. Alive, alive, alive. Yes, ser!"

Aaron had gone off and grown up while Drippy stayed the same, a small child in the shape of a candle, a child who had seen a war for this Kingdom of the mind and heart. Aaron couldn't remember having seen anything so pathetic in his life.

"I'm afraid, ser. If we don't fix it, they'll be like that forever. He'll make us the same way. I don't want to get chopped down to little pieces."

Aaron's gaze drifted to the lights of the village behind them. The choir of anguish wafted on the wind, a terrifying backdrop to the edges of the forest in which they stood. A village of the damned. He looked the way Drippy had been leading them. More trees, like the forest that surrounded the Kingdom's entrance, but thicker. Closer together. The mist wove between everything. This way led to the castle, though the path that had once been there was gone.

"What do you want from me? I can't fix this place." He gazed into the dreamscape as a scream louder than all others rang out from the village. He wasn't seeing the trees or the mist. He wasn't seeing anything. His thoughts returned to when this had been a land of perpetual spring and summer, the sun never dipping below the horizon. "I'm not a prince or a hero."

"But you are!" Drippy pawed at him, tugging on his shirt. "If you can't fix it, who can? The Witch of the Woods will know what to do, ser! She always knows!"

The Witch. The old woman who seemed so familiar but so strange.

It was one of their early visits to the Kingdom. Everything had been new then, but nothing had felt dangerous. On their way to the castle, a woman had stepped out from behind a tree at the center of a clearing, as if she'd appeared from nothing. Thin, covered in gray rags, and filthy. She didn't look like she belonged in the Kingdom, and her presence was *other*. Many people had come from outside and found their way in, but Aaron had never actually seen it until then.

With a warm smile, she held up both hands to show them she meant no harm. "I'm not here to hurt you." Her accent had the same Eastern-European tinge as their grandmother. "Nothing here can."

She bowed before Aimee and Aaron. Drippy returned the gesture formally, even as Aaron stepped in front of his sister.

"Who are you?" He almost knew but couldn't fathom why.

"Just a woman. A traveler, like you."

Drippy hopped from foot to foot, clapping madly. "The Witch! The Witch! The Witch of the Wild Woods! She'll make your aching slow and stop, for good, for good, for good!"

Aimee peeked out from behind Aaron. "You're a witch?"

The old woman bowed low again. "I was curious. I'd never seen this place before. Did you make this place?"

Aaron and Aimee glanced at one another. Aimee answered for them. "No. We found it."

The old woman squinted, but her smile didn't fade. "Did you now? Are you so sure?"

Drippy danced around the three of them. "If they say it's true, it must be, right?"

The witch brought Drippy to a stop by gently placing her hand on his misshapen head. "Is that so? But you know who I am."

Drippy's feet continued to dance as if he were still moving, but his upper body stood stone still. "It's a seneschal's job to know things, mum. Wouldn't do to have royalty running around like a bunch of sillies."

Aimee laughed at his nonsense, and tension eased from Aaron. Drippy was right, of course. He wouldn't lead them into any danger, and he wasn't afraid of her.

"Of course, of course." The Witch released him and let him dance around the glade. "Perhaps I will come back when you're older, Your Highnesses. We will see what there is to discuss then."

With another low bow that belied her apparent age, she stepped behind the tree and disappeared as if she had never been there. Aimee and Aaron searched for her, but there was no sign. Within a day, he had forgotten all about it. The Kingdom was strange, and strange things happened there.

But that had been a long time ago; the blood on his hands and the village behind him attested to that. The Kingdom wasn't strange anymore; it was a rotten corpse full of ghosts. "Will she be chopped up into little pieces too?" He stared off, unable to focus, reeling from the fall and the carnage. So much blood. So much suffering. For what?

Drippy kept pulling at him until Aaron looked down. "I dunno, ser. But we can't go back now."

The woods loomed over them, overshadowing everything, dampening the mystery light that bathed the world. Beyond it would be the castle and the Black Knight.

"She might know more about the princess, if we can find her."

"Aimee?" He'd hoped to see her before, but not now. More than anything, he wanted her to be somewhere else. He needed there to be a heaven instead of being stuck in a hell like this. Anything would be better than finding her here like one of the villagers or the black-eyed thing so much like his mother. That would kill him in a way no monster ever could.

"The Witch will know." Drippy didn't sound sure of it. "Please, ser. We can't stay here."

"How do you even know she'll be there?"

Drippy pawed at Aaron's hand. "I can call her. Leastwise I can try."

The light from the village stopped at the edge of the wilderness, as if a dark barrier prevented it from illuminating whatever lived inside. In the distance, something walked between two trees, disappearing behind the second only to appear twenty feet away and vanish again.

Aaron absently wiped the blood onto his pants. "What's in there?"

Drippy wouldn't let go of him, holding on for dear life or comfort. Maybe both. "I dunno. I haven't been past the village since..." He stared back at the carnage. "Since a long time ago."

"But Aimee went to the castle." Not a question, a statement. If she had returned here, that's where she would have gone. She couldn't leave anything alone.

You're nothing but a bully.

Standing up for him when she thought he couldn't stand up for himself. Both competing to see who could take the most shit for the other. She'd been the only person to do that for him. Brian, Marie, everyone—everyone else saw him as a burden. A junkie. A piece of shit on the heel of society. He wouldn't leave her alone.

"Do you know the way?"

Drippy peeked out from behind Aaron into the maze of wood and shadow. "Things have a'changed, changed, changed. I don't know up from down anymore." He jumped into the air and clicked his heels together, not in a display of joy, but as a twitch reaction, the way a person might crack their knuckles.

He'd been gone, and she had been too afraid to live alone anymore. She'd killed herself, and she was a rotten piece of meat in the ground now, like they would all be one day, magical or not. He didn't have magical problems; he'd had a mental breakdown and bad coping mechanisms, unable to deal with reality. He could get the help he needed in the real world and set everything right if he turned away.

His breath hitched. It was what Aimee would want, if he were being honest with himself. He hadn't been able to give it to her, or Marie and Brian for that matter, before. He could now. If he was just big and strong enough to walk away. Big and strong enough like he'd never been when they were kids.

But maybe, just maybe, Aimee was here. He would spend the rest of his life wondering. Even with all the horrors here, the question of what if would drive him mad if he walked away. If he even could.

Aaron didn't say a word as he led them down the overgrown path, toward the castle he'd once desired to call home.

Chapter 24

The cries from the village ceased immediately as the fog surrounded them. Aaron glanced behind, but the village lights had also vanished. Chills ran through him, and the blood on his hands dried as the trees pressed in, spreading overhead. Whispering and planning as they grew bigger and bigger with each step.

"Bad things live here. Things that came after the Black Knight, and ain't got nothing to do with him." He clung to the back of Aaron's shirt. The confidence he'd displayed leading Aaron in previous excursions to the Kingdom was gone, replaced by childlike fear. He was out of his depth now. Almost as adrift as Aaron himself.

Perhaps worst of all, he thought Aaron could protect him.

Doubts and fears pressed in like the fog under his clothes. Each step seemed to elicit a new, horrible thought. *Junkie. Stain. Disappointment.*

No. He closed his eyes, nearly tripping for the effort. A brother. A friend. A boyfriend. He would get to the bottom of all of this so he could have a life again. A real one, not the crooked, half-thing he'd been living for years now. That steadied him, even as the intrusive whispers continued in his head and the blood froze to his hands and face.

Again, something passed between the trees in the distance. He grew colder despite sweating, as if all his warmth were draining away.

"What do we do if something attacks us?" Horace had shown him how to use a sword, but only in the clumsy way an inexperienced child could. Lacking one, it didn't matter.

"I dunno, ser. We can't run here. The movement draws more. I tried to run through to the castle once..." Drippy trailed off.

Aaron waited for him to finish before his patience finally ended. "Well, what the fuck happened?"

Twigs snapped to their right, and Aaron's heart skipped a beat.

"I used to be taller, ser? 'Member?"

He had been, but Aaron failed to see how it was relevant.

Ghosts of his past dragged him toward memories. He and Aimee riding with Horace to the castle. Picking berries so the baker in town could make a pie. Leading an expedition into the great, wild woods that seemed to last for weeks.

"Do you think we have enough food?" Aimee had asked.

Aaron smiled at her. "Does it matter here?"

Aimee placed her hands on her hips and pursed her lips. "I don't want to go hungry because you're irresponsible."

Even when she was bratty here, it was fun. But the delight he'd once seen in this place was far away, in another kingdom, on another planet. The fog changed shapes as it had when he first returned to the Kingdom. Dinosaurs towering over them as they passed silently by, heads turning to look. Others peered out from behind the timber, as small as dogs but with terrible purpose in their stillness. They were never in the front, instead always on the sides. Watching. Imposing themselves on his mind.

Echoes of laughter, the same he'd heard in the apartment, whispered from the darkness and danced all around before fading to nothing. He spun to see a bank of fog vanish behind a tree and not reappear on the other side.

"Do you think it's safe here, Aaron?" Aimee's voice asked behind him.

He jumped to face the other direction. Someone was standing at the edge of his vision. A young girl dressed in white, blood staining her front.

"Please don't go," she whispered in his ear.

He yelled and turned again, but there was nothing.

Drippy pulled harder on his shirt. "Shh! They'll find us."

His hand shook as he covered his mouth, forgetting the blood still soiling him.

"I waited. I tried so hard to wait for you." His dead sister's voice drifted around him, maddeningly close. "You left me with them. I couldn't handle it." She appeared in the distance, a ghost in a deep mist. "It's your fault. You killed us. You killed all of us." A red

253

crater marked the missing half of her face. Her gaze pierced him. He stood rooted to the spot. Her words weren't a comfort here as they had been in the apartment—they were dark, dripping with accusation.

And she was right. He'd said the same thing often enough to himself. He took a step toward her, bloody hand outstretched.

"Ser, we should keep a'movin!"

Horace and the little girl from the village—piles of mutilated meat, faces barely visible within—tumbled from the white..

"You ruin everything. You always have."

Marie and Brian lurched from the shadows, their black eyes locked onto him. They held hands, leaning in close to stroke one another, touching the way only lovers did.

Marie laughed. "Why would I stick with a loser like you? You're a pig and a junkie. How long until you start beating me like your daddy beat your mommy?" She spit the words at him.

Aaron stumbled back and fell hard onto his butt, his tailbone singing with pain.

"Guess I don't like fat chicks after all." Brian kissed her, running his hands all over her body.

"Please, Your Highness, don't listen."

She kept staring at him, condemning him with her eyes the same way he'd always known she would one day. And she was right; he was a monster. She could do better. They'd both known that all along, but neither had the balls to say it. He was damaged, and she was too good for him.

Aimee wasn't wrong, either. "If you hadn't left, I'd still be alive. If I'd been born alone, the whole world would have been better for it."

A voice he hadn't heard in years joined the chorus. "You always were a little fuck-up." His dad moved with the determined stride that meant someone was about to get hurt. "I should have killed you when I had the chance, you fucking pussy."

Aaron jumped to his feet. Daddy was mad. No, *Dad* was mad. Only Aimee called him Daddy. But it didn't matter that he was an adult now. His legs were rubber, unresponsive and useless. When Dad was mad, you sat your ass still and took your medicine like a man.

Or… that wasn't right. There were no thoughts, just constant accusations. They were right. He was wrong. Everything about him was wrong, and he'd always known it. He grabbed his head, trying to block out the thoughts.

"Ser!"

"You're going to fucking get it. Call the cops on me? You're fucking dead." Dad pulled his belt off, the one with the Confederate flag buckle, and wrapped it around his fist, the blue and red facing Aaron.

Drippy grabbed Aaron's hand, dragging him away from the approaching crowd. He stopped dead in his tracks after a few feet. "Oh."

Aaron tore his gaze away from his father to see his mother advancing, a cigarette in her hand, her eyes black. "I could have been anything if it hadn't been for you. Anything. You ruined my life, and you killed your sister."

"Yes, you killed me."

"You're a fucking disappointment, boy."

"I'm better off with him, Aaron. You never knew what to do with a body like this."

"Ser! What do we do!"

Aaron put his hands over his ears and doubled over, squeezing his eyes shut. "Enough!" He might be a total waste of skin, but he wouldn't hear it from these things. Brian and Marie weren't here. His mother and father were out there in the real world, not in this forest. It was another way for this place to get inside and break him. But this was *his* place. He wouldn't be ashamed anymore. He wasn't a child.

"Go! Get the fuck out of my Kingdom!"

The menacing silence reasserted itself—the almost-sounds on the edge of hearing—but the voices quieted. He opened his eyes. The darkness and the banks of eerie fog surrounded him, but the phantoms had vanished, their voices an echo in the stillness. He sucked in a deep breath. It was as if a thousand people had been in the same closet and then disappeared all at once.

He stood upright, cold sweat covering his body. If they'd touched him, he would have died. Maybe he would have killed himself; maybe they would have done it for him. Whatever this place might be, it could hurt him—he had the cuts on his chest to prove it. He shook as he wiped his forehead.

And still, that hopeless, angry voice whispered in his head. "Liar. Junkie. Murderer." Maybe it had always been there, quiet and poisonous as a snake.

Drippy huddled in his shadow. "Ser? Are they gone?"

The lightless woods, a shadow on a projection from happier times, were bare. "I think so."

Drippy glanced around with his big black eyes. "They come from the cold place between things. They find people and eat them all up. Eat up all they are so there's nothing left but hurt."

Was that what the Black Knight was?

"We should keep a'movin on. They'll be back." He continued in a whisper, "They always return." He glanced behind him as if words might bring the prophecy to fruition.

Forward and back, neither direction appeared any different. Sinister forest blocked the view each way, closing in around them. They could be anywhere.

He tried to ignore the rising insanity inside, the coming freak-out. This wasn't the time for panic. "Which way were we going?"

Drippy shook his head. "Dunno, ser. Ain't no way to tell in a place such as this one."

If it was like the childhood Kingdom, it didn't go on forever. They could pick a direction and walk. They'd hit a cliff, a castle, or a village. From there they could reorient themselves and find their way. He put one foot in front of the other, Drippy just behind.

They had to get to the castle. It wasn't just the idea of Aimee being there anymore; it was an imperative. This place had once been a shining hope that things would get better. That bright light had lit their path until he'd jumped off it and…

He glanced around at the forest. Had he been the one to shut off the lights?

A full minute passed as they walked, then two. He stopped counting after ten. He couldn't be sure he wasn't walking in circles. That burning need to find the center of this place faded into the same cold fear that hung from the branches. The trees all had the same number of limbs, the same height, the same width. The foliage under his feet didn't differ from yard to yard. The pure black sky offered no indication of movement. The only thing that changed was the fog, or the thing that looked like fog. It took the shape of two eyes watching, or a mouth smiling. The mouth gave way to a herd of deer galloping across the treetops and then to a giant winged creature sitting on the ground only a hundred yards away.

He walked faster to avoid it. It would come for them, as it had for all the light and hope in the Kingdom. It would latch onto him and suck him dry too. Cold sweat coated his back as he imagined those things dragging him to a place truly devoid of light. Time lost all meaning as they surrounded him. Crooked fingers pointed into his heart. Dark eyes pierced him, gauging the ugly thing he was underneath. He couldn't see more than a few feet. The maddening sense that something, some unseen claw, was reaching for him from behind wouldn't relent.

"Can you do that light with your mouth again?" He looked down to where Drippy had been at his side just a second before, but there was no sign of him. Aaron spun in a circle, the shock of his sudden solitude washing over him as a wave of nausea. "Drippy!" His words didn't carry in the mist. "Where'd you go!"

No answer except the ever-present silence hanging heavier in the air than any sound.

In the distance, someone called his name.

He hunched low, unsure of the source. More illusions? More crazy thoughts and images bent on doing whatever they did to people they caught?

"Aaron! Come out, man!"

Brian. Alone in the woods just like him.

Aaron stood up and looked around, trying to discern where the voice originated. Fog still clouded the landscape, but things were different. Or had they always been like this? The trees weren't the guardian trees of the Kingdom, just the same ash, oak, and birch seen anywhere in Tennessee. The light was different too. Brighter. The stars shone overhead.

This wasn't the Kingdom at all. "Brian!" Fog stilled closed around him, and the light seemed muted, as if seen through hazy glass, but this was just the woods on the edge of town.

Because the Kingdom had never been real. It had always just been a way to cope with what he'd done.

"No," he mumbled, shaking his head to clear his thoughts. The ghostly haze closed in, preventing him from getting his bearings. It didn't just shroud his vision, it made it hard to think, reaching cold, dead fingers into his skull.

"Aaron?" Marie's voice. "Is that you? Where are you?"

The noise continued, like a distant highway. But the fog seemed to thin. The oppression of the air let up just enough that he could breathe.

He shook his head, but the confusion didn't abate. He'd been in the Kingdom. His butt still hurt from where he'd fallen. "Drippy!"

The word echoed, but neither of his friends responded.

This wasn't right. There had always been...

He finally noticed as he searched for the source of the voices. The trees all had the same number of limbs. In fact, the ground looked the same too. The harder he stared, the less it resembled Tennessee. Which meant—

He spun around, expecting more of those fog creatures moving in to seize him. But he was alone in the darkness. Utterly alone.

More tricks. More bullshit. "Go fuck yourself! You aren't going to trick me!"

The almost-silence continued as the stars stared mutely onto the scene. Brian finally spoke up. "It's all right, buddy. We're here for you. We got a bunch of people combing the woods. Everyone was really worried when you left the apartment."

"Left the apartment?" He mouthed the words to himself. He hadn't left. He'd been pulled out, ripped away from the world like a tick on skin.

No. Another trick. Trying to make him doubt himself. He denied the anxiety. They wouldn't win. "Go fuck yourself! You aren't going to stop me!"

Flashlight beams, muted and frosted like the stars overhead, bobbed through leaves. Doubt assailed him once more, the feeling that perhaps he had finally come as unhinged as everyone accused him of being. Would it be such a surprising thing? How long had he skated that edge of reason and madness, always one needle or bad day from going right behind Aimee?

And if she'd killed herself, what did that say about her? They had the same genes, after all.

"Ser, what's wrong?"

The voice came from far away, but it shook away the doubt for a moment, and with it, the illusions faded a little. The fog was still there, just harder to see. It waited in the periphery of his vision. There were no flashlight beams. Nothing but an unsettling forest. No Brian. No Marie.

His confusion hardened into resolve. "You won't stop me!" Aaron yelled. "I'm getting to that fucking castle."

There was no response, and nothing changed.

A scream rose somewhere in the mist. It began as a human thing, long and mournful, before rising in bass and volume, growing more unearthly. The stars blinked out one at a time, and the trees reached their fingers toward the empty heavens, growing and groaning before his eyes as he backed away. They were no longer the green giants of the Tennessee landscape, they were once more the hideous monsters of the Kingdom. They cried out in pain as they expanded and grew, and Aaron could only watch in fascinated dread.

Something pulled at his arm. Aaron jumped and swung, spinning to face whatever horror approached.

No horror, just Drippy, flinching and afraid. "Ser, don't!"

Aaron stopped himself before his fist could connect with the little creature.

"You was screamin' something fierce, ser! Hollerin'!"

Illusions. Fakery. Nightmares piled upon the nightmares. Aaron stepped back, his breath heaving and his heart hammering. "I heard voices. My friends."

Drippy peeked behind Aaron then looked behind himself. "Nobody here. They do that, ser. They try and lure you out to where the fog is thick and gobble you up. You can't listen."

This was how insane people saw the world. One place one moment, and another the next. Could he sit down here and just wait? Would it just peter out and end when the heroin left his system?

For the first time in a long time, and to his shock, thinking about heroin produced no desire for it. It might have been the terror, but he felt nothing except revulsion and lingering memories of the fool he'd made of himself on it.

He had to get out of here. At least for now, even if Aimee was here. He had to get home and make sure Brian was still there. What if those things showed half-truths, and Brian was out there looking for him? Or worse, what if he was here?

"Let's go." He grabbed Drippy's hand and led him onward. He had no idea if he'd been going the same way they'd been before. It didn't matter. No more stops.

But the mist wasn't done with him.

"Where are we going?" Aimee asked from behind.

He nearly looked back as the hand in his became a little girl's.

He didn't bother to look. He knew what it was even as hearing that voice sent an icy shock through his guts.

"You aren't going to try and find the Kingdom again, are you? It's just pretend. It isn't real. Mommy and Daddy are gonna take you to the doctor if you don't stop. They're going to lock you up in a hole where you'll never ever see the sun again. You don't want that, do you?"

He squeezed his eyes shut and clenched his jaw until his teeth hurt, walking blind. He wasn't going to look back. He'd see her corpse, or a monster, or one of the villagers chopped to pieces and dying forever.

"'Cause I do. I want you to get all locked up before you hurt somebody. You're a bad person. When we're all grown up, I'll never talk to you, 'cause you'll be a useless piece of trash. You'll be everything you hate in the world. I hope you die."

She struggled to free her tiny hand from his. He swallowed the lump in his throat, past all the things he knew everyone thought of him and into the place where he knew them all to be true.

"Don't ruin my life too. I don't want to be stuck with a loser like you. I'd rather kill myself."

His breath hitched. "Please stop." It wasn't a demand but a whimper, acquiescence to all the things she was saying.

"Ser?" A waxy, slick paw replaced her hand.

263

Aaron held his breath for a moment to prevent the sobs. She hadn't felt like that. She'd loved him. There had been no doubt. When they were kids, they'd said it to each other at night before bed. Neither of their parents ever did, and even if they couldn't understand why, there was a need to hear it.

"You're my best friend, Aaron," she whispered into the dark one night when they were teenagers.

He rolled over on the bottom bunk. "I know."

She let out a sigh, a tiny thing in the face of the screaming match that had taken place in the kitchen minutes before. It had ended with Mom on the floor. "I just want to say it sometimes. I love you."

He could imagine her squeezing her pillow to her chest, staring off into space. They'd always be looking over their shoulders and wondering if any place was as safe as it seemed. There would be no happy morning for them. Maybe there never was for people who grew up like that.

He didn't tell her any of that. "I love you too. Go to bed."

But that was a long time ago. He forced down the burning in his throat. There was no place for tears, here or anywhere.

"Look, ser!" Drippy pointed ahead, where the mist didn't cloud so completely and the light shone a little brighter. A clearing with ring of bright red mushrooms circling the whole thing.

"The Witch wanders in places like that, fairy rings. Doors between worlds!"

The fog swirled around them. He needed to get free before his little sister's voice drove him to the ground, choking the life from him until he could never get up again. He walked faster.

The trees creaked and groaned, and the mist moved in closer. No longer taking shape or playing games, it zoomed across the ground as an angry wisp of cloud. A hundred feet away. Fifty. Twenty. Slithering across the ground like water and evoking images of snakes coming to bite him.

Aaron and Drippy were a step ahead. When it was only an arm's length away, they broke through into the clearing. Aaron turned to watch, flinching as the thing behind them collided with the edge of the clearing as if it were a physical barrier.

He took an instinctive step back, pulling free from Drippy's grasp. The mist retreated a few feet, took the form of two eyes, and stared.

"What the fuck?"

"Ser."

The clearing drew Aaron's attention for the first time as more mist things gathered outside.

Chapter 25

At the top of a hill in the center of the clearing, a withered tree stood. The strange almost-light glowed brighter here. The fog waited at the edges, not crossing the line from their little kingdom of horrors onto the open ground.

Drippy giggled. He ran ahead and did a cartwheel, the little pieces of himself that were constantly falling off flying through the air and vanishing in clouds of shadow. "Them woods is the worst! They burst with the worst! They're the worst burst of wood there ever was!"

The air in the clearing was easier to breathe. Everything outside radiated a hot, choking hate, but not here. The dead tree in the center held a place of reverence, less a hill with a dead oak and more an altar where human feet dare not tread. Even as safe as it felt, he wasn't welcome here. Angry ghosts, not so different from the ones outside, stared just as hard. Old things, though not dead things. Even the tree frowned at him.

The living fog pressed against the edge of the glade. He took a handful of quick steps away, glancing over his shoulder as Drippy quipped more nonsense rhymes.

"Shut up, dammit." Aaron gave Drippy a hard glance. "I'm trying to think here." Dad had said the same thing to Aimee and him a thousand times.

Drippy's reaction was the same as theirs had been. The little candle man fell down mid-cartwheel and stopped giggling. But, like Dad or not, Aaron didn't want to hear any of it. He wanted to go home. He wanted to want the heroin so he could find something to hide all of this.

There was no glade, even in the half-buried memories that always returned when he entered the Kingdom. But that wasn't surprising, not here. The Kingdom had always been bigger than two kids. He didn't know how as a strung-out adult, and he sure as fuck hadn't as a stupid kid.

Had always been. Just as bad as believing Aimee was in the castle. In for a penny, in for a pound. "Is this where we'll find her?"

Drippy stopped next to the tree at the center of the glade. "We can try. I can call out to her and see if she'll answer."

Aaron wrapped his arms around himself. "How?"

Drippy arched one of the waxy mounds that passed for eyebrows. "What'cha mean, 'how'? You just *do* here, ser. You know that."

It had been like that as children, and back at the tavern as well. A voice filled with majesty. A kingdom that bent to the whims of children but was still shaped by its own rules. But out here, in the cold of the woods and surrounded by monsters, it was easy to feel powerless. "Whatever, man. Just do what you're gonna do, and let's get the fuck on with it."

Drippy closed his eyes and grabbed the ancient tree with both paws as if trying to shake a piece of non-existent fruit free. The strange little man muttered a few words to himself that sounded strangely like curses, then went utterly still. One minute stretched into two, two into three.

Soon ten had passed as Aaron began to shiver, waiting for something more dramatic to surface. Drippy speaking in some arcane language. A burst of sound and some colossal light leading up to the heavens.

Nothing happened. He stood there quietly latched onto the tree like a moron, and Aaron just stared, feeling foolish for indulging. Outside, more and more of the fog things gathered. They pressed up against the invisible wall now, their not-quite-bodies forming against it like putty against glass. Living smoke coiling and joining to form bigger creatures before breaking apart into smaller ones again.

He sneered at them. Just bad memories pretending to be more. "Fuck you."

A voice purred back at him on the wind, "What a crazy place to find a little prince, wouldn't you agree?"

Aaron's stomach cramped at the sound. No more. No more dead sisters. No more phantoms of the real world. "Who's there!"

The purring voice laughed before moving up the hill. Two yellow eyes and a grin with yellow teeth appeared in the tree. They floated above the branches, shadows around them implying that something else, a body perhaps, might be there.

The terrifying visage forced Aaron back a step, and then another. "No more. Jesus Christ, please, no more."

That laughter rang out again. "Watch your step, little prince, lest you end up back out there with the real monsters."

Aaron turned to see people with black eyes and open black mouths standing behind him. Others were monsters or shapeless things, creatures made of mist that towered above the trees, fading into cloud. All staring. All hoping he'd take those last few steps back into their garden, as he had to eventually.

Aaron drew in a sharp breath.

As if a trance had been broken, Drippy released the tree and marched down the hill to Aaron, grabbing his hand and placing himself between Aaron and the disembodied face on the hill. "You leave him alone now. You ain't got no business in this place. Never have and never will. Never ever, not even when the sky finally falls down and eats the world."

The eyes drifted in circles, a stomach-churning rotation that defied the laws of nature while the mouth stood in place. "Now, now. The little candle shouldn't speak in the presence of its better, lest someone burn him all up." It made a sizzling noise as the eyes reappeared among the branches.

"Are… are you the Witch?" Aaron hated the weakness in his voice, the sound of the little kid he'd been coming from the mouth of the grown man he was.

Drippy answered for it. "No. It's just a parasite. A dingle-berry thing from out in all the blackness that saw something it liked and wormed its way in. It's been following you since you got back here, ser."

A growl rose from the ground, the deep guttural sound of a cat about to strike. The dirt groaned as if something massive were emerging to devour them.

Aaron's blood went cold. They could make it back into the forest, keep running until they hit an edge. Jump off it if it meant it would end of all of this.

But as he looked behind, the army of the fog stared at him. Waiting as it grew one by one, second by second.

He let out a groan of his own. There was no way out.

The creature in the branches laughed again. "Now, now. I say we keep it civil. There's been quite enough madness going on in this place, wouldn't you agree? If I'd wanted to hurt you…" Hot breath brushed Aaron's neck. His eyes widened, and he straightened his back. "You'd already be hurt." The mouth materialized in the branches, still smiling its discolored smile. "Be at ease, little manling. This place is a safe as any in this little piece of world you've made."

Everything here spoke to him as if it knew more than he did. He supposed they did, but that didn't make it any easier to be constantly in the dark. "What are you? What is all this?"

A deep hum issued from all around, as if the creature were pondering the question. More bullshit theatrics. "You don't know? You made all of this after all. You and that adorable little sister of yours. Yesss, I was there from the very first moment. Happened to be nearby when you popped out of your world and into this one."

"Don't listen, ser. He's a liar and a cheat. He just wants what he can't have."

The voice grew ugly and deep. "Let's be done with that for a moment."

Drippy's hand ripped out from Aaron's as he was launched through the air. He flew end over end, a heart-wrenching screech pouring forth, before colliding with the side of the tree on the hill. His little form flattened as it struck with the speed of a car.

"No!" All caution fled Aaron., and he took three running strides to help his friend.

The little man got to his feet, his shape slowly reasserting itself as he stumbled, grasping the tree for support. But when he looked at Aaron, his mouth was gone. He waved wildly, pointing at the place where it had been and back at the invisible creature.

"What the hell did you do to him!" Aaron balled his hands into fists. "If you hurt him, I swear I'll skin your ass and wear you!" He meant every word. He wanted to see Drippy hurt even less than he wanted to be hurt.

The creature clicked its tongue and remained silent for a short moment before responding. "Now, now. I just wanted to stop his rudeness for a moment. I don't feel that's too much to ask. I am, after all, one of only a handful of things you've encountered here that hasn't tried to kill you."

Drippy sat on the ground, a sullen and angry expression plastered across his waxy face.

"Enough games! What are you?"

It purred again, the momentary lapse in confidence gone. "So many questions for a little monarch. Not very regal." It swirled around him. "I'm one of the little pieces of everything that saw your world born. Both this one and the other one you're from."

"You're talking gibberish. Can you help us or not?"

"I'm talking gibberish? Given the company you keep, I hardly think you can throw that accusation around."

Drippy gave the thing a flat look.

"Given what you are, and what you've done, only makes it all the richer."

Aaron's moment of anger spent, the fear returned, though not as strong as before. "What the hell are you talking about?"

"Ooh, I can see everything about you as clearly as you can see a hand in front of your face. You poison yourself and say you do it for fun. You drive everyone away and say it's their fault. You nurture that hurt little heart as if you blame everyone else, but deep down you feel it's your fault. You convince yourself you are at the center of events that have nothing to do with you. And then there's all of this." The voice spread out as if encompassing the whole glade. "You speak nothing but gibberish. You spoke this world into existence, if not with your mouth, then with your mind."

He'd done a lot of bad, and more had been done to him. But this thing wasn't part of that, just another hanger-on, the Goober of the magical world. "Go fuck yourself."

World-shaking growls of anger emanated from below even louder than before, but Aaron stood his ground.

A voice called out from the woods, a harsh Eastern European accent clipping every word. "This is your kingdom. Tell it to go, and it must go."

The eyes in the tree grew bigger, and red. They were the size of apples. Now pumpkins. Now car tires. "You should respect your betters, little man. You think yourself safe from me because you built this place? I've seen gods born and die. I was there when Olympus fell. I watched as the kami were devoured one by one." Giant yellow fangs glowed with saliva in its mouth. The maw opened and rushed toward him.

Aaron's insides scrunched up as he flinched. "Get out!"

It stopped dead. For the first time, Aaron could see its whole body, suspended above the glade. Green, scaly skin awash with blemishes and cuts that oozed yellow. Two red eyes set above a snout like a cat's, and just as full of sharp teeth. It looked like a twisted fairytale dragon.

"Get the hell out of here! Go back to wherever you're from, and never come to my Kingdom again!"

The growling rose in pitch, becoming a whine. "This isn't over, little man. I'll find you." The mouth and eyes rose, slowly at first but gaining speed. The two red peepers glared at Aaron until they vanished from sight.

Aaron panted as though he'd been through some grave physical exertion. He fell to his knees, grasping the ground, sweat pouring off him. The nightmares here never ended.

"The Witch of the Woods," Drippy said, his voice full of awe.

An old woman dressed in rags strode out from behind the tree as if from thin air.

Chapter 26

Scraggly gray hair hung from her head and covered her face. Black rags gave her the shape of a homeless person staying warm for the winter. Despite her age, she walked with a ginger step, her toes barely touching gliding across the ground.

"This is a dead place. Nothing good is here for you. Why would you come back?"

"For you, Mum!" Drippy spun in three tight circles and struck a pose.

She spared him a glance. "Be silent, little light. I talk to your master."

Aaron looked up, unsure who he was seeing. Her voice was that of his grandmother, but she'd been dead for years.

Mom hadn't cared that her mother was dead. They hadn't bothered to go to New York for the funeral.

"At least that old bitch won't be popping in for any more surprise visits," Dad said around a mouth full of pizza.

Mom rolled her eyes. "That's my mother you're talking about."

"And she hated me. I never wanted her in this damn house to begin with."

Aaron kept quiet, but Aimee's eyes misted over. The news had been devastating, and Mom had told them as if she were stating it would rain later. "May I be excused?"

Dad grunted, and Aimee walked into their bedroom. Aaron stayed and finished his pizza, and that night, he and Aimee spoke about it.

"I wanted to go see her before they buried her," Aimee said from the top bunk, her voice thick with tears.

But it wouldn't have been Grandma. A dead body was nothing more than a chunk of meat, rotting faster than it had when it was living. It stung, but they hadn't seen her in years. Even then, they'd been growing into the adults they would be, or might have been. Aaron, too hardnosed and unwilling to bend, and Aimee letting everything into her heart, even when it hurt. "We can do something for her in the Kingdom tomorrow. We'll make a remembrance day."

Aimee was quiet for a long time. Just as Aaron was sure she'd fallen asleep, she replied. "We have to do more than that."

The next day, Aimee sat in the throne room, gazing longingly at the back wall. She hadn't said a word all day at school. Nobody but Brian asked why. The few people that spoke to them seemed to understand their lives were bad. They didn't ask about bruises or tears; they took it as a given that the world would shit on some people.

She finally spoke. "I know what I need to do." She stood up and faced the stone wall at the back of the room, the one with the big glass window that looked out into the sky beyond. Raising her arms, she stared at the window as serious as Aaron had ever seen her.

"I want to see where Grandma is. Open."

Aaron's breath caught in his throat. There had been a time when they'd made wish after wish to change the real world. It never worked. Whatever hope they'd found in this place was for this place only. After a long moment of nothing, Aaron released his breath. Dead was dead, nothing could change that.

Drippy had been waiting near the door. He waddled over and gazed up at Aimee with those big puppy eyes of his. "I don't know if you can—"

"I'm not asking! I'm telling!" She stomped her foot, and the castle shook as if she were a giant. "Open! Now!"

The hair on the back of Aaron's neck stood on end as the stone groaned. The sky outside the window faded to red, then to the black of night. Stars dotted the darkness. Then, in an instant, there was no glass. The castle continued to shift as though it might fall apart.

Aaron grabbed the throne and held on as he nearly lost his footing, but Aimee stood implacably still, the picture of determination. Unmoved even as the world fell apart

"Aimee! What are you doing!"

She didn't reply to him, instead speaking into the night sky behind the throne. "Show me Grandma! I want to talk to her!" Her drive, that look in her eyes, was the same Dad had when he meant to get his way. The one that said she'd tear this whole place to the ground if it meant seeing Grandma one more time.

For one upside down moment, she scared him more than Dad ever had.

The rumbling of the castle slowed and stopped as the back wall fully vanished, revealing the black space and infinite stars on the other side of the Kingdom's blue sky. But there was no Grandma.

"Let me see her!" She stomped her foot again, but this time, nothing happened. No shaking castle, and certainly no Grandma.

For a long time, the three of them gazed into the universe, waiting. Did they have that kind of power? Aaron had never thought about it. The Kingdom did strange things to the mind. The cares of the outside world vanished. There was no desire to make it like Umber Gardens, or to do the things he always imagined he wanted to do there, like flying. Here, desires were different. The light that always shined did more than touch the skin; it seeped inside and made you brighter too.

But Aimee's desire to see Grandma overpowered that. Her eyes misted over. "It's not fair," she whispered to nobody in particular. "I just wanted to see her one more time."

"Aims..." That fear gone, Aaron wrapped his arms around his sister. "I'm sorry."

Her eyes stayed misted as she stared into the unknown beyond the stars. "I just want something to be okay one time. Just one time, Aaron. I want to go home and have everyone be happy. I want to see Grandma. I want to stay here forever."

Drippy sat on the floor behind them and gently pawed at her knee.

"It can't go on like this forever, can it? Is this all we'll ever be?"

A tear fell free and hit the ground between the thrones. In an instant, the stones reshaped into a small pool, rippling like water. A small stream, only a few feet wide, flowed toward the edge of the universe, forming a channel as if it had always been there. It grew wider, and by the time it hit the edge, it was a waterfall cascading over nothing and into eternity.

"Everything will be okay, Aims. I promise, okay? I'll make everything okay."

Aaron remembered it all with perfectly clarity as he examined the woman who reminded him so much of Grandma. He remembered the little notes he and Aimee had made and folded into boats to sail off the edge of that nothing, hoping they would find her in the great beyond being shown to them.

Aimee had asked him if he thought the boats would find her. She had folded them with tears in her eyes, kissing each one as she set it into the water, watching it fade away over the cliff and into the stars.

"I'm sure she'll see them, Aims. She has to, right? Our word is law."

She stared at stars without a word. She'd been so much stronger than he had. Able to reshape the very world while he had never come close to doing such a thing. She'd found this place even after she died, and come here waiting for Aaron.

279

And somehow, he'd convinced himself he was the strong one.

But what he'd thought then wouldn't leave him alone now. There was no talking to the dead. No matter what they had here, there was no going across that veil to see who or what might be beyond. Still, they floated their little boats, some coated in blood from the paper cut on Aaron's finger. And here he stood, trying to talk beyond the veil once again.

As he looked up at the Witch, he wondered if she kept a little paper boat with an eleven-year-old's blood on it hidden away in those rags.

"Get off ground. You should act like you rule this place. It is yours, even if you don't control it as you once did."

He did as she bade, shaking all over. "Why does everything keep saying that? It was just a thing me and my sister made up."

The Witch turned her head and spit as if the words were disgusting. "You may not make the clay, but your words and thoughts set its mold. You make this place as sure as bricklayers make houses."

That accent. Her speech. "Grandma? Is that you?" He craned his neck to see her under the hair, but it was impossible in the darkness.

Her cackle reflected off the mounting fog and endless trees. "I am not your grandmother. I did not make you, and you did not make me."

He didn't know whether to believe her, but more pressing questions were on his mind. "What is this place?" The desperation in his voice made him feel weak. Too many mysteries. Too many questions. Too much fear. "Where is this place?"

"Where is the place you're from, huh? Little bits of rock in an endless black. Hot metal and light screaming through voids of cold. These worlds here are not different." She gestured at the endless dark sky above them. "Just a little world between two bigger ones. The real question is why, and that you have not asked."

"Is it real?"

She cocked her head. "You are smart. Is it? Is anything? Real is context, point of reference in a sea of conflict. The things here can hurt you. That's real enough."

More half-answers. More nonsense like the dribble Drippy was always spitting out. "This is insane. Send me home. Get me out of here."

"I can, but you won't see your sister. Is that not why you are here?"

The words rocked him. "What?"

She hummed and mumbled under her breath. "Do you not know why you are even here?"

"I don't even know where here is! I have no fucking clue what's going on! One minute I'm minding my own goddamn business, and the next I keep ending up in some fucking fantasyland I had as a kid!"

She laughed, his anger lost on her. "Maybe you are not so smart. Did you not question why? Did you not see deeper meaning in this place? In the darkness that spreads across it?" She grabbed a handful of dirt, throwing it into the air. "This filth?"

"Is Aimee really here?"

She arched an eyebrow and sat on the ground, placing her hand on the tree and gazing up at it. "When I was a girl, I made a place like this, too. In it, the animals spoke to me. They told me the secrets of the world. Of how gods make their own realms. I wondered then if our own world, the one outside, was just a place like this. Did some god step from another place into our sky and speak our world into being, like in the stories?" She looked over at Aaron. "Did you never wonder the same?"

He had. Aimee too. They had whispered questions to each other as the memories faded when they came home at night. They'd asked Drippy about it, but he only spoke the same nonsense he always did.

"It'll make sense when you're older, sers. Or it won't. I might not ever make much sense. That's all okay though, in'it? You're here, and that's what matters."

During one of his last trips, he'd tried to command Horace to tell him in the same way Aimee had commanded the throne room to show them Grandma. Horace had only laughed and walked away, leaving teenaged Aaron awash in petulance the way only a teenager could be.

Right now, he needed to know if Aimee was here. And if she wasn't, if she was really gone, getting out of here and making sure Brian was safe was all that mattered. "I don't care. Can you tell me if my sister is in the castle?"

The Witch glared at him, and in the poor light, he caught the barest glimpse of two different colored eyes, same as his. "Young people are ever fools. If your heart was not clouded, you would already know the answer."

Aaron opened his mouth to speak, but she held up a hand to silence him. She closed her eyes and cocked her head the same way Drippy did. Listening, as if voices were telling her secrets nobody else could hear. Drippy did the same from the top of the hill, balancing on one foot, looking every bit like a weathervane.

She didn't do it for very long before she focused on Aaron once more. "I tell you this: You may go now. You can leave and never come back. I can help you. But the gate shuts behind you, and this becomes memory of memory until nothing is left, like when you were baby. Or, you can find what you seek."

He hadn't sought anything here. Or had he? Had he not gone to the guardian trees in the woods the night before all of this started? Hadn't he seen the shack and the string and run away? He'd touched the scar on the trees where he'd tried to break into the Kingdom to find Aimee.

Had he been looking for the Kingdom his whole life? The thought brought on a raging headache as quick as the wind.

"I do not know the inside of you. I don't know what thoughts bring you here, or why this place was ruined. It is yours. It is for you to find out. But your twin is here. The little girl with eyes like a god. You could not be here without her. You two are part of a whole, and even if she has passed in your world, there is still a piece of you and her out there." She waved her hand at the starless sky as she stood, taking it slowly as her old bones creaked. "I can hear her whispers. If you go, you will never find her, I will tell you that now. She will be lost to you, and this place will fall to shadow. Only you can prevent that now, and only perhaps."

"Ser?"

"Not now, Drippy." He felt faint from the revelation. If he could believe this woman, then Aimee was here. It was all true. Aaron had a thousand more questions, a million.

"You should listen to the little light." She stared at something behind him.

He followed her gaze to see a wall of fog so thick it had solid form. It bent the forest over the glade, the wood creaking until it broke. An ethereal humming, as if a woman long tired of doing so were singing a tune under her breath, sounded from the old tree on the hill protecting the last of its domain. The barest hints of words floated from within the melody.

A tidal wave of monsters bore down on them. As wide as the clearing itself, it rose a hundred feet, an endless cascade of damnation to wash him and Drippy away forever. He couldn't look away.

But Aimee was here. *Aimee.*

That thought pulled him out of his terror. He faced the Witch. "Where—"

She was already pointing out a direction in the forest.

"Drippy, let's go!"

He wasn't on the hill. Aaron looked around the glade to find Drippy already fleeing in the direction the Witch had indicated.

"Go. Find your sister. Find the things you seek."

Aaron took two steps before the wood line broke. With a thunderous crack, it split and the fog rolled in like water through a broken levee. The tree at the center of the glade let out an ear-piercing shriek, and then there was only the sound of one long, terrible breath behind him.

Chapter 27

An avalanche of mist as thick as snow rushed toward him, terrible faces and hands visible on its surface. He screamed as he ran. He couldn't outpace it. There was no way. It moved like a force of nature.

Drippy gained ground ahead of him, disappearing into a bank of cloud.

"Wait!" Aaron yelled. Something breathed cold onto his neck.

He hadn't been out of sight more than a moment before Aaron heard him scream, "Ser!" But it came from impossibly far away, and only the echo caught Aaron as he fled.

The trees groaned as he passed, pointing out his position to the army of monsters nipping at his heels. The scent of dead bodies and rotted wood whispered to him.

Look back. See us. Join us.

A stream of white faces and hands caressed him as the fog rolled past, stealing the scream from his lips. It whispered to him, slithering under his clothes and behind his eyes as he grunted in panic and the world became a white canvas.

"Get away from me!" He stopped and swung, but there was nothing to connect with. The world hadn't gone dark; it had gone nothing but light. A sinister glow for miles around, to the very edge of the Kingdom.

"Where are you, Drippy!"

Something whispered behind him, and when he spun, it chuckled behind him again. He exhaled clouds of steam. His fingers went numb, and when he looked down at them, ice crystals had formed.

If he stayed, he died. They weren't coming for him; they were all around him. "Fuck you. You aren't going to have me!" He shoved his hands into his armpits and started jogging the way he'd been facing.

Or the way he might have been facing. He could see nothing, but the presence of *others* pressed in all around him. The quiet whispers rose from the inside.

You're worthless.

Let her die.

He shook his head and picked up his pace. There were no trees anymore, just the eternal, impossibly clean slate.

Did you think this was real?

Abandon your hope.

Whirling, their voices created an endless din.

Everything you have, everything you ever had, is a lie.

287

You are the reason… you are.

"Go away!" He ran, but it didn't feel right. They were right, and he was nothing. A speck. An insignificant thing in a hostile world.

He sat across from Aimee. An adult woman. The person she'd never gotten to be. The person she had been the whole time. The real Aimee, not the one he'd invented.

She was beautiful and tall. She'd always been tall for a girl, nearly Aaron's height. Between that and the old, shabby clothes they wore, the other children had teased her, calling her Rag Lady both to her face and behind her back, but she had blown it off. How she could remain so confident when those things tore him up inside had always amazed him. He'd chalked it up to her thinking she was better than everyone, but he had admired it none the less.

His heart ached at the sight of her. She looked so much like Mom, but different. Healthier. Happier. That ache bit him so hard it hurt, leaving a gaping black hole in his core shaped just like his little sister.

But when he opened his mouth to tell her that, something else came out. "Aims, we have to go."

She clenched her jaw and looked down at him in that severe way Dad always had when he fucking meant it. "It wasn't real, Aaron. Just something we made up because we lived in a literal hellhole." She used her big sister voice. She *always* used her big sister voice, even though they weren't children any longer.

Thoughts that didn't belong to him flooded his mind as he tried to get off the couch. He hated when she said literal like that. She didn't mean literal, she meant figurative.

But none of this was right. He'd forgotten something, or been made to forget. A white fog that carried on until the end of the world and a little candle in the darkness. The same princess in another castle that had fuck-all to do with Nintendo.

Or maybe this wasn't a princess at all. He had to touch her. If she were real, he would know by touch. It would be like reaching out and grasping a piece of himself.

He tried to shake the other parts away as that ache and the cold bit down, but they wouldn't abate. Aimee sat in front of him. That had to be—

"We have to go back, Aims! The Black Knight is going to destroy everything!" No. They didn't need to go back if she was here. He only had to tell her how sorry he was. If it had been him, the world would have been better. Brian would have been happier, and Mom wouldn't have shut down. Maybe even Dad would have been a better man if she'd been the only one born. She'd always been full of hope, and he'd never had anything but anger.

But he couldn't. What he needed to do was to take his medication. He knew that, and she knew that. So they'd go through this fucking song and dance every time just like they had when Aaron had needed to go to rehab and he'd fought her on it for years.

And just like then, she'd be right.

She shook her head at him as she walked to a crib he hadn't seen before and picked up a baby, tiny and swaddled in cloth. Her child? Had Aimee had a child? It was hard to remember anything. She had died a long time ago. She'd only been a kid. She hadn't gotten to live long enough to have a family. Had she?

No. She and Brian had gone to college together while Aaron bummed around Umber Gardens. She hadn't died. The only one who had died was Grandma, and that was when his problems started. Some of them, anyway.

The cold crawled up his arms and into his chest as the drug headache set in.

He glanced around the living room. It was nice. Classy. Brian's stupid comic book posters were all over the living room, but she'd insisted they at least frame them. His gaze lingered on the diploma. Everyone had been at her graduation. Almost everyone. She'd been upset that Mom hadn't come, and he hadn't been able to fathom why.

"She made our fucking lives miserable, Aimee." He lit a smoke as she adjusted her gown. "Why the fuck would you want her there?" Aaron hadn't bothered to finish school. What was the point? He didn't need a degree to be a writer. When he'd told her that, she gave him the same shitty look she was giving him now. The words then had been kind. The words now…

"Do you even hear yourself? Did you take your meds? You know you get like this when you're off them."

He tried not to give her the "you know I hate those fucking things" look that would only spark a fight. Bigger issues were at stake. "We always forgot after we left. Remember?"

"Look, Aaron. There's nothing out there, and I'm not going to buy into this, okay? It doesn't help you."

He jumped off the couch, and she flinched at the sudden movement. The same fear he'd seen on her face a hundred times when Dad raised his fists painted her for an instant before vanishing. It blocked everything else out.

There had been woods. He'd been lost and searching for something. And why was he so cold? He shivered despite the sun outside.

"Listen to me. I can't get there without you. I've tried. We can only go together, and we have to do something."

The fear remained, but there was something else. The other expression she always gave him—pity. The one that said she'd moved on and he couldn't. Her poor junkie brother forever stuck between child and adult. She'd never said it, but she'd always felt bad for him. He'd been the one who took the brunt of the abuse when they were kids. He'd gone out of his way to protect her, even when she hadn't needed it, and even when it was just an excuse to lash out at their parents so they would hurt him and give him reasons to hate them more.

Brian poked his head out from the doorway leading to the kitchen. "Everything okay?" He eyed Aaron up and down the same way someone might a homeless man begging for change.

Aaron opened his mouth to say something else, something beyond his control, but he stopped it. "No." Something wasn't right. This wasn't what he'd been doing. He stared at the wooden floorboards, a lucid dreamer searching for the surface. The white walls, the kids playing outside, the other two members of his three-person gang—all of it just a dream within a dream. Had to be.

He closed his eyes and bore down, holding his breath. Not now. He had somewhere to be. He'd find... someone. She was out there.

He gasped for air as he opened his eyes, his sister and her husband still staring at him.

"What's wrong, buddy?"

But the wooden floorboards had vanished. Dirt, like the ground in a forest, lay under them. His feet were bare and blue, and the shock of it hit him as if he were underwater. They weren't in a house. They weren't here at all. Brian was somewhere else. His apartment maybe, or lost somewhere in the Kingdom. And Aimee...

He looked up. Young again, Aimee stood by the crib. The bullet had shorn away half her head, leaving a pulsing mass of red and pink where golden hair had once been.

"What's wrong, Aaron?" Her voice mocked him, but it wasn't hers. It was Aimee combined with Brian. And something more sinister, like the black lights in the Kingdom. "You look like you've seen a ghost."

He screamed and backed away as the illusion shattered, a broken mirror falling to the ground. In the forest where he stood, a thousand faces made of mist had locked onto his body, sucking out the warmth. Taking away his heat and life one little speck at a time.

Eating him.

"No!" He swung wildly at the faces, and they vanished in a flutter of murmurs.

She'd been right there. Her ghost. Maybe that's all that was in the castle. He ran as the cold seeped the warmth from his very heart. Even now, it beat slower and slower, whatever made him human sapped away. They would devour him—or worse, he'd end up another face in the mist. A dead thing in a dead forest in a dead world.

But still, his heart ached at seeing her. At what might have been. It was almost enough to lie down and die right there. If it were like that, maybe it wouldn't be so bad. Just him, Aimee, and Brian how they shouldn't have been.

But if she was still here, he owed it to her. He would free her from this place. He had to. Without her, there was no hope anymore. And if there was no hope, why not just follow her in the same way?

The cold and frost agreed, crystalizing on his exposed flesh. His feet and toes numb, each step sent a jolt of tingles up his leg. All around, pieces of worlds that might have been loomed in as the fog creatures whispered toward him.

He couldn't see as he ran, each step more painful than the last, his attention wandering further and further. He narrowly missed trees as the sweat on his body froze, dragging down on his thoughts as it slowed his limbs. But she was here... her? He loved her. He had to

293

go to her; it was the only way to end it. And if he had to rip his heart out to find her again, he would. He already had. It beat on the forest floor as he shuffled past. All for her.

Maria? Aimee?

Both?

Brian stood still in the woods as Aaron stumbled by.

"How could you just leave me alone here, man? Do you know what they did to me?"

Aimee appeared from behind a rock formation in front of him. "Why did you leave me?" Her head, still shorn in half, was filled with horrors. Small, wiggling things of blood and bone. Their father and mother standing over two young children with faces like wolves. His eyes staring back at him.

He ran around her, trying not to look as the tears froze to his face.

His mother and father approached from the darkness at the edge of the fog, holding hands. "We were happy before you. If you'd never been born, the world would have been a better place."

Their voices followed him as he grunted and panted, frantic for some way out. They echoed off the trees, gaining volume and speed. A thousand screaming condemnations accosted him as a million murmuring voices closed in on all sides.

"You left."

"You always were a fuck-up, boy."

"Nobody wanted you to begin with."

This was the darkest night of his soul. Still he trudged on, but he couldn't remember why. Ahead, the light brightened as the trees thinned out. Somewhere in the fog, Drippy screamed.

There was a princess to find. She was her. Her. The royal Her. Marie had always been there for him, just as Aimee had been. He had to get to her and get her… Aimee—he had to get Aimee out. He had protected her because she'd been his heart. It had been born beating and crying outside of his body, and he foolishly gambled it away. If he could see her one more time and steal her from this cold, he would let it take him.

He couldn't run anymore. He could barely walk as the edge of the woods appeared in front of him. Ten feet. Closer now. The promise of warmth grasped at his frozen fingers. Spectral arms tried to wrap around him and pull him back. The million voices inside his head that had always been there continued to whisper his worth and how badly it was wanting. Two feet. He reached out as they pulled him back into the cold.

He broke through the mist into an empty field, falling to his knees as the cold released him. Reality flooded back. Drippy, the castle, Brian and Aimee. His thoughts turned to a cacophony of voices and images as he glanced up, shaking violently.

Ahead of him lay the castle, shrouded in black and fog. It towered above him, ready to strike. Once, the gray stone walls had been nearly white, pristine and beautiful. Now soot and substances better left unguessed blackened them. The forest grew nearly to the edge of the walls. Those very walls seemed to march toward him as if they would crush him.

The Black Knight stomped across the lowered drawbridge toward him, each footfall a riot of thunder and lightning. Crows circled as the sky became a blackened, decayed face staring down, while the thing in black armor closed the distance between them.

Chapter 28

The screaming in his head grew louder and louder. The nightmare man stomped across the field toward him. It hurt to look at it.

"No," Aaron mumbled. He struggled to get to his feet, though the ground sang to him to come back down. "You can't do this. This isn't yours." He slurred the words.

The living mists coiled and reached for him from the trees just behind. Plated boots stomped off the bridge and onto the field only a hundred yards away. Somewhere within the castle, Drippy screamed again.

Aaron screamed too—at the hurt the phantoms had done to him with their words, and at the parts of him that knew they were true. None of this was how it was supposed to be. There had been so much more for him and Aimee. The future had been like the Kingdom.

And it had turned out the same way. A sob escaped Aaron.

"You are weak." The knight's voice was familiar even as the sound of it shocked Aaron's brain, like an inversion of a favorite song. "All of this is your fault."

Aaron backed away, trying to escape the doom storming toward him. Nobody could fight this insanity. Icy tendrils caressed his back. On either side, jagged edges of earth gave way to drops down to the bottomless, hopeless ether surrounding the Kingdom.

The impossible blackness of that armor sucked in all light and hope. "You are the cause of all the bad things that have ever happened to you. You're the reason your sister is dead. These people suffer because of you."

Aaron shook his head, still shivering. "Get out. I command you to get out of my Kingdom." The words were impotent. He fell back another step, reeling from the sudden change of scenery, blinded by the torches lining the castle wall. The voices in his head screamed. He slapped his hands over his ears.

Fifty yards away and closing with every stride, a piece of deeper darkness moving inexorably closer. "You have no power here. You are weak. You are worthless. This Kingdom and everything in it belongs to me." The Black Knight reached behind its back and pulled out Aaron's syringe. But instead of the one he always used, this one was a horrifying thing the size of a turkey baster. Even in the dull light, the heroin glowed amber inside.

"This is what you are. You want to forget? You want to wipe yourself out and take all of this with you? So be it."

Ten yards.

Aaron put up his fists, still blue from the cold. Fight or flight. Kill or be killed. He had no idea what he would do, but that part of his mind was numb anyway. He would claw and bite if he had to. Or he would throw himself from the cliffs before he let that thing put a hand on him.

He dropped his fists as he watched his inexorable doom. Both this world and the real one were unkind, hellish nightmares. What did it matter if he gave up? Everyone else had left him; what was one more light snuffed out?

He stepped to the side, intending to do just that. He'd kill himself. Promises to Aimee be damned—anything was better than this. Life had shit on him one too many times. Time to go to whatever home waited after.

"Stop!" Command issued forth from that voice as if the gods of Earth had spoken. The Black Knight ordered, and he obeyed. He froze, his feet rooted to the spot. Even his breath stilled. The icy phantoms grasped him as the Black Knight closed the last distance and stood before Aaron.

"You wretches, be gone. This is mine."

With a shriek, the hands left Aaron, fleeing into the woods. Only the Black Knight remained. His stink of metal and blood. The cold, dead breath coming through the visor in a cloud. The terror that radiated from of him, shaking Aaron even as he stood immobilized, a tear falling down his face.

Time slowed as the Black Knight towered over him. They'd both entered into a pocket realm within a pocket realm. The only things in the universe staring into one another, a visor separating them.

Aaron held his breath and waited for the end. No pain. That was all he could ask now. Let it be over as quickly for him as it had been for his sister.

The Black Knight's armor heaved as he breathed, staring down at Aaron. The epitome of everything wrong with the Kingdom. The thing that had torn down all happiness and left despair behind. Images of him turning the sky dark filled Aaron's mind. Aimee had returned to stop this. She'd come here when she died—or *if* she'd died, to hold this monster at bay. It had removed her from this world the same way a bullet had from the other.

"Where's my sister?"

The gauntleted hand grabbed him around the neck, lifting him off the ground as Aaron's courage collapsed in a gurgle. "She is dead because of you. You bring only ruin and destruction." The other hand slammed the needle into Aaron's neck. He screamed as the Black Knight pushed the plunger down, releasing a full syringe of junk into him. "I will wash away the stain you have made on the universe. I will undo everything you have done."

Aaron gasped for air as the world grayed.

"Everything you have made, I will unmake."

Sirens blared from nowhere, a thousand screaming alarms ushering him into the blackness.

"You are a mistake. If you had never been, the world would be better."

The lights of the castle dimmed. Fear numbed Aaron's limbs. His fingers and toes, already frozen with cold, could be on another planet for all he knew.

"I will do it for her, whether she likes it or not."

Aimee? Did he really have her?

No. Aimee had been dead for years, her young body put into the ground and devoured by worms. Nothing was left of her but bones and scraps of clothes. Soon, there wouldn't be anything left of him either, and he was too tired to care.

But he had to know, even if he died here. He grasped at the fingers around his neck, pulling them loose as the smack settled into his body and the light of the world became a distant pinpoint. "Where?"

He caught a glint of malice behind the visor before the world went away. The hand around his throat released him, and he tumbled toward the ground that never came. He fell downward, past caring, past where land should have stopped him and down into nightmares.

The Black Knight's voice followed him into the void. "You will know nothing. You will get nothing. You have ruined everything. I will enjoy watching you die."

Chapter 29

His throat stung as if the hand were still around it. The words struck again and again, vipers lying in the grass, biting him as he passed by endlessly.

"You have ruined everything."

"You are a mistake."

"This is what you are. Weak. Useless."

The cold, the bone-chilling certainty that there would never be warmth again, pressed in. The junk in his veins filled him. Endless sleep called out. And maybe, as worthless as he was, that would be better.

"No," he muttered into the darkness, trying to deny the hands guiding him to sweet oblivion. It had been too much. A giant syringe. More than he'd ever taken. If the fall didn't kill him, the drugs would. He'd finally become the cautionary tale everyone had warned him about.

Tears started before the first sob escaped him. No weakness now. The dying were allowed tears. Nobody would see them.

Nobody here could call him a wimp or a little bitch. There was no Marie to hide his shame from, and no parents to hold it against him. Nothing but the faceless voices whispering words of damnation and bearing witness to his failure as a man.

"I just want to go home."

All he'd ever really wanted was a home. Had he ever known one? Maybe the Kingdom with Aimee. Or perhaps Brian's house. But not really. He'd never had a place he could call his own, something permanent. Nothing stable in the unstable world.

In the darkness, the past played like a projection on a movie screen. Brian's dining room appeared in the darkness. His mom was there, along with Aimee, Brian, and Aaron. Good china in good cabinets on the wall. The family dog wagging its tail as it gnawed a toy. A real home, with fresh paint on the walls and no echoes of fights from the day before.

"So you're top of your class?" his mom asked Aimee as she passed mashed potatoes along the table.

Aimee flipped her hair in a mock-bashful way. "I am." She left out the part where Aaron was only a hair's breadth behind her.

"That's fantastic, sweetheart! You'll be able to go to any college you want with good grades. Are you excited about graduating in another two years?"

"Yes, ma'am."

Aaron and Brian met one another's gaze across the table. When Brian rolled his eyes, Aaron did his best not to laugh.

"Well, that's good for you. Don't you ever forget you can be anything you want, no matter what anyone tells you." She gave both Aimee and Aaron very direct looks, the kind of look that said they should pay no mind to the troubles at home.

"I won't."

But Aaron took it a step further. "We'll get as far away from this place as we can when we're eighteen."

Silence followed, and he blushed. Brian's mom had never brought up the phone call that had chased Dad from the house. Aaron had been mad at everyone at the time, but when the smoke cleared, he was grateful to her. She had seen what was happening, and she was the only adult to ever intervene on their behalf. She knew, and she understood, and maybe that made her the only adult in their lives worth a damn. She knew what kind of place they lived in, and she'd never once forbid her son from being friends with them despite it. She created a safe space for them, not so different from the Kingdom. Somewhere they could go at the end of the day to be away from the troubles of the world for a little while. Her home had been hope in an ugly world.

He'd never thanked her for that. Not really.

"These potatoes are great," he said instead.

"I'm going to go to the best college because I'm the smartest person you've ever met," Aaron said in his best Aimee voice while the three of them sat in Brian's room later.

She rolled her eyes as she turned the page in her book. "I'm going to be a condescending turd instead because I'm a mouth-breather."

Her impression of him was spot on, and they laughed uproariously, no different from any of the hundreds of other days they'd spent over there after school.

Home. That had been a home, a space where they could find sanctuary and room to grow. But Aimee's death had cut it short. He was still welcome there, and he'd stayed for a few months before turning eighteen, but it had never been the same. Brian's mom did her best to make sure he knew he was loved, but he'd been too blind to see it. Too focused on all that hate and anger inside. And then he'd left. He hadn't seen her in years, even when Brian invited him over on holidays.

It was too painful, the wounds too fresh. Even now, as he fell through the void, those cuts still stung in a deep inside where no healing ever reached.

As the picture faded, he expected more voices to mock him. But the Black Knight's words had disappeared into the nothing, leaving him alone and dying as he fell.

The decaying light of evening caressed him. He tried to open his eyes but managed only to crack them. Everything stank. He wasn't falling. Falling gave the hope of some eventual end. Instead, he was lying. Lying on the ground, and maybe lying to himself that things were ever going to end any other way.

There was ground under him. Carpet, actually—the carpet in his apartment complex hallway. He took in a deep breath, only it was shallow.

"I'd wanna."

Every time he tried to take a breath and speak, something stopped him. A soft, lightless thing on his chest pushed him into a bed of velvet.

He couldn't breathe.

The world swam. Colors shifted, and the dim light hurt. Everything hurt, the place where the Black Knight had stabbed him with the needle most of all.

"Uhhh."

He tried to scream, but only ghostly mumbles escaped.

The terrible reality of the situation settled in. He was OD'ing, dying right there in this old shitty hallway in this old shitty town. Someone would find him like this, choked to death on vomit. Another junkie statistic on the bad side of town.

"No."

He tried to sit up but only managed to push himself up a few feet before he fell back down. Surges of adrenaline coursed through him, only to be devoured by the White Lady and smothered in the same velvet casket as him.

His guts tied themselves into knots. It couldn't end like this. Anywhere but this shitty apartment that had become a microcosm of how wrong everything had gone.

He focused as hard as he could, lifting his arm and managing three weak knocks on the door in front of him. It barely made a sound. He didn't know if it was his apartment. He didn't know if what he was seeing was real anymore. He needed something. Someone. Anyone.

No answer. What a time for nobody to be home. He managed to raise his arm again but only got off two knocks, and that was all she wrote. He wouldn't go out with a bang or a whimper, just five soft knocks on a stranger's door and a throat full of vomit.

Maybe a better person would care, or maybe one not overdosing on heroin. It ended the same either way, didn't it? He settled back onto the floor. Whatever came after had to be better than this. He tried to say something, but every intake of breath was a sack of rice on his chest.

"Aaron?" Brian's voice on the far side of the door. Footsteps followed, and the door opened. Brian peeked his head around the corner before he noticed Aaron on the floor. "Jesus Christ, dude!" He knelt and moved to touch Aaron but stopped short. "What happened?"

He wanted to tell Brian he'd warned him. He tried to form the words, the explanation that would make him understand. He took another breath, but it wasn't enough. The lights grew dimmer.

"Holy fuck, man. Just hang on. Hang on!" He ran into the apartment and grabbed his phone from the couch.

Aaron watched in a passive daze. Unaffected. Uncaring as whatever dark angels belonged to him circled overhead to carry him away. Maybe those angels looked just like Aimee and Marie..

"I need an ambulance. My... Yes." He rattled off the address. "I think he's OD'd. Maybe he was attacked... I don't know! Yes, send the police! Just hurry!" He threw the phone down and rushed back over. Aaron had seen him scared before but never like this. Every time Dad had come to pick them up from Brian's house or the park, that same glint had been in the back of his eyes. Maybe fear, maybe just imagining what it would be like to be them. And after Aimee's death, his eyes had been red from crying. Aaron had pretended not to notice then. Now he couldn't look away.

"Just hold on, man." With a shaking hand, Brian tugged on something behind Aaron. An intense pain shot through his body, dulled by the drugs' sweet siren song. It didn't even register until he saw the huge syringe in Brian's hand, the one the Black Knight had stabbed him with.

Aaron struggled.

"Nughh."

He had to get that thing away. It couldn't be here, because if it was here, it was all real. And if it was all real, then Aimee was there. And there was something more. Some God who should have been watching out for them. Some stupid fucker in the sky who should have made sure they were okay, and that they had parents who loved them, and who made sure Aimee didn't die at sixteen. That meant everything was so much worse.

"Noough."

Tears ran down Aaron's face, and Brian's too as he held Aaron's hand. They could chalk that one up to God too. A guy who did everything right and still lost his two best friends. No more anxiety and nightmares. No more Drippy and Black Knight. No more voices in the dark. The iron taste of blood filled his mouth as he bit his tongue.

Brian wept openly. "Just hang on. Hang on! Help's coming."

Another door opened somewhere in the hallway, and a woman gasped.

The *woo-woo-woo* of the sirens rocked Aaron's addled brain. He groaned at the sudden change in scenery. The struggle to breath had ceased. More than ceased. The opera house was empty, and everyone but him had gone. Nothing made sense.

"Hurgh."

Nobody responded to his question. The acidic boil of panic ignited in his guts, the run or be eaten. He'd become trapped somewhere between the Kingdom and the real world.

And still, that White Lady pushed him back to the bed as he tried to open his eyes and failed twice. Traffic zoomed by going the other direction. He tried to get up, but the restraints on the stretcher held him fast.

A slit of vision appeared. No Kingdom and no shitty apartment. The setting for the latest horrors was an ambulance. A pretty woman, blond-haired and blue-eyed, worked over him, pulling drugs into a syringe and stabbing him with it.

"That did it," she said to someone in the front seat.

Aaron looked up to see the Black Knight driving the ambulance, Drippy next to him.

"Ser, we're gonna fix you right, up, down, and left. Fix this big bastard's big ugly mess." Drippy nodded at the Knight, who stared straight ahead as he drove.

Aaron thrashed against the restraints, and the woman above him, an Aimee in her twenties, pushed him back down.

"Just relax, Aaron. Aaron? Aaron, can you hear me?"

No, not Aimee. A pretty woman with a sad smile and eyes that had seen a lot of bad. No Black Knight and faithful servant in the front seat, just an old man in a black jacket looking over his shoulder as night passed by outside, sirens wailing.

But... It was quiet. No, not quiet. The sirens were gone, but people surrounded him. Some were yelling. He was naked.

"Noo. No more, please." His voice was thick with tears. He had to get away. He'd take Marie up on her offer and leave this wretched place, never looking back. He'd strike the name of Umber Gardens from his mind. Anything to make it stop. He tried to tell the woman above him, but the mask on his face prevented it. An old woman, one of several people working around him. Busy little bees doing their busy little dance. A man in the back shouted at them as Aaron cried on the table. As insane as it was, he wondered if they resented him for it. He wondered if the old nurses told their husbands and wives what a shitbag that doctor was. He would have laughed if he could breathe.

"A fool and his life are soon parted."

The Witch sat in the corner, talking to Mom. For Mom's part, she just nodded and took another puff off her smoke. Maybe it wasn't the Witch. Maybe it was Grandma.

Dad walked through the door, fists balled, his belt wrapped around one hand, buckle out. "Hospitals. You're a goddamn pussy! Did you cry, pussy? I bet you cried."

Aaron's eyes widened, and the machine next to him started beeping at a manic pace. The old woman grabbed him by the shoulders. "Mr. Vasilica, can you hear me? I need you to calm down."

Couldn't she see the monster of a man even now approaching? That hateful gleam in his eyes?

"Aaron, your brain was deprived of oxygen for a long time. Your heart stopped. Do you understand? You're very unwell. You're in the hospital."

She took the mask off him as he tried to explain what was happening. He attempted to back off the table, but a dozen hands prevented it. They held him down and worked faster, just like the ones who had pulled him out the door. These sterile monsters were no different. They'd take him away too, and they'd drug him until he didn't recognize himself in the mirror.

Dad took another step into the room. "You had this coming a long time, boy. A good long time."

311

Aaron screamed right into the old woman's face. She scowled at him, but he didn't have time for propriety. He had to make them understand.

"Don't you see them!" He tried to point at Mom and Grandma. Or maybe the Witch and the Bartender. Whenever he moved his hand, someone placed it back on the table. "You have to look!"

But the people in the room didn't heed him, didn't so much as look him in the eyes. Just vultures picking apart his corpse.

His mother spoke up. "Me and your dad are getting back together."

"*Nooo!*"

"We want you to live with us again. You'll have to. Nobody else will take care of you."

"I hate you! I hate you!" He spit into the face of the nurse above him.

She covered his mouth with the oxygen mask. "Get the restraints."

"We got your old room ready and everything. We're going to have another baby."

"*No!*" He screamed and raged, thrashed and spit. Nothing mattered. Nothing he did made the least bit of difference, now or ever.

"Maybe you'll take better care of your next sister than you did the last one."

He blinked.

When he opened his eyes again, they were all gone. Marie slept in a chair next to him.

He willed his body to jump off the bed and escape before he reappeared somewhere else. He was still in the Kingdom. He had to be. It was the only explanation for the utter madness all around him.

His body reacted with the speed and grace of a slug. Murmured words flowed from his mouth, and he couldn't raise his hand more than a foot before a restraint pulled it back down to the sheets.

He'd done this. All of it.

The soft beep of the machine next to him finally bled into his consciousness. The electric panic of the ambulance and the door step was gone, replaced by the calm only drugs could bring. The good kind of drug. The kind of addiction your doctor prescribed you to get you out the door so they could hook the next sucker. Medical smells—alcohol, sterile dressings, boiled clean sheets, and human sickness—assaulted his nose. The confusion settled down, slowly at first, then a little faster once he realized where he was.

The ambulance. The ER. Finding himself on his own doorstep with Brian over him. All remembered through the mother of fogs. The ultimate bender. Not only had he caught the dragon, but it had also flown his ass all over town.

The bags under Marie's eyes were deep and dark. Even asleep, she shifted and moaned.

"Marie?" He coughed after he spoke. His voice hurt as if he hadn't used it in a long time. "Marie." He said it with more force, but it left his mouth as weak as a ghost's whisper.

313

"Aaron?" The door opened, and Aimee walked in. Grown-up Aimee. The one with the kid and Brian living in her house.

Marie jerked awake as if she'd been slapped. Aimee ran to the side of the bed and grabbed Aaron's hand. "You're almost awake."

No. Every time he'd seen her in the last week, something terrible had followed. It had to stop. "No. No more." But the bed held him fast, and Aimee wouldn't let go. "Just let me die. Please?"

"Aaron?" Marie held his other hand. "It's okay, baby. I'm here."

The socially acceptable hospital drugs slowed him. For a moment, Aimee and Marie became one, though they looked nothing alike.

"You're okay, Aaron." Aimee stared down at him with his own eyes, giving him the same expression she had when he couldn't leave the house for weeks. The one that described all the things they'd silently promised never to talk about again. Pity. Commiseration. Love. Love most of all.

Marie squeezed him as tears fell down her face. "I'm going to take care of you. Do you know where you are?"

Tears fell down his face. "I'm in hell. I'm in hell and it's my fault. It's because I killed you. You're dead, and it's all my fault."

Aimee glanced across the bed at Marie, but she wasn't there anymore. It was just the two of them, like it had always been until he left.

"I'm so sorry, Aims. I'm sorry you never got to have your baby." Snot ran down his face. He didn't care how shameful it was or who could see. "I'm sorry you never got to marry Brian. I shouldn't have left you all alone. I shouldn't have made you go through it by yourself."

"Shh." She stroked his hair and wiped a tear from his eye. "It's not your fault, Aaron. I should have been stronger. I should have held on a little longer. I'm so sorry. I'm sorry it all turned out like this."

"I miss you so much. It hurts every day." He sucked in a deep breath. "I don't want to do this anymore. I don't want to keep being away from you. You're the best friend I ever had." He closed his eyes, shutting out the tears. "I can't go on without you anymore. Please, forgive me. Please."

Her gentle voice surrounded him. "There's nothing to forgive, but you have to let go. You have to learn to be okay with yourself again. All that anger, all the things you hide behind, they aren't helping. They're going to kill you." Her voice cracked. "Please, don't go back."

He shook his head. The drugs turned it into an ordeal, trying to pull him back to the pillow. "No." Anger burned inside him, the same hate he'd always had. The one he'd gotten from Mom and Dad, who'd probably gotten it from theirs. The certainty that every bad thing ever said about him was right. "I'm going to get you out of there. I know where you are now. I can get you."

The world shook. "Just let go, Aaron." Her last words were a whisper.

"Aaron?" Marie's voice chased Aimee's ghost away. "Aaron, wake up, baby."

He struggled, but the bed held him fast. "Leave me alone and let me see my sister one more time." Tears kept falling as he opened his eyes. Gone again. Left. His fault. Always his fault.

"It's okay." Marie cradled his head to her chest as he wept. "It's all going to be okay."

Chapter 30

Two hours passed before he believed he was awake and in the real world. Even then, he had his doubts. A stream of nurses and doctors rushed in and out the door, but every time it opened, he expected fog monsters, candle men, evil knights, or even more evil parents. By the time Marie walked back in after stepping out to call Brian, he finally felt something like himself again.

She glanced at him tentatively, the way someone might eye a grumpy stranger, not a longtime lover. "Brian's on his way. He's going to grab a few things and come by."

She might have always looked at him like that. He might have deserved it. As he stared at the ceiling, there was no certainty in anything, and it didn't matter. Not really.

"I'm fine." Already the wheels were back in motion. Aimee was in the Kingdom, sure as the sun would rise tomorrow. And Brian had been there when something had ripped Aaron out of the apartment. He'd seen that syringe and the return to Earth. He had to accept something was happening, and that meant Aaron had someone in his corner.

But doubt nagged him until he huffed and rolled onto his side. Brian had seen it with his own two eyes. No shitty looks that suggested Aaron had lost his mind. No comments about rehab or a new life. But Brian had never been one to leap in for a friend, and without Brian... Could he do it alone?

"Baby, you okay?" Marie placed a hand on his shoulder before running it down to his hand. Gentle mist after a morning rain. No sign of the angry woman who'd stored out of the intervention... only days before? It felt like forever. But she would never believe that he needed to find Aimee.

Marie squeezed his hand. "Will you look at me, please?"

He turned his head, staring through her as if she weren't there.

"I can't lose you. I don't know what I'd do if something happened to you."

"I'm all right." He thought of the million ways he could tell her about it all. *A secret Kingdom in the woods where my childhood was turned into a nightmare.* Or maybe... *It's like Disneyworld if Walt had been on acid instead of just a Nazi.* But she wouldn't believe a word of it. He knew exactly what she'd say too. *Are you fucking high?* And it would be a valid question, because he'd been high or drunk as often as not in the years he'd known her. He'd been high as long as she'd known him.

She was still here.

He grunted and wiped his eyes with his hands.

"Do you need some water?"

"No, babe. I'm fine."

Brian knew. That would be the confirmation he needed. He would go back one more time. Brian would understand if he told him Aimee was there, some part of her trapped in a nightmare. Even if she didn't want to be saved. *Let it go.* How? Why? What did that even mean? He owed Aimee the saving of her soul. It was the least he could do after taking her life.

Marie didn't see the missiles launched in his internal war, and she continued as if there were peace across the continent of Aaron. "We can go away. I'll call my boss right now and say I want to transfer to Seattle or Kuttawa. We can be there in two weeks."

"Marie."

"There are treatment places there. We can get you in and get you taken care of."

"Marie."

She kept talking over him, drowning out the objections that would follow. "Tacoma is amazing. My parents have that place in town. We'd spend every other summer there visiting my grandparents—"

"I'm not going anywhere. This is my home. I grew up here. I'm not leaving."

Her mouth opened once, twice, and the third time was the charm. "So what are you going to do? Are you going to go to rehab or not?" The soothing tone vanished, replaced by the one that always charged out before harsh words.

319

"Marie, listen. I—"

"No, you listen!" And there was the temper. "You almost died. Your brain went without oxygen for five minutes. Five damn minutes!"

"I'm fine."

"No, you fucking overdosed. I know you don't want to hear it, but you have a problem. I'm not going to sit around and watch you kill yourself."

And there was the perfect opening. *Follow the fucking exit signs then.* Or maybe, *Don't let the door hit you where the good lord split you.* But he kept them to himself. Too tired. Too much bad already going around. Too much doubt and self-loathing. If she wanted to think he was just a crazy junkie, so be it. Brian would know the truth.

Her tears began. His were spent. He'd cried more in the last few hours than he had in his whole life. That was done. He had a mission. Aimee was hidden away somewhere, and he would find her.

But even if Marie knew that, she wouldn't understand. "You're the only person I've ever loved. I'll die if something happens to you." Dramatics. Always with the dramatics.

"Marie…"

"I mean it. Please. Let me help you."

Even as he sat in that bed, he wanted to fix. He wanted to get going already. Go back and find some way into that castle. He was scared too. Of course scared. But when had being stupid and scared ever stopped him?

But watching her cry, just like Aimee…

"You think things have gotten that bad?"

She pulled away and sneered—almost snarled—at him. "We're sitting in a hospital room post-overdose. Yes, things have gotten that bad."

He stared out the door as nurses and other harried staff walked by. They must have thought him a junkie too. The old nurse in the ER as well. Had he really spit on her?

"If I stopped using, would you get off my case?"

"What?"

"If I told you I wasn't going to use anymore. Would you believe me?"

The tears stopped. She gave him the look he'd seen a thousand times, not so different from Aimee's before she decided to be snobby. Eyebrows up, neck back, and that sparkle in their eyes like they wanted so badly to believe but knew better. Both of them could smell his bullshit from a mile away. "Go to rehab. Go and get better."

"I'm not going to rehab."

She threw her hands in the air. "So what? You just up and quit cold turkey after all this time?"

He shook his head. "Give me one week."

"Oh my god." She buried her face in her hands.

"Give me one week to sort out what I need to sort out, then I'm done."

"You are so full of shit."

"Have I ever lied to you?"

She wiped her mouth and barked a humorless laugh. "Only lies of omission. Exactly like this crap. There's always some workaround. 'Heroin doesn't count. I only drink socially. I sell pot to pay the bills.'"

She wanted to bait him into a fight, but he wouldn't have it. "Believe me or don't; I'm not going to rehab either way." He wasn't sure if he believed himself. Even now, especially now, he didn't see why they couldn't just let him be him. But hadn't Aimee said it too? Hadn't she told him to let go?

"I just don't believe—"

Brian knocked on the doorframe before stepping in. "Bad time?"

Aaron covered his eyes. He couldn't deal with this. Not now, not ever. "Never a good one."

Marie scoffed.

"I grabbed a book from your place." Brian tossed *The Shining* onto the stand by the bed. "Just in case you were in here a while. Got your toothbrush and a few other things too." He threw the bag on the floor and sat in the same chair phantom Aimee had occupied a few hours before.

"Maybe you can talk some sense into him."

Brian put his hands in the air, a man held at gunpoint and robbed of his good will by his best friend. "Not involved."

Marie's jaw dropped. "Are you kidding me? After everything that's happened, that's your response?"

"Look. If he wants to kill himself, he's welcome to. I've always done everything I can for him, and that's all anyone can ask."

The words were a splash of cold water. "I'm sitting right here!"

"Yes, I know. And I need you to hear it."

Marie stood, knocking her chair against the wall with a bang. "You're a cold bastard, Brian."

"It is what it is. I've thought a lot about this, and I'm not going to get on his case. He's a grown man. He can do what he wants."

The words hurt more than Aaron could admit aloud. Brian had given up. After everything, he'd really given up. "Can I talk to Brian alone please?"

Brian shook his head. "Nothing to talk about."

Fuming, Marie shifted her gaze from Aaron to Brian and back again. "What? That's what I get after coming here and sitting with you all day?"

Aaron's patience vanished. "Marie, get the fuck out."

She froze, an expression of rage plastered across her face. Without a word, she walked out. And for the first time in a long time, his little barbs at her cut him too. He opened his mouth to call out to her, but she had already slammed the door.

Boom!

323

Brian watched her go too. Dispassionate. Disconnected. The perfect Buddhist monk, looking at it all with an impassive eye.

Aaron spoke up as soon as the door closed. "What the fuck, man?"

Brian closed his eyes as if he were barely tolerating an insolent child. "I don't know what else to do. Do you have any idea how bad you scared me when you just vanished? When I found you with that big-ass needle in your back? How did you do that?"

Aaron's mouth went dry. Brian didn't believe any of it. "I told you what's been happening. The Black Knight that is ruining the Kingdom, he—"

"You ran out of the apartment. I came out of the bedroom and you were gone, the front door wide open. I looked everywhere for you. Your car was still there, but you weren't. Poof, puff of smoke. I thought you were fucking with me for the first few hours." He clenched his jaw. "And you know what? I don't owe you an explanation. We had a deal. Either you stick with it or you don't. I can't do anything else for you."

The drugs didn't do shit to slow Aaron's temper. "We did have a deal. You're going to tell me you didn't hear the laughing or see what happened?"

Brian paused mid-breath, gazing into the middle distance. "Yeah. Like I said, I thought you were fucking with me."

Aaron tried to throw his hands in the air before the restraints stopped him. "What the absolute fuck, man? If you aren't going to even try and see anything, how do you ever expect to actually see it?"

Brian's jaw set once more, his eyes disinterested. The patented "fuck you" without saying "fuck you" look he wore so well.

"So that's it? No questions? No wondering what the noises were? No wondering why I'd have a fuckin' syringe bigger than my dick?"

"I'm done. I'm not doing it anymore. You either get help or you don't. I've done everything I can for you."

Aaron nearly jumped out of bed. "Aimee is there! He has her!"

For the first time, real anger crept into Brian's voice. "Do you even hear yourself? She's dead. Gone. She has been for years. It's all in your head." But maybe nothing ever really died. He'd been elsewhere, some pocket reality where magic and monsters roamed free. None of them could see it, but that didn't make it any less real. If he was on his own, so be it. That wasn't new. "Fine. Get out."

Without a word, Brian did as Aaron said. No last look. No final comment. Nothing like the heartfelt parting of best friends in the movies.

Marie returned as he left, watching him go as if it were business as usual. "Are you done screaming?"

Aaron lay back down.

"They won't keep you here, and they won't refer you to a rehab facility. They need your consent."

He didn't respond. Nothing left to say. One more time, maybe two. He'd be able to find Aimee again and tell her all the things he never got the chance to.

"I can't babysit you all the time, but I want to come back to the apartment."

That snapped him out of his thoughts. "Why? So you can ride my case?"

She took a deep breath, ready to let him have it. Instead, she blew it out slowly, staring at him with the victim expression she had perfected over the years. "One week?"

It didn't register. "What?"

"You said one week, and you'd be done. No more heroin. No more nothing, right?"

"I have something I need to do. Once that's done…" Take the plunge. Now or never. "I'll quit. All of it. If I can't do it on my own, I'll go to rehab."

She stared at him, weighing his words. To believe or not to believe. A truthful attempt to make life better, or Tinkerbell sprinkling bullshit dust on more lies? More drama, heartache, and everything they didn't need.

"Okay," she whispered.

"No questions, either. I can't explain it, and I don't want to try."

She looked at the floor. "Are you… Will there be more drugs?"

"No questions."

"Because I won't sit around and watch you kill yourself."

Almost the same words Brian had spoken, and maybe they were right. It *had* gone too far, but the stakes were higher too. It didn't change the fact that there was some problem he couldn't see. A giant monster loomed over him, so big he had mistaken its shadow for night. This wasn't any way to live. He didn't want to die in a hospital bed, and he didn't want to die alone.

Once he found Aimee, that would be the end. The real end. No more bullshit. No more excuses.

Just one more week.

Chapter 31

He couldn't get out of there fast enough. Marie had tried to have him committed. He could see it in the nurses' glances, the way they whispered in the halls as they walked by. He could almost hear it.

Might have tried to kill himself.

Crazy, you know.

It's always the handsome ones.

He never asked her about it, even though she visited often during the two days he was cooped up. Doting over him while trying to make him comfortable. More aggravating, talking to him when he didn't want to talk back.

His mind reeled over the last week and its existential implications. The craving for junk reappeared, stronger than he remembered it ever being. Itching and sighing. Scratching inside his veins and climbing up the walls, knowing it would be a few days before he could give in and that it might be the last time.

He wanted to believe he was scared because of what he might find when he used. The ideas kept him up in the darkest watches of the night wondering if he could die there. But he had to know. And did he want to go as well? Was that what the feeling was?

As he walked to Marie's car two days later, wearing clothes she'd brought from the apartment, he wasn't sure. That scared him more than anything.

"I've moved some of my stuff in. You don't mind, do you?"

He shook his head. He wasn't there. His gaze locked onto something miles or universes away, wherever the Kingdom was.

"I cleaned too. It stank like shit in there. It still kinda does. That carpet hadn't been cleaned in years."

She'd never cleaned when she lived there. He could see what she was doing as clear as day. The quiet places where tender moments were supposed to grow had been loud and raucous as long as they'd known each other, irascible piece of trash that he was. So she filled in the spaces where the silence might creep out and bite her. Always trying to batten down the hatches before the storm moved in.

"I got us dinner. Cleaned up your closet."

He stopped with his hand on the top of the car. "Did you touch any of my stuff?"

She froze halfway into the car. The deer in the headlights look that followed stank worse than his apartment ever had. "I mean, I cleaned."

He pursed his lips. "Did you throw out my stash, Marie?" If she had, she could blow. He didn't need this shit, least of all now. His blood pressure rose at the thought of her finding his rig where Brian had almost certainly left it and throwing it out. He had shit to do and places to be.

She looked away. "No, I…I put it away. But I wanted to. I sat on the couch for an hour just staring at it. I wanted to throw it away and watch it burn in a landfill. I hate what it's done to you."

"Don't."

He couldn't remember her ever looking more pathetic as she blinked for longer than normal and sat in the car. "I won't." It tugged at his heart in a way it never had before. "Just remember your promise."

He stared at the hospital as they drove away, gazing into his own eyes as much as the million windows. He'd never thanked any of the doctors or nurses for helping him. Besides checking on him and getting him to sign paperwork confirming he'd be poor forever, they'd barely spoken to him, but they'd also saved his life. He couldn't remember the last time he'd said thank you to anyone.

It didn't sit right after the last few weeks. What had the Witch said? There was something more behind it all. Things had to change.

"Thanks."

Marie glanced at him. "For what?"

"For coming out here after everything. I know I haven't been easy to be around, and the last few years have been…" He groped for the right word. Had it been hard? Had he been terrible? Had taking care of himself been more important than anyone else? "Have been tough."

Nobody really looked out for other people. They did things because they wanted something. You loved your kids so they would love you back. You took care of other people so they would take care of you. People held the doors for one another because they wanted doors held for them.

Still, Marie was there. Even when Brian had quit the team, she was still catching shit for him.

She shifted in her seat. "You'd do it for me."

Would I?

"But if you really wanted to say you're sorry, you wouldn't wait to quit. You'd do it today. Right now. You'd tell me you'll never touch that shit again."

He stared out the window at the cloudless sky. Just like her. Keep pushing. Cover just a little more ground. "I have to do this."

She drew in a sharp breath, as if getting ready to start the good ol' fight all over again. Instead, she blew it out and let the quiet settle in for a second, but only a second. "You don't. You can just let it go. We have a free pass. We can leave all of this shit behind."

Her words mirrored Aimee's. *Just let it go.* How anyone ever did was beyond him. "It's not open for discussion."

But wasn't it?

"Aaron—"

"Don't."

And she didn't. She let it hang out there. There was no sullen silence, and no punishing him with passive-aggressive bullshit. Just acceptance. Something he could never have.

331

By the time they reached the apartment, neither had spoken for nearly thirty minutes. He looked up at the wreck of a place he called home as she grabbed his bag from the back seat. The dead grass, the smokestacks across the highway, and the tang of human depravity in the air. It felt more miserable than he ever recalled, exactly the kind of place you'd find a half dead junkie in a stairwell. Now that someone had, maybe they could put a fucking plaque up.

"Good job picking a place without an elevator, by the way," she said as she walked into the building.

The hopelessness of the place didn't affect her. Why would it? It was *his* doing, and he was the asshole still coming back here every day. She'd moved on.

Maybe she had a point. He could give it all up now and be done with it, do like Aimee said and let it all go. He expected doubts to assail him once inside, reasons to keep using, to keep trying to catch that dragon. They didn't.

She helped him up the stairs. He'd been woozy since the incident. Drugs aside, he couldn't stand for long. The doctor told him it would pass with time. Unfortunate complication of his *problem*, as the man had ever so delicately said. *His problem.*

She really had cleaned the place. He couldn't remember the last time the carpet looked like something approaching white. The stale reek of an unwashed human with a total disregard for self-preservation still hung in the air. The metal taste of the factory smoke clouded everything, but less than before.

It just didn't look like home anymore.

"Frozen pizza in the fridge. We can order out if you want. I have the money." She had always had the money between the two of them, and she never hung it over his head. One more thing he'd never thanked her for.

"That'll be fine." He slowly lowered himself onto the couch, afraid the dizziness might knock him on his ass if he did it all at once. "I don't remember the last time there was food in the house."

"There's a shocker."

He lit a cigarette. Three or so days without them had been torture. After binging for the better part of a month, three days without smack had been ugly too. Ugly and climbing.

A fucking month. He paused with his smoke halfway to his lips. His leg shook as he thought about it. Give one of those assholes on Broad Street a few thousand dollars and that's exactly what they would do. Rent a room and get their fill. They might even skip the rent-a-room part and just do it right there on the street. More money for junk, or maybe some of Aaron's pot to help take the edge off the come down.

But he wasn't like them.

"It's pepperoni. Is that all right?"

"It's fine." The ashes from his Marlboro fell onto the couch.

Let it go, Aimee had said. The real Aimee, or at least the Aimee he imagined she might have been one day. But how? How did people go on after that, even years later? It was giving up. People moved on because they stopped caring. They killed their favorite friends and family twice when they did, as sure as if they held the gun themselves.

And if they had that chance to save them, wouldn't they?

Marie stared at him. "Are you all right?"

The cigarette in his hand had burnt away to nothing. He flung the ashes off. "I'm fine."

She didn't have to follow it up. *Let's go. Let's get the hell away from here.* She said it all in that almost-hurt glance.

They washed the pizza down with plenty of water as per the doctor's orders. TV filled the silence until they both had enough, and then it was off to bed. It had been a long time since she'd stayed over, but it was still as familiar as breathing. One leg curled up, the other straight down. One hand under her pillow, the other at his side.

She was out within minutes, probably exhausted from dealing with his shit. But no matter how tired he was, sleep wouldn't come. His doubts wouldn't relent. The questions and the countless voices that asked them wouldn't cease.

He had his validations. But if Aimee could visit him in his sleep, if it really had been her, did she need saving? Shouldn't he just save himself?

No sooner had the question entered his mind than the closet creaked in the corner of the room. Just a little one. Maybe a finger cracking it open so something could peek in.

He sat up as the hair on his neck rose, his vision blurring from the sudden movement. The light from outside barely penetrated the gloom. Shadows washed everything in black, leaving hints for the imagination to turn into horrors. He eyed every corner of the room, staring into the blackness until stalking shapes of monsters and madmen became dresser drawers and baskets full of clean clothes. Panic, dull and lifeless after so much fear, pinged up and down, up and down.

And it was just that. Imagination. Nothing else. Old building. Old closet.

As he lay back down, he heard, "Ser," somewhere far away. Distant but unmistakable.

"No. Not tonight. I'm not doing it."

"Ser, help." Drippy. His loyal friend. "Please, ser, don't leave us."

Aaron grabbed Marie's arm and shook her, trying to be discreet in doing so. Get her up. Let her see and hear this for herself.

That quiet, out-of-the-way panic began to stretch outward, repainting the nightmares into the corners and cracks of the room.

"Fuck. Fuck." Aaron rubbed his eyes with his palms. Not now. He couldn't even run away now.

"He'll hear me soon. I need, need, need you to come and help."

"Marie. Marie!" No stealth. He shook her with both hands, but she didn't stir.

The closet door slid open further, and the chill seeped into his bones. The growling that had rumbled under the earth on the lonely hill in the Kingdom filled the room. "Well, well, well. Not so regal out here in this world, are we?"

"Help, ser!"

He stared at the closet as it opened further. These things from another world were invading his, and if they could hurt him, they could hurt Marie.

"No, not so tough at all now. No witches to save you from yourself. No little candles to mouth off. I told you I'd find you."

The lamp on his nightstand rattled, and his teeth chattered. "You aren't here. You aren't…" But he no longer doubted its reality.

It laughed, and he caught the barest glimmer of teeth in the dark. "Oh yes, you know now, don't you? Can't unsee the things you've seen, can you? Down the rabbit hole, little manling."

"Get out!" His words possessed power, or they *had*. He had cast it away. "Get out now!" But there was no power in his proclamation, only a wavering voice and fear so ripe he smelled it.

The laughter circled him. "You've no authority here. Just another piece of meat. This isn't your kingdom. You can't even lick the boots of the people who command *this* place."

"*Ser!*" Drippy's voice fell away, and a slam shook the apartment.

The growling tapered off as something stomped toward the bedroom door from the living room, each vibration shaking his bowels.

"Ooh, you're in for it now. The king is dead; long live the king." A cackle echoed then vanished abruptly, but the walls continued to tremble. Something drew closer.

The lamp vibrated against the stand with each thud as the neighbor above screamed at him. Aaron pulled himself up, bringing

336

his knees to his chest and the blanket with them. Too weak to fight but too scared to run. Mist poured through the edges of the window. Red light rained in from outside. The beams from the sky, the Black Knight's searchlights. The lamp fell and broke apart on the floor.

The door bashed into the wall and rocked the apartment. A figure cloaked in black stood in the frame, still and cruel. The sirens wailed, a terrible prelude to terrible things. That thing, that Black Knight that shattered every piece of his past, had come.

"I told you I would watch you die."

He took one step forward, and the apartment quaked again.

Aaron screamed as everything went dark.

Chapter 32

"Aaron."

Gut-ripping panic seized him. He shouted and swung, his eyes still closed. His fist connected with the side of a head. A monster, a thing from the Kingdom here to carry him away.

Something crashed to the floor, followed by Marie gasping.

He opened his eyes, and nothing made sense. The light pouring in wasn't the sign of a beautiful Sunday morning; it was a trick or a drug. Marie, lying on her back, stared up at him. That wasn't real either. Kingdoms and dead sisters, perhaps, but the earth-shattering calamity of him striking the woman he loved?

He blinked twice before it registered. She held her jaw. They both stood still as stone, trying to grasp the enormity of what had happened.

She spoke first. "It's fine."

The dream from the night before fell away, and the guilt replaced panic, and he threw the covers off. "Marie! Oh my god!"

He climbed out of bed, and a piece of the broken lamp lodged in his foot. "Fuck!"

She shook her head and looked from him to the glass on the floor. "No, really. I shouldn't have startled you… When did that happen?"

He'd hit her. The blood on the carpet, the open doors, and the shattered lamp he barely noticed. He'd punched her right in the goddamn head. Just like Dad.

Just like Dad.

"It's okay. You didn't mean it."

Just one more incident in a long line of treating her badly.

Just like Dad.

"I'm going to go get ready for work. Really. It's fine." She stood up and kissed his cheek before walking out of the room as if nothing had happened.

He watched the creeping spread of red on the almost-white carpet, broken glass scattered across the floor. A normal person would get a tetanus shot. Or more likely, a normal person would vacuum more than once every year or two. The whole place stank of shit, and not just the kind that fell out of an ass. It smelled of the kind of shit who punched his lover and subjected his friends to emotional waterboarding.

And the worst part was that it couldn't be over yet. He glanced at the closet, and despite the sun coming through the window, his butt puckered. They'd been here to take him away last night. A little hand of the Kingdom had reached out to grab him and pull him back. Drippy had begged for his help.

Would life be like that forever if he just walked away?

And by god, he'd hit her. After everything else he'd done, he finally crossed that line.

That stank like shit too. He'd crossed that line years ago. He'd been the one to declare war on life when it hadn't gone his way, and he'd dragged her down with him every step of the way. And she stayed, because she was either wonderful or fucking stupid, maybe both. What was punching her in the head by accident when he'd been raining blows on her for years?

He pulled a chunk of glass out of his foot, throwing it at the wall. Tiny splotches of red dotted the paint where it struck. He threw the next piece even harder. Everything hurt. His head, his body, and most of all his shoulder where that needle had dug in. He wanted to get wasted. It was a goddamn cure-all for anything that ailed you, no matter what anyone said. It was a Band-Aid on a bullet wound but better than nothing. A couple beers? A little weed? Fine. But heroin? That took you places. That shit made you a fucking star.

Maybe that was the only way to stop it all.

He pulled open the drawer on his nightstand. True to her word, Marie had put everything from the living room with the rest of his stuff in the drawer. His little treasures. Right on top was the bag of junk he'd use for the next few weeks.

Or maybe the next week, then done, like he'd said.

Or maybe not at all.

His leg shook as he rubbed his face. The thought of not using jolted his stomach and made his chest ache. Even the thought of it made it harder to breathe, as if the walls had closed in. They'd been closing in for a long time now. Maybe since those days when he'd been dumb enough to believe he could have a normal family and a normal life. Or perhaps only since he'd discovered heroin could cure him of those delusions.

The results would be the same either way. Those walls would close in, those stomach cramps would kill him, and he'd die choking on his own vomit, heroin or no.

Marie called to him from the kitchen. He shook away the thoughts, blinking twice when he saw the walls right where they'd been before. He closed the treasure chest behind him before joining her.

"I'm heading out. Are you going to be all right?"

She'd mentioned taking the day off, but he wanted to be alone. Needed to be, really. "I'll be fine." He couldn't meet her eyes.

"It's okay, really. It was an accident. I know that." She kissed him. "It's going to be fine."

But nothing would ever be fine. It never had been. Not since the day the snake sold some dude's wife an apple just before their kids clubbed one another to death. The smile she gave him felt as weak as the promise.

She left without looking back, and the building's quiet set in immediately. Across the street the *beep, beep, beep* of trucks backing up filled the silence. The *booms* as people unloaded freight.

341

The blaring horns from the highway that often drowned out the TV filled the absence left by her going. And still, it felt too quiet as his guts rioted in waves and sudden nausea nearly overcame him.

He tried not to think of the stash as he gazed anywhere but the bedroom. The TV. The window. His shaking hands. Finally, he glanced back to his treasure chest. He had to finish this. If he didn't go back now, if he didn't try to find Aimee and at least attempt to make things right in the Kingdom, he'd always wonder. Either that or it would keep bleeding into the world until it finally drove him mad.

He wasn't shivering because he was jonesing for a fix.

Or was it?

"It's not." But his denial didn't stop him from going in and pulling out his gear.

Big, stinking fear oozed out of him, covering the apartment in its stink; the kind a person saw as an oncoming trucker made eye contact before the collision. The terror before oblivion. He'd almost died last time.

It didn't take him long to fix up his hit. He made all of it. A total waste of supply, but he had to do something. He'd rip the fucking syringe open and drink the shit. Junkies did that.

"I'm not a fucking junkie," he mumbled as he worked. Keeping his hands occupied. Running out the clock and hoping some heroic thought would save him from what he was about to do.

He stared at the syringes laid out on the table when he finished. Enough to stay well supplied for a good long while. Enough to get him to the Kingdom right now. Enough to fucking kill himself if that's what needed to happen.

But he wouldn't. He couldn't, not until he made it back to that throne room. Because if she was there...

He glanced at the picture of him and Aimee by the old trees—a snapshot of what might have been, taken in better times. And he would have done *anything* for her. He would have killed for her. And instead, he'd killed her like the dumb, selfish shit that he was.

Hot tears ran down his face. "Not this time, Aims." The picture couldn't hear him, but he spoke as if it could. "I'm going to set you free from that nightmare just like I should have done with the one we grew up in." He sniffled, staring despite the water blurring his eyes. "I'm going to save you whether you want me to or not. Because you'd..." He swallowed as his voice broke. "You'd do the same for me."

His guts rumbled as he glanced down at the golden keys in front of him. However many it took, then he'd be free. Once the two of them were reunited, he would never use it again. Maybe he'd be dead, and he wouldn't have to anyway.

He caught sight of Marie's things stacked neatly in the corner. Fastidious to a fault. Always put together just so, even for a man who would kill himself and kill her with him.

Just the way Aimee's death had killed him—the real, honest him.

He wiped his eyes on his sleeve. Aimee needed him, and Marie would understand when he explained it to her one day.

343

This time, however, he would go smart. He waited for the crying to stop and his eyes to dry before putting his shoes on. His resolve hardened as he grabbed a knife from the kitchen. It might not do anything against the Black Knight, but it was better than going in like an unshod jackass. Not on this last trip to save his sister. His sword a kitchen knife, his steed made by Nike. He couldn't write it better himself.

He sat down and tied off the band on his arm. Leaning back, he slipped a syringe into himself, injected, and threw it on the floor. Marie would understand if she knew. Aimee wouldn't have told him to let it go if she knew they'd chase after him.

He closed his eyes. No nightmare journey this time. He wouldn't look. Whatever angry god or fucked-up demon loved to torture him could wait until he landed to get their jollies this time.

The gold candy that wiped away memories of monsters in the closet and dead sisters set to work. He fell a little deeper into himself, to a happy place in the back of his mind. Still, anxiety had its foot in the door, as if the world was all happy rainbows but a homeless dude was pissing on one in the corner.

It didn't get better when the bedroom closet squeaked open.

He tapped the arm of the couch. The serenity of being blitzed disappeared in a puff of smoke. All that remained was the loss of control, that feeling of otherness in his own body.

"Fuck," he whispered.

Something skittered in the room, the sound of a dog on the kitchen tile, followed by laughter on the other side of the apartment. The jingle of little voices *tee-hee-heeing* from somewhere nearby.

What would he see if he looked? Dead eyes staring back at him? Scattered pieces of villagers? The Black Knight?

Sweat beaded on his forehead. His throat clicked as he tried to swallow and found a desert in his mouth.

"Fuck."

A sudden, deafening silence took hold.

Aaron jumped out of his skin and screamed as a cannonball struck the floor behind the couch, making a hole where his apartment had once been. He screamed over the boom but held his eyes shut tight. Not this time. He knew what it was now; he just had to hold on.

The world shook, and the couch slid back. He nearly fled to save himself, his leg twitching. But there was more than him at stake. He stayed put, butt in seat, as the couch slid slowly at first, then all at once. He gripped the butcher knife for dear life.

The black, hungry place between worlds opened its mouth and sucked him in. The sensation that had become so familiar over the last week took over, as if he'd left his body behind and a physical manifestation of his soul was being hurled through a hateful void. He sat on his shitty old sofa as it plummeted through inscrutable fathoms of nothing, his stomach flipping with it. He couldn't breathe, but he didn't need to. Up was down. Left was right. Reason and knowing unraveled into something and being elsewhere. Two times two took him to the drinking fountain, and his stomach screamed at him while it ran away with the spoon and the cow jumping over the moon.

And still, even as the couch tumbled end over end, he stayed where he was. He finally opened his eyes, but it made no difference. Black on black, darkness on darkness.

And still it flipped, over and over. Would it crush him if it landed wrong? Break his neck in ten places? Would Marie find him like that on the floor of the apartment and wonder what happened?

Cold anxiety exploded in his stomach, now back in his body. "Oh fuck, oh fuck." He wasn't floating through nothing; he was falling now.

He shouldn't have come back. What if he never found his way home? What if he spent eternity spinning through nothing, moving but never arriving? Could he cut his wrists to escape a fate like that?

"Fuck, fuck, fuck."

The air in the void tasted of burning metal, but the flavor of smoke and decay whispered across his tongue. The atmosphere changed, and for the first time, he heard the noise of the wind.

The Kingdom rushed up toward him from below.

"Fuck!" He grabbed onto the couch for dear life, squeezing his eyes closed and waiting for the splat.

Wind rustled leaves around him, and the air stopped whistling by. The sour rot of vegetation left in the sun forever and ever replaced the metallic taste of the void.

When he looked again, the drawbridge to the castle lay open, the Kingdom's sky as barren as ever. Still gasping for breath, he glanced at the couch under him, then at the forest behind. White mist snaked around the trees, but there were no tidal waves of the stuff as there had been last time.

The churning in his guts worsened. He'd arrived.

Chapter 33

Without Drippy to greet him, the desolation became palpable. This had been a good place. This had been his. He stared at the castle where he and Aimee had once ruled. The place where she was still lingering, somehow. A million eyes watched him from arrow slits and ramparts, sending the junkie bugs crawling across his too-cold flesh. The open drawbridge beckoned him forward to crash upon its unseen defenders. But there was nothing there, nothing real. No Black Knight, no monsters, no anything. Just the aftermath of dreams gone bad and a slab of stone looming over him. He sucked in a deep breath, calmer.

So be it. He'd made the plunge, and there was nothing to do now but take the steps. He walked across the ground separating the forest from the walls. His shoe hit the wooden drawbridge but made no sound. The knife was gone too. He patted his pants and looked back to where the couch had been, but it had vanished as well.

He ran a hand through his hair as he turned back around. It wouldn't let him cheat. This was some grand cosmic game, not a real place.

The castle doors were a dark wood he hadn't seen before, and as thick as stone. Aimee had once asked Drippy if an army could break them down. "What if another kingdom attacks?"

Drippy fell to the ground and rolled with laughter. "What other kingdoms?"

Aimee did not approve of mockery. "We hear about war all the time where we're from. What if it happens here?"

Drippy sat up and cocked his head, considering her. "There are no other armies. Well, really, there are no armies at all. Whatever would you need one of those for?"

The question struck Aimee dumb. Aaron, who sat nearby, was equally put off. Why would they need one? Why did anyone? Back when things had been bright here, they hadn't. Would things have been different if they had imagined themselves an army to take care of this place?

Someone had etched words into the dark wood in the years since he'd been here last. Jagged and uneven, they looked as if they'd been scrapped there with a stone, not a knife.

> *Betwixt the shadows, lie all that's seen,*
> *all the things that shimmer and gleam.*
> *They stay and wonder for a time,*
> *'Til in the end, all things die.*

An involuntary shiver that had nothing to do with the cold ran through him. He reached out to touch them when the entire portal shuddered, raining dust from the stone arches above. With the heavy creak of wood and a sigh, the doors swung outward. A gust of arctic air washed over him, and the castle's all-consuming mouth gaped open. One long hallway appeared, lit with low, burning torches. It vanished into shadow far, far away. Once-grand furnishings lay broken on the floor. Where once it had been filled with wonder and possibility, now it had the air of a morgue—quiet and sullen, filled with things better left unseen.

It was too late to go back. Whatever had done this still waited inside. He stared down at the hands of a junkie, the same ones that had once held Aimee's hands as they found this place. He stepped inside with his head held high, trying to feel a pride he hadn't since he was a boy.

The doors slammed behind him as some part of him knew they would. The air of finality chilled him further, and its boom carried down the hall. His breath hung in clouds as soon as he passed the threshold. He held himself as goose flesh puckered his arms.

But the cold didn't bite as hard as the memories that superimposed themselves over the world. Aimee ran past, Aaron just behind, as they had the first time they'd visited.

"Is there a throne?" Aimee clapped and giggled as she sped down the hall.

Drippy skipped in behind them. "Two, actually, one for each. Twin thrones for the twin rulers."

Aaron approached with more caution, watching every corner. They'd taken the trip and trusted strangers like they'd always been told not to, but how could they not? This was magic.

"And from that throne you can do as you please! Why, I daresay everyone here has been waiting for you, sers." He hopped in circles around them, his dripping skin never quite touching the ground.

Aimee glanced over at Aaron. Under her smile was an anxiety he knew all too well. Nothing good lasted. Even then, they'd known. It seemed nice here, but the question hanging in his mind was the same as the one in hers.

"Will we have to go back?"

The memory fell away as a draft blew from deeper in the castle. A bellow shook the floor from a roaring, angry thing he felt more than heard. The stones beneath his feet shivered. When it was silent again, only the lonely howl of the wind filled the void.

He couldn't imagine what might make a sound like that, but he wasn't as afraid as he should be. This place had sucked the fear from him and left him with nothing but resolve. He had a mission, and he would get it done. The throne room wasn't far, but first he needed his steward.

Drippy would be below, where that bellow had come from, if he were still alive. The dungeons had been there. They'd never used them. Aaron wasn't sure they'd ever been below the first floor.

That ground quaked again; ice in a nearby doorway cracked and shattered. The noise echoed down the hall. Several booms followed, and this time he couldn't ignore it. He glanced behind. No fog monsters or giants. Nothing but the memories and the pain that came with them, pushing out even the fear as if it were playing across a movie screen.

Heroin did that too. It set everything so far away that he couldn't reach it if he tried. Brian, Marie, his writing career, and his apartment… all of it vanished into a hedonistic haze. And without that, he couldn't face those expectations and disappointments. He couldn't handle being less than what he always said he would be.

Where had it landed him now? Purgatory? The deeper levels of Hell where Dante had once roamed, his own Virgil nothing more than a bloated theme-park mascot and his Beatrice a sister with a bullet wound to the head.

He moved on regardless, past the rotted pictures and broken statues. Doors led into rooms either collapsed and filled with stones or destroyed like the main hall, echoes of the calamity that had rocked this world while he'd been away. Snapshots in time of the thing Aimee or her ghost had journeyed here to prevent. It played across his vision too, like the memories of his childhood. Men and women running to the castle to escape. Caught in rubble as the ceiling sagged to meet the floor, or overtaken by a black cloud of decay and lost forever.

The chill deepened. Frost covered glass. In one doorway, a single icicle stretched from the top of the frame to the bottom, linking the two. The pressure increasing with every inch weighed him down. A diver going too far. A submersible about to explode.

A roar rocked the building, and the beast responsible rampaged just below. Stone breaking, glass shattering.

Aaron's blood froze, and he stopped. Behind, the hall stretched forever, and dancing wisps hinted at something following. Ahead, the same black shadow that had overtaken the people of the land pooled across the floor, waiting for him.

The castle had never had a floor plan per se. What might have been a garden on one visit became a swimming pool the next. They'd had free reign to change it as they saw fit, speaking words that erased walls to reform them as windows or doors. What whims the world bent to now, he didn't know, but he felt it standing over him. The very shadow of the specter of decay cast itself across his body, and the world went frigid.

A door opened in the blackness ahead with the same squeal as his apartment closet. Another answered it, then another. Soon the whole hall sang with the noise of a thousand doors opening. A thousand eyes watched from the shadows.

The hair rose on his neck as he ran, caution be damned. Reach the end, the throne room. Find Aimee, and he could make this right. One foot in front of the other, ignoring the quiet steps behind and the shadowy images of frozen men and women half-hidden in ruined rooms and hallways. Maybe people who had sought shelter when the Black Knight came, maybe just more ghosts. He focused on anything

353

but the incessant whispers and building, building, building echoes of the slamming doors.

The floor erupted from below in an explosion of stone. He screamed as he struck something, and all sense failed him. Floor became ceiling as masonry the size of microwaves fell on and around him. Gravity pulled him down, down, down.

He floated, but not between worlds, between stone and sky. An impossible grind of stone on stone and bursting wood filled the halls as he struck the floor, knocking the breath out of him.

A hulking figure draped in shadows loomed over him before knuckle-walking away and howling. The ear-splitting roar bounced off the walls, reverberating louder, deafening him to everything else as he gasped for air and choked on dust.

He groaned as he rolled onto his back, the dark of unconsciousness sweeping before his eyes. The light from the grand hall shone down, fifteen feet above.

For all its distance, it might as well be on the other side of the Earth world. Dust clouded the hall. Shackles on the wall held skeletal arms. He coughed and tried to make sense of it. The dungeons. Black halls and blacker arches holding them up. Bars on wooden doors long rotted.

"So weak!"

The words assailed him from every angle.

"You've always been weak!"

That critical voice screamed at him from everywhere. A ghost, long dead and buried, back from the grave to haunt him. Just like then, Aaron hunkered down and waited for the blows to come.

"You were always a disappointment!"

Dad.

Chapter 34

He couldn't catch his breath. Maybe he'd broken a rib in the fall. Maybe blood poured into his lungs, drowning him.

His father laughed in the dim light of the lower level. The echo made it impossible to tell where it originated. *"I should have killed you. You're still as big a bitch as you ever were."*

Footsteps shook loose dirt from overhead. Closer. Closer. Right on top of him.

He rolled over and pushed off the ground. The effort worsened the spots in front of his eyes. He fought the urge to pass out and searched for somewhere to hide, something to defend himself with, anything but standing there in pants-shitting terror.

"Your mother wanted to get rid of you. A coat hanger up her snatch to pull you little bastards out. I should have let her."

Aaron staggered toward a door, just like when he was a boy. Run, run, run, but there was nowhere to hide. There never had been. The cold numbed his toes and fingers, but not as much the sound of that voice froze his insides. Dad should be dead by now. That fucker had walked out of their lives and should have died quietly of lung cancer or liver failure.

Maybe he had. Maybe it was another monster. That didn't mean he wasn't six again and flying off the porch to land on the rock. The sickening crunch of his bones screamed from the past over Dad's stomping, and a whimper escaped Aaron's lips. He opened the door. Another room full of broken things.

His mind blanked as something hit him hard enough from behind to send him spiraling inside, tumbling across the ground and crashing against the stone wall on the far side. It moved him as if he were a child. Outside, bigger than the doorway, stood a monstrosity with his father's face, its enormous body obscured by shadows.

Gray skin, scars, and arms as big as Aaron's torso. It didn't look like his father except in those eyes. Those two terrible eyes stared at him with so much loathing. They burned into him, pulling out that little boy that had once hoped it might turn out okay.

If I'm a pussy, it's 'cause I have a pussy for a dad!

It wore no clothes. It wasn't a man but the beast he had always been, the one that crushed any happy thoughts that dared intrude on his domain.

"Look at you! Still a crybaby after all this time!" A sickening grin wormed across its face. Then it slunk back the way it had come, its footsteps rocking the castle.

"No, please." Not after all this time. He'd never really escaped that house as an adult. It lived inside him, slithering out to coat everything good in the same filth it had covered him and Aimee in.

He carried it with him everywhere he went, the seed of the failure he would become planted in the soil of youth.

His arm hurt terribly where it had bashed the wall. He held it while he searched the room. He had to find something to defend himself. Just like before. Just like all those years ago.

"We have to protect ourselves. The cops won't arrest us for that." Aimee's gaze had shifted back to the gun cabinet Dad never locked, the same one where he kept all the bullets.

For once, Aaron was the less brave of the two. "We shouldn't even be in here, Aims. If he sees us, we'll get it worse than ever." He told his feet to carry him out, but they wouldn't. They kept him firmly rooted, staring at the cabinet and considering her crazy plans.

"He'll kill us if we don't. I know it. He'll kill us both." Her voice wavered.

They faced each other. Her swollen lip and his bruised cheek were a perfect match. The same eyes stared back at one another, eyes that had seen too much. He didn't dare touch her, lest the steel in her cut him down.

He'd dreamed for years after Dad vanished what he would say or do if he ever saw that old bastard again. Kick him right in the nuts, maybe. Stab him in the neck. For a while, he considered carrying a gun, pointing it at Dad while looking into his pig eyes and saying, "This is for Aimee," as he pulled the trigger.

But he wouldn't have. He would have seen Dad and remembered that boxing match in the back yard. He would've heard the stories all over again, and maybe he would have seen a little bit of himself in that tired old man. But he never saw him.

Until now.

His mind raced. There had to be something to defend himself with. He limped toward the center of the room, giving the door a wide berth.

The wall exploded behind him, showering him with rocks and shattering his nerves as he screamed. He'd lucked out when the floor fell, but not this time. A giant piece of masonry hit him in the back, flinging him toward the hall.

By some miracle, he kept his footing. Stomps rushed toward him from behind. He turned to see the nine-foot-tall form of his father careening toward him, hunched over to avoid hitting the ceiling.

Aaron shrieked the same way he had when Dad nearly killed him for having the audacity to stand up for himself. Parents were gods, and his were the angry deities of some forgotten pantheon. He dashed through the door as an arm reached out behind him. A breeze from the quickness of the snatch brushed the nape of his neck.

His father roared in rage. The cold intensified. The air moved like a hurricane, from still to crazed in an instant. The sound drowned out all others until he couldn't hear. He slapped his hands over his ears and screamed too, but it did no good. The wind picked up pieces of debris and flung them around the hall.

It stopped as suddenly as it began. The father-creature stalked back through the hole it had made, and the debris dropped to the ground. Aaron ran, blind with panic. He went straight, made turns, checked doors that were all locked, as the rumbling footsteps grew closer.

"Take it! Take the whoopin' you got comin', you little faggot!"

As a child, there had been no escape, and there wouldn't be now. The realization struck him the same as those stones. Animal fear turned his stomach. The dungeons stretched on forever in every direction, and this was where he would die.

The presence bore down on him, a shadow on the wall. A menace surrounding him. The circle drew tighter, the breath in his lungs sparser.

"After I left, my life got much better."

Another locked door. Aaron ran on, his father growling a laugh behind him.

"Found some pretty young slut that put your mom to shame."

Another short turn. The hair on his neck stood on end at the sensation of a massive hand grasped at him. He glanced back, but there was only the darkness and cold of the hall.

"And ain't had no kids to fuck up my life in years!"

Ahead on the wall, a sword.

Cold sweat and terror. Pain and fear. He didn't know if he could hurt the thing behind him, but to keep running would be to die here, killed by the man he always knew would be the one to do him in.

"I should have left years before, as soon as I saw your mom shit out you two little ingrates."

360

He closed his hands around the hilt as a massive kick caught him in the small of the back. He hadn't heard Dad approach, but it didn't matter as he flipped through the air, his back a tangle of pain.

There were no walls to catch him. He hit the ground and tumbled end over end, hitting his head repeatedly as the Dad-creature circled closer like a shark. By some miracle, he still held the sword.

He stood, though something inside hurt. Dad had never pulled punches, and that hadn't changed in the last decade. Aaron faced him, ready to do what needed to be done. For him. For Aimee. For every day they'd spent under his thumb. They'd stood in front of that gun case as children, after all. He'd said for years that he'd knock is old man out if he ever saw him again. And here he was.

But as he spun, his back screaming, it was just Dad. No giant monster. No wall-breaking creature. Just his dad, though still bigger than Aaron by a foot. His belt was wrapped around his fist, like always when he didn't want to leave a mark. His eyes were black as coal.

"What're you gonna do, Ariel? You gonna cut me?"

That name had been his way of making Aaron even smaller.

"You're a little bitch!" He'd hit Aaron again and again, screaming at him, making him less with every word and every blow. "Ain't gonna call you, Aaron. You're Ariel! How do you like that name, ya little bitch?"

But Aaron wasn't a child anymore.

He stood straighter. It hurt, but if he was going to die, he was going to die like the man he'd become, not the scared little kid this asshole had beaten half to death. Staring at that face, all the ghosts flooded back. Every slap. Every punch. The noise of them echoed off the walls. Even louder, Aimee and Aaron's screams as kids, and the crunch of his breaking bones.

"Don't call me that." He spat the words as anger bubbled over. It pushed out the fear and cold, leaving only a gaping black hole of rage that had been there as long as he could remember.

Dad took a few steps forward. "Oh! You manned up while I was gone, huh? Your little nuts dropped and you're a big man now? Gonna take a swing at your old man?" He threw his head back and laughed.

He'd said that the day he left too. "Why don't you take a swing, huh? Why don't you little shits nut the fuck up and say what you got to say to my face?" He'd towered over them, his shadow blocking the light. The only thing stopping him from beating them senseless was fear of the social workers that would soon be at the house. The only thing he was more than mean was cowardly.

Aaron tightened his grip on the blade. "Yeah, I think I will." The first step hurt his ribs so badly he nearly fell, but he caught himself.

Dad kept laughing. He'd always be the same arrogant, fat slob, but Aaron had the cure for that. After years and years of beatings, he would finally do what he'd wanted to do his entire life.

He'd kill his old man.

The fear changed into the anger that had always been there. The rage that had choked him at night while he listened to Aimee sob above him. The simmering discontent that boiled over every time he was ashamed of the marks on his arms or the ratty clothes.

No regret. If he traced the lines of his tragedies back far enough, he'd find this man standing over them with a belt while screaming in a blind rage. He'd be holding Aimee by the throat when she'd tripped over an empty bottle of beer in the living room and woken him. His ghost would be beating their mother over a cold dinner.

He'd fantasized about this moment his whole life.

He walked toward his father, sword at his side.

Dad returned his stare.

He swung with his whole body, arcing it like a baseball bat.

Dad smiled and reached to grab the blade, but Horace had taught Aaron a trick or two. "If your opponent doesn't except a punch, punch them to get them off their guard. If they don't expect a kick, kick them."

Aaron kicked him in the crotch. The old man let out a groan and doubled over, catching the sword swing in the head. The blade rang against his skull, a meaty thwack that surprised Aaron as the vibration went up his shoulder. The old man fell to his knees as Aaron dropped the sword not out of anger or guilt but pure shock.

Blood dripped from his head as he knelt on the ground. Savage joy filled Aaron.

"Who's the pussy now?"

He reared his foot back and kicked forward—

"Looks like it's still you." His father exploded upward, taking Aaron's other foot out from under him and spilling him onto the ground. His wounded side burst into world of pain. His vision grayed, and electric wires hummed in his ears. He stared up at his father, who grew in size again to the monster he was deep down. The ugly thing he hid from the outside world ripped him apart and formed his real visage.

The fear returned—not just the fear Aaron had known in the Kingdom, but that childhood terror. The dawning sense of doom that overcame him and Aimee every time they walked home. He might not be a kid anymore, but here he was lying on his back and looking up at the man who had ruined them.

"Finally got the nuts to take a swing, huh?" The monster of a man grabbed Aaron by the neck, lifting him off the ground as if he were a small animal. He set Aaron on his feet. "I'm gonna give you to the count of ten, then I'm going to kill you like I should have years ago." He cackled again, his voice bouncing off the stone at Aaron over and over and over.

"One."

Aaron took a step back as he gaped up at his father. This place wouldn't give him any more closure than the real world had. Just more nightmares.

"Two. Better run, boy!"

He turned and fled as best as his aching side would let him.

"Three."

The blocked doors flew by as he passed, the shadows behind the veils of ice staring out at him, beckoning him to join them as the mist in the forest had.

"Four."

He groaned in panic, searching for some escape. He was a child again, never free and never able to grow up. Beaten and bloodied, soon to be killed by the man supposed to protect him.

"Five."

Ahead of him, a door stood half-open.

"Six."

How could he run from something that could break walls? How could he hide in this Kingdom?

"Seven."

He pushed the door open.

"Ser!"

"Eight."

Drippy stood behind the rusted iron bars of a cell, as fitting a place as any to hide. Aaron slammed the entrance closed.

"Ser! You came to—what happened to you?"

"Nine."

Aaron put his back against the door and closed his eyes, sliding down. It wasn't supposed to be like this. Mom had always said, "Fair is a way you describe the weather, not life," but that didn't make it any more palatable.

"Daddy's home!"

Deep down, he was glad Aimee hadn't lived to see this.

"It's the beast, ser! The beast!"

Outside, the manic grunts and growls of something bowling down the hall grew louder and louder. He'd be here in seconds. There was no out this time.

"Get away, ser!"

Aaron looked up at the little candle man. "How?"

The first kick rocked the door, shaking it in the frame. "Come out and take your whoopin'!"

Drippy searched his cell, as if some tool or escape he hadn't noticed before would appear. Outside, Dad screamed, rattling the wall.

Aaron shivered as he held the door, staring at the floor and covering his ears. "Shut up! Shut up and go away, you old prick!"

"Daddy isn't done talking yet, Ariel!" The frame bulged with each kick.

"Ser! You have to go, go, go! Run away!"

He'd spent his entire life running, but it was over. Any escape he'd hoped to find had vanished the moment he'd set foot back in this Kingdom. This was his punishment, and it was time he took it like a man. His father had given up when things got hard. His mother. Even Aimee. The family tradition had to end somewhere. He'd be the first one not to run away.

"Just let me go, ser!" Drippy's candle form oozed around the bars but never quite passed through. "It's all right, ser. I understand. You can go home."

Just let it go.

Another pound on the door and the wood splintered, digging into his back.

Let it go. Aimee's words from the hospital. The warning that anger and sadness would one day consume him like it had everyone else in the family.

A calm as cold as the room settled over him. *Is that what she meant?*

He didn't have time to think about it. With one more kick, Dad destroyed the door, and Aaron flew through the air to bash against the bars of Drippy's prison. His head bounced off the iron before he struck the pile of broken wood that had been the entrance. When his senses returned, something hot ran down his head and arms.

His father walked in, ducking to fit through the frame. "Daddy's home, you little shit." He spread his arms wide. "Why don't you come over here and give him a hug?" His black eyes gleamed from across the room as Drippy touched Aaron's shoulder.

"There's still time to run away, ser! Go! Go!"

But there wasn't, not anymore. Maybe it had been about this from the beginning. If there were a greater meaning in the madness, maybe that was it. "No." Aaron struggled to get to his feet as his father drew closer. "No more."

The monster bellowed a laugh. "Speak up. Someone should hear your last words."

Calm settled over him. Battle high. A soldier facing down enemy forces after all his friends had been killed. "No more." He held onto the bars for support, every breath labored. He stood as defiantly as he could, facing his old man. No fear. No anger. Not anymore.

"You beggin', boy? I raised you to be tougher than that. Why don't you show me what kinda man I raised?"

Aaron shook his head. Waves of dizziness nearly knocked him off his feet. "It's done, Dad. I won't be like you."

That condescending smile only Dad could wear so well faded. "What'd you say?"

"I grew up hating you. You took away everything good we had in our lives. You and Mom even took away Aimee." He stopped to catch his breath. Talking hurt the place where he thought his spleen was.

"*Ohhh.*" Dad rubbed away pretend tears. "Little baby—"

Aaron held up a hand. "Not done."

His father's mouth snapped closed. The anger, the simmering rage that had ignited into violence a thousand times, spread across his face.

"I almost became you." No, that wasn't right. All the things he'd done since he'd grown up. The way he'd given up and drank away his trouble. The way he'd hit Marie. By god, the way he'd treated her for years. "I *did* become you. But it's done. I won't be like you or Mom anymore. Not to spite you, and not because I hate you. I just don't want it." The world dimmed around the edges from the effort of talking. "I don't want to be you. I would hate myself." He looked at the floor, unable to hide his shame. "I do hate myself. But it's done."

His father grew with every word. As big as the room now. As big as the Kingdom. As big as the world. He swelled until he became one of the monstrous planets in the darkness, the things lurking between worlds to devour those who fell between the cracks.

And still Aaron wasn't afraid. The hate that had filled him evaporated, and without it he was empty. Empty, but serene for the first time he could remember.

"I forgive you."

Dad stood where the monster had been, an overweight old man who had learned to hate himself from his father and passed it off to his children. A pathetic man who'd seen his own worth and run away from it. "What?" No bluster. No veiled threat.

"I don't know if I ever loved you, and I don't think I can now, but I forgive you. For Aimee and for me."

Let it go. Let that hate out. Make that anger vanish. It would be the death of him; Aimee had said so herself.

"You..." Those black eyes stared at him in a way his father's never had. Awe and respect, and somewhere inside both of those, fear. "You ain't no son of mine."

The effort of speaking and standing had taken its toll. Aaron slid down the bars. Maybe this is what it felt like to die. It terrified him but not in the way he thought it would. Comfort radiated out to him, like the warm smile of a friend not seen in a long time or a sudden view of a valley after a cold ride through the mountains.

"You." His father kept repeating it, trying to find some threat in it. "You."

With every word, he grew smaller and further away.

"You."

He became less important. He became never important, as if he'd not been there at all.

"You."

And then he was gone, turned into wisps of shadow.

"Ser." Drippy pawed at his shoulder and stroked his hair, nuzzling him through the bars like a goddamn cat. Aaron hated cats, but he breathed a sigh of relief. "You'll be all right, ser. All right as rain and rum."

The bars snapped open, but Drippy stayed where he was. Darkness deepened around Aaron. Everything grew far away and dull. "Am... Am I dying?" It didn't feel appropriately dramatic for a death, if closure ever did.

"I dunno, ser. But I don't think so. You haven't—"

An explosion rocked the castle, and air raid sirens blared. Red light, like the searchlights from the village, spilled in from the little window in the back of the cell. A streak of crimson hit the treetops outside the window. They erupted into flame and upset the castle's foundations again.

"No, no, no! It's the Black Knight, ser! He'll destroy everything!"

More booming eruptions and another flash of light. Grainy dust shifted loose from the stones overhead, showering down and burning Aaron's throat. He coughed as the blackness deepened and the sirens swelled. He wasn't a man; he was a stone and the darkness underneath now. Up, up, and away, living to shoot junk another day.

"No, ser!" Drippy grabbed on as if his life depended on it. Maybe it did. "Please! Don't go now!"

His father posed no threat to Drippy. But this could be the end of the world as he knew it, the very foundations of the Kingdom torn asunder by some weapon of unimaginable scope.

This was Armageddon.

Aaron couldn't stay. Those invisible hands already pulled him down into the stone, the dream between worlds devouring him. He held Drippy's hand as he faded away, trying to care. "I'll come back. I promise I won't leave you." But his thoughts were thick and dull. It felt like a lie even as he spoke it.

"Ser!" Another explosion cracked the stone in front of him, and the pile of rubble that Dad had crashed through loosened and dropped through a hole in the floor.

But Aaron was somewhere else, and Drippy's voice was suddenly far, far away.

"Ser Aaron!"

He was back in that endless black between worlds. The pain in his side and back followed him all the way down, down, down, but there was no bottom.

Chapter 35

Before he had time to fathom what was happening, someone's hand was in his. Aimee's.

They walked back from the Kingdom, weaving through the woods as the dark settled in. They had to return home before sunset. Out of sight, out of mind, but never out of reach of Daddy's belt. The Kingdom's shimmering, tingling magic held while it could, but as always, it faded. The first memory to go was the happiness. Soon the only thing left was the desire to be out of the real world once more and into something more pleasant.

Because no matter what happened there, the real world always hurt more. Aaron wore a bruised eye as a reminder. Don't sass. Don't back talk. Be meek, demure. Dad was the alpha dog, and Mom made damn sure everyone knew she was number two.

"One day we'll run away," he blurted out as he ducked under a half-fallen tree.

"What?"

"Yeah. We'll get out of here and find someplace where nobody acts like they do. We'll find somewhere of our own." He looked at her as they walked. "We can bring Brian, too. Just get away, you know?"

Aimee stopped, and Aaron stopped a few feet past here. When he turned around, she was nothing more than a wisp of shadow, her face half illuminated in moonlight. A phantom before her time.

"What about Drippy, and Horace? I…"

"What?"

"I don't want to leave there. I want to stay forever. We can just live there."

But they'd tried and been ejected. He shook his head, his jaw setting. The spitting image of his dad—he could see that now as he watched like a ghost. How had he not then? How could he have been so blind? "No. We'll go away."

Don't! Don't you stupid little shit!

Whatever had taken his emotions when the castle was attacked had returned them. He had no hands that he could see, but he reached out to grab his younger self anyway. Nothing happened. He couldn't stop the past.

Stop, you dumb fuck!

"No." Little Aaron turned and kept walking. "We'll go away."

Years later, he was ready to do just that. The scene melted like water thrown over fresh paint. Colors ran down, and the world itself peeled away to reveal another world behind it.

Adult Aaron shook, or tried to. If he didn't come up from this lucid nightmare, he knew what he would see, and he couldn't. Not again. He already relived it every time he closed his eyes.

"Come with me. Let's go, please."

She had taken to wearing makeup in the last few months of her life. Now it ran down her face, smeared and ugly. "No." She wrapped her arms around herself. "No, please. Let's just stay. We can go to the Kingdom."

His temper had already started to show by then. Flashes of anger. Not as bad as Dad, or even Mom, but nobody had failed to notice, least of all him. "I don't want some fake shit! I want to live a normal life!" He felt bad as she flinched, but he didn't lower his voice. "This place is hopeless, and that one is just a dream. We can have something real, Aims!"

Things had seemed so much better after Dad left. No more beatings. No more wondering if they were going to live to see the next year. But in many ways, things were worse. When Mom wasn't drinking, she was bringing home losers almost as bad as Dad. There was never food. The power had gone out twice because of unpaid bills.

Enough was enough. The time to go had long passed.

But it hadn't been. Enough should have been enough, but he'd over reached. He hadn't been willing to see the obvious as it spit in his eye, too caught up in his own desire to be free. And he'd gotten his wish. He'd been freed of every stable shore he'd ever known and cast out into a starless sea.

Please.

He tried to look away but couldn't.

"Please, Aaron. I…I won't go."

The words cut through his anger. "What?"

She wiped at her eyes, further smearing her makeup. "I won't go. I don't want to leave the Kingdom, and—"

"And what? We need to get out of here, Aims. We need something real. I can get a job. I'm big enough to pass for eighteen now." He had to shave the hair on his face every day. He'd already started to look like Dad in build and features.

"I can't leave."

He stood up from his bunk and leaned against the dresser, staring at her across the same room they'd shared for years. November cold had set in, and the heat hadn't worked in months. Curled up. Shivering. Wondering if they could pick up more meals at Brian's house. Some excuse or another usually did the trick.

Anything would be better than this.

But that wasn't true. It never had been. That little brat didn't know rock bottom; neither of them did. As bad as it had been, it would get so much worse.

Aaron screamed it from his spectral prison, shaking the bars that weren't there with arms he didn't have. Where were the planets in the blackness between worlds? Why had he been sent to this Hell?

Let me go! Please! Don't make me watch… don't do this. Please. You can have the Kingdom!

But there was no reply.

"I'm going."

They could have heard a mouse farting in the walls in the silence that followed.

"What?"

His resolve hardened as soon as the words left his mouth. "I'll find a job. Then you won't have to worry about it. We won't end up homeless; you'll see."

In the ghostly dream vision, he could see the horror on her face, her mouth opening and closing in the wake of his declaration. How had he not seen it then?

"Don't leave me. Please."

How could he have been so blind?

"I can't be here alone."

She'd cried herself to sleep in the cold every night. She'd leave the house when Mom's boyfriend came over. Everything had been so clear, and he'd been so blinded by his own needs he hadn't seen hers.

And she was he. Grandma had said so. They'd always been one flesh, and he'd left it to die only to return later and kill himself further.

He began to cry, but there was no sound and no tears.

"Please."

Then she was crying too, and Little Aaron missed the point entirely.

"There's nothing to be scared of. I'll find us a place far away, somewhere you won't ever hear of Umber Gardens again. We'll go out to the West Coast or Florida. Maybe New York! You always wanted to go there, right?" His wheels were in motion. Already planning. Already looking ahead. He'd failed to see the pitfalls right under him or read the writing on the wall. Ever the fool. Already shutting other people out and focusing only on himself.

"Aaron. I…" She'd wanted to say more, hadn't she? But she didn't. And as it faded, other images appeared.

Brian and Aimee holding hands in the park.

Brian and Aimee kissing for the first time after school behind the gym.

Brian looking into Aimee's eyes as they sat at the park bench without Aaron, the same bench where Aaron had once called her story "unicorny bullshit". "We can't tell him. He might get mad. He trusts me too much, and I don't want to hurt his feelings. He'd think we're shutting him out."

He knew the look on Aimee's face as that perfect spring day framed the young lovers. Nobody did pissed-off teenager better than her. Her eyes went as hard as steel. She was going to ask if Brian was afraid of Aaron or ashamed of being with her. Before she got the chance, the world faded to smoke. The blackness consumed him once more, but he still had no flesh as he wept.

I don't deserve this.

He never had; neither of them did. Was this some Faustian bargain made when they were children? Given a Kingdom for the price of their torment?

The whispered conversation he was never meant to hear followed him down, down, down as the monstrous, planet-sized creatures regarded him. But whatever held him here wasn't done yet.

Blackness gave way to blinding light. It was the kitchen at Brian's house. The cute little pictures on the wall. The wallpaper. The stove that was older than Brian's mom was. He knew all of it almost as well as he knew his own house.

"Why didn't you tell me sooner?" Aaron couldn't remember ever seeing Brian that angry, not before or after.

And Aimee, her makeup still smeared, cried. She held herself the way she had the night he'd planned to leave. Only he was already gone, and she was alone. She leaned against the counter, unable to look at Brian. Outside, birds chirped and cars went by. The neighbor mowed his lawn.

Brian held himself at a distance, staring at her with…revulsion? Anger? Contempt?

"I didn't know what to do. I'm so scared. I miss Aaron."

She covered her eyes and cried, but Brian didn't move. He stared at her across the kitchen as if the village leper had knocked on his door begging for change. His every move said he wanted to go to her and hold her as he had a thousand times before, now in the full light of day instead of behind closed doors. He wanted to kiss her and tell her everything would be fine. But he didn't. He was still only a child. They all were then. He couldn't know what to do.

"I can't go back to that house. I can't let him touch me again. He… I won't let him… I'll never touch him again." Unable to say it, ashamed that it happened, she closed her eyes.

As if to torture him further, there it was. A small revelation, but a revelation nonetheless. The last piece of the puzzle.

Call the police, you dumb fuck!

Aaron tried to swing at Brian, but there was no substance. The entire world had turned into a projection of the past, ghosts on celluloid flashing across the skin over and over.

Tears burned the back of his eyes. His throat hurt as if he were yelling, but there was no sound. There would be no phone call like there had been with Dad. Nobody had rescued his sister in the real world, and they wouldn't here.

Nobody had rescued her because he had left her all alone. The only person who might have saved her had been sleeping in a car in Florida the night she died.

Then she was screaming. He didn't care about her. Nobody did. Aaron had left, and Brian didn't care that she'd been raped.

He was screaming. She didn't know everything. She should call the cops. *Don't get mad at him; he didn't do it.*

Then, what always came next.

She stood alone in the bathroom back at home, the gun in her hands. A cold acceptance settled over her features. She looked so fragile and thin, but so brave. She stared at herself as Aaron screamed and begged her to stop, but she couldn't hear him. She hadn't been a scared little girl at the end. She'd been a woman.

She'd been an Amazon, or a warrior princess. Maybe she had been all along.

Please, Aims. Don't. I'm so sorry.

But ghosts couldn't hear ghosts.

If her last thoughts were of Aaron, or the Kingdom where they might have been free, he couldn't blame her. And if she hated him for leaving her to kill herself, he would agree. Nobody hated him for it more than he did.

She placed the gun to her temple, breathing three deep breaths in quick succession before squeezing her eyes shut.

By some miracle, the scene faded before she pulled the trigger, but the sound followed.

Bang!

A body hit first the counter and then the floor as Aaron wailed and the world dissolved.

The last words he'd said to her before he left chased him as he fell through the endless nothing. Then he was there again, seeing her for the last time.

"Please don't go, Aaron."

He'd looked at her as he walked out the door, his mother's car keys in hand.

"I'll come back. I promise."

Chapter 36

He hadn't known. He couldn't see it then. That house had been bad, and only bad things every happened there. Aaron should have paid attention; he should have made her come with him, or never left at all. It wasn't her fault, and it wasn't Brian's. It was his for leaving her, for being so selfish he couldn't see the pain she suffered. His and only his.

A key fit into a lock. A door opened, and Marie's voice followed. "Aaron... What the hell?" Footsteps as she walked in.

The light blinded him as she opened the curtains and daylight washed in. The pain from the castle, forgotten in the fall and the memories that followed, returned with savage force. He collapsed on the ground, sobbing. Crying like a child, just as he had in the hospital.

"Aaron?" Marie dropped the bag of food in her hand. "Oh my god." Her hands went to her mouth.

Huddled and bloody, he stared at her through tears. Dust from the castle covered him, and his shirt hung off him.

She opened and closed her mouth a few times, but all she could muster was, "What happened to the couch?"

He squeezed his eyes shut and wept. That last image was seared into his brain. Aimee, holding the gun. So brave and so small.

Marie rushed over and embraced him, rocking back and forth. "Shh. We'll get you to the hospital. It's going to be okay. What happened, Aaron?" A tear, not his, hit his cheek. He looked up to see her crying. "What's going on, Aaron? What happened?"

He sniffled. "I have to go back. I'm close. I can feel it. She's there."

"What are you talking about? Who?"

He couldn't tell her. She wouldn't understand. Just like Brian. But if Aaron called him now and told him about that last conversation, would he believe then? Would he break down and cry, claiming every terrible thing that had happened in the last ten years was his fault? Would he beg Aaron for forgiveness?

Did it matter anymore?

"Get up." She wiped her face and hooked her arms under his. "It doesn't matter who did this to you. I'm taking you to the hospital."

He shook his head but didn't push her away. "No. I can't. They wouldn't understand. Nobody does."

"Aaron, please." The same words Aimee had said to him. Crying the same way Aimee had. "You're hurt really bad."

If he went back in the hospital now, they'd lock him up. They'd tell him he was a danger to himself. He couldn't allow it. Too close

382

now. Too close to Aimee. Too close to the Kingdom's truth. He had to see her one last time.

"Baby, I can't lose you." She kissed his cheek, her tears dropping onto his face. "I don't know what I'd do if something happened to you. I love you. Please, please just go to the hospital."

"No." The weeping slowed, then stopped. "No hospitals. I'm fine." He sat up and embraced her legs. "It's going to be okay." So much like that last talk with Aimee.

"Tell me what happened. Who did this to you?"

He wiped his eyes. "No questions, remember? One week. You promised."

She pulled away. He'd never seen a woman as horrified as she was then. "No! No way! You don't go and get yourself killed, then tell me it's not my business. That isn't fair!"

But he'd made up his mind. One more trip, even if he found the Kingdom in ashes, those red rays having reduced everything to cinder. It didn't matter if he found the Black Knight in a burning hole where the world had once been. It had to end, and it could only end one way.

"I'm calling 9-1-1." She grabbed her phone from her pocket.

"I'll be gone before they get here."

Her fingers hovered over the dial pad, her face a mask of disbelief.

"I have to do this. I have to, and then it's over. We can go just like you wanted and start over somewhere else."

She dropped the phone, and tears fell once more.

"Just let me finish this one thing. One more thing, and I'll be free."

"Listen to yourself. This is crazy talk."

The upstairs neighbor pounded on the floor, assuring them he would end their lives if they didn't pipe down. She didn't move to pick up the phone. But she didn't leave, either.

He stood, the pain in his ribs nearly sending him back to the floor. She didn't pull away as he limped over and embraced her, but the tears didn't stop.

She helped him wash away the dirt and blood in the shower. Bruises covered half his body, and his head pulsed with every movement. His vision blurred when he bent over. Still, he wouldn't go to the hospital, wouldn't even entertain the notion. Marie played mother hen over him the rest of the night, holding him, talking to him to fill the silence. She was always so afraid of that silence. But wasn't he too? She filled it with words; he'd filled it with drugs.

The Kingdom called to him, an elongated shadow in the mirror reaching from the corner of his eye. A soft whimper in the space between commercials on the TV. But he couldn't go, not with her here. Soon, though. He was close, so damn close to whatever was at the end he could taste it. And Drippy needed him. Everyone there did. The fate of a world hung in the balance.

They watched TV sitting on the floor that night, the couch conspicuously absent. They stared at images as they flashed by, but of the four eyes in the room, he suspected not one saw a thing. He certainly didn't, and every time he glanced over at her, she appeared to be in her own world. Maybe a private hell like the one he'd found in the Kingdom. By the time eight rolled around, they were safely tucked in bed.

But sleep didn't come for Aaron, not for hours. He didn't think she was asleep, either. What must she be imagining while lying there? That he had finally come unhinged? That drugs had scrambled his brains after years of walking the razor's edge? That she could do better?

He couldn't stop picturing Drippy waiting in that dungeon, surrounded by the ruins of the Kingdom. When sleep finally found him, he saw Aimee imprisoned by a Black Knight in the Kingdom's tallest tower, looking down on their empire of destruction and wondering what they'd done to deserve it.

Chapter 37

The morning light—or maybe mid-afternoon—woke him. Hard to tell lying naked on his back. He rubbed the sleep from his eyes. All night, he'd dreamed of the Kingdom. And broken or no, he had to do it. Today. This had to end now, for Aimee and for him.

Pots banged in the kitchen.

"Hello?"

"It's just me."

Marie. He hadn't expected that. "Don't you work today?"

The sullen silence of a child caught doing wrong followed. His temper flared, that agitation that started in the spine and—

No. A condescending drug addict thought that way when he took everything for granted. Maybe her silence was that of a woman feeling guilty for caring about a man more than he cared for himself. At length, she broke it. "I called off."

He threw the covers on the floor. He'd tell her to go, get the hell out of the apartment so he could do what he had to do. There were souls at stake—and his sanity too.

The aches stopped him halfway off the bed, and the sudden desire to do none of those things overcame him. Neglect had gotten him here to start with. His callous disregard had already killed his sister. She could be right. Maybe running away was the right answer this time. If he could get away, if he could start a new life, maybe he could feel like a person again. He'd never fix what was already done. That was true no matter what happened in the Kingdom.

He rested his hand on his treasure chest, the little drawer with all the cures for what ailed him. He didn't want to use. The need was still there, but the desire was gone even as his hand shook on it and his mouth went dry. A nightmare trip would do that to anyone.

But wasn't it more than that?

Because he was a junkie. A Broad Street crackhead, just like Marie had said only a week before. He would tear apart any love in his life and kill any good will anyone had for him so he could get his fix and go on his trip. So what if that trip was literal? That didn't make it any less disgusting that he pined for it between doses.

He pulled the drawer open to look at his stash. The last bit that would get him where he needed to go. One last time, and it would be over.

He slammed it shut. "Where is my shit!"

Amazing how quickly that junkie rage ignited when the old horror story surfaced. *Came home and my family had thrown out all my junk!*

A pot set down on the counter in the kitchen.

"Where the fuck is it, Marie? I…" *I need it.* He wanted to say it, but the words wouldn't come.

She saved him the trouble. "You don't need it. Not after whatever happened yesterday."

He got out of bed, the pain forgotten. Naked, he stormed into the kitchen. His chest heaved from trying not to fly off the handle. "Give it to me. Right now, or you can just walk out the door. We had a deal."

She watched him without a word, her lips had the hard set of a woman about to be an obstinate bitch. "No."

"We had a deal." He spit every word, taking great pains to keep his voice level.

"No."

Boom. Another fist through the wall. He didn't have time for this shit. He had a mission. There was a… Aimee needed…

He saw himself from the outside. Naked, his eyes bloodshot as he punched holes in his apartment.

He finally saw Her too, because there had always been a Her. This time in the form of the long-suffering girlfriend looking every bit like the woman in a *Don't Be the Dick That Abuses His Wife* movie on Lifetime.

And the Him? That man looked just like his father.

Aaron's shoulders slumped, and he walked back to the room. "I'm not done yet, Marie. Almost, but not quite."

She stomped her foot as if this fighting was as disgustingly intoxicating to her as it had always been to him. "Not done with what? Killing yourself? Why don't you just grab a gun and get it over with?"

A sly reference to Aimee, but he wouldn't rise to the bait. "If you don't give it to me, I'll just get it somewhere else."

The pot from the counter flew into the hallway behind him. "Damn you. Goddamn you!"

And like that, they were back to the same old tragedy. She the reformed party girl, he the burnt-out loser. One always pulling away, one always running to catch up. The same old story anyone who'd been around the block had heard once or twice. The same people who would ask her why she stayed when he was so clearly a piece of shit.

One more time. One last trip in every sense of the word. He put on his last pair of good jeans and a dirty shirt from the floor. He'd rob Devon if he had to. He'd bust into the place with a ski mask and a gun, hold it up Old West-style. It wouldn't fool anybody, and finding a gun would be rough. A guy like him walking into a gun store set off too many alarms, and the kind of people who sold them out of their homes weren't in the business of selling to addicts. Either way, Devon would know exactly who did it. But by the time anyone found him, he would be free.

"I'm done. This is it. The heroin or me?"

He walked back into the kitchen, his mind made up before he saw the tears in her eyes. "Always you, but I need it one more time."

"One more time! One more time! It's always just one more time! I'm done!"

He held out his hand. No threats. No posturing. Maybe never again.

She shook her head, and tears fell free. "You want it that badly? Fine." She grabbed her purse off the table. When she upended it, his filled syringes and gear fell to the floor.

"There you go, you goddamn junkie." *Junkie.* That stain of a word. Her go-to insult when she wanted to cut deep. Before he could respond, she was pulling the door open. "I can't watch you die. I…" Weeping now. "I can't. You're breaking my heart."

He wanted to go to her, to let all of that anger free and just run away. But he had a responsibility to all the things he'd left behind. He couldn't turn away now, not at the end when he was this close. "I'll call you when it's done, I promise. We'll go away just like you wanted."

She screamed, and it broke his heart into pieces just as small as hers.

The door slammed, and he was alone once again. Truly alone. No Marie. No Brian. Nothing except him, the habit, and dead dreams, but he would fix those things today. He'd finally put them all away and be really, truly free.

All the filled syringes but one went into his pocket. He got ready. Band on his arm, shoes on his feet, bladder feeling as though piss would run down his leg any second. He couldn't recall ever wanting to do anything less.

Aimee.

A few deep breaths. Eyes closed. Calming thoughts. He might die this time, but it would be over one way or the other. He pushed the needle into his arm and released the heroin, throwing it and the band aside when he was done. With that, he lay on the floor and waited.

He didn't know what he would do when he met the Black Knight. No confrontation in the Kingdom had gone anything like he imagined, not that he had ever imagined such things, even in his best writing. If it came to a fight, he would lose. But then it would be just as over as if he won, if winning were even a thing. What did that word even mean in a fucked-up world like this one? Maybe it was a tomorrow word. When he wasn't shooting up, he'd have won. When he ran away with Marie, he'd have won. If he wrote a bestselling novel, he'd have won.

Maybe it was always tomorrow, and that was why he always lost.

The drug tickled the edges of sensation. The tingling in the toes and fingers. That calm cool, like Patrick Swayze in *Roadhouse*, rained over him.

But those dreams would have to remain tomorrow dreams. There could be no peace until this was over. He wouldn't be able to love himself until he looked Aimee in the eyes and told her all the things he'd wanted to say—the real Aimee, not a dream or an illusion. If he couldn't love himself, he couldn't love anyone else. It had to stop.

The heroin seized his mind in a velvet grip, cushioning him from the harsh vibes of a mad world with its mad hold. He didn't want to be alone anymore. He didn't want to end up like all those assholes on the street. He'd be just like his parents then. They grasped and grasped but never grabbed hold. Both of them had dreams that they would have one day lived, but they never did. Both of them had run away when things got hard. He had too.

Everything spun in a manner befitting a drug that took the sharpness out of the world. It dulled everything down so it would be okay. So easy to fall into that trap. What better bait than peace of mind?

And if there were no Aimee? If he reached the end to find only a dead dream world and a knight in black armor? He'd kill himself.

What was one more broken promise at the end of a lifetime of them?

He waited for the final journey, lying there facing the ceiling. Any moment now, the walls would collapse and the floor would vanish. A pool of ink would suck him out of this world and spit him into the one he sought.

The minutes stretched on. Something tugged at his edges a few times but petered out quickly—as if he'd pulled on a door so rotten and swollen it couldn't open. He closed his eyes and pictured the Kingdom in his mind. The castle on the hill. The forests. The village. Drippy waiting for him like always. The Black Knight prepared to face him on the tallest tower for his soul and the soul of the world.

Nothing. Sweat broke out across his forehead, and his guts teetered dangerously on the edge of sickness. Panic seized him as he felt his face and arms to make sure this was real. What if he'd waited too long and the Kingdom was already gone? What if he couldn't go back?

An anxiety attacked manifested instantly, ratcheting to ten before it had even hit a two. He couldn't go back. After all that, he wasn't allowed to return. He would have to accept the world for what it was, failures and all. He would rather be dead.

He sat up and tried to catch his breath. There had to be some reason it wasn't working. He grabbed a second syringe out of his pocket. He needed more. Three days post-overdose or no, he had to finish this. The hospital. The nurse he'd spit on. He didn't care. Even if he died, he didn't care.

He yanked the cap off and stared at the needle point as the drugs in his veins tried to drag him back down to the floor, humming the same carefree bullshit it had been singing for years now.

Someone knocked on the door as the tip touched his skin. "Aaron?"

Marie. Marie had come back.

"Aaron, I'm sorry. I didn't mean to get so mad."

His thoughts were slow. "Go away."

He heard the soft intake of breath, same as every time he cut her a little deeper. It hurt him more than ever. She was a part of him as much as Aimee had been, and he treated her as poorly as every other part of himself.

"Please. I know we aren't the strongest couple in the world, but it doesn't matter. You're enough. You exactly as you are. You don't need to be anyone else for me. I just get scared of what my world would become without you. I have nightmares about it."

His tongue stuck to the top of his mouth. How could she lay this on him now? "I love you too, but I have to do this. I have to make it okay. I don't expect you to understand. But I'm sorry I didn't always love you the way you loved me, and that I couldn't love myself. I'm sorry I haven't always been strong enough to do the things I needed to do and say the things I needed to say."

Again, that pause, but not the same as before. "What are you doing?" A note of caution entered her voice.

"If I can get there again, and if I make it back, I swear things are going to be different. Not different like the last ten times, but really different. I'm going to be the man I always wanted to be for you."

"Aaron." The jingle of keys. Did she still have hers? "Aaron, please don't do anything crazy. I'm here for you, baby."

Now or never. He slammed the needle into his arm and shot the plunger down, injecting the skag. He couldn't wait, and he couldn't let her see him like this. He meant every word, but there was no going back now. He stumbled to his feet as a key found its way into the lock. He shoved the extra junk into his pockets.

"Answer me!"

The world dimmed as he shuffled toward the bathroom. He had to get away and find the Kingdom. The front door opened as he closed the one to the bathroom. He flipped the light switch to no

394

effect. The lock clicked into place as Marie gasped in the living room.

"Did you take all of this?"

He didn't sit on the floor so much as collapse. The edges of reality softened as they did when he had fallen between worlds before. No ink stains or couches tumbling through the void yet, but he felt lighter. His body wasn't as solid as it had been a moment before. The squiggles and spirals of his brain unraveled. Not enough to get him to the Kingdom, maybe, but there was more in his pocket.

She tugged on the knob. "Aaron! Answer me! Did you take all of this?"

He wanted to answer, but his mouth wasn't working. When he opened it, all he managed was a low moan. There should be fear, but there was just the cold tile under his back and that dragon circling overhead.

When had he lain on the floor? Where had the light gone?

Marie's voice didn't fade, nor did she stop pounding. "Open this right now! Please!" She tugged again before kicking it. "Open the door right now!"

Her voice grew distant. The light under the door had disappeared completely. The tile under him sailed away in a void of utter night.

A ghost of a whisper reached him from far away. "Aaron, don't leave me! Please!"

Not Aimee's words, but close.

Chapter 38

This wasn't the darkness of a bathroom in a junkie's house. It had character to it. Depth. The colossi that watched him fall every other time wept silently as he passed, lamenting the poor fate of a poor fool. Marie's spoke from everywhere and nowhere, calling out to him even as she spoke to the police on the phone, begging them to hurry and telling them to send paramedics. Her words were distorted and slow, a tape played at half-speed.

And he wasn't falling anymore. It took him a moment to realize his eyes were closed, his back to the ground in some windswept place. Opening them didn't help him understand where he was.

The desolation of the Kingdom spread out forever above and around him. Where once there had been land were now pieces of castle and earth floating in the void. Some of them enormous, the size of small islands. Some tiny, no more than a fist. Half were aflame, and a deep, grainy haze surrounded everything. It looked like pictures of cities after a bombing, so much dust in the air that it was hard to see.

And still Marie's voiced drifted on the wind, begging him to open the door and let her in.

He rubbed his eyes as dread wound around his throat. This had to be a mistake. He'd ended up in some other kingdom, or a surrealist painting in a gallery. The front half of the bar, ripped free from the ground and hovering in the void, collided with the shack that sat at the edge of the forest. The remains of dozens of guardian trees drifted in the void too, all of it an impossible visual mess, an M.C. Escher painting of the Kingdom.

He sat on the largest remaining piece of the world, a huge chunk of the rear of the castle, its insides laid bare through destroyed walls.

"Aaron! Please, baby! I love you!"

His knuckles popped as he balled his hands into fists. There was no more Kingdom. Whatever that Black Knight was, he'd destroyed it.

"Ser," a voice croaked behind him.

Aaron spun to find Drippy, burnt and wounded, limping up a set of stairs behind him that led to nowhere.

"Oh my god." He knelt beside his most loyal servant, who leaned against him.

"Things not going so hot here, ser." He chirped out a laugh. "Or maybe they is, and that ain't such a good thing."

His wax was more black than yellow. The parts of him that dripped to the floor were smaller, and they didn't return to the top as they had before.

A hard lump formed in Aaron's throat. "I…"

"I'm fine, ser. Just a little crisp is all." But he didn't stop leaning on Aaron.

Aaron mouthed the word several times before it found its way out. "How?"

"Black Knight, ser. Says he'll burn this place down if he can't have what he wants. Take everyone with 'im." Drippy looked at the wasteland that had once been the happiest place Aaron had ever known. "I think I'm the only one left."

Aaron wiped the tears from his eyes. Any thoughts of them being weak were gone. The old Aaron let his old life control him, and that Aaron died tonight. "I'm so…" He swallowed. "I'm so sorry, Drippy. I would have come back sooner if I'd known."

"Aye, and you'd be dead too. But you're here now, ser. You can fix this. You can set things a'right again."

Aaron stared into the eyes of the strange little thing that had watched over him and Aimee as they'd laughed and played here. He was the guide they'd always taken for granted, and the thing—the person—Aaron had called a monster when he returned.

His little friend.

Aaron stood and grabbed Drippy's hand, steadying him. "We'll finish this together. You can show me the way."

Drippy looked up, the fear he'd displayed before gone, though his gaze didn't rest on anything anymore. A man-child who had seen too much. A veteran of a war of the soul.

Marie's voice drifted to him from nowhere. "Please, Aaron! Don't do this to me!"

They walked down the twisted hallway leading deeper into the castle. Wisps of mist parted as they proceeded. Pieces of creatures that had once tried to devour him, unable to survive the incredible destruction visited upon this place. Were burnt chunks of Horace floating through the hazy void too? That little girl? The Witch?

He pushed those thoughts aside as they passed holes in the castle wall big enough to drive through. He couldn't imagine what the Black Knight must be to have such unfathomable power. It was as if a thousand nuclear bombs had bombarded the tiny planet and set the pieces floating in the void of space.

"Do you hear it, ser?"

He did. The waterfall in the distance—the same one Aimee had spoken into existence so they could watch the stars shine over it from their thrones.

"I ain't seen the falls since last time you and the princess was here together. Seems like a life ago now."

He recalled it, though barely. Aimee insisting he say goodbye to the Kingdom, and him going along to humor her as he made plans to leave. It had been a dream that time, vaguely seen and vaguely recalled. It had given up on him the moment he gave up on it.

But he was here now. He would find his sister make this right. He expected to be afraid, or to make some excuse. But that was the old Aaron too, and there was no room for him anymore. Not here, and not out in the real world.

Drippy squeezed his hand as if he could sense his prince's resolve, and they walked on, the roar of rushing water ever closer.

Pieces of the world floating, lost in time and forgotten. He could feel her there. He could feel *it* as well, that malignant presence sullying the place that belonged to them. Even Marie touched the edge of his mind, screaming for him to spare her the grief of his death.

He didn't intend to die today, not if he could help it.

They trod on, past broken rooms and crumbled walls until the great bronze doors that led to the throne room appeared in the haze. No designs. No adornments. Drippy had made it clear on their first trip that a room where royalty entertained guests had to appear regal. It was the one thing he had ever insisted on besides them leaving before dark.

But he had allowed the waterfall.

"It's mighty, magically, and magnificently majestic, Your Majesties." He put a leg out and bowed to them.

Even after years in this place, seeing the world bend to their whims had scared Aimee. If someone could do this in their world, was there a person who could do it on Earth? Was God just a cruel child wishing things in and out of being?

But on that trip, there were no questions of God or man. Aimee hadn't stopped crying since Grandma died, her tears even then mixing with the water that fell off the universe into some other place, one outside of this world or any other.

"We should make paper boats."

He had stood by silently. Long before thirteen, he'd been taught that boys who cried were given reasons to cry. "Why?"

She wiped her eyes on the sleeve of her coat. "We can write notes on them and send them to Grandma."

He stared at her, his expression carefully blank. "I don't know if it works like that."

But her face had brightened already. He hadn't seen her eyes shine like that in a while. "But it might! I made the waterfall, didn't I? We can say where it goes, right?" She looked over at Drippy, who had been sitting quietly on the floor. In one fluid movement, he jumped up, stood on one foot, and cocked his head, always listening to things they couldn't hear. He stayed like that for a long, silent minute.

Aaron opened his mouth to remind Aimee Grandma was gone, but that didn't mean she had to be forgotten, when Drippy spoke up. "Can't say. That goes somewhere else. But if you want it bad enough, it might work."

And so she had him retrieve pens and parchment. They wrote their notes and folded them into little boats. Aaron cut his finger, and his blood sailed over the edge of fantasy into the nothing between it and the waking world.

If they wanted it bad enough, they could have it. He helped his limping companion down the long hall to the throne room. More than anything, he wanted that waterfall to be the place where he found Aimee. No little boats, no bloody messages, just him and his sister reunited for one moment. For one second. For anything at all.

The doors loomed over them as two giant pieces of the Kingdom collided and shattered above, pieces flying off in every direction. *Boom!* The sound of it was deafening in the quiet void.

"Ser." Drippy stopped, forcing Aaron to do the same.

"What is it?"

The little candle man looked up at him, dwindling by the second, his burnt pieces sloughing off to the ground. "You don't have to do this." His whimsical tone vanished.

The sudden change startled Aaron. "What?"

Drippy grabbed Aaron's hand in both of his, the warm wax of his body sliding over rough skin. "You can go away, I think. Not much left here anymore. You can let us go. I wouldn't hold it against you. I don't think I'll be around much longer to do so anyhow. I know you want to find the princess, but she died, and even if she came here after, she's somewhere you can't go. I see that now, don't you?"

Aaron blinked and looked away into the endless pieces of his Kingdom. Gone? It took a moment to process. He'd seen her out there, in the real world. She'd been visiting him since this whole thing started. She'd told him to let it go, even as the demons of this hell chased him into the real world. That was just like her too. Always so damn bossy, and always looking out for him over herself.

His jaw set, and he squeezed Drippy's hand harder without meaning to. Part of her was here. Even now, he could feel it on the far side of the door. Maybe just the little piece of that little girl soul it had taken to build this place when they found it all those years

402

ago. Maybe nothing more than her smile in a reflection on the waterfall. Either way, he wouldn't leave her behind. He owed her that.

Drippy frowned. "You've got to accept the things you can't change. I've known you your whole life, and you never could before. But you can now. You can walk away."

And to Aaron's surprise, he could. The gentle breeze of a door opening him behind touched the nape of his neck. Not a bronze door, but a door between worlds. Somewhere in the distance, Marie cried, begging him to open the bathroom. That voice grew closer through the portal.

He couldn't ignore it any longer. He'd never heard anything so pathetic and desperate. He could go back to her now and end that pain. The Kingdom wouldn't chase him anymore. There was nothing left but one room and a Black Knight.

But he couldn't. Or he wouldn't. He wasn't sure which.

He shut his eyes and pictured the door closing.

Closing.

Closed.

And so it was. He knelt before Drippy and grasped both of his small hands. "We're going to finish this. You, me, and Aimee, just like it started."

Drippy held his gaze for a long time, a serious expression on what had once been a silly creature. Finally, he gave Aaron the slightest of nods.

They turned to the bronze door as it swung open without a sound. No hands needed. This was his kingdom, and it was well past time he remembered that.

Chapter 39

The ceiling inside stood fifty feet tall, arches and pillars holding it up all the way to the waterfall in the back. Murals of dragons, fairies, and noble knights covered the walls. At the far end, the castle opened into a black nothing dotted with a million points of light. Two arches framed the river that bubbled forth from the stone into oblivion, rushing toward the lights of the universe. Aimee's tears, forever flowing out to grieve for the only member of their family who had mattered besides one another.

Between the two thrones on either side of the falls, the Black Knight pounded his mailed fist on a golden door that appeared to lead nowhere. That was new, but the rest were fresh from Aaron's childhood memories, untouched by the dark hand that had painted the rest of the Kingdom into nightmares. He could almost feel Aimee and his younger self running past him to their thrones on a thousand summer days.

As if he could sense it too, the Black Knight stopped pounding. "I didn't expect you to come back." His voice filled the room and spilled out into space as the bronze door swung closed behind Aaron and Drippy.

Aaron said nothing. There was nothing to say. They were past the point of words and threats. He'd gone this far; he would finish it.

"I thought you too much of a coward. I figured you'd take a few more hits of that junk you put into yourself and finish the job." He cocked his head the same way Drippy and the Witch did. "Maybe you have."

As if on cue, Marie screamed in the distance.

Aaron ignored her, but the syringes of heroin in his pocket grew heavier with each word. "This place doesn't belong to you."

The person behind the mask laughed and finally faced them. "Doesn't it? Do you think it belongs to you?" He nodded at Drippy. "To that?"

Aaron gazed down on his friend. One leg had nearly melted off. Drippy sat down and panted. "It's all right, ser. You can do this."

Aaron walked toward the Knight, who approached him in turn. "Yes. It belongs to me. Get out." He poured every ounce of majesty he could into his voice. "Throw yourself off that cliff."

The Knight cackled, his laughter bouncing off the walls and growing with each echo. "You think to command me? He who has ruined paradise? The Devil returned to the Garden of Eden to give God a piece of his mind? I think not." Both men stopped ten feet apart in the center of the room. "You. Ruined. *Everything!*" The Knight balled his hands into fists. "We had it all. We had the perfect paradise!"

We?

The Black Knight reached up and removed his helmet. Aaron's face, black-eyed and contorted in rage, stared back at him.

He thought his heart would stop. A terrible moment of cognitive dissonance threatened to tear him asunder and cast him over the waterfall into the universe. *He. Me. Him. We.* He could almost see through his doppelganger's eyes.

The Black Knight sneered. "Did you forget that we never came here alone? Did you think that Aimee's ghost was allowed to roam these hills without you?"

Aaron's mouth worked, but he couldn't speak. He had forgotten. Never once had they come to the Kingdom without the other. There was no Kingdom without both of the twins. If her ghost had come here, then his had created this thing. His guilt maybe, or by the piece of his childhood that hadn't been able to let go. Aimee had come here to find safety, and his angry spirit had followed and sowed ruin.

He really had destroyed the Kingdom. In his anger and grief, he had killed the one perfect place he'd ever known.

He swallowed hard as he stared into his own black eyes. Just like Mom and Dad. Every awful thing he'd ever known had come home to roost in his Kingdom. But that meant...

"Aimee. She really is here."

The Black Knight stomped his foot, and the throne room shook. "You killed her! You killed her and drove everyone away. You took all that you were and twisted it into a nightmare, and now you're back to pour salt into the wounds. You should have died! We should have died, you no-good junkie!"

Every awful thing he'd ever said to himself, thrown back at him. Even the word he hated. The one that described him perfectly.

Aaron took a step back. "No, I didn't do this."

The Knight pointed back at the golden door. "I've almost reached her. I'm so close. If you would just finish the job and kill yourself, we could be together again and start over."

The junk in Aaron's pocket weighed him down, pulling him to the earth with its gravity. He was right. Every bad thing that had ever happened was his fault. The Kingdom. Aimee. Marie. Brian. All of it.

"Yes! Do you see? We could have had it all, and you ruined it. You ruin everything."

Aaron took another step back, then another. "No."

But he had. He had done everything wrong, every time. Even simulacrum that had killed the Kingdom was his responsibility.

For one clear moment, he saw back in time to the path that had led him here. All the hate and lies. The disregard. The junk in his pocket called to him. Maybe this inversion of himself was right. Maybe he should put those needles into his arm and just end it. Why not? The Kingdom was gone, but Aimee's ghost still floated beyond that waterfall somewhere. He could be with her. He could let this thing open the golden door and free her, or free himself. Aaron reached into his pocket.

Drippy touched his leg. Aaron looked down to see the little creature at his knee, a trail of wax from where he had dragged himself across the floor behind him. "It isn't your fault."

The Black Knight screamed, shaking the chamber again. "Shut your mouth!"

"You have to let go of the things you can't change."

Let it go.

How could he? How did anybody?

"Forgive yourself."

So easy to say, but…

Aimee had sat across from him in that studio, telling him it wasn't his fault. She said it was hers. She told him to let it go. Marie had wanted to run away and start over. A fresh start was a clean one, free of self-blame for things that weren't his fault.

He'd been nothing but a scared child looking to protect his little sister as best he could. Not a monster. Not the devil in black armor, destroying all the good things he'd ever known. Just an unhappy boy who'd grown into an unhappy—

The gates in his mind broke. Every childhood memory filled him up, threatening to tear his head apart. His father's beatings. His mother's neglect. The Kingdom. Grandma.

He and Aimee on the hill. "If it doesn't matter, why not go?"

In their bedroom at night. "I love you, Aaron."

Grandma holding their hands as children. "Too much fear makes you weak. Don't be scared."

Brian at the park with Aaron and his sister. "I love you guys, you know that?"

Marie holding his hand as they stood on top of the tallest building in town, her other hand hovering over the edge. "I love you this much."

It all filled him up so completely that the black muck inside had nowhere to go. It shot out of him, a beam from his mouth and eyes expelling the nightmares over the waterfall and into the universe beyond. It tasted of demons and self-hatred. It reeked of original sin and the sins of his fathers.

And then it was gone.

The Black Knight—Aaron's darker half, or maybe his lighter one—stopped his advance.

It burned away everything, same as the fires that had consumed the Kingdom. The force of it staggered him, and only Drippy's steadying hand on his leg prevented him from falling down.

The dark-eyed Aaron stared in awe as the light-eyed one righted himself. Their self? Them? There had never been just a him; it had always been an us, and it had never been the monster he thought it was.

One moment stretched into a thousand years, then back down to a single second. The static vanished, and all that remained was the one thing he'd come to do. "I should never have left her alone. But it wasn't our fault. None of us. Not you, not me, and not her."

Those black eyes bored holes into him. "More excuses from a crackhead. Will wonders never cease?"

No more self-recriminations. The doubt and pain had to stop. "It's okay. We can fix it now. We can put all of this behind us and start over." He stepped forward, and this time the Black Knight retreated.

"No, I'm nothing like you. You're a monster. A thing. You ruin everything you touch."

Aaron kept moving forward, even as Marie screamed again. "No. It isn't your fault. It's nobody's fault. You can't fix the things you can't control. The past. The future. You have to let it go."

Drippy laughed behind him—not the humorless sound he made when he did his dances or made his faces, but the laugh he'd bellowed in these halls a million times, ages ago.

"No. If you would just die, things would be better. They'd be better for everyone." The Black Knight backed up against the golden door above the waterfall. Behind him, the universe waited. Open and calling.

Three feet away.

Two.

One.

They stood face to face, the darker half and the lighter. The one who could have been a great man and the one who had failed.

"Aaron, I forgive you."

As the Aaron in black armor screamed, the one without it embraced him. Then they were both screaming. Then there weren't two, only one seeing through four eyes. The loser. The winner. The one who might have been and the one who was.

Then there was just Aaron, and the Black Knight was no more.

He stared out into the endless something beyond the waterfall, seeing nothing and everything. Whole, or almost whole, for the first time since Aimee died.

"Ser." Drippy's voice was little more than a whisper behind him.

Aaron walked in a daze back to his constant companion. His mind flooded with thoughts and memories from his childhood. The night he went to the guardian trees and gouged a scar into their bark, some dark piece of him had stepped past the barrier and into the Kingdom to try to make things right. But you couldn't build with hate. He saw that now. Those seeds bore only bitter fruit.

The intervening years were still there, but it felt as if he were waking up from a long sleep. As if he'd closed his eyes the day Aimee died and kept them that way until this very moment. In many ways, he had.

"You did it. Yes you did, did, did."

He knelt down beside Drippy, who was little more than a pile of goo with a face, and even that was evaporating. For once, his tears weren't of self-pity. "Can I fix you now? Can I fix all of this?"

Drippy closed his eyes. He didn't open them again. "I don't know. I can't hear the whispers of the Kingdom anymore, but I don't think so."

Aaron stroked the face on the floor, his tears falling into the pile of wax. His little friend. "I'm sorry I didn't get here sooner."

Drippy's lips curled into a smile. "Now, now, no need to be sorry. You fixed it. You fixed everything. You made this place whole again." He cleared his throat. "Even if it was you what messed it up in the first place."

They both laughed. Real laughter! How many years had it been?

"Make me a promise."

"Anything." Aaron's heart broke as Drippy spoke his last words.

"Promise me you won't forget. Promise if you make another Kingdom, you'll bring me to that one too. You and the princess were the only friends I ever had."

Another Kingdom. Grandma had told him that his eyes meant he was special. The Witch spoke of countless worlds beyond this one.

Tears turned to full grief as his little friend breathed his last and faded away. But he didn't burst into shadows and smoke as the others had. He became a wisp of cloud that floated over the waterfall and out into the place between worlds.

"I promise. I'll bring you back if I can." Aaron covered his eyes and wept as he'd never been allowed as a child. "I'll never forget what you did for me."

Aaron stood there, the last thing in the Kingdom. Just he and the throne room in the world two kids had once created. Even the river of tears was silent as it slid out and over the edge into forever.

The soft click of a lock rang out. A dazzling light flooded the room as the golden door opened.

Aaron's heart skipped a beat. Aimee…

He tried to shield his eyes but couldn't make out anything beyond the door. Just a blinding glow.

At least at first.

He held his breath, tears streaming down his face from more than the light. A path. And in the distance, the silhouette of a woman with long blond hair, staring at him from atop a wooded hill. And was that a little shack in the woods nearby? He couldn't tell what lay beyond that cliff at the edge of sight. Too bright. Too much light. Too many things happening too fast.

She moved, but he couldn't see how as the overwhelming waves of comfort washed over him from that golden land. Beckoning to him, or gesturing for him to stay away?

He wiped his eyes and stood, taking one step toward it.

Another door opened behind him. A soft breeze blew on the back of his neck. Marie cried as she spoke to someone, begging them to get the door open.

"He's been in there for twenty minutes. He hasn't said a word. Please! Help him!"

When he looked that way, he saw light under the bathroom door. The real world, the one with the real people who cared for him. Brian and Marie. They hadn't given up on him, they just hadn't always known how to help him.

He stood between two worlds in the remains of a third. The old, the new, and the dead. The past, present, and future. The boy he'd been, but not the man.

He knew where she was. He had never failed her, but he had lost her. And now she stood there, in the distance. It had to be Aimee, and that meant that door led over the waterfall and into the beyond.

Horace had said it. Your time ending in one world didn't mean it ended in all of them. He could find her there.

Or he could turn back. Go to Marie. Make good on the promises he could still keep, and make the world out there the Kingdom he wanted it to be.

He waited for an eternity as the question raged inside of him. Heavens were born and perished as he made his decision. He weighed his love for his sister against his newfound self. His guilt versus his forgiveness. The woman he loved versus the sibling he'd lost.

He reached into his pocket and pulled out the heroin, dropping it on the ground. The syringes shattered, and the pieces melted into shadow and smoke before vanishing.

With one final look at the place they'd created all those years before, he stepped through the door.

Authors make their living thanks to readers such as yourself. If you enjoyed Aaron and Aimee's story, please take the time to leave a review on Amazon. Help someone else find this book.

If you'd like to read more of my work, be sure to look up *Darker Shadows Lie Below*, *All That Remains*, and *The Ghosts We Leave Behind*.

From The Author

Before I say anything else, let me say thanks to you, my reader. I always said I would write even if nobody read it, but it would be significantly less enjoyable to do so. While on the subject of thanks, I also owe a big one to Jenn Loring for being patient with me and my weasel words. (And even more patient when the story grew by about 50k of them) Megan, my wife, also deserves some gratitude, and maybe the most of all. She's as patient as ever, and this book wouldn't have made it to this stage without her. Turns out I'm a real bitch to be around when I'm plodding along on a project close to me, who knew?

And this one is very close to me. This is what I like to think of as an "old project". I think any writer would understand the idea. It's a story that has its roots in the soil of our –pre-storyteller lives. It's been bouncing around in my head since my early teenage years, and it rooted from a simple question: What would it be like to lose a twin?

I'm not Aaron, but I did my best to answer the question for him. This book went through many, many iterations, and the story changed a dozen times before pen even hit paper. It changed twice that once I began to scribble it out. I love how much this project surprised me, even if I hate that it took me nearly three years to finish. Honestly, I could have kept going and refining it again and again, but there comes a point where you have to let the little birds fly free. I like where this ended. In fact, this might be my favorite Al Barrera story.

A big part of that was the end. Frankly, it came as a shock to me. I always thought I knew which door Aaron would ultimately chose once I knew there were doors to choose. I was wrong. Did he follow through on his change and self-reflection? Did he wind up too broken to go back to the real world? Did he leave Marie in the same sorry state we found him in at the start of the book? I have no idea. Don't ask me, ask Aaron if you ever meet him.

Maybe you won't. Maybe he and Aimee, or he and Marie, found a new kingdom they never have to leave. The kind of place where the addictions and miseries of the real world don't exist. And maybe a little candle man lives there with them too, and they end every day smiling in a way they never got to here on Earth.

It might be fantasy, but all magic has to start somewhere.

Al Barrera
December 2017

www.ingramcontent.com/pod-product-compliance
Lightning Source LLC
Chambersburg PA
CBHW070723280626
47159CB00023B/2312